Carried Forward By Hope

April – December 1865

Book # 6 in The Bregdan Chronicles

Sequel to The Last, Long Night

Ginny Dye

Carried Forward By Hope

Copyright © 2014 by Ginny Dye
Published by
A Voice In The World Publishing
Bellingham, WA 98229

www.BregdanChronicles.net

www.GinnyDye.com

www.AVoiceInTheWorld.com

ISBN # 1507887523

Printed in the United States of America

For Bogey – my four-legged best buddy and the joy of my life! He lays beside me every day while I write. Surely he deserves to have a book dedicated to him!

A Note from the Author

My great hope is that *Carried Forward By Hope* will both entertain and challenge you. I hope you will learn as much as I did during the months of research it took to write this book. No one was more surprised than me when it ended up portraying just the last eight months of 1865 – instead of a whole year like the other ones have.

When I ended the Civil War in *The Last, Long Night*, I knew virtually nothing about the first year of Reconstruction. I wasn't even sure it could carry an entire book. I was shocked and mesmerized by all I learned. When I got to December, and I already had more than 500 pages, I knew I needed to close the door on 1865 and start fresh in 1866 with the next volume of *The Bregdan Chronicles*!

Though I now live in the Pacific Northwest, I grew up in the South and lived for eleven years in Richmond, VA. I spent countless hours exploring the plantations that still line the banks of the James River and became fascinated by the history.

But you know, it's not the events that fascinate me so much – it's the people. That's all history is, you know. History is the story of people's lives. History reflects the consequences of their choice and actions – both good and bad. History is what has given you the world you live in today – both good and bad.

This truth is why I named this series The Bregdan Chronicles. Bregdan is a Gaelic term for weaving: Braiding. Every life that has been lived until today is a part of the woven braid of life. It takes every person's story to create history. Your life will help determine the course of history. You may think you don't have much of an impact. You do. Every action you take will reflect in someone else's life. Someone else's decisions. Someone else's future. Both good and bad. That is the **Bregdan Principle**...

**Every life that has been lived until today is a
part of the woven braid of life.
It takes every person's story to
create history.
Your life will help determine the
course of history.
You may think you don't have
much of an impact.
You do.
Every action you take will reflect in
someone else's life.
Someone else's decisions.
Someone else's future.
Both good and bad.**

My great hope as you read this book, and all that will follow, is that you will acknowledge the power you have, every day, to change the world around you by your decisions and actions. Then I will know the research and writing were all worthwhile.

Oh, and I hope you enjoy every moment of it and learn to love the characters as much as I do!

I'm already being asked how many books will be in this series. I guess that depends on how long I live! My intention is to release two or three books a year, each covering one year of history – continuing to weave the lives of my characters into the times they lived. I hate to end a good book as much as anyone – always feeling so sad that I have to leave the characters. You shouldn't have to be sad for a long time!

You are now reading the sixth book - # 7 (*Glimmers of Change*) will be released in the Fall of 2014. If you like what you read, you'll want to make sure you're on our mailing list at www.BregdanChronicles.net. I'll let you know each time a new one comes out so that you can take advantage of all my fun launch events!

Many more are coming!

Sincerely,
Ginny Dye

Chapter One

April 15, 1865

Carrie Borden fought to control the shudder that rippled through her body when she stepped out onto the porch. The polished boards gleamed in the early morning light filtered by the looming magnolia tree, and a soft fragrance from the milky white blooms perfumed the air. Cardinals offered a splash of brilliant red, but they couldn't distract from the starkness that permeated the still, somber air.

Abigail Livingston and Rose Samuels moved out onto the porch beside her. Carrie reached down to grab hold of their hands as they stared down at Richmond's charred remains. A gentle breeze tossed soft strands of her long, ebony waves around her face as her bright green eyes clouded with tears.

"Can you feel it?" she whispered, somehow not able to make her voice sound normal. On a day like today, surely it was necessary to speak differently.

Aunt Abby nodded her head as she gripped Carrie's hand tighter. "I can feel it," she replied heavily, her soft, gray eyes misting as she took deep breaths.

"There is trouble in the air," Carrie said, her voice still a strained whisper. "What is going to happen?"

Rose stepped forward to gaze down the dusty road, aware that most of the people stepping out of their houses had no idea what had happened. "Who will tell them?" she asked quietly. Her black eyes, usually snapping with life, were heavy with sorrow. "He was a hero to my people. He gave us our freedom." Her voice trailed off as the tears flooding her eyes escaped to create rivulets down her glowing ebony skin. "I can't believe he's gone," she groaned.

Matthew Justin and Peter Wilcher walked out to join them.

Aunt Abby turned to Matthew. "What is going to happen now?" she asked. "I realize you just discovered the news yourself, but as a journalist, do you have a feel for what the ramifications will be here in Richmond?"

Matthew ran his hand through his thick red hair, his blue eyes dark with concern. "I wish I knew," he said somewhat helplessly. "I still can't believe President Lincoln is dead..."

"Assassinated by a Southerner," Carrie added, still not able to believe any of it was true. "Dead... President Lincoln is dead." She turned and stared into Matthew's eyes. "What's going to happen to our country now?"

"There's not a person alive who knows the answer to that question," Peter replied, his dark brown hair tousled as he leaned his tall, muscular body over the railing to peer down the road. "Matthew and I will head down into the city to get some answers, but I truly believe it would be best if all of you stay here until we can get a feel for what is going to happen," he said gravely. His dark eyes revealed what his words did not.

Matthew nodded his head in agreement. "I do believe my fellow journalist is being wise," he admitted. "I suspect the Union forces are all aware now of what happened. In the midst of all the pain, there is going to be a lot of anger..."

"And they're going to look for a way to vent that anger," Aunt Abby finished in a flat voice.

Matthew didn't make an effort to correct her or alleviate her concerns. Instead, he reached down to squeeze her hand warmly. "We'll go into town soon and bring back news as quickly as we can," he promised.

Carrie shuddered again. "Is there to be no end to the trouble?" she cried, her voice rising to full strength as stark reality settled into her mind. "Four years of horrid war have just ended. How will we find our way back without President Lincoln? How will our country heal all the terrible things that have happened?" Despair dripped from her words as tears clogged her throat.

Aunt Abby wrapped a comforting arm around her waist. "We will find a way," she said. Her voice was both determined and tremulous. "We will be carried forward by hope."

"Carried forward by hope..." Carrie whispered, trying to hold on to the words Aunt Abby had first uttered into the stunned pain they all felt when Matthew brought the news of Lincoln's assassination. The power of Aunt Abby's simple statement slowly filtered through her pain once more. Her tears dried as she straightened her shoulders. "Yes," she said more firmly. "We will indeed be carried forward by hope. We will survive this darkness, just as we have survived the darkness of the last four years."

Rose moved forward to let Aunt Abby embrace her with her free arm. "The future isn't going to look like what we thought, but the future is still going to come. We have no choice but to continue to move forward. We have no choice but to find our way. President Lincoln gave us so much. Now it's up to us to continue forward."

"And so we will," Aunt Abby whispered, her voice thick with love as she looked around the porch. "All of you young people represent the best of what both the North and the South have to offer. All of you have found a way to choose love in the midst of incredible violence and hatred. I have to believe there are others who will step up to bring healing to a damaged land—a divided country."

"So many questions," Carrie murmured. "So many things to learn about what we can expect to happen now that President Lincoln is dead." Her forehead crinkled in thought. "I know absolutely nothing about Vice President Johnson."

"President Johnson," Rose interjected, disbelief still ripe in her voice.

"I'll tell you everything I can," Aunt Abby said, "but I'd prefer to do it over the breakfast I'm sure May is fixing inside. I'm rather ashamed to say I still have an appetite."

Matthew managed a chuckle. "I've never known anything to keep you from eating," he teased. "Not even when men in Philadelphia were trying to destroy the business your husband left you when he died."

"I had you to protect me," Aunt Abby said fondly. "What was there to ruin my appetite?"

Carrie smiled softly. She knew the real story of the terror her beloved friend had faced and just how lucky she was to be alive, and not to be gravely injured. She had long admired Aunt Abby's strength. It didn't matter that the woman wasn't really an aunt to any of them—all of them had adopted this amazing woman full of love, passion and wisdom. That they were all standing together on the porch after four years of separation during the war was still pure amazement to Carrie.

The creak of the screen door announced Jeremy's arrival on the porch. "May has breakfast ready," he said. "I think some of her tears are mixed in with the eggs, but she was determined to fix it."

Rose moved over and wrapped her arm around her twin, leaning into his strength.

Carrie smiled again, hoping she never lost the feeling of wonder she felt every time she saw them together. What a miracle that the two had been reunited after more than two decades of neither of them even aware the other existed, and both of them bi-racial—Rose living as a black woman, and Jeremy living as a white man for his entire life.

"Do you ever think the day will arrive when our niece stops staring at us?" Jeremy asked Rose, his eyes dancing with mischievousness, obviously grabbing on to an opportunity to ease his pain and worry.

Carrie smiled back at him. "Since my uncle and aunt are only two weeks older than me, and I had no idea of the relationship between Rose and me for most of our lives—and didn't even know you existed until *after* that— I'd say my staring may last for quite a long time. Add to that, the reality that you and Rose have only known each other for a matter of days, and I say I'm entitled to do whatever I want. I suggest you get used to it," she retorted, thankful for even a moment of brevity to take her mind off Lincoln's assassination.

"And I suggest we go in to eat May's cooking," Matthew said, taking Carrie's arm and steering her through the front door. "It was a very long night, it's going to be a very long day, and I happen to be very hungry!"

Carrie sobered at the thought of the day ahead, and allowed herself to be led into her father's elegant Richmond home. She missed the plantation more and more now that the war was over and spring had blanketed the trees with fresh green. The hillsides of Richmond were covered with glowing white dogwoods and brilliant azalea blooms. It was beautiful, but while she dearly loved his large three-story brick home overlooking the city, it wasn't the same as the plantation calling her name

The morning sun caught on the chandelier in the foyer, breaking into millions of dancing lights on the floor. Aunt Abby moved up beside Carrie and took her hand. "No matter how dark it is, the sun will shine again," she murmured.

They watched the dancing lights for a moment and then hurried into the dining room to sit down to breakfast. There was a new day to live, whether any of them were ready for it or not.

****

Carrie thought she might never get used to the sight of a real breakfast on the table. After three years of severe deprivation, she had grown quite accustomed to daily breakfasts of thin porridge. Since the end of the war, groceries had slowly begun to make their way in from the North, filling the few stores left standing after the inferno that destroyed most of Richmond's business district less than two weeks earlier. Aunt Abby, who insisted on buying their food in return for their hospitality, was responsible for the eggs, bacon and toast gracing their table. Carrie had quit trying to argue with her, and decided to simply be grateful for Abby's love and generosity.

Carrie had taken only a few bites of her eggs when May hurried into the room, her eyes wide with concern. "Miss Carrie!"

Carrie pushed back from the table immediately and stood. "Robert?" she asked, trying to control the fear in her voice. What more would she have to endure today?

"Yessum. I went up to take him his breakfast. I found him with a right high fever. I done sent Micah out to get some cold water out of the well."

Carrie was already halfway up the stairs when she paused to give a tight smile. "Thank you, May. I will need some—"

"I know, Miss Carrie. I'm goin' right now to get them rags and a bowl. I be havin' them up to you in a jiffy. Then I be's right up with some o' your potion." May spun into the kitchen, the door snapping shut behind her.

Janie appeared on the steps behind Carrie. "I'm coming to help you," she said, and then looked back at Rose and Aunt Abby who had already pushed away from the table. "Both of you go ahead and eat. Carrie and I can handle this. If you could bring us something when you're done, that would be wonderful. We'll need both the food and the moral support."

Carrie was already entering the room when Janie caught up with her. She barely managed to suppress her groan when she saw her husband's flushed face and his confused, fever-bright eyes. She had so hoped the fever was behind them. Forcing her tightened lips into a smile, she hurried to him and laid a cool hand on his forehead.

"I'm so hot," Robert whispered. "Where am I?" He looked wildly around the room, panic shining in his eyes and thickening his voice.

Carrie's heart sank even while she managed to sound calm and cheerful. "You're at home with me, Robert. Your fever has gone back up, but we'll get it back down. Lay back and relax," she said soothingly.

Robert stared at her for a moment and then his eyes cleared a little. "Carrie," he gasped.

"That's right, my love. It's me." Carrie worked quickly as she forced her voice to remain level and slow.

May eased up behind her with a bowl of cool water and fresh rags.

"Thank you," Carrie said. "Please tell Micah to keep bringing them up."

"Don't you worry none, Miss Carrie," May replied. "Me and Micah done know how to help you. Ain't we been doin' it for a while? You focus on taking care of Mr.

Borden. We gonna make sure you gots ever'thing you need."

Carrie and Janie worked in tandem soaking the rags in cool water, laying them on Robert's hot body until they warmed, and then replacing them. Time ceased to exist. The horror of Lincoln's assassination was replaced with the current battle for life.

Carrie prayed fervently as her hands moved. Robert had only been home with her for a week. He had put on a few pounds, but he was still a gaunt caricature of the laughing, vibrant, handsome husband she had sent off to war. He had given his all for the Confederacy, but she was determined it would not claim him entirely. He had returned home in a medical wagon weak and sick with pneumonia. She had been waging a battle ever since.

"He's unconscious again," Janie whispered.

Carrie nodded grimly. She would have been relieved if he had simply slipped into sleep, but she knew his body was shutting down against the fever. "We've got to bring this fever down," she replied, trying to keep the desperation out of her voice, knowing that Robert could somehow feel her through the darkness. She wanted him only to feel confidence and love.

"We'll get it down," Janie assured her.

Carrie managed to smile. "You've been my strength for four years. What am I going to do when you and Clifford return home to Raleigh?" She and Janie had been like sisters ever since Carrie saved her from a drunken attack the first year of the war. "I'm so happy to be reunited with Rose and Aunt Abby, but so very sad that you're leaving."

Janie's gentle blue eyes glistened under her brown hair. "I can't bear to think of it, so I'm not," she replied, her lips set firmly. Only the tremor in her voice revealed her true feelings.

"We'll always be sisters," Carrie promised, reaching out for a moment to squeeze Janie's hand. Then she went back to wrapping and unwrapping, dismayed there was no reduction in the fever.

She forced herself to take deep breaths, refusing to give into the panic. She had fought this same battle over thousands of soldiers in the last three years of serving in

Chimborazo Hospital. She lost some, but she had won most of them, sending soldiers home to their families or back out to the battlefield.

She would not lose this most important battle!

"I love you, Robert," she said softly, smoothing her hand over his chalky, hot face. She could feel death trying to enter the room, slinking in on misty fingers of darkness.

Her back stiffened. "I love you, and I'm not giving up on you. We've still got too much living to do," she said, her voice suddenly fierce and defiant. "You have to fight. You have to come back to me."

The battle waged for another four hours. Carrie was aware when Rose and Aunt Abby entered the room with plates of food, but neither she nor Janie eased their efforts for even a moment. She could sense when Matthew, Jeremy and Moses hovered by the door, but she didn't look away from her husband. She could hear soft prayers flowing through the room, but her own heart had no room for anything but a relentless hope that kept driving her forward.

"Live," Carrie pleaded in a whisper as she replaced another rag. *"Live..."*

As the morning dragged on, weariness claimed her, sapping her energy and her hope. Her movements were simply mechanical now, as fear battled her attempts to hold it back. Tears sprang into her eyes and her hands shook with fatigue, but the rags continued to be replaced steadily, and her voice continued its soft stream of soothing talk.

The sun was high in the sky when Janie grabbed her hand. "His fever is going down," she said triumphantly, her voice cracking with weariness.

Carrie stared at her with glazed eyes and then looked more closely at Robert. Hope crawled back to life when she realized Janie was right. Robert's color was better and his breathing was easier. "Live," she said yet again, her voice stronger. *"Live..."*

Micah moved into the room with a fresh pan of cool water.

Carrie reached for it, but Aunt Abby pushed in and took it from her hands "Enough," she firmly, her eyes shining with compassion and concern. "You've had enough, Carrie. You, too, Janie," she added. "Rose and I are going to take over for a while."

"But..."

"But, nothing." Aunt Abby gently pushed Carrie down into a chair. "You're about to fall over. You've done the hardest part. Rose and I are going to take over now," she repeated.

Rose had already pushed Janie into another chair. "We may not be medical people like you and Janie, but we're good with rags and cool water. You can sit there and tell us if we're doing something wrong."

Aunt Abby looked up and beckoned May into the room. "Please bring them both some food."

"Yessum," May said. "I be's right back. I been keepin' some hot food for them, ever since they started workin' on Mr. Borden."

Carrie stared around helplessly and sagged back against the chair, realizing just how exhausted she was. She fought to control the trembling in her arms and hands, and struggled to keep her breathing even.

Moments later, Moses entered the room with two plates of hot food. Carrie stared at the mounds of steaming vegetables and the thick chunks of hot cornbread glowing with melted butter, not sure she had the energy to pick up the fork and move it toward her mouth.

"Eat it all," Moses commanded.

Carrie gazed up at Rose's towering hulk of a husband, who was also one of her closest friends. Staring into his strong face infused her with hope. Moses had been so close to death a month ago when she found him with an infected, gaping hole in his chest in a wagon full of wounded Union soldiers. Richmond's medical personnel refused to give care to the black Union soldiers— members of the first units to occupy the city. She and Dr. Wild had saved Moses' life, along with many of his friends.

Moses read her mind. "You saved me, Carrie. I don't reckon God is going to let you lose Robert. I know this is going to be a long battle, but I believe Robert is going to make it."

Carrie took a deep breath and let his words wash through her, somehow knowing it was a message that came from a place deeper than him. She saw that Robert's breathing was almost back to normal, exchanged a long look with Janie, and reached for her fork. "Thank you," she said, and then she began to shovel food in.

****

Matthew and Peter made their way through the crowds thronging the streets in the defeated capital of the Confederacy. Black soldiers in Union blue mingled with the growing number of former slaves pouring into Richmond looking for a better life. They had done nothing but add to the overpopulation of a city that had finally collapsed under the barrage of four years of constant attacks. Crowds of white people; despair and confusion clouding their faces, roamed the streets, while many were only willing to peer out from behind their heavily curtained windows. Fear and uncertainty vibrated through the very air of the city.

Peter gazed at several frightened faces peering out from behind curtains. "Their whole world has disappeared," he said sympathetically.

Matthew nodded. "That's for sure," he said, glancing quizzically at his friend, uncertain how to say what he was thinking, and not sure he should say anything at all.

Peter interpreted the look and smiled slightly. "I know I was eager for the Confederacy to fall, and I know we felt differently about how things happened in the Shenandoah Valley. All I could think about then was having this crazy war end so I could go home to my family. I was willing to inflict whatever damage it would take to make that happen, but…"

"But…?" Matthew prompted. He hoped he knew what Peter would say, but he wanted to hear the words that would give him a belief that things could change.

Peter glanced around at the remnants of charred buildings that were a terrifying testament to the fire that had almost destroyed Richmond. "Being with Carrie, Janie, and everyone else has put a human face on everything. Those people are no more my enemy than you are. They are simply people who got caught up on the southern side of the Mason-Dixon Line, swept into the consequences of decisions made by hot-headed politicians and business leaders."

Matthew nodded, a hope surging through him that more people from the North could gain the same understanding with time. "Unfortunately, the people of Richmond are going to be dealing with the consequences for a very long time." His eyes sharpened as he gazed around the streets. "There are a lot more soldiers here than there were yesterday," he said, his gut tightening. He raised both his hand and his voice when he saw a fellow journalist making his way down the road toward them. "Sam Kremer!" he shouted.

Sam stopped, his face flushed with an odd mixture of excitement, despair and anxiety. "Matthew! Did you hear the news about Lincoln?"

"I'm afraid I did," Matthew said, swallowing his grief because his senses were screaming a warning. "There seems to be an increased presence of soldiers. What is going on?"

Sam's eyes flashed with anger. "The news about Lincoln came through to Union commanders last night. They rushed extra regiments into the city early this morning. They have doubled patrols and street guards."

"They expect trouble?" Peter asked.

"They don't know *what* to expect," Sam snorted. "You know it was a Southerner who killed Lincoln?"

"John Wilkes Booth," Matthew replied, his voice heavy with regret. "I got the news early this morning."

Sam nodded. "He's an actor. That's why he was able to get into the theater. He walked right into President Lincoln's box and shot him in the head. Then he leapt from the balcony box down onto the stage, yelling '*Sic semper tyrannis! The South is avenged!*'"

"*Ever thus to tyrants,*" Matthew interpreted in a troubled murmur.

"They still haven't caught him?" Peter asked, his own eyes sparking with temper.

"Not that I've heard," Sam replied. "He escaped by jumping on a horse, but there are a lot of troops after him. He won't get away," he said angrily, his eyes glistening with both sorrow and rage.

There was a sudden rush of Union blue toward where they were standing on the street.

"Get back!" Sam yelled, pulling them behind a burned-out wall.

Matthew and Peter stumbled, barely missing being knocked over by the charging Union soldiers.

"Get him!" one of the soldiers yelled, fury ripe in his voice and eyes. Anger was echoed on all the faces of the men with him.

Just before they reached their target - an emaciated-looking Confederate soldier wandering up the street in search of food - he suddenly realized the danger. His head jerked up, his eyes betraying his fear as he looked around and saw there was no route of escape.

Matthew watched in sick dismay, knowing there was nothing he could do to help. Just yesterday, he had seen Union soldiers handing out food to their returning Rebel counterparts. He had witnessed both admiration and pity from the conquering soldiers to the defeated army returning home in tattered clothes with emaciated bodies. "How things can change in a day," he muttered as the swarm of Union soldiers fell on the unlucky Rebel, beating him and driving him back down the street. His helpless cries rose into the air before he collapsed and lay still. "My God..."

"Does he have any idea why he was attacked?" Peter asked.

"Probably not," Sam replied. "*The Whig* just put out an edition of the newspaper, telling people about the assassination. The soldiers being attacked have no idea of what is going on, or they would be hiding somewhere."

"Is it happening everywhere?" Matthew asked, wincing as he saw another Rebel soldier attacked. He was very glad he had kept Carrie and the rest away from town. When mob violence took over, there was no telling who could get hurt.

"Yes," Sam admitted, a hard light in his eyes. "The entire Union adored Lincoln and the soldiers were committed to him, but the black soldiers saw him as their savior and hero. Learning of his assassination has released an anger that has been brewing for a long time."

"Aren't the commanders doing anything to keep them in line?" Peter asked. "Surely they know uncontrolled anger could easily turn into a full-scale riot. There's no telling what could happen then. Haven't enough innocent people been hurt?"

Sam shrugged. "Everybody is trying to figure things out. There is a strong belief that President Lincoln's assassination is part of a much bigger conspiracy. They fear his death was the first blow in a much bigger uprising."

"So soldiers that deserved pity yesterday..." Matthew started.

"...are now suspects in a wide conspiracy to begin the war again," Sam finished.

Matthew looked at him with disbelief.

Sam raised his hands. "You and I both know the South has no fight left, but you have to admit you expected backlash to Lincoln's death."

Matthew nodded. "I knew it would be bad," he admitted reluctantly, aware of his own growing anger. "What else is happening?" he asked, more to bring his own feelings under control than because he really wanted to know. It was his job to learn the details, but suddenly he wanted to pretend Lincoln wasn't dead...that the long-fought war hadn't descended into a chaos perhaps more destructive than the one that just ended.

Sam grimaced. "Grant also suspects a wider plot. He had been invited to be at Ford's Theatre with Lincoln last night. He suspects he would have been killed as well had he and his wife attended." He paused. "We know so little right now, but more details will be filled in as we learn more."

"So, what is Grant doing?" Peter asked.

"I know he ordered General Ord to arrest Mayor Mayo, the Richmond City Council, other officials, and the paroled Confederate officers in the city," he responded. "He demanded they be locked into Libby Prison." Sam shook his head. "Grant stated that extreme rigor will have to be observed while assassination remains the order of the day with the Rebels."

"But surely..." Matthew began in protest, his mind spinning through what would happen if the order played out.

Sam managed a tight smile. "Ord refused to follow the order," he said. "General Lee was to be arrested as well. Ord said he feared the rebellion *would* be reopened if the city's beloved General Lee was arrested."

"Thank God!" Matthew said. "Ord is quite right."

"Let's hope Grant sees things your way in time," Sam replied. "Ord said he would risk his life so that the paroles in Richmond would be honored, and that no one in the city has any clue about the assassination."

"Let's hope that feeling can spread before more violence is done," Peter muttered. "This is hardly the way to generate goodwill among Richmonders."

"And assassinating President Lincoln is hardly the way to build goodwill in the North," Sam said. "Look, I don't think all these Rebels should be attacked, but I also understand how the black soldiers feel. They have given years of their life to fight for a man who gave them their freedom. They finally have it, and now they get the news that Lincoln has been killed—by a Southerner. They're angry."

"And they're afraid," Matthew added. "They're wondering what will happen to them now that their savior has been killed. They realize there are a lot of politicians in the North that don't care about them the way Lincoln did."

Anger faded from Sam's eyes. "They have a right to be afraid," he admitted. "The fellows and I have been talking. President Johnson..." Sam paused, his eyes clouding with pain. "It will take a while to get used to saying that."

"What do you know about him?" Matthew asked, eager to add to his own knowledge.

Sam looked to him as a band of Union soldiers ran past on their way to ambush another unsuspecting Confederate victim. "You really want to know whether President Johnson will carry forward Lincoln's plans for the reconstruction of the United States?"

"Yes," Matthew replied, afraid he already knew the answer.

Sam shrugged. "Only time will tell, but I don't see it happening. Johnson is not Lincoln. They didn't think the same, and they didn't see things the same. As long as Lincoln was in charge, he could make things happen. Now...?" His voice trailed off as another fearful scream rent the air.

****

Carrie woke with a start, realizing she had fallen asleep in the chair. She stared, bleary-eyed, at the soft yellow blanket that had been laid over her.

"Robert's fever is completely gone," Aunt Abby said.

Carrie jerked her head up, remembering. "It's gone?" she asked, her voice still groggy.

"Gone," Rose assured her, grasping Carrie's hands. "He even woke up and took some sips of soup. He looked over, saw you sleeping, and asked us not to wake you. Then he dropped off into a peaceful sleep of his own."

Carrie smiled, allowing the relief to wash over her in waves. A quick glance told her Robert was sleeping peacefully, his breathing steady and even. Sudden tears filled her eyes. "Thank you," she whispered. She looked around. "Janie?"

"Clifford came and took her to their room so she could get some sleep," Aunt Abby replied.

Carrie started to smile but then stopped, struck by the look in Aunt Abby's eyes. "What is it?" she asked.

Aunt Abby hesitated and looked down at her hands.

"Aunt Abby? What's wrong?"

"Perhaps nothing," Aunt Abby said, raising troubled gray eyes. "I hope nothing."

Carrie looked over at her husband again. "Is it Robert? Are you not telling me something?"

"No, no!" Aunt Abby said quickly. But then she stopped again, her eyes dark with distress.

Carrie looked up at Rose. "What is going on?" she demanded.

Rose opened her mouth and closed it again, her eyes troubled.

Carrie pushed aside the blanket and stood. "I really must demand you tell me what is happening," she said. "I may be tired, but I assure you I am not fragile."

Rose chuckled. "You are most definitely not fragile," she said. "And you do so sound like the heir to the Cromwell fortune right now."

Carrie fought to control her sudden hysteria. Only she knew how little was left of the Cromwell fortune. She did, however, realize how imperious her voice had sounded. "I'm sorry," she said. "I've gotten rather used to giving orders after three years of being in charge of my ward at Chimborazo Hospital."

She took several deep breaths and forced her voice to remain calm and even. "I know you are both trying to protect me from something. I'd rather you didn't. I've discovered during four years of war that I would much rather know the battle I am fighting. Hiding from reality never seems to serve a purpose."

"You're right," Aunt Abby said with a heavy sigh. "It's just that we hope we're wrong, and we don't want you to worry about something that might not even be a problem." She glanced at Rose. "Tell her."

Carrie turned to Rose and took a steadying breath.

"We're concerned about Janie," Rose said. "Clifford seemed so angry when he came to get her."

Carrie stared at her, confused by this sudden turn of events. "Janie?"

"She was afraid when she left with him," Aunt Abby added. "I'm sure of it. I could see it in her eyes."

Carrie gazed at both of them, snippets of images from the last week flooding her mind. She nodded slowly. "I guess I didn't see it. Or maybe," she admitted, "I didn't want to see it. The war changed him."

Moses picked that moment to enter the room. Rose nodded at him. "You've told her?" he asked.

Carrie jerked her head around. "About Janie?" She eased back down into her chair. "Please tell me everything," she insisted, leaning forward to look into all of their faces.

Moses settled down in one of the sturdiest chairs, easing his muscular frame forward. "Clifford is a man with a lot of hate in him," he said. "Especially against us black folks."

"Clifford?" Carrie echoed. She wanted to deny what she was being told, but now that she was forced to hear it, supporting images were telling her it was the truth. Her shoulders sagged. "But, Janie..."

"She's got the same kind of love in her that you do," Aunt Abby said softly. "That's why we're concerned for her. Clifford is going to feel threatened by his wife feeling differently than he does."

"But he knew who she was before they married," Carrie protested.

"This war has changed a lot of people. The South lost," Moses said. "Clifford's whole world has changed. He's got to find a way to vent all that anger. He knows better than to vent it against the North, so he has to find another target."

"The freed slaves," Carrie said. Her heart raged, but her mind told her it was true.

Aunt Abby nodded and gripped both her hands. "It's going to happen everywhere," she said sadly. "We're in for a long battle."

"She's right," Rose said. "We may have our freedom, but we don't yet have the freedom to live our lives in this country."

"You sound very calm about it," Carrie observed, her mind whirling as she thought about Janie.

Rose shrugged. "We've talked about it at the contraband camp for the last three years. We knew that when the war finally ended, it would be the beginning of the slaves' fight to truly be free. Our goal was to equip our students so they could fight their battle."

Carrie nodded, but her heart and thoughts were with Janie. "She's leaving to go back to Raleigh with Clifford any day now. What will happen?"

"Do you think you can convince her to not go?" Aunt Abby asked.

Carrie stared at her. "Convince her to leave Clifford?" She shook her head. "I don't know." She thought about the joyful wedding just months before. "They've been married such a short time," she murmured.

Aunt Abby squeezed her hands again tightly. "We might be completely wrong," she said.

Carrie gazed at her, knowing Aunt Abby was trying to make her feel better, and also knowing the older woman didn't believe a word of what she had said.

"Carrie..."

Carrie leapt up as Robert croaked her name. "Robert!" Pushing aside thoughts of Janie, she rushed to his side.

"I'm hungry," he said weakly.

Carrie smiled for the first time that day. "Well, I can certainly do something about that," she said as she looked into his clear eyes.

"I'll go down and get something," Rose offered.

Carrie nodded and continued to gaze down at her husband. She couldn't bring Lincoln back to life, she couldn't know what was happening in Richmond right now, and she couldn't change how Clifford thought, but she *could* love her husband. She stroked his hair gently as she took hold of one of his hands. "I love you, Robert," she said. "You're going to get well," she added, forcing the fierce tone out of her voice, but doing nothing to keep it from resonating within her heart.

She longed to return to Cromwell Plantation, but she knew it was too soon to move Robert. It was enough to know it still stood. Captain Jones, Moses' commanding officer, had sent out a squadron of men to check on it and bring back news. Moses claimed the captain did it for Carrie because he had such respect for how she escaped the plantation on Granite three years earlier. She didn't really care why, she was simply glad to know her home remained. Everything in her wanted to be there right now, but it wasn't time.

"I've been very sick," Robert murmured.

Carrie took hope from the awareness in his voice. She settled down on the bed next to him, still stroking his hair. "Yes, you've been very sick," she agreed. "But I believe the worst is behind you now," she said. "Now you're going to get better."

Robert gazed at her for a long moment and then looked around the room.

Carrie's heart leapt with gladness. Her husband's eyes were actually looking—they were *seeing* for the first time. He gave a brief smile to Rose and Moses, recognizing both of them, but his eyes grew confused when they settled on the older woman.

Carrie stood, took Aunt Abby by the hand, and drew her to the bed. "This is Aunt Abby, Robert," she said happily.

Robert's confusion cleared. "Aunt Abby," he said. "Carrie's Aunt Abby."

Aunt Abby's joyful laugh filled the room as she laid her hand on Robert's arm. "I am so very glad to finally have the chance to meet you. I've only heard about you for five years. It's nice to know you weren't just a figment of Carrie's imagination," she teased.

Darkness fled the room as the breeze brought in hope and light. The curtains swayed and danced as hope replaced the despair that had filled the room minutes before.

Robert stared up at Aunt Abby. "You have good eyes," he said, but then his head slumped back against the pillow. "So tired..." he whispered.

Aunt Abby stepped back as Carrie placed her hand on his head again, relieved beyond measure to find it cool to the touch. "You've had quite a long day."

May entered the room with a bowl of soup.

Carrie lifted Robert easily until he was sitting partially upright, still stunned that her robust husband was now frail and light enough for her to lift. She kept her voice cheerful, encouraged by his awareness. "Take a few sips of this soup. Then you can go to sleep."

Robert took the soup obediently and then closed his eyes, his face going lax.

Carrie smiled at Aunt Abby and Rose. "It's a healing sleep," she whispered. "We'll go down now so that he won't be disturbed."

****

Carrie looked at the two empty seats as May brought steaming platters out to the table. Robert's awareness had lifted her spirits more than anything could have, but the conversation she'd had earlier with Aunt Abby and Rose had played through her mind all afternoon.

"Where are Clifford and Janie?" Matthew asked, reaching for a piece of cornbread. "This is too good of a meal to miss."

Carrie pushed back from the table, aware of Aunt Abby and Rose's gaze on her. "I'll run up and check on her," she said casually. "She must have been so tired after helping with Robert. I want to make sure she's all right."

Moments later, she was easing down the hallway of the east wing, wondering why she was walking so quietly, but loath to make noise. She would analyze it later. She padded down the hall past Jeremy's room, slowing as she heard angry voices coming from the end room. Frowning and no longer concerned about stealth, she moved more quickly.

"I tell you, those soldiers have no right to be here in Richmond!"

Carrie heard Clifford's voice easily through the closed door. She raised her hand to knock, but dropped it and decided to listen.

Janie didn't respond, but Clifford continued on. "Those niggers have no right to tell white men what they can and cannot do!" He paused. "I tell you, we won't have it! Something has to be done."

Janie said nothing.

"Don't you have anything to say?" Clifford asked. "Can you do no more than look at me?"

"What would you like me to say?"

Carrie stiffened when she heard the fear in Janie's voice. Aunt Abby and Rose had been right! Indecision tormented her. She wanted to knock, but what if her presence made it worse for Janie?

"Surely you must agree with me," Clifford said scathingly. "Clearly you see that having blacks in control of whites is simply not acceptable."

"The North won," Janie said. "I suspect everyone in the South is going to have a lot to adjust to."

"*Adjust* to?" Clifford snapped. "You think I will *adjust* to having a nigger tell me what I can do?" Scorn and anger dripped from his voice. "You're even more stupid than you look."

Carrie gasped and knocked boldly on the door, stepping back a little when Clifford flung it open.

"What?" he snapped, his face changing immediately when he recognized their visitor. "Well hello, Carrie," he said calmly.

Carrie stared at him, wondering how such rage could so quickly become a civilized expression. That, perhaps more than anything else, scared her for Janie. What was hiding within the man they had all grown so fond of? "Dinner is ready," she said, stepping into the room and smiling at Janie. "I was afraid Janie was too tired after all she did to help me with Robert today."

"Yes," Clifford said smoothly. "Janie was quite exhausted. We thought we would skip dinner tonight."

"Oh, that would be so sad," Carrie said, determined not to leave her friend in the room with Clifford's anger. "Everyone is quite eager to have you there." She took Janie's hand and looked at Clifford. "You're going back to Raleigh so soon. We don't want to miss a minute with either of you." She almost choked on her words but managed to keep her voice casual and light. "Please do join us for dinner. The rest sent me to bring you back."

Janie remained silent.

That alone made Carrie grit her teeth. She hated the look of fear lurking in Janie's eyes as she gazed at Clifford, waiting for his decision.

"All right then," Clifford relented. "You're right that we won't be here much longer. We want to spend as much time with you as we can." Only his eyes revealed his tension.

Carrie squeezed Janie's hand comfortingly before smiling and releasing it. "Wonderful!" She stepped back out into the hallway and stopped, not willing to leave Janie alone for even a moment, and sick at heart that she felt that way.

Carrie saw Clifford's eyes narrow with anger, but he kept a pleasant expression on his face as he stepped out into the hallway to join her.

Chapter Two

"We saved you some dinner," Matthew said pleasantly as Carrie, Janie and Clifford claimed their seats.

"Wonderful!" Carrie said brightly. "These two were going to hide in their room tonight, but I convinced them we wanted their company too much to let them do that."

Clifford nodded as he took his seat. Janie gave a small smile and slipped into the chair next to his.

Matthew almost frowned when he saw the expressions on their faces, but a quick warning glance from Carrie stopped him. "You're just in time to hear our news," he said instead.

Carrie took a bite of steaming beans. "What news would that be?" she asked, trying to keep her voice calm and steady, while her insides churned with fear and anger. She barely kept her hand from shaking when she remembered the fear she'd heard in Janie's voice behind the closed door.

"Matthew and I have decided to return to Washington, DC for President Lincoln's viewing and funeral procession," Aunt Abby said.

Carrie put down her fork slowly, her throat suddenly tight. "You're leaving?" was all she could think to say. The long day had left her physically, emotionally and mentally drained. She'd only had Aunt Abby back in her life for a short time. She couldn't bear to lose her again so quickly.

Aunt Abby, reading her thoughts clearly, reached over and took her hand. "Yes, my dear, but I'll be returning as soon as the formalities are over. Only something like this could pull me away from Richmond right now."

The pain in Aunt Abby's eyes sliced through Carrie's own pain. "Of course," she said immediately. "You must be there." Her gaze landed on Matthew. "You too," she murmured.

Matthew nodded. "The *Philadelphia Inquirer* has asked me to cover it, but I would want to be there regardless."

"Will you be coming back, too?" Carrie asked, still desperate to be surrounded by all the people who mattered to her. Janie was leaving and her father was still in hiding from Union forces, but she wanted to pull everyone else close. After four years of having to be strong, she suddenly felt fragile and weak. It was not a feeling she liked nor welcomed, but she also couldn't seem to conquer it.

Matthew shook his head. "No. I'll be leaving from Washington to accompany the funeral train to Illinois. I won't go with it all the way, because I've also been called down to travel with a boatload of freed prisoners from Vicksburg up the Mississippi."

"They're going home," Carrie said softly, understanding how much that would mean to Matthew after his stays in Libby Prison. She still had memories of his emaciated condition when she and Robert helped him escape.

"Yes." Matthew nodded, his expression showing his gratitude for her understanding. "They are going home."

"Then of course you must be there," Carrie replied. "No one can tell their story better than you can."

"When is the viewing?" Rose asked. "People must be coming from all parts of the country."

"You're right," Matthew agreed. "The trains will be crowded. The procession will be on the nineteenth so that people have a chance to get there."

"He's not going to be buried in Washington, DC?" Moses asked.

"No." Matthew answered. "I received news today that a delegate from Illinois came to the capital and asked Mrs. Lincoln to please have his body returned to his home in Illinois. She agreed."

"But not until there has been a procession and several days for people to view him," Aunt Abby added. "He was greatly loved."

"He was a tyrant," Clifford snorted.

Everyone jerked around to stare at him.

Aunt Abby was the first to speak. "You're angry," she said simply.

"Angry?" Clifford echoed. "I don't think there is a word strong enough to communicate my feelings. It was

Lincoln who declared war on the South. It was Lincoln who sent troops down here to kill off the best and the finest we had to offer." His voice grew more heated. "It was Lincoln who set all the slaves free. It was Lincoln who made sure the South was left in complete chaos and turmoil when the war ended." He pounded his fist on the table and leapt to his feet. "Angry?" he shouted. "Yes, I guess you could say I'm angry. And I certainly won't say I'm not glad he's dead!"

Shocked silence met his tirade.

Janie sat frozen as a statue, only her trembling shoulders revealing her pain and embarrassment. Her eyes were fixed on her empty plate.

Matthew was the first to find his voice as he sought to defuse the tense situation with reason. "I think I understand why you feel the way you do," he said slowly, "but I think you'll find Lincoln's death will only make things more difficult for the South."

Clifford snorted again. "I hardly think that is possible."

"Then you don't know President Johnson," Matthew responded blandly, not wanting to go into all he had learned today, and hoping against hope it had been wrong.

"And you don't know the Southern people," Clifford responded. "We may have lost the war, but we have not lost our dignity or our self-respect. The Yankees have taken or destroyed our lands, but they have not taken our spirits."

"I certainly hope not," Aunt Abby said fervently.

Even Clifford quieted and turned to stare at her. "What?" he muttered.

"Four years of war have left bitter feelings on every side," Aunt Abby said calmly. "There are people in the North who feel just as strongly as you do. It is going to take a very long time to reconstruct this great country. It's only going to be done by people who hold on to their dignity and their self-respect." She paused for a long moment. "It's also going to be done by people who can appreciate the dignity and self-respect of the other side. Hatred and misunderstanding is what got us here in the first place. I hardly think continuing down that road will create different results than what have already been created."

Clifford stiffened but remained silent.

Aunt Abby fixed her eyes on him and continued. "You are a very intelligent man, Clifford. You have a law practice you plan to revive. You can be a leader for positive change, or you can continue to promote hatred and prejudice. The choice will be yours."

Silence filled the room, but Aunt Abby wasn't done. "Anger and hatred will only poison you, my boy," she said. "They will poison your heart. They will poison your relationships. They will poison your business. And in the end, if you choose to let them, they will destroy all you hoped to be or become."

Carrie could hardly breathe. She saw Clifford's eyes flash, but he remained silent.

Aunt Abby took a breath and turned to smile at the rest of the table. "Now, I do believe May prepared a special dessert for tonight." She looked over to the housekeeper staring at her with wide eyes. "Would you be so kind as to deliver it to the parlor? I believe all of us need a change of scenery." She rose quietly and moved into the other room.

"Yessum," May squeaked, before she disappeared back into the kitchen.

Everyone pushed back from the table and followed Aunt Abby—all but Clifford and Janie.

Carrie looked back, her heart torn by the misery in Janie's eyes and alarmed by the fury in Clifford's. She'd seen that look before in Ike Adams' eyes. Memories of the old overseer at Cromwell Plantation made her shudder. She couldn't leave Janie alone with Clifford right now.

Carrie turned and moved back into the dining room, taking her place across from Janie. Janie's eyes were pleading with her to leave, but she couldn't do it. "I'm sorry, Clifford," she said quietly. "There are a lot of intense feelings right now."

Clifford snorted but looked at her with something akin to respect. "You came back in to talk to me?"

Carrie smiled tightly. "Aunt Abby said there has been enough hatred and prejudice. She's right. I don't pretend to understand or agree with all you feel, but I certainly accept your right to feel that way." She took an easier breath when she saw some of the rage fade from his eyes. She had endured many difficult conversations with her father and with Robert over their feelings regarding slavery.

The difference was that neither of those men had spoken to her with the complete scorn and disregard Clifford had directed at Janie. Neither of them had caused her to be frightened by their anger—especially not frightened they would direct it toward her. She sensed Clifford was a dangerous man. She had to calm him before Janie was alone with him again. Only then could she think about a more permanent solution.

"You are my friend's husband. You are someone I've come to care a great deal about. Those are the things that are most important to me."

She reached out and took Janie's hand, tears springing to her eyes when she felt how cold and trembling it was. "You're going home soon. I will miss both of you."

Clifford's anger faded away as he stared at her. "You're a fine woman, Carrie Borden. I fear you will not like the world the North has given us to live in."

Carrie shrugged. "I fear I will not like the world both the North and the *South* have given me to live in, but I learned long ago that I can't let circumstances rule my life. I have to acknowledge them, but I don't have to let them control me. My only real choice is to try to live a life of love and integrity in the midst of chaos."

Janie's eyes shot up to meet hers. Carrie breathed a sigh of relief as she saw the fear fade, replaced by a glimmer of hope and strength. She gazed into her friend's eyes, willing her to accept the confidence and strength she was passing on to her through her hand.

Carrie stood after a long moment. "Please join us in the parlor," she said gently. "It may be awkward," she added when she saw Clifford's eyes flare with resistance, "but if you truly meant what you said about living with dignity and self-respect, then you must be willing to stand up for your beliefs without apology."

She turned and walked into the parlor, praying Clifford and Janie would follow. She couldn't imagine

Janie having to go up to their room with Clifford right now. She simply wouldn't allow it, though she had no idea how she would stop it.

She almost cried with relief when Clifford followed her. He stood stiffly by the fireplace, but accepted the plate of dessert Aunt Abby handed him. Janie sank down on the sofa, looking as if she couldn't stand one more minute. Carrie sat down next to her, staying close to give her moral support.

She looked up to see Aunt Abby gazing at her with warm approval and pride.

Carrie flushed and had to stiffen herself against the total exhaustion that swept through her body. Had it really only been that morning when Matthew arrived with news of Lincoln's death? It didn't seem possible, yet she knew it was true. She sat quietly while conversation ebbed and flowed around her, everyone trying to ease the awkwardness for Janie's sake.

****

Carrie had just finished feeding Robert breakfast the next morning when a knock downstairs caught her attention.

Robert caught her quick look of concern. "Go see who it is," he said.

Carrie shook her head quickly, glad beyond relief that Robert's eyes were clear and his skin was cool. "There is nothing more important to me than being here with you," she protested. "I'm so very glad you're better."

Robert's smile was weak but genuine. "Now that I've eaten, all I want to do is go back to sleep. You won't tell me anything that is going on, but I can tell there is something."

"I don't want to give you anything else to worry about."

Robert shook his head wearily. "I find I don't have enough energy to care, much less *worry* about what might be happening in our country right now. I'd rather not know."

The words were dark with despair, but they gave Carrie a bright hope. It was the longest statement Robert had made since they carried him in so close to death. It was also the most coherent he had sounded. He may not care, but at least the fevers had not burnt through his intelligence and clear thinking. She could wait on everything else.

"All right then, my wonderful husband," she said. Carrie leaned down and kissed him softly. "You sleep. I'll be back up later."

Robert nodded but gripped her hand. "Aunt Abby? Is she still here?"

"Why?" Carrie cast about for how to answer him

A look of confusion marred his clear features for a long moment before Robert simply shrugged. "I don't know..." he murmured. "I thought perhaps she could come to see me." He paused and seemed to struggle for words, the fog seeping back into his eyes and voice. "She has very good eyes," he finally said, before he sagged back against the pillow and closed his eyes.

Carrie pulled the blanket up around his thin shoulders and gave him another gentle kiss, glad she didn't have to explain why Aunt Abby was gone. She didn't know how Robert would respond to Lincoln's death. She had no intention of letting him hear anything that would upset him. All she cared about was him getting better so they could leave Richmond and return to Cromwell Plantation.

****

Rose was waiting out in the hallway for her. "He's better this morning?"

"Yes. We actually had a short conversation. It wore him out, but it convinced me my husband is still in there." Carrie looked back at the room. "I don't care how long it takes—Robert is going to get well."

Rose wrapped her arm around Carrie's waist and squeezed. "I believe that completely," she assured her.

A giggle sounded from the room two doors down.

Carrie smiled. "John is awake?"

Rose laughed. "That boy wakes up the minute his daddy opens his eyes. He not only looks exactly like him, it's as if there is a cord between the two of them. All

John cares about is being with Moses. It's like he doesn't want to miss even one moment."

"Can you blame him? They've been apart for most of his life. John only saw Moses when he could slip in from serving in the Union Army. Every time he's seen him, he had to say goodbye again so quickly. He probably can't really believe, or understand, that his daddy is home to stay."

"You're right," Rose said quietly, tears of gladness pooling in her eyes. "Seeing the two of them together gives me so much joy I can hardly stand it sometimes." A lone tear escaped and trickled down her cheek. "When I think about how close Moses came to dying... If you hadn't saved him..."

"Well, I did!" Carrie said, determined to banish dark thoughts from the house. She decided to change the subject. "Do you know who is downstairs?"

Rose wiped away the tear and smiled. "I know what you're doing, Carrie Borden, but I'm going to let you change the subject because you *did* save my husband. I will forever be grateful," she added softly. She cocked her head and listened. "I believe that is Dr. Wild's voice I hear downstairs."

Carrie also listened, but her expression remained blank. "You can hear that? I can hear a murmur, but I can't detect any voices."

"Spend most of your life as a slave," Rose said blandly, "and you'll learn to listen harder. Always knowing what was going on was necessary to making it in the big house. You's sho 'nuff didn't want to be caught by no surprise!" she said, slipping into the slave lingo.

Carrie laughed merrily. "You never talked like that in your life," she said. "You were reading before I was—probably speaking better English before I was, too."

"That's true," Rose agreed, her eyes sparkling with fun. "But I did know how to fit in down in the quarters," she said. "Now, are you going to sit up here and jabber with me, or go down and find out what Dr. Wild wants? I'm quite sure he didn't come down here to see anyone but you."

Carrie turned to run down the stairs, but spun back around to give Rose a resounding kiss on the cheek. "I do love you, you know! I'm so very glad to have you back in my life again." For a moment, the loneliness of the four years they were separated pressed down on her, but she pushed it back. The war was over.

"And I love *you*," Rose replied, her eyes wet with emotion. "Now go!" she commanded.

Carrie was still smiling when she entered the parlor. Her smile disappeared when she saw Dr. Wild's sober eyes. "What's wrong?" she demanded, stiffening to prepare for whatever else was coming.

"We're short of help," Dr. Wild said. "So many of our boys were injured yesterday by the retaliation of the Union troops for Lincoln's assassination."

Carrie frowned. "Matthew told me a little of it. I suspected he was either hiding the whole truth, or simply didn't know. I didn't realize it was so bad," she murmured.

"He might not have known, but it doesn't matter. A lot of our medical personnel have left to return home to their families. I'm afraid I'm desperate for some help."

Carrie nodded. "Of course. I will need just a minute to get my things."

"I hate to take you away from Robert right now."

Carrie shook her head. "It's quite all right. I just fed him breakfast. He'll sleep the morning away, and Rose will be able to feed him lunch." She suddenly saw the answer to another problem. "Let me go get Janie," she said impulsively.

"I thought she and Clifford were leaving tomorrow for Raleigh," Dr. Wild protested. "I couldn't possibly ask her for help right now."

"Nonsense," Carrie returned. "You know she wouldn't forgive either one of us if she didn't have an opportunity to assist." She turned toward the east wing, praying that Clifford would allow her to go.

Fortunately, Clifford had left the house to take care of some business. Janie grabbed up her medical bag with a look of utter relief when Carrie explained the situation. "Of course I'll help," she responded.

Carrie gripped her hand as they walked down the hall. "We have to talk later."

Janie stiffened and nodded. "I know," she said hesitantly. "But right now, we have men who need us."

****

Moses settled back in the big porch swing, smiling down at little John fast asleep on his shoulder. Soft spring air flowed around them, bringing with it the aroma of magnolias bursting forth from their tight white buds. The creak of the swing kept rhythm with the carriages rattling past the house. He watched idly as May picked early spring vegetables from the garden for dinner that night.

There had been so many times in the last four years when he wondered if he would ever feel peace again. Even the knowledge of Lincoln's death couldn't overshadow the sheer joy of holding his sleeping son on a warm spring day.

"He's going to be as big as you before you know it," Jeremy teased. "It seems like he gets bigger every day."

Moses nodded. "I'm glad this war ended in time for me to still hold him like this." His voice was rough with emotion. "I've missed so much already in the first two years of his life."

"Your son adores you," Jeremy responded. "It's like the two of you have never been apart a day in your lives."

"We're making up for lost time," Moses agreed. "Your father was a fine man," he said, changing the subject.

Jeremy's face tightened for an instant. "Well, the father who raised me anyway. I still can't get used to knowing Thomas' father is my real father, or that Carrie is actually my niece..." His voice trailed off as his eyes grew thoughtful. "There are times when I can only hope to God that I'm a better man than he was."

"Times were different," Moses observed.

Jeremy stared at him. "You can't possibly be all right with the fact he raped Sarah."

"Of course not, but I've also learned enough to know it happened a lot. There are more men and women around this country like you than anyone would like to admit."

"Half black and half white," Jeremy said. "That is easier to get used to than the reality of who it was."

"Is it?" Moses asked, his eyes sharp and focused. "Is it really easier? Do you have any clue what your life is going to be like now that you're not a white man?"

Jeremy shrugged casually, but took a deep breath and settled back against his seat. "Probably not," he admitted. "The only thing I've really thought much about is getting to know Thomas and Carrie, and having the joy of getting to know my twin." He smiled. "Rose is really something."

"That she is," Moses agreed, but continued to press. "Your life isn't going to be the same, Jeremy. Are you ready for that?"

Jeremy took another deep breath. "How can I be?" he asked. "I have no idea what it means. I've spent my entire life as a white person. I've worked in the Virginia government as a white man. I've earned respect as a white man. I've never experienced anything else..."

"You have no idea what to expect," Moses finished for him.

"How could I?" Jeremy asked again, only his eyes revealing his tension. He looked at Moses for several long moments. "What can I expect?" he finally asked quietly.

Moses opened his mouth, but then closed it again.

"You started this conversation," Jeremy reminded him. "You asked me if I'm ready. I think it only fair you give me some idea of what I need to be ready *for*." He leaned forward. "You're right that I need to know. I can't think of anyone I would rather hear it from than you."

Moses frowned but knew he could be nothing but honest. "The fact that you're a white man won't matter once people find out you're half black," he said bluntly. "They will still be looking at blond hair and blue eyes, but they'll see you differently." He paused. "And they'll use it to look down on you."

Jeremy nodded. "I experienced that because of my father's work. There were people who looked at me differently because he chose to be the pastor of a black church."

"It will be different," Moses said sadly. "Especially now..."

"Now?"

"Because the South lost the war. There are a lot of people who blame it on the slaves—on the black people. They figure if the North hadn't come down here to set us free, then none of this would have happened."

"And if the South hadn't made you slaves in the first place, none of this would have happened," Jeremy countered.

Moses shook his head. "Reason doesn't matter to way too many people. You'll come to understand that. People are angry," he said simply. "And when they're angry, they need someone or some*thing* to be angry at. We're going to be it for a very long time."

He shifted John on his shoulder and looked down at his sleeping son. "It's going to take a long time for things to change, and I'm afraid they're going to get worse. My son is free, but he's certainly not yet free to live his life. People want a target for their anger. Staying in the South is going to make us their target."

"What do you think will happen?" Jeremy asked.

Moses shrugged. "Slavery meant white people had the right to do whatever they wanted to us. Control us...beat us...kill us...rape—"

"Slavery is over," Jeremy protested, his face tightening.

"But hatred isn't," Moses said, his eyes flashing with anger. John, sensing his temper even in his sleep, stirred restlessly and whimpered. Moses took a deep breath and kept his voice calm. "Prejudice isn't. The belief that we are less than them isn't. I don't believe the fact that we are no longer slaves is going to change those realities. It may actually make them worse."

"Worse?" Jeremy shook his head. "How?"

"Worse," Moses insisted. "It was bad enough when the South was successful and wealthy. Now they have lost everything. There is a lot of pain and a lot of anger."

"And people want a target for their pain," Jeremy finished for him.

"Yes," Moses agreed, "but it goes even deeper than that. Slave owners truly believe blacks are an inferior species. They believe we are simply not capable of controlling our own destinies. It appalls them to think we are being put on equal footing with them. And it scares them," he added. "They controlled us through slavery. Now suddenly we're free. They're going to be looking for every way possible to keep us in our place. They'll do whatever it takes," he finished.

"You paint an ugly picture," Jeremy said, protest in his eyes.

Moses eyed him sympathetically. "You said you wanted to know." He paused. "It doesn't have to be that way for you, though."

"What do you mean?"

"There's only a few people who know who you really are." Moses took a deep breath. "It can stay that way. You can keep living your life as a white man."

Jeremy stared at him hard, and managed a tight smile. "I hate to admit I've thought about it."

"And...?"

"No."

"Why not? It would make things so much easier for you," Moses insisted. "It doesn't mean you have to give up your relationship with Rose."

"Have you talked with Rose about this?" Jeremy asked.

Moses nodded. "She knows what I know. She loves you too much to want you to be hurt."

Jeremy nodded and smiled again, a genuine smile that lit his face. "I know." He looked out over the street and watched a carriage roll by with an elegantly dressed woman who smiled up at him until she saw Moses. Her smile vanished and became an angry look of disdain, her anger obvious at the impertinence of a black man sitting with a white man on a front porch in a white neighborhood.

Jeremy stared at her and turned back to Moses. "There has been too much hiding. Too much deception." He drew a deep breath. "My father hid the truth for all my life. My mother hid the truth. The Cromwells hid the truth. The trouble is that the truth has a way of always coming out."

He reached over, plucked a leaf from the magnolia tree, and twirled it between his fingers. "What would happen if I chose to live as a white man?" he asked. "I would have to deny who Rose is to me. I won't do it. I also know that, even if I marry a white woman, I have the chance of fathering a black baby. It would be totally unfair to hide that from someone I love."

He tossed the leaf over the railing and watched as it settled onto the grass. "I will not be the cause of more deception. I am who I am. I am the son of a wonderful black slave named Sarah and a careless, arrogant slave owner who only viewed her as property. I have a remarkable twin who has beautiful, ebony skin. I am the half-brother of a man I have tremendous respect for, and the uncle of one of the finest women I know. I would never deny my connection to Carrie. I am also the son of two wonderful adoptive parents who loved me and who also loved the black people they served. I will not hide behind white skin and blue eyes. I don't know exactly what all of it will mean, but I will live it as it comes."

"You've thought about it more than you admitted," Moses said after a long silence.

Jeremy shrugged and smiled. "I'm also rather fond of my brother-in-law and nephew. I'm afraid you're stuck with me."

John chose that moment to wake up. He reached up and patted Moses' face. "Hi, Daddy," he said sleepily. He looked around and spotted Jeremy. "Hi, Jer'me!" he said brightly, holding out his arms.

Jeremy grinned and scooped him over to sit on his lap. "Hello there, nephew. Want to go play in the backyard until dinner?"

John nodded happily. "Play!"

Jeremy winked at Moses as he set John on the ground and took his hand. "At least I have a little while before I have to try to explain it to him." He laughed and swung John down from the porch in a giant arc that sent the little boy into spasms of giggles.

****

Carrie and Janie worked until long after dinner. They treated bloody wounds, set broken arms and legs, and dispensed food to starving soldiers. After four years of war, they could do it almost without thinking. It was the questions that were the most difficult. How did one respond to questions that simply had no answers? Certainly ones she couldn't comprehend herself.

Carrie supposed she understood the anger that had resulted in the attacks, but she also knew it had been completely misplaced—black anger spilling over onto white men who had nothing to do with Lincoln's assassination. She also knew it would do nothing but make it harder for Richmond to heal the deep divisions over race.

"Are you Mrs. Borden?" The question came from a skinny lad with shaggy, dark hair and piercing brown eyes. His right arm was splinted, and bruises and welts covered his body.

"Yes, I am," Carrie said gently. "What can I do for you?"

"My name is Alex. I served with your husband."

Carrie reached down to grasp his hands. "I'm so sorry you're hurt."

Alex shook his head. "I'll be all right. I been hurt worse lots of times. I called you over here to ask about Captain Borden. I was the one who got him to the hospital wagon. He was pretty bad off. How is he, ma'am?"

Carrie's heart swelled with gratitude as tears filled her eyes. "Alex..." she murmured as she squeezed his hands tightly. "I've always wanted someone to thank. All they told me was that someone got Robert into the wagon and said to make sure he got help quickly."

"I wish I could have done more, ma'am." Alex hesitated. "The captain...?

"Is doing fine," Carrie said, deciding not to reveal how tenuous his health was. "He was very sick, but he's getting better every day." She leaned down to kiss Alex softly on the brow. "He has you to thank for that. As do I."

Alex smiled. "I sure am glad, Mrs. Borden. Captain Borden is a fine man." He looked up into her eyes shyly. "He used to talk about you all the time. Now I know why. You're even prettier than he said."

Carrie smiled softly.

Alex wasn't done. "The captain wouldn't stop," he said. "I knew he was getting real sick, but all he could think about was all of us. We didn't hardly get to eat anyway, but he ate even less. He wanted to make sure we had all we could. I tried to get him to eat, but he would just say he was fine." He frowned. "I knew he wasn't. He held on until it was all over, and then it was kinda like he gave up. I knew all he wanted was to get back home to you."

Carrie made no attempt to stop the tears rolling down her face. "Thank you so much, Alex," she whispered. "It's because of you that my husband is still alive." Her breath caught. "And then you were attacked!"

Alex shrugged again. "Like I said, I been hurt way worse. Can I get out of here soon? I'm eager to get back home to my farm." He paused, a shadow coming into his eyes. "If it's still there. I know lots of places aren't."

Carrie could tell his thoughts were far away. Her heart ached at the look of yearning on his face. "I hope it's still there for you, Alex," she murmured, unable to keep her thoughts from flying to the fields of Cromwell Plantation. "You are going to get a chance to start over."

"Yes, ma'am, I reckon I am," Alex said wearily. "Things sure didn't turn out the way we hoped, but at least I'm still alive. My arm may be broken, but at least I still have it. That's more than I can say for a lot of the fellas."

Carrie pressed his hands again. "You've got a whole life ahead of you," she whispered through her tears. "If my husband or I can ever do anything for you, please let us know."

Alex smiled. "Thank you for that, ma'am. It's enough to know the captain is okay. You tell him I said hello."

"I will," Carrie promised. "I know he would want to come down, but he's still too ill."

Alex nodded. "Just knowing is enough. I reckon I'll be out of here in a day or two. I'm going to head home right away. I'd already be close, except for them soldiers attacking me. But then I wouldn't have found out about Captain Borden, so I reckon some good came out of it."

Carrie looked at him more closely. "You're rather remarkable," she said suddenly. "I've met so many soldiers who are bitter and angry. Why aren't you?" she asked.

"You can thank your husband," Alex responded. "We used to have right long talks while we were waiting for battles, or while we were marching to escape the Yankees." He paused, remembering. "I had me enough bitterness and anger for a bunch of men, but the captain told me it would eat me up and leave me with nothing. He told me things would always happen that would be hard, but it was up to me how I dealt with it." Alex was the one to give Carrie's hand a tight squeeze. "He told me his wife taught him all that, so I reckon I got you to thank, too."

Carrie smiled through her tears, only moving away from Alex's bed when she was called by another soldier. "I'll check on you later," she promised.

When she finished caring for her last patient and everyone was asleep, she slipped over to say goodbye to Alex, smiling softly when she saw he was sleeping soundly. His face had softened, and she laid her hand on his forehead gently, said a quick prayer, and turned away.

Janie was waiting for Carrie by the door, her eyes clouded with fatigue, but her face peaceful.

Only then did Carrie realize how tired she was. "Long day," she said simply.

"It felt good," Janie replied. "It will be hard when I get to Raleigh and I don't have a way to make a difference."

Carrie's gut tightened as she gazed into her friend's eyes and saw the pain and fear she was trying to hide. She grabbed Janie's hand and pulled her over to stand under a tall oak tree next to the hospital entrance. Spencer was waiting in the carriage across the street, but she knew he would wait as long as she needed. "We need to talk before we go home," she said.

Janie opened her mouth to protest and then simply nodded.

"I'm so worried about you, Janie. So much has happened that I almost missed how angry Clifford has become."

Janie's blue eyes shimmered with tears. "He has changed. Losing the war has changed him."

"*Losing* the war?"

"Yes. Losing his arm was hard, but he still believed the South would go back to the way it was, and he would pick up his life where he left it in Raleigh."

"And he no longer believes that?"

"He believes losing the war has destroyed everything he holds dear," Janie explained. "He is terrified of what will happen now that all the slaves are free. He is afraid of them revolting against the white people, just like they have in the last day when they attacked all the soldiers."

Carrie looked at her more closely. "And you? How do you feel?"

Janie stared into her eyes and shook her head helplessly. "His fear is rubbing off on me," she admitted slowly, her eyes begging for understanding. "You know I don't have a prejudice against black people, and I'm so glad the slaves are free..."

"But...?"

"I guess I never really thought of what it would be like in the South if two million slaves suddenly had their freedom." Janie searched for words. "What do you believe is going to happen?"

Carrie spoke carefully. "I don't believe there are any easy answers," she said. "I know that slavery simply had to end. Now that it has, I think everyone is going to have to figure out what life will be like."

"Are you scared?" Janie asked. "Are you scared of what will happen?"

Carrie made sure her answer was true before she gave it. "No. I believe there are two million slaves who are way more frightened than any of us are. I believe they simply want an opportunity to become educated, and live their lives as they want to. I believe they want to know they will never be separated from their loved ones by the auction block, and that they want to reunite from the people they have been torn apart from." She paused and looked up into the leaves of the tree as a wind sprang up to toss them in a merry dance. A glance over Janie's shoulder revealed the last glimmer of light on the horizon before darkness cloaked the day.

"I don't believe they are looking for more fighting. I'm sure there are some who are angry and looking for revenge, just as there are white people looking for the same. But that's not a racial issue, it's a morality issue. Those of us who believe in their right to freedom have to stand up for them and do everything we can to help them live as free people."

"But what if the white people won't let it happen?" Janie asked.

Carrie looked deeply into her friend's eyes and saw something that troubled her. "Do you know something?"

Janie hesitated but shook her head. "Clifford talks all the time about how the Southern man will never allow blacks to be their equal. He doesn't tell me how, but he tells me there are already plans to make sure that doesn't happen."

Carrie's heart squeezed with sorrow and regret. "So they're not going to let the war end?"

Janie only shook her head again. "I just don't know," she whispered, fear and pain shining in her eyes.

Carrie gave her a warm hug. "None of that matters right now," she said bluntly. "Right now I'm only worried about you. Clifford's anger is growing. So is your fear." She stepped back to stare into Janie's eyes. "You're afraid of your husband."

Janie opened her mouth in automatic refusal but closed it, her weight sagging against Carrie as tears filled her eyes. "Yes," she admitted, her voice raw with pain. "I am afraid of him."

"What are you going to do?" Carrie asked, fighting to keep her voice calm.

Janie looked at her now with confusion. "Do? What *can* I do? Clifford is my husband."

"Has he hurt you?" Carrie asked, hoping the unexpected question would illicit an honest response.

"Physically?" Janie replied. "Not really. He has grabbed my arms a few times, but he has never hit me. I can't believe he would ever do that," she protested.

"Yes, you can," Carrie responded, "or you wouldn't be afraid of him."

Janie closed her eyes for a long moment. "Yes, I'm afraid he will, but it's more than that..." She paused for a long moment. "I'm disappearing," she finally murmured. "I can't seem to remember who I am, or what I want, or what I dreamed of during the long years of the war."

Tears spilled over to run down her cheeks. "Everything is getting swallowed by his anger and bitterness."

Carrie prayed for wisdom and the right words. "You don't have to go back with him," she said gently. "You can stay here in Richmond and come out to the plantation. We'll figure things out together."

Janie stared at her blankly. "Leave him? Divorce him?"

"It's been done," Carrie replied. "Times have changed. It used to be you could only get divorced because of adultery, but Thomas Jefferson began to change things. Now you can get a divorce for incompatibility."

Janie was staring at her, her eyes now dry. "Divorce? It can be done, but how women are viewed hasn't changed. Do you know what the life of a divorcee is like? People would scorn me."

Carrie searched for what to say. "This from my liberal friend who defied so many societal conventions to work at Chimborazo Hospital?" she asked. "You suddenly care what people think?"

Janie's eyes flashed with quick anger. "This is different," she insisted. "I married Clifford for life."

"Yes," Carrie said, with a growing anger of her own that she fought to control. "You married a man who promised to love, honor and cherish you—not frighten you with threats, anger and abuse." She took a deep breath to control her anger. "I heard the things he said to you last night, Janie. I heard him call you stupid. I heard the rage in his voice."

The tears that filled Janie's eyes now were ones of shame. She lowered her head as sobs shook her shoulders.

The anger vanished as quickly as it had appeared. Carrie wrapped her friend in another warm hug. "I'm so sorry," she whispered, "but it's not your fault. Clifford is a very angry man, and he's allowing his bitterness to spill over you. You don't have to let him."

"Would you leave Robert?" Janie asked. "Would you divorce him and fail at marriage?"

"Yes." Carrie had already thought it through. "If Robert returned from war abusive and destructive, I would divorce him. It would break my heart, but I can't expect anyone else to have respect for me, if I don't have it for myself first," she said gently.

Janie stared at her for long moments before she shook her head. "I can't," she whispered. "I can't leave him." Her voice broke as she shook her head helplessly. "I'm sorry, Carrie, but I can't."

"It's all right," Carrie whispered back. "You're making a choice. I'm praying you'll find the strength to live with it." Her voice grew stronger. "But you have to make me one promise, Janie."

Janie peered at her through tear-filled eyes but remained silent.

"You have to promise me that if it gets too hard, you'll come back here. That you'll let me help you." She grasped her hands tightly. "And you have to promise to stay in communication. I'll write every week. You have to let me know what's going on."

Janie hesitated for a long moment and then nodded. "I promise." She stepped back. "We have to go home," she said. "It's getting very late. I have some things to finish up before we leave tomorrow. I'm sure Clifford is getting quite anxious."

Carrie opened her lips to say more but realized she had said all she could. She raised her hand and signaled to Spencer.

Chapter Three

Matthew leaned back against the train seat and closed his eyes for a long minute. When he opened them, Aunt Abby was gazing at him with tender compassion.

"Long few days," she commented.

Matthew nodded, rubbing his stiff neck to try to release the tension. "Long few days," he agreed. Then he smiled. "I'm glad you're coming to Washington, DC with me."

Aunt Abby smiled back. "Me, too. I hate the circumstances, but I'm so glad to have this time with you, and I wouldn't want to experience this with anyone but you. I know that you know what I'm feeling right now. I'm old enough to be your mother, but I simply think of you as my friend."

Matthew reached across the seat and took her hand. "We are friends," he said simply. "But you are also my rock. There were so many times during the last five years that I wasn't sure I could keep going. You were always there to encourage me and make me believe it was possible to keep pressing on."

"We did that for each other," Aunt Abby assured him. Her clear, gray eyes suddenly filled with tears. "Oh, Matthew...it's really true that President Lincoln is dead. We are really going to his funeral."

Matthew frowned. "It's true."

Both of them sat quietly, watching as trees flashed by. The train was crowded but eerily quiet. Every person on the train was headed north for one reason—to attend Lincoln's funeral. Each person sat with their own grief and uncertainty about what the future held.

Matthew had expected the trains coming from Northern cities to be congested, but he was surprised the train leaving Richmond was so crowded. It didn't take him long to realize the train was full of Northerners who had come south when Richmond fell two weeks earlier. They were all returning to say a final goodbye to the man who had held the Union together against all odds.

Matthew's chest tightened as the reality of Lincoln's death hit him once more. His eyes blurred as he tried to imagine the future without Lincoln's steady presence and political influence.

"What do you know about President Johnson?" Aunt Abby asked. "I'm afraid I know so little, other than he was inaugurated as vice president just six weeks ago on March fourth."

"And no one has seen much of him since then," Matthew responded ruefully, glad for the question because it set him free from his own thoughts. "I'm afraid his inauguration was something of a debacle."

"Oh?"

"He was already hungover from a party the night before, and then a few shots of whiskey that day had him quite drunk when he got up to give his speech. I understand he rambled on for quite a while, not making any sense for periods of it, before he finally sat down to let Lincoln speak."

"Oh dear..." Aunt Abby murmured.

"He's been hiding out at a friend's house from sheer embarrassment since then," Matthew continued. "He showed up in the Senate a time or two, but other than that, no one has seen him. I heard from a colleague at the station this morning that he had his first meeting with Lincoln since the inauguration on the morning of April fourteenth."

Aunt Abby grimaced. "And that night President Lincoln was assassinated." She took a deep breath. "Well, it's certainly not a grand beginning, but there must have been good reason for Lincoln to put him on the ticket last fall."

"Yes, there must have been a reason," another man said.

Only then did Matthew realize their conversation had drawn an audience. Several men and women in the seats surrounding them had turned to listen, their eyes full of avid curiosity about the man who was suddenly the president of a country that had just ended a four-year civil war.

"I'll tell you what I know," Matthew replied, glad he had recently finished an article on Johnson for the

Philadelphia Inquirer, and also thankful for what he learned from Sam in Richmond. "President Johnson grew up in poverty in North Carolina. His father died when he was three years old. When he was ten, his mother apprenticed him out to a tailor until he was twenty-one, but when he was fifteen, he ran away."

"Rough beginning," Aunt Abby murmured. "And now to be president..."

"Yes. He went back after a few years and tried to buy out the rest of his apprenticeship, but he and the tailor couldn't reach an agreement, so he headed west to Tennessee and started a new life."

"I heard he was quite successful as a tailor," one of the listeners offered.

"And that he made even more money by investing in real estate," another added.

Matthew braced himself as the train took a sharp curve and then nodded. "All true."

"I also heard he was a slave owner," another added angrily.

"And there is also rumor that the three children from his first slave are very light-skinned. People believe he is their father."

Matthew nodded again, knowing that most of the people who had come down to Richmond were abolitionists eager to help the slaves start to rebuild their lives again. "That's true, too," he agreed. Then he launched back into his explanation. "Johnson fought for the right to own slaves his entire political career."

"Then why did President Lincoln select him as his running mate?" Aunt Abby asked, aware her own personal affairs in the last several months had kept her oblivious of Lincoln's choice—a fact she now deeply regretted.

"President Johnson was a staunch Union man," Matthew informed her. "He fought hard for Tennessee to stay with the Union. When they chose to secede with the Confederacy, Johnson was the only senator from the South who actually kept his seat throughout the war." He stared out at the darkening sky, and then continued. "Lincoln made him military governor of Tennessee when the army claimed the western and middle parts of the state. The Confederates were less than thrilled."

"I imagine," Aunt Abby murmured. "I understand his home and his business were in eastern Tennessee. What happened?"

"The Confederates confiscated all his land, took away his slaves, and turned his home into a military hospital," Matthew said ruefully.

"Johnson also fought for slavery," one of the listeners protested.

"That's true," Matthew agreed, "but he also created the Homestead Bill that became law in 1862."

"President Johnson was the man who created the legislation that made homesteaders able to claim a hundred sixty acres of land on public lands?" one of the men listening asked with surprise. "That has sure helped a lot of people."

"Yes. He tried to pass it in 1860, but Southern congressmen rejected it because they were afraid most of the land would be claimed by Northerners, who would then ban slavery in that state."

"Tipping the balance of power," Aunt Abby observed.

"Exactly," Matthew said. "After a long hard fight, Congress actually passed it, but then President Buchanan vetoed it."

"Why?" Aunt Abby asked in surprise.

"Buchanan was not willing to go against his Southern backers," Matthew said. "It would have been sure political death for him to alienate all the Southern leaders, and he was also trying to hold the country together."

"But it passed in 1862?" The question came from an immaculately dressed woman with sharp, intelligent eyes.

"Yes. It had already passed easily through the Northern part of Congress. Without pro-slavery involvement, it quickly became law."

"If Johnson was so pro-slavery," another man asked in confusion, "why did he introduce something that alienated so many of his colleagues?"

Matthew shrugged. "Our new president is a very complex man. I have no doubt he loves this country, but..."

Aunt Abby leaned forward. "*But what*, Matthew? It's better for everyone to know the truth about the man now leading our country."

"He has no sympathy for the Negro population," Matthew said heavily. "He finally came around to the belief that slavery had to end because it was hurting the United States, but he has never pretended for a moment that he thinks slaves can ever be equal citizens with white people."

"But why would Lincoln put someone like him in power?" Aunt Abby's head was spinning as she considered the ramifications of Matthew's last statement.

"Lincoln was impressed with how Johnson administrated Tennessee. He also believed that having Johnson, a Southern War Democrat, on the ticket sent the right message about the folly of secession and the continuing capacity for union within the country." Matthew paused. "Lincoln believed Johnson was a good man."

"And he never thought Johnson would end up running the country he fought so hard to keep together," Aunt Abby said.

Matthew nodded. "That's true." His face said everything that his words did not.

"But what is going to happen to all the freed slaves?" a woman demanded. "Is he going to use the power of the federal government to make sure they get their rights?"

Matthew shook his head. "I don't know," he said bluntly, weariness in his voice. He had thought of little else since he had heard of Lincoln's death. His mind had been full of thoughts of Rose, Moses and all the other friends he had made. He feared for what their lives would be like if President Johnson still carried his same attitude. He feared what would happen in the South without Lincoln's leadership. His excitement over the future had dulled to an uncertain dread.

Aunt Abby watched him quietly. He already knew she was reading his mind. Her clear gray eyes were dark with their own troubled thoughts.

A long silence followed Matthew's final words.

"Only time will tell what the future will bring," Aunt Abby finally said. "I've learned not to borrow trouble before it comes."

Matthew nodded along with the others as they murmured their agreement, but his dread did not diminish. There were times when being a newspaperman gave him a sense of pride and purpose. There were other times when knowledge was nothing but a reason to dread the future.

******

Carrie and Janie climbed out of the carriage and waved goodbye to Spencer.

Carrie glanced longingly at the barn behind her father's house. It was on days like today that she would give almost anything to be flying across the fields of Cromwell Plantation on Granite, her towering gray Thoroughbred. The carefree days of her youth seemed to belong to another person, yet the memories called her and intensified the longing to go home.

Janie caught her wistful look. "Nothing more from your father?" she asked.

"No," Carrie said. "I think about him all the time. I hope he is still safe in Danville. I don't know how strongly the Union Army is going to go after former officials in the Confederate government. At least Father was only involved in the Virginia government, but I'm afraid it might be more dangerous now that Lincoln has been killed," she said, her voice catching on her fears. Tears blurred her eyes. "He just wants to come home," she murmured. "I so hope he can do that soon. He needs to be on the plantation again." She knew it was the only place he could begin to heal from the agony of the war years.

"And so does Granite," Janie said sympathetically. "At least your wonderful horse is where he has food so he can gain back the weight he lost during the war."

"I'm hoping that is still true," Carrie said fervently. "It tore at my gut every time I couldn't feed him enough, or every time he had to go off to battle." Her voice tightened. "I'm so glad this blasted war is over," she said.

"You and me both!"

Carrie jumped as a voice sounded from the shadows of the porch. "Moses!" she gasped. "I didn't see you there."

"I was waiting for you and Janie."

Carrie tensed at what she heard in his voice. Long years of suspense, waiting and tragedy had made her quite adept at reading voices and situations. "What is it?" she asked.

Moses sent Janie an apologetic look before he answered. "Clifford was upset when he came home and found Janie gone."

"I was taking care of our soldiers," Janie said.

"Yes," Moses agreed, "but he was still upset."

"Because she was with me." Carrie provided the words he wasn't saying. She knew Clifford was threatened by her closeness with Janie, and afraid that Carrie's influence would lessen his hold on her.

Moses looked at them, knowing his silence would reveal the truth. "Clifford has gone into town to get a wagon. He's decided to leave tonight."

"Tonight?" Janie gasped. "We're scheduled to leave tomorrow morning. What difference could a night make?"

Moses' eyes flashed his anger, but he kept his voice calm, seeming to know Janie would need it to hold on. "It seems to matter to Clifford. He had May and Micah pack up the last of your things and put them in the foyer. He should be back any moment."

A sudden rattle of wagon wheels had Janie spinning around to peer down the road. Her face was a bewildering mixture of anger, pain and fear. It was easy to identify Clifford's erect body on the wagon seat. Even with one arm, he handled the team proficiently. Janie shook her head helplessly and straightened her body as the wagon rolled to a stop in front of the gate.

"We're leaving," Clifford announced, only his eyes flashing his anger.

The anger dissolved from Janie's face. Only the pain and fear remained.

Carrie gritted her teeth but kept silent. She'd said all she could. Janie was going to go with Clifford. There was nothing else she could do. She watched as Micah and Moses carried the boxes and luggage down from the house and stacked them in the wagon. She almost cried when May bustled out with a big basket of food for them, because she knew it had been made strictly for Janie.

Everyone remained silent, but grief shone from every pair of eyes.

When the wagon was full, Carrie turned and grabbed Janie in a tight embrace. "You are my sister," she whispered fiercely, forcing the words around the tears in her throat. "You promised to write, and you promised to leave if things get really bad." She swallowed back her tears and gripped her even more tightly. "I love you, Janie. I don't know what I would have done without you all these years."

Janie gripped her back just as tightly. "I love you, too, Carrie. You are the sister I always dreamed of. I will write you every week."

Clifford stared down at them, his face a tight mask. "It's time to go, Janie," he said calmly.

Carrie forced herself to look up and smile. Increasing his enmity by saying everything that boiled in her would only make things more difficult for Janie. "Goodbye, Clifford. I'm so sorry you feel you have to leave now, but I hope you have a good journey back to North Carolina." She paused and took a deep breath. "And I hope you find all you're looking for."

She was almost mesmerized by Clifford's cold eyes when he stared down at her. How had they gone from warm friends to obvious enemies? Her heart tightened at the brief glimpse she was seeing of how relationships could change over the racial issue. Aunt Abby was right. The war had been won and the slaves were free, but the battle for racial equality had only just begun.

Clifford nodded curtly, but his eyes softened slightly. "Thank you for all your hospitality, Carrie."

Carrie fought the urge to laugh hysterically. She had saved Clifford's life. She had arranged the wedding ceremony between him and Janie. They had lived as family for the last months. How had all that been reduced to *hospitality*? She swallowed back her hysteria and smiled. "You're welcome, Clifford. And you're always welcome here," she added graciously, determined not to let his anger create any more of a divide between her and Janie. Already, her heart was breaking.

Carrie battled tears as she watched Janie climb onto the wagon seat beside Clifford, her face etched with dark sorrow and confusion. Carrie stepped back beside Moses, thankful for the feeling of his strength beside her. "Goodbye," she said softly, gazing into Janie's eyes so that her friend would see all the love bubbling from the depths of her heart.

Janie stared back almost wild-eyed, as Clifford raised his hand and urged the horse forward. In moments, the wagon had disappeared into the near darkness.

Only then did Carrie collapse against Moses and let the tears come. Sobs wracked her body as Moses enfolded her and let her cry. "How could she go with him?" she cried. "How could she go with him?" she repeated, her voice a hoarse whisper.

"He's taken her courage," Moses replied.

Carrie pulled back to stare up at him with drenched eyes. "She told me today that she was afraid she was disappearing..." she whispered.

Moses nodded. "A man like Clifford controls through fear. Janie is afraid of him. Until she can reach down to find her own courage and remember who she is, she won't be able to stand against him."

"And if she does?" Carrie asked, fresh fear springing into her heart. "What will he do then?" Visions of Janie being beaten, or worse, filled her mind. She choked back the groan that wanted to escape.

"There's nothing you can do now but pray," Moses said gently. "Janie is going to have choices and decisions to make."

Carrie wanted to scream out against the injustice. Anger rose in her that God would allow Janie to be in this situation, but then the truth of Moses' words sank in. Janie had *chosen* to leave instead of staying where she would be safe. She was an adult woman who had made her choice. Only she could live with the consequences. Carrie clenched her fists and fought to control her breathing. "You're right," she finally admitted.

"At least Janie has a safe place to come back to if she's ever ready," Moses added. "My guess is that you tried to convince her to stay."

Carrie nodded.

"And you also told her she could come back here."

Carrie nodded again; still silent, but his words gave her a small surge of hope. If Janie ever decided to make another choice, at least she wouldn't be like so many women with nowhere to go—nowhere to escape.

Moses gazed down at her. "You've done all you could do, Carrie. Now it's up to Janie."

"You're right," she whispered, staring down the road into the darkness.

May stepped forward then. "You come on in now, Miss Carrie. Dinner be on the table. Rose be upstairs feeding Mr. Robert. You gots to put some food in your belly, chile." She stepped back to stare into Carrie's face. "You ain't eaten nothing since you left here this morning, have you?" she demanded.

Carrie forced herself to focus on the loving woman's concerned eyes. "No, ma'am," she admitted. She was suddenly aware of her stomach rumbling as a deep wave of fatigue rolled through her. "Dinner sounds good."

Within moments, she was sitting in front of a plate full of cornbread slathered with butter, and heaps of hot vegetables picked fresh from the garden that morning. A plate of fresh lettuce topped with carrots and radishes had her almost salivating as she gave thanks for the warm days causing the garden to produce so early.

Carrie remained silent as she dug into the meal, knowing she needed the strength it would provide. Her day was not over yet. She knew Robert was waiting for her. She brightened slightly as she thought of how pleased he would be to hear she had met Alex. She had a lot to tell him—if he could stay awake.

*****

Rose joined Carrie just as she was finishing her meal. "Janie is gone?"

Carrie nodded, feeling a fresh wave of grief and anger. "She's gone."

"Janie is a strong woman, Carrie," Rose replied, her eyes soft with knowing.

"Not right now," Carrie replied, her words almost a groan.

"No," Rose agreed, "but I'm willing to bet she will find her strength when she needs it," she said. "Right now, fear is controlling her decisions, but at some point she will get tired of the fear and reach down to grab the strength that is waiting."

Carrie smiled slightly. "You sound like your mama."

Rose smiled back at her. "You couldn't give me more of a compliment. My mama helped me through so many of my own fears. Every time my fears would grab hold of me she would remind me of how strong I was, and that I just needed to decide to *be* strong."

Carrie sighed. "I would so love to sit down and talk with your mama right now."

May walked in with a huge slice of cake. "I done heard so much about Old Sarah," she said as she put it down. "I sure wish I could have known her myself. She sounds like she done been quite a woman."

"That she was," Carrie agreed. "Rose's mama was one of the wisest women I've ever known. Besides helping me grow up, she taught me almost everything I know about herbal medicine." She shuddered. "I hate to think how bad the suffering would have been in the hospital if we hadn't had the herbal treatments I taught the women to make. Once the blockades stopped all medical supplies, it was all we had."

"Mama was a saint," Rose agreed softly. "Every time I look at little John, I think about her. She would have loved him so much."

"She sho 'nuff would have," May said just before she slipped into the kitchen. "That young'un is really somethin'."

Carrie closed her eyes in delight as she ate the first bite of cake. She talked around her food, grateful no one was around to see her lack of manners. "I think your mama sees John every day. And," she added, "I know John sees *her* every day because you're becoming just like her." She reached out and gripped Rose's hand. "She would have been so proud of you."

Tears shone in Rose's eyes for a brief moment. "Thank you," she said. "I pray every day that I can be as fine a woman as my mama was."

Carrie reached over to grab another fork. "You have to help me with this cake. There is no way I can eat all of this, and if I do, I won't be able to waddle up the stairs."

Rose laughed. "It's not possible for someone as slender as you to waddle, but I'm happy to help you out of your dilemma, especially since no one is here to watch me eat off your plate!"

Moses walked into the room just then. "What's that I hear? Two Southern women sharing a plate? I'm fairly certain the etiquette gods will come after you," he teased as he sat down and reached for another fork. "Since you've thrown all manners to the wind, do you think I could have a bite of that?" he asked hopefully.

They heard the snort of laughter before the door to the kitchen flung open again. May slapped another huge slab of cake on the table, smiled at them, and disappeared back into her domain.

"Bless you!" Moses called as he pulled the new plate close to him and began to eat, pure satisfaction covering his face. "That May cooks like my mama," he announced.

Carrie watched as the satisfaction faded away to be replaced by pain. She reached forward to grab his hand. "You'll be strong enough to go after your mama soon," she said. "You're getting stronger every day." She saw the spark of protest in his eyes. "To try to go after her now would be a mistake," she said. "It would be too easy for infection to set in. What good would you do your mama then?"

Moses stared at her and nodded reluctantly. "You're right," he admitted. "I know the war has only been over a couple weeks, but I've been wondering about my mama and Sadie for the last five years. I've got to find them."

"And you will," Rose assured him. "You will. But first you have to let your wound heal. And," she added, knowing this would temper his restlessness more than anything, "John would be heartbroken if you were to leave now. He needs more time with his daddy."

Moses' frustration was replaced with a look of warm love. "You're right. I can't imagine saying goodbye to him right now." He smiled as he looked at Rose. "Don't think I don't know how you're handling me," he said. "I guess I'll have to be okay with it, because I know you're right."

"I'm always right," Rose said smugly, sticking her tongue out at him.

Carrie laughed, the sheer normalcy of their conversation easing the pain of Janie's departure. She jumped up from the table. "I'm going to leave you two children to fight it out," she tossed over her shoulder as she ran up the stairs. "I'm going up to see Robert!"

Chapter Four

Matthew was waiting for Aunt Abby when she entered the dining room of the National Hotel. "Good morning," he said somberly. "Did you sleep well?"

"I slept much better than I thought I would. The hotel is quite nice. This is my first time here." She gazed around at the white-columned dining room, appreciating the linens covering the tables and the many beautiful plants that lent splashes of green. Then she frowned. "It's hard to believe God would create such a perfect spring day for Lincoln's funeral procession. I think I would prefer it to be cloudy and stormy. It would certainly be more fitting."

"That may be," Matthew agreed, "but it would also certainly be harder for the horses to pull the funeral wagon through the mud, and I daresay it would be rather uncomfortable for everyone."

Aunt Abby sighed and took her seat at the table. "I know you're right. It's just that my thoughts are so dark this morning. I'm trying my best to find some sort of comfort and understanding, but it continues to elude me."

"As it does the thousands who are here to watch the procession," Matthew responded. "I'm afraid there is nothing to feel but sadness."

"And anger," Aunt Abby added, her eyes sparking. "I still can't believe that John Wilkes Booth killed the one man who should be putting our country back together again. Everything he stood for...everything he came to believe and understand during the war...the love he had for the United States..." Her anger crumpled as her eyes filled with tears. "A waste...such a waste."

Matthew reached forward to take her hand and decided the best thing to do was offer a distraction after a long time of silence. "I do believe it's at least safe to eat here this morning."

Aunt Abby pulled her thoughts back to the table as she stared at him. "Excuse me?"

"You're not aware of the mysterious sickness that seems to have come from this dining room about eight years ago?"

Aunt Abby frowned. "A mysterious sickness? I'm afraid I've not heard of that."

Matthew was glad to see curiosity replace some of the trouble in her eyes. "Eight years ago, the National Hotel was the largest in the city."

"The war has certainly changed that," Aunt Abby replied. "I can hardly even remember the capital the way it was before the war. It's changed so much."

Matthew forged ahead, wanting to keep her distracted. "The illness made four hundred people sick. Nearly three dozen died."

"What?"

Matthew was satisfied he had Abby's full attention when he looked into her wide eyes. "The disease caused a persistent diarrhea, along with intense colic. Many were prostrate with nausea."

"Food poisoning," Aunt Abby murmured. "I was sick with that once when I was in my twenties. I was miserable."

Matthew grimaced in sympathy. "People were indeed miserable. Thankfully, most of them did not die." He paused, determined to be a good storyteller. "Some medical experts believe it was an attempt to poison hotel boarders."

"But why?" Aunt Abby leaned forward and fixed her eyes on him.

"What is known for sure is the epidemic happened at the same time as President-elect Buchanan's first stay at this fine establishment. When he went home, reports of new cases stopped." He paused for dramatic effect. "When he returned two weeks later, the illness flared up again."

Aunt Abby gaped at him. "Someone was trying to kill President Buchanan?"

Matthew shrugged. "We'll never know, but among those who were killed were three members of Congress."

"But surely there was an investigation," Aunt Abby protested. "I seem to remember hearing something about this, but I was in the midst of the attempted takeover of my business back then. I'm afraid I was rather distracted."

Matthew frowned, remembering much too vividly just how much danger she had been in. Certain men in Philadelphia had not taken kindly to the idea of her taking over her husband's business. They had tried to force her out with intimidation, threats, and finally an attack he had been there to thwart. "You had good reason to be distracted," he said gruffly and then remembered why he was telling the story.

"There were doctors who believed there was someone in the hotel trying to poison the guests. Their investigations couldn't prove that. They did discover that arsenic was used to try to eliminate rats in the hotel. One of the poisoned rats was discovered in the water tank after guests became sick."

Aunt Abby carefully put down the glass she had just picked up.

Matthew laughed. "I believe it's quite safe now." To prove his confidence, he took a long swallow from his own crystal goblet. "Anyway, they never found evidence of arsenic in the autopsies they did. They did, however, put forth the theory that a poisonous miasma could have caused the illness."

Aunt Abby stared at him. "*Miasma*? I'm sorry, but you're going to have to enlighten this old lady. What is a miasma? It sounds hideous."

"It is," Matthew agreed. "A miasma is a poisonous gas that originates from the decomposition of vegetables and animals. The committee thought the infection could have entered the hotel from the Sixth Street sewer line. Evidently, they discovered a leak coming into the building that was strong enough to extinguish a candle flame."

"Disgusting!"

Matthew laughed. "I couldn't agree more. The committee could never find evidence of water, food or arsenic poisoning. People quit getting sick, so all the furor died down. Since then, it's simply been referred to as a mysterious illness."

"Are you ready to order?"

Matthew looked up at the elegantly attired waiter. "Certainly." He placed an order for both of them and then leaned back in his chair.

Aunt Abby spoke first. "Thank you."

"For what?"

"For distracting me. I know what you were doing," Aunt Abby said fondly.

"It worked?"

Aunt Abby smiled slightly. "For those few minutes." Her forehead creased again. "I heard people in the lobby talking about Secretary of State Seward, but I didn't catch much of what they said. Did something happen to him as well?"

Matthew sighed, knowing he would have to tell her sooner or later. "Yes."

"What happened?" Aunt Abby asked quietly, bracing for more bad news.

Matthew knew better than to give her anything less than the total truth. "They tried to kill him the same night they killed Lincoln," he said bluntly.

Aunt Abby gasped and covered her mouth with her napkin, tears sheening her eyes. She stared at Matthew, waiting for the rest of the story.

"Earlier this month, Seward was injured when he was thrown from his carriage during a ride with his family around the countryside. He was hurt severely and had been restricted to his bed."

Aunt Abby nodded. "I heard he had been hurt. Didn't it include a broken arm and a broken jaw that had to have an extensive metal splint?"

"Yes. Four days ago, the same night Lincoln was shot, a man named Lewis Powell arrived at his home claiming to be from the pharmacy. He told the butler he had medicine for the secretary. It took some persuading, but finally the butler cleared Powell to go upstairs. At the top of the staircase, he was stopped by Seward's son, Frederick. Powell told Frederick the same story, but evidently the son didn't believe him, so he said Seward was sleeping." Matthew stopped and took a drink of water.

Aunt Abby held her breath and waited for him to continue.

"Powell stabbed Frederick, and the butler shouted, 'Murder! Murder!' before he ran away in complete terror."

Aunt Abby gasped. "No!"

Matthew nodded grimly. "Seward's daughter Fanny heard noises, but couldn't tell what was going on, so she opened the door to let Frederick know his father was awake. She didn't realize what Powell was doing, but she had alerted him to which room Seward was in. Powell had evidently turned around to leave, but he suddenly changed his mind and whipped out his pistol to shoot Frederick. He pulled the trigger, but it misfired. Instead of pulling it again, he used the gun to bludgeon Frederick around the head until he collapsed."

Aunt Abby gasped again but remained silent, gripping her napkin tightly.

"Fanny looked out again, saw her unconscious brother, and screamed. Before she could do anything, Powell ran down the hallway, shoved her aside, and began stabbing Secretary Seward around the face and neck."

Matthew stopped, frightened by the stricken look on Aunt Abby's face.

Tears poured down her cheeks, but Aunt Abby shook her head. "Finish. I want to know what is going on in my country."

Matthew hesitated but continued. "The splint in his jaw is evidently what saved him, because it kept Powell from penetrating his jugular vein. A guard and another of Seward's sons, awakened by Fanny's screams, tried to drive him away. The only thing that saved Seward," he said, "was that the blows forced him off the bed and onto the floor against the wall. Powell couldn't reach him. That didn't stop him from stabbing the guard, his other son and Fanny before he ran downstairs and headed for the front door."

"Oh, Matthew!"

Matthew felt sick to his stomach as he finished the story. "A telegram messenger had just arrived. Powell stabbed him, too, as he ran out the door. I've heard the man is now permanently paralyzed. Before Powell ran out the door, he cried, 'I'm mad! I'm mad!' and then he jumped on his horse and disappeared."

"Secretary Seward?" Aunt Abby whispered through her tears.

"His face will be permanently scarred, but he's very much alive and recovering."

"And Powell?"

Matthew smiled grimly. "They arrested him two days ago. He showed back up at the Surratt House where he planned all this with Booth. The detectives were waiting for him. He's under arrest, along with Mary Surratt, the woman who owns the inn."

"Booth?"

"Still at large," Matthew admitted. "But they'll find him—no matter what it takes."

Aunt Abby sat back and stared out the window. She could hear the singing birds. She could see the fluffy clouds in the blue sky, but none of it penetrated the darkness surrounding her heart. She shook her head numbly. "Is there to be no end?" she murmured. "No end to the madness? No end to the senseless death?"

Matthew sat quietly, knowing there was no answer to her question—at least not an answer he had the wisdom to offer her. He had just learned about Seward the night before. He had not been able to sleep much since then. Fatigue fogged his mind as weary grief seeped deeper into his heart.

Aunt Abby reached forward and grabbed his hand. "How long have you known about this?" she asked tenderly.

"Since last night."

"And you haven't slept a wink, have you?"

Matthew didn't bother to deny it, but a noise in the distance had grabbed his attention. A quick look at his watch told him it was time. "We have to leave. The funeral procession will begin soon. I've arranged with a friend to watch it from the second floor of his building along Pennsylvania Avenue, but we have to get there before it's too congested."

Aunt Abby looked down at the untouched food sitting in front of both of them. "I know we should eat, but I can't imagine swallowing a bite right now."

Matthew nodded his agreement and reached out his arm. Aunt Abby took it firmly. Both of them knew it offered equal comfort and strength. They remained silent as they left the hotel, joining with the crowd that had already formed along Pennsylvania Avenue for the funeral procession that would not begin for four hours.

Aunt Abby gazed around her as they made their way down to Matthew's friend's house. Thousands already lined the broad dirt thoroughfare, but the silence was deep and profound, grief and confusion radiating from every face. Black crêpe decorated the front of every building, mocking the bright sunshine. Militia units had already begun to gather in the distance, but nothing happened to mar the almost total silence.

Aunt Abby gripped Matthew's arm as they wove through the crowds. She was relieved when they reached his friend's house. She hated the fear that trembled in her heart—hated the constant watching to see if there was someone else in the crowd with intent to kill. She hated knowing that after four years of war, they were probably worse off as a country than before the conflict had started. The war had done nothing but intensify the hatred and division. She bit back the groan that wanted to escape as she tried to imagine how the country could possibly come together without Lincoln's steady leadership. "Was it all for nothing?"

Matthew's understanding squeeze of her hand made her realize she had spoken her thoughts aloud. She gazed up into his warm blue eyes and took strength from what she saw there. She knew he could offer no answers, but the strength she saw gave her hope that somehow the country could find its way from darkness into light.

She took a deep breath as they turned to walk up brick stairs lined with elegant wrought iron railings. When they reached the top stair, she stopped to look over the sea of people who waited solemnly. Every rooftop was full. Trees labored under the burden of people clinging to their limbs. Rows of people lined the street, a veritable wave of black-draped buildings standing guard over it all.

******

The funeral procession for the assassinated President Abraham Lincoln began at two o'clock in the afternoon on April 19, 1865.

Matthew and Aunt Abby, along with all the others occupying the rooftop, straightened to rigid, sorrowful attention as the bells began to toll.

Aunt Abby jolted when the minute guns fired, but she was determined tears would not blur her memory of the event. She gripped her hands together as she stood quietly, her head held high.

The crowds watched silently as the procession left the White House, and preceded up Pennsylvania Avenue to the Capitol. Women dabbed at tears with embroidered handkerchiefs, but nothing marred the silence. It was as if everyone knew President Lincoln deserved somber control after four years of intense effort to hold the Union together. Wild crying and wails of despair would not honor his memory. It would not bring him back, and it would not set the tone for the work that remained to be done. There was as much steady determination, as there was grief resonating through the air.

Aunt Abby held her breath as the funeral car drew close. She hadn't expected it to be so large, though she knew she had no basis for any expectation whatsoever. The entire thing looked to be about fifteen-feet tall—high enough where everyone in the crowd could see the coffin that held their beloved president. The canopy itself was topped with a glimmering gilt eagle and draped with black crêpe. The hearse was entirely covered with cloth, velvet, crêpe and alpaca. The seat was bordered by a splendid lamp on both sides. It was being pulled by six gray horses all holding their heads proudly, as if they understood how precious their cargo was. Each of them had a groom walking at their head to make sure nothing could go wrong.

Aunt Abby reached for Matthew's arm as the coffin filed past them. It was at that moment the stark reality of Lincoln's death truly penetrated her heart and mind. The knowledge filtered down into her heart, bringing a pain so stabbing she could not breathe. Vowing not to shed a tear, she straightened her shoulders even more.

It will not be in vain, she promised the president as his body rolled by. *You gave your all to hold this great country together. You gave your all to grant freedom to millions of slaves. It will not be in vain. You may be gone, but there are others of us who will take up the mantle and carry on. We will not let the last four years be for nothing.*

She remained rigid as the long lines of government officials and troops filed by, the sound of muffled drums beating out their challenge and comfort to all those who watched.

The silence remained long after the funeral car had reached the steps of the Capitol, long after the coffin had disappeared up the stairs into the Rotunda. No one moved, as if by staying in place they would delay the reality of the president's death.

Finally, the crowds began to disperse. They would return the next day when the coffin would be open for a viewing, but there was nothing more to do other than gather in small knots of people and talk, trying to make sense out of something that was totally senseless.

Chapter Five

Carrie pushed her hair back from her face and stared north. She knew from newspaper reports that Lincoln's funeral train had departed Washington, DC that day, April 21. The train was going to wind its way through Northern cities, allowing the grieving masses an opportunity to say goodbye to their beloved president for thirteen days, before it would finally arrive in Illinois, where the president was to be buried. She couldn't help wondering how many Southerners shared her grief, and how many of them rejoiced that Booth had killed the man they saw as their enemy.

May's head appeared from the back door. "You gonna just stand over them peas, Miss Carrie, or you gonna actually pick a few so I's can fix dinner tonight?"

Carrie shook away her thoughts and managed to smile. "I'll have them right in to you," she promised, realizing she needed to hurry. She had to feed Robert lunch before she rode with Spencer to the train station to pick up Aunt Abby. The telegraph with news of her return had arrived the night before. The smile on Carrie's face was genuine this time as she bent down to fill her basket with peas, adding in some carrots and radishes. She could hardly wait to see Aunt Abby again. She'd been surprised she was returning so soon, but was thrilled to have her back.

Her basket was finally full when she turned back toward the house. She felt, more than heard, the bundle of energy rushing toward her. She had just enough time to swing the basket to her other arm before John barreled into her and grabbed her skirt.

"Aunt Carrie! Aunt Carrie!" John squealed, laughing with delight when she almost toppled over.

Carrie laughed and managed to squat down to eye-level with the excited boy. "Hello, John. Where have you been? I've missed you."

John nodded, an important look on his face. "Me and Daddy had to go to town. I wanted to walk, but Daddy said you would skin him good if he did, so we went down in the thing that horse pulls."

"You mean the carriage?" Carrie guessed. She was glad Moses wasn't pushing too hard, but she realized he was probably going crazy being confined to the house.

"Yes! That's what he called it. It was just me and Daddy," he said proudly, his face shining. Then his face puckered. "This place don't look so good," he said. "Where I came from looks better," he said firmly.

Carrie hid a chuckle that John could think the shacktown built around Hampton, Virginia for escaping slaves was a better place than Richmond. She quickly sobered when she realized how desolate the burned-out buildings made Richmond look. A lot of cleanup had been done, but charred buildings still reached for the sky and huge piles of rubble waited to be hauled away. It was going to look bad for a long time.

John suddenly twisted away. "Daddy taught me how to play chase last night," he boasted. "I bet you can't catch me!"

Carrie opened her mouth to explain she had to get the vegetables into the house for May.

"I figure you're too old!" John added impishly, his grin lighting up his face.

Carrie laughed, swung the basket down, gathered her skirts, and ran toward John.

John squealed with delight, dashing behind a tree as fast as his little, pudgy legs could carry him. "You can't catch me!" he yelled.

Carrie pretended to let him outrun her until she was almost out of breath. The last time she had played chase was with the children down in the slave quarters on the plantation. Sorrow gripped her throat for a moment before she banished it, sped up, and scooped John up into her arms. "I got you!" she cried, tickling him and laughing just as hard as he was.

******

Robert was awake when Carrie entered the room, but a quick look at his face had her heart sinking. The joy from her fun with John vanished as she gazed at her husband. His eyes were clear of fever, but they were dull with apathy.

She knew his nights had become a long series of nightmares and flashbacks. She still wasn't sharing a bed with him, but her cot against the wall swept her into his world of horrible memories. Every time he had a nightmare, she would sit on the side of his bed and rub his arm or hold his hand until the worst of it passed. Most times he didn't wake up. When he did, he very seldom knew who she was. He would just stare at her with terrified confusion, until he finally closed his eyes again and drifted off to sleep.

He was stronger physically, but the apathy seemed to suck him in a little more each day. The fever that had burned his body seemed to have dipped into the recesses of his soul and left nothing but dead embers. She had told him nothing of what was going on in the country, but it was as if he knew, and decided to distance himself from everything and everyone.

"Hello, dear," she said softly.

Robert gazed up at her but didn't speak.

Carrie's heart sank further. She was sure he knew who she was, but there was nothing she could say that pierced the veil of indifference. His brief period of clarity and communication that had given her so much hope had vanished. She knew the nightmares and memories were destroying her husband's soul, just as surely as the war almost destroyed his body. She gritted her teeth but kept her voice calm and loving. "I brought you some lunch."

Robert nodded. His willingness to eat was the only thing giving her hope that the man she loved would claw his way back from the darkness. There had to be some part of him that wanted to live, or he would have simply quit eating. Or maybe he was just aware enough not to want to cause her more pain. Whatever it was, she was simply glad he was still eating.

Carrie was grateful for the warm spring air blowing in through the window, billowing the white curtains, and causing sunlight to dance on his soft, blue bedcover. She insisted on plenty of fresh air. "It's a beautiful day," she said brightly. "The garden is coming along very nicely. I picked a huge basket of vegetables right before I came up."

Robert gave no indication he had heard her.

Carrie kept on, determined not to let his apathy numb her into non-communication. "I heard from Janie this morning as well. A brief telegram came with the message she and Clifford made it back to Raleigh safely." She said nothing about her fears for Janie's safety. She knew he didn't have the energy to care, and she didn't want to introduce more trouble into his already burdened heart.

"I'm picking up Aunt Abby at the train station in a little while," she continued, surprised when his eyes flashed a spark of interest, and his head turned toward her. "Would you like her to come up and see you?"

Robert stared at her for a long moment and nodded his head once. "She has good eyes," he said quietly.

"Yes," Carrie agreed. "She's told me more than once how much she would like to spend time with you. I'll have her come up when she gets here."

Robert nodded again but then closed his eyes and turned his head away.

Carrie stifled a sigh as she picked up the bowl of soup, tucked the blankets around him securely, and kissed him on the forehead. She stood over him for long minutes, wondering if she would ever have her husband back, or if he was going to waste away for months and then die like her mother had. Blinking back tears, she banished the thoughts from her head. *Robert will get well!*

Before she left the room, she moved to the window and stared southeast over the fresh green emerging on the trees; over the housetops; over the spires of the churches below her; over the blackened remains of buildings; over the vibrant white of the dogwood trees exploding into bloom. None of it held her anymore. After three years of being locked in the crowded, turbulent capital city of the defeated Confederacy, she wanted nothing more than to return to the open, lush fields of Cromwell Plantation. She wanted clean air to breathe. She wanted open spaces in which to roam. She wanted to see new growth in the tobacco fields of her childhood.

Tears filled her eyes as she thought of Sam and Opal. She frowned briefly as she thought about Eddie. Imprisoned in the infamous Castle Thunder prison for three years as a suspected Union spy, he had escaped just days before the fall of Richmond. He was staying with friends in the city until he could return to the plantation with her and see his children. He had been heartbroken when he discovered his wife, Fannie, had been killed in an explosion at Tredegar Iron Works, but the hope of being with his children again kept him going. Would all of them still be on the plantation? Captain Jones had sent word the plantation was still there, but what condition would they find it in? What would life be like now?

Carrie pressed her hands to her head. She had little more than questions with no answers. She took a deep breath to steady herself. She had learned to survive years of war by refusing to look beyond the day ahead. The end of the war had produced as many questions as the war itself, but all she had to focus on was the day in front of her. And this day had Aunt Abby arriving at the train station in little more than an hour.

A rumble of wheels on the road outside made her take her eyes off the horizon. A smile flitted across her lips as she identified Spencer sitting erect on the seat of his carriage.

Carrie looked at Robert one more time to assure herself he was sleeping peacefully before she moved from the room and ran down the stairs.

Aunt Abby was coming today!

When Carrie reached the bottom of the stairs, Rose moved forward and wrapped Carrie in a warm hug and gave her a big kiss on the cheek. "Good morning, Carrie."

Carrie smiled. "What did I do to deserve that?"

"Nothing. than living," Rose added. "I'm simply making up for lost time. I spent so many hours in the contraband camp staring toward Richmond, wondering how you were...if you were still alive...if I would ever see you again..." Her voice caught before she forced a laugh. "I have no idea why I'm thinking of all this today. I'm here. We're together. That's all that counts!"

Carrie understood completely. She stepped closer to give Rose another huge hug, adding her own kiss on her friend's cheek. "I'm all for making up for lost time. Every time I see you, my heart wants to sing. I missed you so very much during all those years! As much as we have talked in the last couple weeks, I still feel like we haven't even scratched the surface of telling each other all that has happened."

"That will take a very long time," Rose murmured.

"Good! At least we won't get bored," Carrie said teasingly, her earlier heaviness evaporating.

"You have a point," Rose said, laughter dancing in her eyes.

Spencer poked his head in from the kitchen, his hand wrapped around a big piece of cornbread. "You 'bout ready to go, Miss Carrie?"

"Yes, Spencer. Is it warm enough to go without my coat today?"

"Oh, yessum, you won't be needin' no coat. Spring done really sprung. I's gonna finish up this here cornbread May fixed for me, then I be meetin' you out front in a few minutes."

His head disappeared, but the door flung open to reveal May's shining face with a wide streak of flour down her cheek. "I be fixin' Miss Abby a right special meal," she announced. She looked at Rose. "You done brung me that chicken, Miss Rose?"

"Have you brought me that chicken?" Rose corrected.

May gave her an exasperated look. "How could I have brung you a chicken? You're the one who went to town."

Rose laughed but shook her finger at their housekeeper. "This is a new world you're living in, May. Learning how to speak correctly is important."

May scowled. "You know what dey say 'bout teachin' old dogs new tricks."

Rose scowled right back at her. "You're not an old dog. You're an intelligent, middle-aged woman who is free for the first time in her life. You've learned how to read this past year. Paying attention to how you speak is the next step," she said.

"Don't you neber get tired of bein' a teacher?" May demanded.

"No," Rose replied, a warm smile on her face. "Now, what were you asking me about?"

May stared at her for a few moments, laughter lurking in her eyes, before it finally broke out into a smile. "I would like to know if you brought me a chicken from your shopping in town," she said very properly.

Rose clapped. "Very good! And, yes, I have your chicken. It's in the boxes Spencer brought in."

"Good!" Still speaking slowly as she thought about the words before they came out of her mouth, May turned to Carrie. "We are going to have a very special meal to celebrate Miss Abby's coming home. I'll have it ready when you return."

Carrie smiled broadly. "I will tell her, May. Thank you so much. We're so lucky to have you!"

"You got dat right," May said, delivering a wink before the door swung shut again.

Carrie and Rose were laughing when they moved out onto the porch. The fine, spring weather had lured most Richmonders outside. Mothers called to children playing in their dirt front yards. The wind flapped sheets and clothing on the lines. Garden patches were all coming alive with green plants. The war years had taught everyone to have as big a garden as possible. The war might be over, but still no one had money. It would take a long time for things to get back to normal.

Carrie stepped down from the porch when Spencer pulled the carriage to a stop in front of their gate. "I'll be back soon with our favorite woman," she told Rose. Then she stopped. "Where is Moses?"

"He went back into town to meet with Captain Jones. He is getting more and more restless. When he was out this morning, he saw more and more freed slaves coming into the city. They are all excited, but seem equally bewildered and lost. He wants to find a way to help." She raised her hand to stop the question rising to Carrie's lips. "He's taking it easy, but he feels he has to do this."

Carrie closed her lips on her comment and nodded. "I know. I'm probably being far too cautious," she admitted. Her eyes darkened. "We came so close to losing him. I don't want to take any risks."

"None of us does," Rose agreed, "but I also understand how he feels. We have worked for this time for so very long. Now that freedom has come, he doesn't want to be on the sidelines. I don't believe he'll be foolish, but he can't keep just lying around the house."

Carrie smiled. "I understand. I'll check the wound in his chest every night to make sure there is no infection." She shrugged. "It will make me feel better."

Rose laughed. "You and me both." She waved her hand. "Go get Aunt Abby. I've missed her terribly."

*****

Carrie had not been out of the house in several days. Already so much had been done to restore the city. She saw hundreds of men, both black and white, clearing debris from the burned buildings. Wagon after wagon was being filled with charred wood, while bricks were being cleaned for reuse when it was time to build again.

The Union military was everywhere. The primarily black troops that had marched into Richmond after the surrender were now mixed with white troops that had been sent to bolster their numbers. They were patrolling the streets, making sure no Confederate veterans lingered on street corners or gathered in groups to talk, still suspicious that more Southerners had been involved with the plot to assassinate Lincoln.

Just as Rose had said, she saw many more black people on the roads. Spencer had stopped at an intersection when a group of black people disembarked from a wagon. Carrie smiled as they raised their hands in praise to God as they stared up at the white Capitol Building that had been untouched by the fire.

"Looky dat!" one man exclaimed. "We be here in Richmond at last. And we be here as free people! We ain't slaves no more!"

A young woman, her eyes shining with delight, clapped her hands together and began to sing. *"Slavery chain done broke at last; slavery chain done broke at last. I's going to praise God 'til I die."* She swayed her hips, raised her arms high, and did a joyful little dance step.

The rest of the group joined in with her. It only took moments for the song to spread through the meandering crowd.

Carrie's smile changed to a frown when she saw the scowls from white people on the streets. She felt something tighten in her chest when the scowls turned to glares of hatred and resentment. She was quite sure it was only the heavy presence of Union soldiers that kept order in the midst of such intense feelings.

Her thoughts flew to Clifford's growing hatred, and fear for Janie sprang afresh into her mind. She took a deep breath and forced it back out again. She had decided to live just this day. She wasn't going to borrow trouble she had no control over. She was relieved when Spencer directed the carriage through the intersection and left the crowds behind.

She heard the train station before she saw it. The fact that the station survived gave at least a small sense of normalcy. There were still people coming and going into the city. Supplies for the few remaining businesses were making it through. Everything looked horrible now, but time would change that. They would rebuild—that she was certain of. The people of Richmond would not remain defeated. They would grieve all they had lost, and then they would rebuild. The biggest question that remained in Carrie's mind was what kind of city they would build. Would it be a city based on hatred and revenge, or a city based on equality?

*****

Carrie spotted Aunt Abby as soon as she stepped from the train. She stood up in the carriage and waved her arm, directing Spencer to claim her baggage. "Aunt Abby!" she cried, rushing to give the older woman a warm hug as soon as she drew close. "I'm so happy you're back!"

Aunt Abby grabbed her close. "Oh, I am, too. It's so very good to see you again!"

Carrie stepped back and peered into her face. "It was bad," she said softly, saddened by the grief lurking in her eyes.

Aunt Abby sighed and nodded her head. "It was bad," she agreed. "But I wouldn't have wanted to be anywhere else," she said, stepping into the carriage and settling her soft gray dress around her. "We have so much to talk about."

Rumbling carriages, the shriek of train whistles, and the shout of porters and baggage boys made it difficult to hear anything. "We'll be out of this in a minute," Carrie said loudly, glad when Spencer strapped down the last bag and climbed back into the carriage seat.

Ten minutes later, they were far enough away from the train station to have a conversation.

"Will you tell me about it?" Carrie asked.

"Certainly, but I prefer to wait until we're all together over dinner," Aunt Abby replied. "I would much rather tell you about what I decided while I was in Washington."

"I'm listening," Carrie leaned back against the seat.

"I'm going to open a factory here in Richmond," Aunt Abby began.

"Here?" Carrie asked. "Richmond? What about your factories in Pennsylvania?"

"They will continue to run with the managers I have in place. I can make trips there when needed to oversee everything."

"But..." Carrie stammered, stunned by the sudden announcement. Then a wide smile broke out on her face. "Then you're staying? You're not leaving?"

Aunt Abby squeezed her hand and smiled. "That's correct. Now, let me tell you why." She took a deep breath. "Without going into any details of the funeral procession, I will say I had a life-changing moment of epiphany when the funeral wagon passed beneath the balcony I was standing on." Her eyes glistened with tears as she remembered.

Carrie waited quietly, her own heart aching as she watched the waves of sorrow sweep over Aunt Abby's face.

Aunt Abby shook her head. "With President Lincoln gone now, there is some doubt that President Johnson has Lincoln's same feeling about equality for the newly freed slaves." She held up her hand before Carrie could interrupt. "I'll tell you about that later. Just know that I have discovered enough to be gravely concerned about his intentions and course of action in the future. When Lincoln's wagon was rolling by, I had moments when I wondered if the last four years—if all the years we have fought for freedom for the slaves—had all been in vain."

"Aunt Abby!"

Once again, Aunt Abby raised her hand. "Hear me out. Lincoln may be gone, but we're all still here. President Lincoln signed the Emancipation Proclamation and passed the bill to abolish slavery, but it took thousands of us to bring it to that point. It was the work of thousands over the years that truly created freedom for the slaves. We are still here," she repeated, her strong voice ringing out into the air.

Carrie felt the passion in her words and realized the truth in what she said.

"I made a promise to the president as his body rolled past the balcony. I promised him that everything will not be in vain. Lincoln gave his all to hold this great country together. He gave his all to grant freedom to millions of slaves. It will not be in vain. He may be gone, but there are others of us who will take up the mantle and carry on. We will not let the last four years be for nothing."

Carrie took a deep breath, the older woman's words piercing her heart. "What is your plan?" she asked, already knowing there was one.

Aunt Abby smiled, squeezing Carrie's hand. "I knew you would understand," she said gladly. The carriage made a turn and joined the stream of people passing the burned-out buildings. She nodded toward one of the buildings as they passed. "That used to be the First Bank of Richmond."

"Yes," Carrie murmured, staring at the blackened rubble that was all that remained. "All the banks of Richmond burned."

"Yes, they did," Aunt Abby said, "and lots of now useless Confederate money went up with it."

Carrie nodded again, confusion showing on her face.

Aunt Abby smiled. "I met with some colleagues from Philadelphia when I was in DC. They are stepping forward to make investments to open another bank so

Richmond can begin to get back on its feet." She paused. "I have become an investor as well."

Carrie stared at her. "You've invested in a bank?" She looked at Aunt Abby more closely. "I've just realized we have never talked about your business interests. They didn't seem important at the time, but now I find I'm wondering just how much my dear Aunt Abby is worth."

Aunt Abby merely smiled. "Enough," she said simply. "It's imperative that Richmond get back on its feet. That won't happen unless there is a bank with money to lend to those who want to start rebuilding."

"Why?" Carrie asked. "Other than my personal interest because I love this city so much, why is it important enough for Northern investors to make sure we have a bank to help finance rebuilding?" She was quickly realizing how little she knew about business. When she looked over at Aunt Abby, Carrie caught a glimpse of the woman who had stood against a multitude of men to protect her deceased husband's business.

"Before the war, Richmond represented the most advanced economic development in the South. It's a center for transportation to the rest of the South. It was a manufacturing center that processed regionally available materials. There were industries here, from barrel-making to building construction. In the decade before the war, Richmond's factory workforce grew by five hundred, eighty-one percent."

"Really?" Even with her limited understanding of business, Carrie realized that was a lot.

Aunt Abby nodded. "It will take the South getting back on its feet to provide jobs not only to freed slaves, but to all the veterans struggling to create a new life. I can help."

Carrie continued to stare, not sure how all of this fit with being sure the fight to end slavery had not been in vain. "I see..." she murmured, feeling totally out of her comfort zone. If Aunt Abby had come back and wanted to talk about new surgical procedures, she could have conversed with intelligence. As it was, she merely felt inadequate, though she was mesmerized by the shining passion in Aunt Abby's eyes.

Aunt Abby suddenly laughed. "I see I'm not being clear, my dear."

"Or perhaps I'm too dense to understand," Carrie protested.

Aunt Abby snorted. "That is certainly not the case."

Spencer spoke up from the driver's seat. "You's plannin' on opening up a factory to give jobs to black folks. But not just any job," he continued. "You's plannin' on paying them what they really be worth."

Aunt Abby beamed. "That's correct!"

Carrie mulled over what Spencer had said. "You're concerned that other people rebuilding in Richmond won't be fair to the freed slaves. You are afraid they will take advantage of them, and try to keep them in the same slavery mode by paying them little and treating them badly."

Aunt Abby nodded solemnly. "That's exactly right."

"Why are you so concerned?" Carrie asked. "What did you learn in Washington?"

Aunt Abby frowned as she gazed into her eyes. "You may not know business, but you certainly know how to read me, my dear." She sat back with a heavy sigh. "Yes, I learned a lot while I was in Washington. The government knew it was time for the slaves to be free, but I'm afraid no one has carefully thought through a plan for how they can become equal citizens—especially those who remain in the South."

"Just cause we be free don't mean people done changed how they think 'bout us," Spencer drawled, his flashing eyes betraying his calm voice.

Carrie thought about the resentment and hatred she had seen shining from Richmonders' eyes just that morning.

"I'm afraid you're right," Aunt Abby said sadly. "I believe there are already plans in the works here in the South to control the freed slaves in much the same way slavery did."

"And it will take all of us to make sure that doesn't happen," Carrie said softly. "I understand." She straightened her shoulders. "What kind of factory are you going to open?"

"A clothing factory," Aunt Abby said. "I have already purchased the property down by the river where three warehouses stood before they burned. I'll be hiring men to clean away the rubble, and then I'll have some equipment sent down from Philadelphia. It will take time to get ready for production, but I think it will move quickly. Everyone is eager to see Richmond recover from this disaster and the years of the war."

"You certainly move quickly." Suddenly, Carrie laughed.

"Why are you laughing, my dear?"

"I've never seen the business side of you before," Carrie admitted. She laughed harder. "I almost feel sorry for those men who tried to intimidate and threaten you out of business. I'm sure they had no idea what they were up against."

Aunt Abby joined in her laughter. "Sometimes it's best for men to believe women are weak. That way you can sneak around them and catch them completely unprepared with your brilliance and scheming."

Spencer snorted with laughter while peals of merriment rang out from the two women. They were still laughing when the carriage rolled up in front of the house. Rose and Moses were waiting on the porch, little John bouncing with excitement in his daddy's arms.

The aroma of fried chicken, mingled with some kind of cake baking, rolled out from the front door.

Aunt Abby turned and wrapped Carrie in an embrace. "It's so good to be home," she whispered. "You have no idea how wonderful it is to feel I have a family to return to."

Carrie gazed after her as she jumped from the carriage to greet Rose and Moses.

"That be one fine woman," Spencer observed, his eyes shining with admiration.

"That she is," Carrie murmured, her heart pounding with gratitude that they were all together. It still seemed surreal at times.

"She gonna have a hard time down here," Spencer said.

"What do you mean?"

"The white men down here in Richmond ain't gonna take kindly to a woman with a heart for black folks."

"She already knows that," Carrie assured him. "We've talked about what I went through during the war."

Spencer nodded, opened his mouth, and then shut it again.

"Go ahead, Spencer," Carrie encouraged him. "What do you want to say?"

He shrugged his wide shoulders. "They sho 'nuff hated you takin' care of the sick black folks," he agreed, "but Miss Abby comin' down here to give jobs to people they figure still be slaves, is gonna be somethin' else." He stared up at the porch with worried eyes. "I sho hope she smart enough to be real careful."

Carrie stared up at Aunt Abby, who was laughing as John bounced in her arms. She tried to push down the sudden uneasiness that gripped her throat. She had a sense that all of them were going to have to be careful.

Chapter Six

Carrie was just coming in from the garden with a brimming basket of greens when Aunt Abby entered the kitchen. "Does Robert need me?" she asked quickly.

Aunt Abby shook her head. "I read to him for a while, and then he drifted off to sleep after he had some soup."

"Did he say anything?" Carrie asked hopefully, though she was almost sure of the answer. Robert had done nothing but nod or shake his head since Aunt Abby had arrived three days ago.

"No," Aunt Abby said softly, her eyes radiating compassion. "I can sense he is feeling and thinking things, but he doesn't seem to have the energy to put anything into words."

Carrie nodded, doing her best to hold on to hope. Sometimes she thought she saw a spark of life in Robert's eyes, but mostly he just stared dully, or simply escaped into a world of sleep.

"Are the nightmares still as bad?" Aunt Abby asked.

"Yes," Carrie admitted. "That's the only time he speaks. He mumbles about blood and death and watching people be blown up." She shuddered. "Even after treating all the soldiers and seeing for myself how horrible the wounds were, at least I didn't have to watch them being blown up or shot. I only dealt with the aftermath."

Aunt Abby nodded. "None of us, except Moses of course, can possibly understand what he has been through. He hung on until there was nothing in him to hold on with."

Carrie swallowed back her tears and placed the basket on the long counter. "I am trying to believe there is enough left in him to come back."

Aunt Abby stepped forward and gripped her hands. "You keep on believing, Carrie. Your belief will get through to him." She paused and chose her words carefully. "I sense there is a part of him that wants to keep living. I believe it's the part that loves you so much.

He wants to come back to you. He simply doesn't know how."

"And I don't know how to help him." Carrie groaned. "I've tried every herbal remedy Sarah ever told me about. Nothing seems to be working."

Aunt Abby smiled gently. "I don't believe it's a problem that can be treated with an herbal remedy. He's dealing with a problem of the soul. The death and suffering he has seen have almost destroyed his will to live. Yet, there is something in him that is reaching for the light of your love for him. Just love him," she said tenderly. "That is what he needs most."

Carrie's eyes glistened with tears. "I'm trying," she whispered. "I love him so much, but what if I don't show him in the right way? What if I don't communicate it in a way he can hear? What if I'm the reason he dies?" Her voice broke as her shoulders slumped.

Aunt Abby wrapped her close and stroked her hair. "Nonsense, Carrie. You are the most loving person I know. You are pouring such amazing love into him, but..."

Carrie leaned back when she hesitated. "But what?"

"But it's still up to Robert. No one can make us do, or not do, anything. Every action we take is a matter of our own will," she said firmly but kindly. "If Robert gives up, it won't be because you didn't love him in the right way. It will be because he makes a decision, deep within his soul, that he is too afraid of the light to leave the darkness."

"He's been through so much the last five years. He has changed so much and overcome so many challenges. It's just not fair that he has to go through this now."

May stepped forward then. "Ain't nothin' bout life fair, Miss Carrie. I done lost my man and my fine babies 'bout twenty years ago when my master sold me to someone else here in Richmond."

Carrie gasped. "I didn't know that, May! You never told me."

"No. I didn't reckon there be any need to. Ain't nobody can change the past. I learned a long time ago, that all I could do was live my life right now. I could let the bitterness and regret eat me up, or I could choose to live.

I reckon I chose to live. It weren't no easy decision, but it was the right one." She took a breath and continued. "I saw a bunch o' people make a diff'rent decision. I saw some of them people waste away with a broken heart till they were mostly dead themselves."

"Like Robert," Carrie said softly.

"Like Mr. Robert," May agreed. "But," she continued in a strong voice, "Mr. Robert got somethin' them other people didn't have. He have you. It ain't been long at all since Mr. Robert got home. I know it seems like a long time, 'cause you want things to be diff'rent, but it only been a couple weeks." She moved forward and laid a hand on Carrie's arm. "Two weeks ain't nothin', Miss Carrie. You just keep right on lovin' Mr. Robert. I reckon he'll come back to you when he's ready, and his heart done healed from all de bad things that man seen."

Carrie took a deep breath and gazed at the two strong women looking at her with so much love. "What would I do without the two of you?" she murmured. "I am so very lucky."

"That you are!" May snapped with satisfaction. "Now, it's time to get on out of my kitchen so I can make some food for the army that's about to show up." She reached over, grabbed a handful of molasses cookies, and shoved them into Carrie's hands. "You and Miss Abby go on out to the porch and eat these while you watch the storm that will be rolling up soon."

"A storm?" Carrie asked in surprise. "I was just outside. I didn't see evidence of a storm."

"That's 'cause your heart be too stuck in your problems," May snorted. "You go on out there and see if I be right. And don't you let them cookies spoil your appetite or you won't get any more!"

Carrie and Aunt Abby were laughing as they walked out on the porch and settled on the swing. Carrie's eyes widened as she looked at the horizon and saw a boiling mass of gray clouds scurrying in their direction. "May was right!" she exclaimed. "There is a storm coming."

Aunt Abby looked at her and then glanced at the approaching storm. "You sound rather happy about it."

"I love storms," Carrie replied. She looked closer at Aunt Abby. "You seem a little nervous."

Aunt Abby shrugged, trying to hide her concern. "I think storms are best experienced from within the house."

"You've never been outside in a storm?" Carrie asked in astonishment.

"I've chosen to experience them differently," Aunt Abby replied, jumping when a roll of thunder was followed by a bolt of lightning. She eyed the front door longingly.

Carrie laughed and moved closer to her in the swing, taking her hand. "It's high time you learned to enjoy a powerful spring storm," she replied. "Father and I used to always sit outside on the porch to watch the storms."

"Where was your mother?"

"Hiding in the house," Carrie admitted, grinning when another bolt of jagged lightning split the sky. She squeezed Aunt Abby's hand when a rumbling roll of thunder seemed to wrap around them, the air almost electric.

"I'm thinking your mother was the sane one of the family," Aunt Abby muttered, but she didn't close her eyes when the next lightning bolt struck. She leaned forward and stared up at the sky. "The clouds are rather amazing," she said slowly. "They seem to be swirling in their own kind of dance. I must admit they are rather beautiful."

"Now you're catching on," Carrie laughed.

"When will it start to rain?"

Carrie cast a practiced eye at the sky. "Oh, I'd say we have a few more minutes of the light show before the rain obscures it." She smiled at Aunt Abby's look of astonishment. "Don't forget I'm a country plantation girl, my dear lady. My father taught me everything he knew from the time I was quite little. Just because I didn't want to stay on the plantation, doesn't mean I didn't love it and learn all I could."

"And now, Carrie?" Aunt Abby asked. "What about now? I know how much you want to go home."

Carrie took her eyes away from the sky and gazed into Aunt Abby's eyes. It was time to talk about what she was feeling. "Yes, I want to go home," she replied. "I want a sense of normalcy. I want to get out of the city. I've felt trapped here for so long. I long for fresh air and open spaces." She paused. "And I also believe the plantation will help Robert. That's his world. He needs to be able to breathe real air that isn't clogged with dust and fumes." She stopped and gazed at the sky as the first huge raindrops plopped onto the dusty roads, creating their own kind of dance. "And I want Father to go home. He will need me," she said simply.

"But..."

Carrie smiled, not bothering to ask how Aunt Abby knew there was more. "But, I don't want to stay there," she admitted. "I still want to go to medical school. It seems even more impossible now than it did before the war," she said, "but everything I did in the hospital only made me hungrier to learn more—to do more." She took a deep breath. "I'm meant to be a doctor," she said simply. Then she flushed. "Does that make me bad?"

"Excuse me?"

"I have a husband who is gravely ill. My father needs me to help him rebuild his life on the plantation. I fear I am incredibly selfish to still dream of being a doctor."

"Rubbish!" Aunt Abby snorted.

Carrie shook her head. "I'm not a girl anymore," she protested. "I'm a woman who has responsibilities. Perhaps I was supposed to help in the hospital, and then relinquish that dream so that I can care for the people who need me."

Aunt Abby reached forward and turned her head, forcing her to look into her eyes. "I don't believe you mean that," she said softly.

"I believe I *should* mean it," she whispered, tears filling her eyes.

Aunt Abby sighed and pulled her into her arms. "Carrie, I know life can be nothing but a confusing mess at times, but I believe with all my heart that you're meant to be a doctor. God would not have given you your passion, or your gifts, if it was not the plan for your life. But that doesn't mean we can understand the timing of everything." She paused. "I've discovered over and over again that life is what happens *after* I make my plans. I have to be willing to roll with whatever is happening and believe the time will come if something is meant to be. I simply have to keep walking toward my dream."

"Keep walking..." Carrie murmured.

"Yes," Aunt Abby replied firmly. "You can't go to medical school right this minute, but that doesn't mean your chance isn't coming. You have to continue to do all you can right now to prepare for that time."

Carrie sighed. "I would love nothing more than to get my hands on the latest medical books," she said longingly. "I know there must have been huge advancements in the last four years that I know nothing about."

"Then you're going to love the shipment coming in on the train tomorrow," Aunt Abby said smugly.

Carrie gasped when she saw the dancing light in Aunt Abby's eyes. "You mean...?"

Aunt Abby laughed. "I spoke with Dr. Strikener while I was in Washington, DC."

Carrie's eyes widened. "The good-looking doctor I met in the hospital ward? The one who seemed to be quite taken with a certain gray-eyed businesswoman from Philadelphia?"

Aunt Abby snorted. "I suppose that would be the one," she admitted. "Anyway, he agreed to put together a box of all the books being used in the first year of medical school right now. They should be here tomorrow. I believe they will keep you busy for quite some time."

Carrie was both laughing and crying when she fell into Aunt Abby's arms again. "You are wonderful!" she cried. "If I ever become a doctor, it will be because of you."

"Nonsense!" Aunt Abby responded, her eyes shining with pleasure. "It will be because you have persevered through enormous challenges to make your dream come true. All I will have done is lent a helping hand." She smiled. "And I will be the proudest person in the audience when you get your medical degree."

*****

The storm had blown out its fury by the time May put a fresh plate of molasses cookies on the table for dessert.

A strong breeze swirled through the curtains as lamplight flickered and danced on the walls. The smells of rain, magnolias and spring drifted in, mingling with the lingering odors of ham, biscuits and collard greens.

Rose leaned back in her chair and sighed deeply. "I used to dream of times like this when I was in the contraband camp. All of us together..."

Moses nodded. "The idea of it kept me going through the worst of the war. I had to believe that someday it would be over, and I would get to sit around a table like a normal person."

Jeremy chuckled. "It seems rather surreal to me. It wasn't that long ago that I was an only child with a single father. It still amazes me that I have a big family. Most of the time I feel I'm living in a fantasy world, but it's one I hope never ends."

"It will never end," Carrie said firmly. "You're stuck with all of us, my dearest uncle."

"Ah..." Jeremy said smugly. "It does my heart good to hear my strong-willed niece acknowledge me as her wise uncle."

Carrie snorted. "I remember saying dearest—the wise part must be another segment of your fantasy."

Everyone was laughing as Micah walked into the dining room holding an envelope.

"You's got mail, Miss Carrie."

"My father?" Carrie asked eagerly, reaching for it.

"Not unless Master Cromwell be in West Virginia."

Carrie took the envelope but still looked at Micah. "You know you don't have to call my father Master Cromwell anymore, don't you? You're free now."

"Yessum," Micah agreed.

Carrie was concerned by what she saw in his eyes. "What is it?" she asked quietly. "You can talk with us," she added when he hesitated.

Micah stared down at her for a moment before he answered her. "It's gonna take a while for things to be right down here," he said.

"What do you mean?" Carrie pressed.

Micah shrugged. "Just 'cause I be free don't mean folks see me that way. It ain't smart right now to go 'round callin' Master Cromwell anything but that."

May swung in through the door carrying a fresh pot of coffee. "You know Micah ain't gonna tell you nothin', Miss Carrie," she snapped.

"But you will," Aunt Abby prompted.

"Yes, I will. There's talk about a lot of black folks being beaten the last few days because they wasn't showin' the proper respect for their old owners," she said bluntly.

"What?" Carrie gasped.

May nodded her head briskly. "Micah be right. Just 'cause we be free don't mean folks are gonna see us that way. The black folks who gonna make it through this time are the ones who are smart. We's been playin' the game for a long time. We knows how to play it for a while longer."

"But you're free now," Carrie protested. "You don't have to—"

"They're right," Moses interrupted.

"But..."

Moses held up his hand. "Right now, there are soldiers here to keep the peace. They're doing a good job, but they can't be everywhere. There are a lot of white men who are determined to make sure our kind remembers their place."

"They ruled by fear for a long time," Rose added. "Just because the slaves are free doesn't mean they have walked free of that fear. It also doesn't mean they don't have a reason to be afraid, Carrie," she said. "A Constitutional Amendment is a wonderful thing that has changed the law, but that doesn't mean it has changed people's hearts. That's going to take a lot longer."

Carrie wanted to protest again, but the quiet acceptance in Rose's eyes stopped her. "It's wrong," she said.

"Yes," Moses agreed, "but we all knew freedom was only the first step. We aim to do everything we can to make sure that freedom means something, but it's a good idea to do what we can to live through the transition," he said.

"How bad is it?" Aunt Abby asked.

Moses shrugged. "Everything is so new right now, but I can promise you that white men aren't going to sit back forever and let us be. The soldiers won't always be here. The government won't always be around to take care of things. We have to prepare for that time."

"And how are you doing that?" Aunt Abby asked.

"We're forming societies," Moses replied. "The identity of everyone in them will be kept secret. The freed slaves are pouring into Richmond because they think there is more opportunity here."

"Is there?" Carrie asked.

Moses shrugged. "For some, but it's going to take a long time for Richmond to get back on its feet. In the meantime, every black person who comes to town is seen by the whites as competition for a job. They're seen as a slap in the face to the Southern way of life."

"You sound rather calm about it," Aunt Abby observed.

"Not calm," Moses admitted. "I think I would prefer to call it resigned. I had to resign myself to a lot in the military. Instead of wasting my energy fighting it, I looked for ways to work around it."

"And that's what the secret societies are for?" Carrie asked.

"Yes. Black folks have known for a long time how to take care of each other. We've always had only ourselves to count on. We don't see that changing anytime soon. The societies will be in place as an insurance policy. Everyone will contribute what they can, and then they will take care of people who need it."

"There are lots of freed slaves who are too old to work," Rose added. "There are people who are sick. There has to be a way to care for them."

"But isn't the government going to take care of them?" Carrie asked, her head spinning as she gazed at Aunt Abby for help. "What about the new Freedmen's Bureau?"

"It's not going to be easy," Aunt Abby said carefully. "There is a lot of fear, a lot of anger, and a lot of battered pride. When you add all that together..."

"You gots a big mess!" May said.

"I'm afraid you're right," Aunt Abby agreed. "There are certainly plans being made to get help to all the freed slaves, but it's a daunting task to provide for over two million people, while also working to get people to see things differently." She straightened her shoulders. "It doesn't mean it can't be done, though. The government will do what they can, but each one of us needs to step up to do what we can."

"Like starting a factory," Carrie said.

"Yes, that's what I do," Aunt Abby agreed, "but every one of us has something to offer. Rose will be teaching. Jeremy's expertise in finance will be critical. Moses will be a leader for those who are lost and confused. Carrie will provide medical care." She paused. "The most important thing we all offer are hearts of love and compassion. It will take massive amounts of love to offset the hatred and prejudice that are still rampant throughout our country."

A thick silence fell on the room as everyone thought about those words.

Carrie remembered the envelope in her hand. She smiled when she looked at the return address. "It's from Hobbs," she said, using her knife to open it. She smiled as she envisioned the red-haired young man who had become like a little brother to her during the last four years. He had been her friend and her protector. Robert had saved his life during battle, and Hobbs returned the favor during Antietam. From that time on, he gave his all to take care of Carrie while Robert served.

It took her moments to scan the contents. "He made it home safely," she said with relief. "He's glad to be back with his family and says his farm was mostly untouched. He just finished helping plow the fields."

"On that leg?" Jeremy asked in astonishment.

Carrie smiled. "I didn't suppose Hobbs would allow a shortened leg and crutches to keep him from farming. He always found a way to compensate."

"Has he gone camping with his dog yet?" Rose asked. "I remember him saying how much he wanted to do that."

Carrie grinned. "First thing when he got home. He and Bridger took off for three days into the woods. I imagine that was the best possible thing he could do to begin to wash away the memories of the war." She grew thoughtful. "He's just one of hundreds of thousands of men who are being forced to rebuild their lives."

"And women," Aunt Abby added.

"Yes," Carrie murmured, her mind drifting back.

"Have you heard from Georgia?" Jeremy asked.

Carrie shook her head, thinking of the young woman from the Deep South who had dressed as a man, and gone into the Confederate Army with her brother. He was killed, but Carrie had saved Georgia's arm, as well as saved her secret by taking her out of Chimborazo Hospital and treating her at home. "I keep hoping a letter will come, but nothing has. I don't know if she lived through the last battles in Petersburg. I haven't wanted to ask Robert."

Another silence fell on the room as their thoughts drifted to Robert lying in the bed above their heads.

Moses cleared his throat. "Is he any better at all?"

Carrie shrugged. "I don't know," she admitted. "His heart and mind are still closed down, but he seems to have put on a little weight." Her eyes sharpened as she realized Moses' eyes held more than his question. "What's on your mind, Moses?"

Moses gazed at her steadily for a few moments and then spoke with the ease of an old friend. "I've got to go after Mama and Sadie," he said gently. "Before I do that, I need to get Rose and John settled on the plantation."

Carrie nodded. "You should do that," she said. "I'm afraid to move Robert until he's stronger, but that doesn't mean you can't go." Once she had thought that far, her mind flew forward. "There's no reason for you to stay here in the city. If you went, you could also take Eddie. He would be safe with you."

Moses nodded. "Captain Jones said he would send some of my men out with us."

Carrie eyed him sharply. "You're worried about what could happen if you went alone."

Moses shrugged. "Let's just stick with what I said earlier about being smart."

Carrie pushed aside her uneasiness, realizing that Moses' men were seasoned veterans who had come through the war. Surely they could protect Rose and John. "I think it's a good idea for you to go," she said.

"You can let Sam and Opal know I will be coming home with Aunt Abby and Robert as soon as I can. If they are still there, they can help get things ready."

"I have a feeling they're still there," Moses said. "Sam didn't want to leave, and Opal is waiting for Eddie to be reunited with his kids."

Carrie shrugged. "I've learned not to take things for granted," she said with a slight smile. "Regardless, you need to go get your mama and Sadie." She cast an eye at Jeremy. "What do you want to do?"

Jeremy sat quietly for a moment. "This is the first I heard of them going out, but I think I'm going to stay here for a while longer and see if Thomas returns. He'll want to know everything going on in the government. I'm the best person to fill him in. I would like to first experience Cromwell Plantation with him." His voice thickened. "He's told me so many stories." He looked at Rose. "Do you understand?"

Rose nodded quickly. "Of course! I'm glad you want to be here for him. And it makes me feel better to know you'll be here for Carrie."

Carrie didn't try to stop the tears that welled up at the thought of her father. She reached over for Jeremy's hand. "He will be so glad you're here," she whispered.

Chapter Seven

Matthew breathed in the humid Mississippi air as he stepped from the train.

Peter appeared in front of him almost immediately. "Welcome to Vicksburg, old man! I thought you were going to miss the excitement all over again." His grin disappeared almost as fast as it had flashed. "How was President Lincoln's funeral?" he asked. "I would have been there, but the paper sent me down here to cover this story instead."

Matthew smiled and gripped his hand. "It's good to see you, Peter. Thanks for coming to meet me." His expression darkened. "The funeral was a fitting tribute to an amazing man. His funeral train is still winding its way through the Northern states right now. It won't arrive in Illinois until May third."

"Nine more days," Peter murmured. "I'm glad so many people are able to pay their respects."

Matthew nodded. "It's only right." He glanced around the train station. "Did I get here in time to accompany some of our soldiers on their trip home?" He was caught off guard by the flash of fury on Peter's face. "What is it?"

Peter shook his head angrily. "Calling them soldiers almost seems a farce," he snapped. "The men that are being loaded onto the steamboats are little more than caricatures of the soldiers they once were."

"I know what that's like," Matthew said grimly. His two times as a hostage in Libby Prison had indoctrinated him to deprivation and starvation. He barely had the strength to escape, and it took him months to return to his old self. The nightmares still haunted him, but they were fewer, and they weren't as intense. He could only hope time would heal the rest of his scars. It wasn't something he talked about. Peter shared the second experience with him but hadn't been confined to Rat Dungeon, in the hold of the prison for months, like Matthew had been.

Peter's shoulders slumped. "It's bad, Matthew. It's really bad," he whispered roughly.

"These men came from Andersonville?"

"Yes," Peter ground out. "I met with a group of men last night. They are nothing but skeletons. One man went in to Andersonville weighing one hundred eighty-five pounds. He came out weighing about eighty."

Matthew grimaced.

"He's just one," Peter continued. "Grant arranged for the sickest ones to be released first. A lot of them didn't make the trip here. They died on the train, or during the thirty-mile walk from Jacksonville."

"They made them walk thirty miles?" Matthew asked angrily. "In their condition?"

Peter nodded, his lips a tight line. "The ones who made it are counting the minutes until they're on a boat and on their way home. Most of them have already written letters telling their loved ones they will be with them soon."

Matthew took a deep breath. The war was over, but the horrors were not done. He wondered how many men would die on the boat, unable to withstand the rigors of several days of travel. His job was to tell the story of the return trip, and the men who had lived to experience it. He forced himself to think like a journalist.

"When is the next boat out?"

"Tomorrow."

"Have any of the men already been sent home?

Peter nodded. "Yes. The *Henry Ames* shipped out on the twenty-second with thirteen hundred men on board. The *Olive Branch* left on the twenty-third with seven hundred."

"Why didn't you leave with one of them?"

Peter grinned. "I was waiting for you," he answered. "We've experienced so many horrific things together. I decided it was time we experienced something good in this war. I can't think of anything better than watching these men reunite with their families."

Matthew clapped his shoulder. "Thanks, old man. That means a lot." He stepped into the waiting carriage Peter had tossed his luggage into. "What boat will we be going on?"

"The *Sultana*. It arrived in port last night."

"I know it well," Matthew responded.

"You do?"

"I had the pleasure of being onboard the *Sultana* about a year ago. She was just launched in January of 1863. She is one of the largest and best business steamers ever constructed," he said enthusiastically. "She's about two hundred sixty feet long, forty-two feet wide, and her hold is seven feet deep. She has a capacity of a thousand tons, but only trims on thirty-four inches of water. This makes her ideally suited for trade on the Ohio and the Mississippi Rivers." He smiled at Peter's look of amusement. "I kind of have a thing for boats."

Peter laughed. "I can tell."

"I don't suppose we're being lodged in one of the staterooms?" Matthew asked hopefully. "They are quite luxurious."

Peter laughed. "My guess is, we'll be on the open-air deck with easy access to the men we're reporting on."

Matthew shrugged. "Hope is a good thing," he said lightly. "But I've learned to deal with reality."

"Were you in one of the staterooms before?"

"Yes. I was writing a story about the steamboats transporting freight and men for the Union Army."

Peter whistled. "Profitable, I hear."

"Yes, but not without its hazards. We were part of a convoy of four other boats a couple of years ago in May. We were fired upon by a Rebel battery near Island number eighty-two right here on the Mississippi."

"Hit?"

Matthew grinned. "No. Thankfully they weren't very good shots!" Then his grin disappeared. "They weren't so lucky that July. They were fired on again near Memphis. The Rebel's aim was much better that time. There was a lot of damage to her upper works."

"It's all been repaired now," Peter said promptly. "She really is a beautiful boat. I felt better about my decision to stay behind when I saw her."

"It will be good to be on her again. If I remember correctly, she can hold close to four hundred passengers, along with her crew of eighty."

Peter nodded. "Don't be surprised if they load more than that. These men are eager to get home, and the government is eager to get them there."

Matthew shrugged. "I'm sure they'll set safe limits," he said. "These men have already been through so much." He was struck by something on Peter's face. "Do you know something?" he asked bluntly.

"I don't know," Peter replied hesitantly. "I've been hearing rumors. It might not mean anything."

"Newspapermen live off determining if rumors are true or not. What have you heard?"

Peter answered with a question. "Was Captain Mason on board when you traveled?"

"Yes. He's been the captain from the date of her launch. He's also part owner."

Peter nodded. "One of my sources told me Mason is in financial trouble. He's sold some of his rights, and rumor says he pushing hard for as many soldiers as he can get."

"Nothing wrong with that," Matthew replied. "A full contingent of soldiers must provide a nice profit."

"You could say that," Peter said ruefully. "Five dollars per enlisted man, and ten dollars for every officer."

Matthew whistled. "That's a nice profit," he admitted, "but I still don't see the source of concern. It's just business. It's how Mason has made his living for the last two years."

Peter hesitated. "Are you familiar with General Reuben Hatch?"

Matthew furrowed his brow in thought and then frowned. "The brother of O.M. Hatch, the Illinois Secretary of State who was a good friend of Lincoln's and helped him win the presidency?" He sorted back through his memory of all the news stories he had heard. "Isn't the general the one who was under investigation for fraud?"

"That's the one," Peter agreed. "They eventually cleared him, but rumor has it that it was only his brother's plea to Lincoln that got him off. The evidence was quite compelling. He's been under investigation a few times and was made to resign once. His brother and Lincoln got him his job back."

"I do remember that," Matthew replied with a frown. "Politics at work. What does that have to do with now?"

"Maybe nothing," Peter admitted, "but General Hatch is now the chief quartermaster for the Department of Mississippi."

"So he's in charge of all these steamboats taking our men back."

"Yes, and while it may mean nothing, I wouldn't put it past him to allow things that shouldn't happen."

"I see," Matthew mused. "Are you suggesting anything in particular?"

"More a feeling," Peter said a little sheepishly. "I also discovered this morning that repairs have recently been made to the boat." His voice was much more serious this time.

"On what?"

"The boilers."

Matthew looked at him closely. "What was the problem?"

"That's still somewhat of a mystery. I was near the boat yesterday when a man named Taylor came off the *Sultana* looking upset. The chief engineer caught up with him, talked to him for a little while, and then went back on board."

Matthew waited, knowing there was more.

"I saw Taylor grabbing a meal in a restaurant right before I came to get you. He didn't want to talk at first, but he finally opened up. Evidently, there was a problem with one of the boilers leaking."

Matthew frowned. "That could be serious."

"That's what Taylor said. He told Mason and the chief engineer he had found a bulge on the middle port boiler."

"The left boiler?"

Peter nodded. "Taylor told them that, for safety reasons, two sheets on the boiler needed to be replaced. He also told them that if they wouldn't let him make the repairs he thought were necessary, he didn't want anything more to do with the *Sultana*."

"Did he fix it?" Matthew asked sharply.

Peter shrugged. "They talked him into limiting his repairs to a patch measuring eleven by twenty-six inches. When he got another beer in him, he also told me he had recommended forcing the bulge back on the boiler. They wouldn't let him do it. He just put the patch over the bulge."

Matthew frowned, his stomach rolling uneasily. "Does he seem to think it's safe?"

"No," Peter said bluntly. "He also said he had concerns about some of the other boilers."

"I see," Matthew said slowly. "Will anyone else be inspecting the boat? Surely they won't let it travel with a load of men if they aren't confident it is safe?"

"Here's hoping," Peter said, his eyes showing his nervousness more than his voice did.

Their carriage was just arriving at the waterfront. Matthew took deep breaths of the humidity-laden air and stared out over the bustling port. The sheer pleasure of being there pushed back his feelings of uneasiness. After the grief-filled days of Lincoln's funeral, it was good to be covering a story full of life and hope.

"I'm sure it will be okay," he said. "Someone else will inspect the *Sultana*. They won't let it leave until it passes inspection."

Peter smiled. "You know more about boats than I do, so I guess I'll believe you." He looked up as he heard his name called, and raised his hand in response. "Hey, Jakes!" He waited until the slightly overweight blond with a cheerful grin reached them. "This lanky drink of a West Virginian is Matthew Justin. He's a reporter for the *Philadelphia Inquirer*."

The two men shook hands. "The prisoners are on their way here. They're being brought in from Camp Fisk, where they have been held since their release from Andersonville and Cahaba," Jakes explained to Matthew.

"How many?" Matthew asked.

Jakes shrugged. "We won't know until they get here."

Matthew frowned. "They haven't done a count? Isn't that standard military procedure?"

"Yes, but there seems to be a rush to get them here so they can head home. They decided to get them on the boat and then do a count."

Matthew frowned but nodded. It only made sense that everyone was eager to get the men back to their families.

Their decision was against procedure, but he could understand the motives to bypass it.

"There's another steamer that has just arrived," Jakes added. "My understanding is that the *Lady Gay* can take some of the prisoners if there are too many for the *Sultana*."

A whistle shriek had all of them looking toward the water.

"Isn't that the *Lady Gay* departing?" Peter asked. "I don't see anyone on her."

Jakes shrugged but looked discomfited. "They must have decided the *Sultana* could handle everyone."

"You don't agree?" Matthew observed.

"I don't know," he said hesitantly. "I was at Camp Fisk early this morning, before they started to ship the men. More have come in. I don't know exactly how many are waiting to head north, but it seems more than can fit on one steamer." He stared out over the water and shook his head. "What do I know about steamers and their capacity? I'm sure they won't put more men on the *Sultana* than it is safe to transport." He laughed lightly. "I just hope they leave enough room for us."

Peter chuckled. "I have General Hatch's word that we'll have a place. Everyone is eager to hear the stories we'll be able to tell."

Matthew pushed down his fresh uneasiness, calming himself by looking out over the busy port. He loved the shouts and calls as the stevedores unloaded and loaded the boats. The war had brought down massive shipments from the North, but its end would result in renewed shipments from the South of cotton, tobacco, rice, sugar, and so much more that the Confederacy provided. It would mean stabilization of the Southern economy and the beginning of reunion. The return of the prisoners was just one more sign of the healing between the North and the South. He could hardly wait to hear and tell their stories.

"Are those men being loaded onto the *Sultana*?" he asked suddenly, his attention caught by a column of men, most being transported on stretchers, moving toward the waiting steamer.

Peter gazed down at the boat and nodded. "Yes. Those are the men from the hospital. They were already in Vicksburg, so they are being loaded first." He grinned. "That's also our signal to board. You got here just in time." He grabbed his own bag and headed toward the steamer. "Come on, my boys. We have a job to do!"

*****

Matthew gazed around the boat as he walked on board. It was just as he remembered. He grabbed Peter's arm and pulled him toward the main cabin. "I know we won't be staying in the staterooms, but you have to check this out before it gets too crowded."

Peter whistled his appreciation when they walked through the long, narrow saloon. "Nice chandeliers," he commented, and then stopped to admire the fine china, glassware and tableware. "Classy accommodations," he murmured. "I hope I'll get another chance to travel on this lady in style someday. My wife would love this."

"The staterooms are the epitome of luxury," Matthew said with a hint of longing in his voice. "I'm sure Amanda would love it." He glanced out the window and pulled Peter toward the open deck. "There are more soldiers loading. I'd say it's time to get to work."

"I'll take the right side of the boat," Peter replied. "You can cover the ones on the left."

"That would be the starboard and port sides," Matthew corrected.

Peter shrugged. "You're the one with a thing for boats. You can call it what you want, as long as you stay off my side of the boat."

Matthew chuckled, pulled out his notepad and pen, and headed to the port side of the steamer. He was surprised by the long line of men he saw stretching down the wharf, but he had work to do. The first group he spotted was a row of men laid out on stretchers. He hesitated for a moment, not sure he should disturb them, and then decided to let them tell him if they didn't feel up to an interview.

He bit back a groan when he looked down at the first man in the row. His new uniform was draped over his skeletal frame, his cheeks and face sunken in and his Adam's apple in sharp relief. He managed a smile, though, when he saw Matthew.

"I reckon you look like a reporter," he said weakly.

Matthew managed a smile in return. "And I reckon you look like a man who is glad to be going home."

"You have that right." The enthusiastic response resulted in a jagged bout of coughing, but he held up his hand to keep Matthew from moving on. When he finally caught his breath, he said, "My name is Abner Crosstree."

Matthew squatted down to meet him at eye-level. "Hello, Abner. My name is Matthew Justin. I'm a reporter with the *Philadelphia Inquirer.* Where were you freed from?"

"Cahaba Prison," Abner replied, a deep shadow filling his eyes. "You don't have any idea what it was like."

"Not Cahaba Prison," Matthew agreed, "but I spent many months as a guest of Libby Prison in Richmond."

Abner looked at him more closely. "Then you do know what it's like."

Matthew nodded. "Unfortunately, I do."

"That why you're here to talk to us and tell our stories?"

"Yes. They need to be told."

Abner nodded. "I hear tell a group escaped Libby Prison a couple years back. Me and some of my friends tried to figure out how to escape from Cahaba, but we never did. Probably a good thing, because there wasn't anywhere to go. We just tried to survive instead."

Matthew didn't bother telling him he was one of the escapees. He was there to tell Abner's story, not his own. "How did you end up there?" he asked.

Abner grimaced. "My commander was tricked into making us surrender."

Matthew poised his pencil over his notepad and waited for him to continue.

"I was part of the guard at the fort in Athens, Georgia. We were making sure the railroads supplying Sherman stayed secure after he captured Atlanta, so they could keep getting supplies to him." Abner spoke slowly, taking deep breaths between sentences.

"You sure you're up for this?" Matthew asked, concern making him lower his pencil.

Abner nodded. "A bunch of the fellows didn't make it from the prison camps once they set us free. They died on the road, or they died in Camp Fisk waiting for their ride home. I know I'm not doing too good," he wheezed. "If I don't make it, I'd like to know my story is being told."

Matthew understood. "No more interruptions," he promised. "Your story will be told."

Abner nodded, drank some water to stop his coughing, and continued. "Our fort was strong," he said proudly.

Matthew nodded, thinking of Fort Athens. It had been considered the strongest fortification between Nashville, Tennessee and Decatur, Alabama. A quarter of a mile in circumference, the fort was surrounded by a ditch fifteen feet wide. The walls were seventeen feet high, and the whole thing was surrounded by a palisade and a wall of felled trees. They had enough supplies to withstand a siege of ten days. He'd been surprised when he found out how easily its 571 soldiers had been taken. He was about to find out why.

"The Rebel's General Forrest showed up on September twenty-third. The next morning, they shelled us with artillery for a couple hours, but didn't do any real damage." Abner tightened his lips against the pain rampaging through his body.

Matthew waited quietly. He would write for as long as Abner could talk.

"Me and the boys wanted to laugh when Forrest sent in a soldier equipped with a white flag to demand our surrender. Colonel Campbell refused. We didn't find out until later, that Forrest met with him and convinced him there were at least ten thousand men and nine pieces of artillery ready to make the assault."

"There weren't that many?" Matthew asked, in order to give Abner time to breathe.

Abner shook his head, his weary eyes snapping with disgust. "Nah. We found out later he had less than half that. They knew they couldn't take us, so they tricked us."

"Campbell fell for it?"

"Yes. He told the officers that the jig was up, and told them to pull down the flag. Then all of us marched out of the gates and became guests of Cahaba." He coughed a while longer and then added, "Relief was on the way. There were seven hundred men coming to help. They fought their way through to get to us, right as we were marching out of the fort. The only thing they could do was surrender, too."

Matthew grimaced. "I understand General Forrest captured another eleven hundred men at the Sulphur Branch Trestle."

"By the time we headed to Cahaba, there were twenty-three hundred of us. Getting there was no picnic," he wheezed, the shadow growing deeper in his eyes. "It was pretty cold last December when they finally marched us to the prison. The Rebels had taken a lot of our clothes, so most of us marched through snow and ice in bare feet."

Matthew winced but didn't interrupt.

"We didn't eat for a while. They finally threw us some raw corn from a wagon. A bunch of the fellas died from eating that. We thought things would be better when we finally saw some train cars. They crammed us into unheated cars lined with a half-foot of horse manure." Abner's voice faltered. "I reckon most of us were near dead by the time we got there. Probably would have been better if we'd died," he said weakly.

Matthew waited for him to regain his strength, watching as the flow of men continued up the gangplank and crowded onto the boat, spreading out to make room for themselves. There hadn't been a break in soldiers loading the boat since Matthew had gotten on. He had no idea how many had been loaded, but he was quite sure it was over the legal limit the *Sultana* was allowed to carry. He had been warned the final number would be higher than the legal limit, but he wondered just *how* much higher. He pushed away his uneasiness when Abner continued.

"We were hoping we would be inside when we got to Cahaba, but only about half the prison was covered with a roof. It didn't do anything to keep out the rain and cold." He shivered as he remembered.

Matthew searched his brain to remember what he had read about Cahaba Prison. It was on the Alabama River, not far from Selma. It had been built as a cotton and corn shed measuring roughly 193 feet by 116 feet. The walls were eight to ten feet high and only partially roofed. The entire center area was left open. "All twenty-three hundred of you were there?" he asked.

Abner shrugged. "I heard one of the guards say there were three thousand of us."

Matthew scowled. "You were practically on top of each other."

"Felt that way," Abner agreed. "The water wasn't worth drinking, and food was pretty scarce. I guess I lost a lot of weight."

Matthew stayed silent, hoping Abner didn't know just how bad he looked. His family's eyes, when they finally saw him again, would reveal the truth. His family would also be there to help him get better.

"Things got really bad back in February when the river flooded. It came right up into the prison. We had to stand in water up to our waist for four days."

"It had to be freezing!" Matthew exclaimed, the vision forcing the shocked words through his lips.

Abner nodded. "It was right cold," he said flatly. "The guards finally let us out to gather some driftwood. Me and some of my buddies hauled back enough wood to stack on top of each other. We got it high enough to sit on top and stay above the water. We crammed back to back for two more days until the water finally went down." His eyes grew sadder. "Lots of men didn't live through that flood."

And maybe they were the lucky ones, Matthew thought, but again remained silent.

"Anyway," Abner finished. "I made it, and I'm glad to be going home."

"Where is home, Abner?"

"Cairo, Illinois," he said. "Lots of the men have to travel more when the boat puts in dock. Not me. My wife and parents already know I'm on my way home. They'll be waiting for me."

"What did you do before the war?"

"I ran the post office in Cairo. I'm hoping I can get my job back when I get home." He frowned. "I reckon it may take me a while to get my strength back."

Matthew smiled gently and laid his hand on his shoulder. "I wish you the best."

Abner shook away his heavy thoughts and stared at him. "Are you gonna tell my story?"

"I promise," Matthew said. "Your story will be told."

Abner smiled, closed his eyes, and drifted off to sleep.

Matthew became aware of something happening at the end of the row of cots. He made his way down through arriving men so he could hear what was being said. As he approached, he could tell the argument was heated.

"You may *not* take these men from the boat, Dr. Kemble!"

Matthew gazed at the angry, red-faced man confronting Dr. Kemble, the medical director for the Department of Mississippi. He finally identified the speaker as George Williams, the commissary of musters—the man in charge of allocating prisoners onto the *Sultana*. Mathew edged closer.

"These men are certainly not staying on the *Sultana*," Dr. Kemble snapped. "This boat is already too crowded. Men in their condition cannot travel like this."

Captain Williams thinned his lips. "They cannot be removed," he repeated. "Their names have already been added to the rolls," he said stubbornly.

Dr. Kemble merely shrugged and beckoned some waiting men forward. "Then remove them," he said. He turned to the waiting men. "Take these men off this boat," he ordered.

One of the men waiting on the cots, in about as bad a condition as Abner lifted his head weakly. "Don't keep us here, Dr. Kemble," he pleaded. "My wife is waiting for me to get home."

Dr. Kemble's eyes softened, but his voice remained firm. "And it's my job to make sure you get there in one piece," he responded. His tone became gentler as he moved forward to take the soldier's hand. "I'll have you on a boat tomorrow," he promised. "One that has room for you." His scowl was directed toward Captain Williams.

Captain Williams scowled back at him, but didn't try to interfere as the men on the cots were picked up and transferred to stretchers.

Matthew watched as Kemble led the procession down the gangplank, glad that Abner was asleep and unaware he wasn't headed home. Matthew was still watching when the doctor stopped at the head of a large line of men who all appeared to have just been released from the hospital. Dr. Kemble spoke to an officer who, after an intense conversation, turned around to direct the men to head back to the hospital. Evidently, the doctor didn't feel good about *anyone* else being added to the boat.

Matthew frowned, wishing he could hear what was being said. His frown deepened as he saw that the line of men waiting to board the vessel hadn't diminished at all. What was going on? Why were so many men being loaded on the *Sultana*? A look at the wharf revealed there were other boats that could have transported some of the men. A glance behind him at the crowded decks of the steamer increased his discomfort.

Another conversation caught his attention. He watched as a bone-thin man with erect bearing approached another whose clothing identified him as the captain of the *Sultana*, Captain Mason.

Matthew moved closer, every sense on alert now.

"Captain Mason, I am Major William Fidler of the Sixth Kentucky Cavalry. I am in command of the soldiers aboard the *Sultana*."

Captain Mason nodded. "I was informed. You were a prisoner as well."

"Yes, and now it is my job to make sure these men get home safely. I fear there are far too many men on this boat for us to proceed safely," Major Fidler said.

"There is nothing I can do about that," Captain Mason said smoothly. "All the men have to go through on the *Sultana*." He hesitated. "I believe I can carry them all through."

Matthew's blood chilled when he heard the hesitation in Captain Mason's voice. Even the captain wasn't convinced his steamer could handle the increasing load.

"I tell you, they are packing us on here like hogs!"

Matthew turned in time to hear the comment from an angry soldier.

"There is no place to lie down. There is no place to even relieve ourselves. Did we suffer through the war and the prison camps to be treated like this?"

Matthew listened as the indignation rose around him. He was quite sure he agreed with all of them. What he was not sure of, was what he could do about it. The alarm bells ringing in his head said all of them were in danger, but he had no idea how he could stop what was happening. He looked around for Peter, but was already quite sure he had little chance of finding him in the mass of men crowded on the boats.

He scanned the sea of men swarming around him. How many? The boat was cleared for four hundred people. There had to be more than two thousand on this boat. His frown deepened into a scowl as he moved past women, children and families who seemed completely bewildered by what was happening. Passengers were everywhere—on the hurricane deck, on the wheel-house, the forward deck, and guard.

He listened as he shoved his way to the front of the boat, knowing there was too much commotion to attempt an interview.

"They gave the slaves more room on the slave boats," one man muttered as he tried to slide down into a sitting position by the rail."

"Do you see the hurricane deck sagging? This is madness!"

"What will happen if this steamer catches fire?" another man demanded.

Matthew shuddered and continued to push forward. He wasn't sure why he was working so hard to get to the front, except that perhaps it would give him a feeling of not being so closed in if the front were open to him. His anxiety and anger were making it hard to breathe.

He continued to overhear conversations as he moved forward.

"I just spoke to the steamer's clerk," one dignified man stated.

Matthew slowed when he realized the man speaking was William D. Snow, a senator-elect from Alabama. He listened eagerly.

"I went to him with my concerns about the number of passengers. He showed me the boat's certificates and books." Snow scowled. "He also told me the *Sultana* is transporting the largest number of passengers ever carried upriver on a single vessel."

Matthew ground to a halt.

"How many passengers are on here?" another man asked.

Snow hesitated before he answered. "Twenty-four hundred soldiers, a hundred citizen passengers and a crew of about eighty."

Matthew almost gagged. "Twenty-five hundred passengers on a boat built for four hundred?" he blurted.

The men turned to stare at him, but no one responded. Matthew knew they felt as helpless as he did. He turned and continued to push forward.

"This steamer isn't only carrying passengers," a round-faced man growled as he fought for a handhold on the railing. "There are almost one hundred mules and horses and a hundred hogs in a pen toward the stern. Not to mention all the sugar and wine they are carrying."

Matthew's steps faltered, but he was being pulled forward by a force he didn't understand.

Chapter Eight

Janie stared blindly into the vibrant green of the newly leafing maple trees surrounding Clifford's home. It was odd to be in a city virtually untouched by four years of violent war—no battles, no destruction, no charred buildings. If she were so inclined, she could almost believe it had never happened.

She was not so inclined. In spite of the horrors of the war, at least she had felt alive. She had felt purpose. Now there was nothing to break the monotony of one mindless day after another. Shifting her chair, Janie reached over to pick up a cold glass of iced tea. She sipped it thoughtfully as the sun caused shadows to dance across the lawn.

Clifford's home was beautiful. The sprawling white clapboard structure with gleaming green shutters was bordered on both ends by a wide brick fireplace. The circular gravel drive in front of the house was rarely empty of fine carriages transporting important men. She hated every inch of it.

Janie's eyes narrowed as she thought of these *important* men. *Self*-important was a more apt description. She had come to loathe the purposeless days that spread out like the never-ending flow of a river, but she truly dreaded the nights when Clifford's beautiful home rang with the angry voices of *important* men determined to regain all they had lost during the war. She could not help but hear their hatred and bigotry, and she had learned their violence spawned even more anger in her husband. With nowhere else to direct it, Clifford always released it on her.

It had taken only a few days before she greatly preferred the boredom of daylight to the terror of the evenings. She could hardly remember the tough-minded, independent woman who had left Raleigh five years ago to work at Chimborazo Hospital against the wishes of her family. Undaunted, she had taken the train and started a new life. That new life included Carrie Cromwell, her family, and all the patients they treated together over the years.

In less than a week, that world had been dimmed by the brutal reality of the one she was in now. Why had she not listened to Carrie? Why had she been so determined to return to Raleigh with Clifford? Why had she thought she could change the anger that grew in him daily?

Janie swallowed the sob that wanted to burst from her throat and blinked back the tears that wanted to break free. She knew to hide the fear that beat at her breast on a daily basis. She had learned quickly that any show of fear or weakness only fed Clifford's anger. Defiance had the same effect, so she was learning how to walk a very fine line to escape his insults and rage.

The sound of carriage wheels on the drive caused her to take a deep breath and straighten her shoulders with determination. A glimpse through the trees told her Clifford was home from his law office. The others would arrive shortly. Janie stood, took a final deep draw of tea, and walked into the house. It was a matter of principle that she not be on the porch when Clifford arrived home. She refused to give him the satisfaction of thinking his dutiful wife was waiting for his return. It was a non-significant victory, but she grasped for whatever would allow her to hold on to her rapidly dwindling self-respect.

"Janie!" Clifford called for her as soon as he entered the house; his sharp eyes scanning to make sure everything met his high standards of excellence.

Janie watched him for a moment from the protection of the dining room. She felt a moment's fear when his sharp eyes scanned the ornately carved rosewood furniture upholstered with soft blue velvet. Two Boston rockers perched on the edge of the dark blue carpet in front of the fireplace. In spite of the bright sunlight pouring in through the spotless windows, she had already lit the lanterns, anticipating Clifford's demand that his house be ready for guests at every moment. She forced herself to relax, knowing her careful cleaning had removed even a speck of dust.

Finally, Clifford stopped his perusal of the room. Just as he opened his mouth to call for her, Janie straightened her shoulders and walked into the parlor.

"Hello, Clifford," she said calmly.

Clifford's eyes scanned her carefully, analyzing her coral crinoline dress and her hair pulled back into a tight bun. He demanded she look the part of a successful attorney's wife at every moment. Even when cleaning, she had to always be ready to accept company. In only a week, Clifford had already taken great strides to rebuild what had been a powerful law practice before the war. She had no doubt his unscrupulous determination would open many doors.

Janie stood straight, forcing herself to breathe evenly, taking pride in such a small accomplishment. She met his eyes directly and waited for him to speak.

There was no greeting and no fond welcome for his wife. "I have an important meeting tonight," he announced. "I expect drinks in the study in one hour."

Janie nodded calmly but chose to not respond. She was fairly certain he would not expect her to, as long as she met his wishes. She had a wild moment of wondering how he would respond if she were to say, "Yessuh, Masser."

Clifford's three slaves had disappeared well before the end of the war, and his fledgling business could only support part-time housekeeping, so he expected Janie to do almost everything. She didn't really care. At least it gave her a way to pass the tedious days. And on the days Wanda was there, at least she had someone else to talk to, though their housekeeper was clearly not comfortable with carrying on a conversation with her white employer.

"Where is my dinner?" Clifford demanded, a scowl appearing on his face when he glanced into the dining room and saw an empty table.

"We're having chicken and dumplings," Janie replied. "I left it in the pot until you returned home, to be assured it was hot." She knew it wasn't as good as May's, but her cooking skills were improving. It was something she had never had need of until recently. Her family's servants had always cooked when she was growing up, and then May provided delicious meals at the Cromwell home. Even when all they had was months of beans and cornbread, she always managed to do something to vary the taste, and it was always delicious. "I prepared a sweet potato pie for dessert," she added.

"I would like to eat now," Clifford said imperiously, his look clearly indicating he was disappointed not to have found something to accuse her with.

Janie nodded. "Go ahead and be seated. I'll have it out in a moment."

Dinner passed quietly, though Janie could feel anger and resentment boiling in Clifford. She could only guess at what knowledge he had gained during the day that ignited the latest fire. She could hardly remember the days in the beginning of their relationship, and even in the early months of their marriage, when they would have wonderful conversations and discuss what was going on in the country. The defeat of the Confederacy had changed all that, sparking a rage within Clifford that closed her out.

Still, she was anxious to know what was happening. Clifford forbade her to leave the house without him as an escort, and since he was never free to go anywhere, she had not left the walls of his home, except to walk in the yard, since arriving in Raleigh.

"Any news from General Johnston?" she dared to ask, desperately wanting to know if the war was truly over. Lee and Grant had signed the infamous surrender at Appomattox, but the last she knew, General Johnston still had active troops in North Carolina.

"And what could you possibly care about that?" Clifford asked scornfully, his eyes flashing as he shoveled in a mouthful of steaming chicken and dumplings.

"Since I helped return a good many of those soldiers to the battlefield," Janie responded, forgetting for a moment to keep her voice subservient, "I would like to know if they are still fighting, or if the war is truly over."

"So you can gloat over the complete demise of the South?" Clifford snapped angrily. "I'm sure you're sorry not to have Carrie Borden to celebrate with."

Janie swallowed back her bitter retort and closed her heart to the stinging pain of missing Carrie. She'd had her chance, and she had foolishly walked away. She also knew better than to press for more information.

"You are nothing but a stupid woman," Clifford sneered, his eyes boring into her. "I ran into your father at the courthouse," he offered, his eyes shifting to become more calculating.

Janie stiffened. She'd seen her family only once since returning home. Clifford insisted she invite them over for dinner the second night, acting the part of a dutiful, loving husband. Janie, not wanting to alarm her parents, played along. Her parents, she knew, were so proud she was married to an influential attorney, who was also a war hero in their eyes.

"I chose not to tell him that his beloved daughter is a nigger-loving traitor without a brain in her head," he snapped.

Janie continued to gaze at him. He knew before they married that she carried no prejudice in her heart, and that she longed for the slaves to be free. Only one of them had changed in the last months. Clifford's bitterness was growing on a daily basis. She was desperate to know what was fueling it, but instead she asked, "How was Father?"

"As well as could be expected," Clifford ground out. "Everything he has worked for is gone, most of his money is gone, and now he has nothing but a woman who longs for the destruction of the South for a daughter." He slammed his fist down on the table. "As well as could be expected is really not so well, is it?" he taunted.

Janie's color rose in her face as she swallowed back her fear and anger. She forced her shoulders to remain straight as she stared back into his eyes directly, so as not to betray her fear, and calmly, so as to not appear to be challenging him. All she wanted to do was bolt from the table and hide in her bedroom, but even there she wasn't safe.

The sound of carriage wheels signaled her rescue. Clifford spared her a scathing glance, took two quick bites to finish his meal, and slid back from the table. "Stay away from the study once you have brought drinks," he ordered before he strode from the room.

Janie blinked back tears as she pushed away her full plate. If Clifford cared enough to notice, he would see that she had lost quite a bit of weight in the last month or so. Even at Carrie's, it had become increasingly difficult to eat. Now that she was back in Raleigh, she was hardly able to swallow a bite around the constant tightness in her chest.

Within twenty minutes, there were five gentlemen in Clifford's study. They smiled pleasantly at her when she delivered the drinks, but she could tell by their distracted eyes that they didn't really see her. They were already thinking about what they had come to discuss. "Have a good evening," she said graciously before she left the room.

Janie did not go to the back of the house as ordered. She moved out of sight of the study door, inching closer when Clifford closed it. She would have to take her chances. The only way she could get information was to stay close enough to try to overhear any conversation. Right now, their voices were muted behind the heavy oak door, but if history repeated itself, they would soon be yelling with passion.

Janie waited restlessly while the murmuring continued. Her head jerked up when the first statement was made that she could understand.

"I'm telling you, General Johnston will be forced to surrender!"

Clifford's voice rose above the rest. "That's nonsense! Johnston signed a surrender armistice with Sherman."

"Yes, he offered him the same surrender terms Grant offered Lee," another man snorted. "Give up their weapons and promise to fight no more, and then they could go home."

"That's only part of it," another protested.

Janie crept closer so she could hear the conversation clearly. She was sure she would hear footsteps and be able to hide before she was discovered snooping.

"He's right," Clifford said. "Johnston refused to accept the terms. He told Sherman he had the power to surrender all the Confederate armies in the South, but would only do it if Sherman gave him what he wanted."

"Which was?"

Clifford sounded quite proud to be the one with the information. Janie could envision the cold gloat on his face as he proved his superiority over the other men. "Instead of surrendering, the Confederate armies will break up and go home, taking their weapons with them. In exchange, President Johnson will recognize state governments in the South that promised to support the Constitution." Clifford paused. "Sherman said the president will protect our political rights and will not interfere with the Southern people, if we remain peaceful and obey the laws."

There was a long silence. Another man, someone Janie had not heard speak yet, was the next to raise his voice. "I hear Sherman was called up to Washington. I'm not sure everyone up there is happy with the arrangement he made."

"Well, they should be," Clifford retorted angrily. "The North had better give us the right to live our own lives down here, or they'll find themselves right back in battle!"

An even longer silence reigned. Janie, safe from discovery, smirked with disdain. Just exactly how did Clifford think the South could go to war again over anything? They had already been soundly defeated and had no resources to take action of any kind.

"How exactly do you propose that happen?" one of the men asked.

Janie smiled, knowing she wasn't the only one to find Clifford's statement ridiculous. The smile faded as she listened.

"There is more than one way to fight a war," Clifford said. "The North might think they can come down here and tell us how to run our lives, and they may send the military down to control things, but they won't be here forever. There are already plans being made," he added mysteriously. His voice rose again. "Do any of you intend on letting your old slaves be your equals?" he snarled. "Are you ready to let the niggers invade our cities and leave our plantations to go to ruin?"

"No!" The voices of the other men in the room rose in unison.

"But what do we do now?" one of them asked.

"We wait," Clifford responded. "First, we wait to see if Johnston's armistice sticks. President Johnson was a slave owner himself. I sense he is sympathetic to our cause, though he may have to do some posturing to catch the Yankees off guard." His laugh was brittle and cold. "John Wilkes Booth did us all a huge favor by killing Lincoln. It may take some time, but I predict we'll be back in control of the South before too long. They may have beaten us militarily, but that doesn't mean we don't still have ways to protect the grand Southern lifestyle."

"Slavery is dead," one man protested. "There is no changing that."

"You're right," Clifford agreed, "but there is more than one way to make sure the nigger stays in his place."

Janie stiffened, not wanting to believe it was her husband she was listening to. Had he truly deceived her so completely when he courted her? Had she been totally blind to what was truly in his heart? Or had he radically changed when confronted with the reality of a crushing Southern defeat? Tears filled her eyes when she accepted the kind of hatred she heard oozing from his voice had not been born overnight. It had long been felt and nurtured. Perhaps once, he had cared enough about her to stuff it inside and even believe he could feel differently, but he was no longer making any kind of pretense about how he truly felt and who he really was.

The sound of footsteps had her scurrying down the hallway. She slipped into the kitchen just as the study door opened. Knowing the meeting would go on for hours but unwilling to risk being detected, she slipped out onto the back porch and slumped down on the steps to lean against the railing. Protected by the darkness, she let hot tears rain down her cheeks.

******

"We're here!" Susie called out as the spires of Richmond appeared on the horizon. She leaned forward as the crowded wagon approached the outskirts of the city, and then frowned when she saw the blackened walls standing out in stark relief against the blue sky. She heard about Richmond's burning, but seeing it in person was different from hearing about it. She sucked in her breath when she saw the destruction, and felt bile rise in her throat.

"You know Richmond right well?" a woman in the wagon asked anxiously. "You know how to get us down to the black quarter?"

"Don't worry," Susie said soothingly, forcing her nausea down. "That's where I grew up. I have friends there."

"You sho dey still dere?" a wiry, older woman asked, her eyes wide and anxious as she gazed at the burned buildings. "The black quarter still eben be dere?"

Susie hesitated. "I got news that the black quarter didn't burn," she said. "And my friends can't all be gone," she added, her confidence slipping a little. She grew quiet as the wagon full of twenty slaves from the contraband camp neared the outskirts of town. They had loaded up the wagon and headed for the capital city as soon as they heard word of blacks pouring into Richmond from the countryside. She was the only one who knew anything about the city, but all of them were confident that there was opportunity to be found.

"I wonder if Simon is here."

Susie looked back at June, smiling at her friend as she juggled two-year-old Simon, Jr. in her arms. June's eyes were frightened but filled with determination to find her husband. "The last letter you got from Moses said he and Simon were here in Richmond. We've seen black troops patrolling the roads. I believe they're both still here."

June tried to smile naturally, but it didn't reach her eyes. "You think Zeke is here?"

Twenty-year-old Susie frowned slightly, her pretty face twisted with concern. "I haven't heard from Zeke for a while, but I know it's hard to get letters through right now. I don't know where he is, but if he comes to the contraband camp, he'll know I came here looking for my daddy."

June nodded. "You reckon your daddy is out of that Castle Thunder place?"

Susie nodded. "I heard it's empty, but that doesn't tell me where he is. They took the prisoners up toward the mountains before Richmond fell. I'm sure they've been released, and I'm sure Daddy will come back here, but I don't know how long it will take."

June laid a hand on her arm. "You'll find him," she said.

Susie stared at the city, remembering the day her father had been hauled off to prison for suspected spy activity, on the very same day her mother died in an explosion at Tredegar Iron Works. She and her three siblings had ended up at Cromwell Plantation, away from the violence and wrapped in safety. It had done her heart good to watch her brother and two sisters grow healthy and strong from plentiful food. It took months for the haunted expressions to leave their eyes, but finally laughter returned. When she met Zeke, married, and left the plantation, she promised them she would return to Richmond after the war to find their daddy.

"Where we going?" June asked. "Are we going to stay with some of your friends down in the quarter?"

Susie shook her head but didn't say anything else. She had to get everyone else settled first. She stiffened when a soldier in Union blue approached the wagon, but relaxed immediately when she saw he was black.

"Howdy," the soldier said. "Where you folks comin' from?"

"The contraband camp at Hampton," Susie replied, not offering any more information.

The soldier, his eyes sharp but kind, nodded. "Lots of people comin' into the city," he said.

"I imagine they are," Susie replied, sensing there was something else behind his casual conversation. "Anything we need to be aware of?"

The soldier shrugged. "Won't everybody be glad to see you," he commented. "The city is getting a mite crowded."

Susie frowned. She wondered about that when she had seen the number of wagons heading toward Richmond. "Problems?"

The soldier looked at her, seeming to realize she was the leader for their small group. "You know the city?"

"I grew up here."

The soldier nodded with relief. "Stay out of the white part right now," he said. "Take everyone directly to the black quarter. We're keeping control of things, but they are gettin' right tense. When it gets dark, it's harder to watch things."

Susie nodded. She knew exactly what he meant. There was no longer a legal curfew for blacks, but that didn't mean you should do something stupid to put yourself at risk. "Thank you," she said.

The soldier lifted his hand and rode on.

Susie turned to everyone in the wagon. "Did you hear him?" she demanded, waiting until everyone met her eyes and nodded. "We're free, but that doesn't mean we can stop being careful. I want all of you to be around to enjoy your freedom. Everything is still right new. I'll make sure you're safe, but then you'll be the one to *keep* yourself safe."

****

Susie and June lifted their hands and waved goodbye to the wagonload of people standing on the dusty road in front of the First African Baptist Church. They looked excited and bewildered, but they were already surrounded by several women from the church who assured Susie they would help them get settled. Susie had asked about her father, but no one she spoke to knew anything.

"Where are we headed?" June asked again.

Susie smiled. "Just follow me. We have enough time," she said as she glanced at the sun still well above the horizon. She shifted her bag in her arms and headed out of the black quarter.

Two miles of walking had them approaching a hill. They had remained quiet as they passed throngs of white people on the road who stared at them with undisguised hostility but did nothing more than mutter. Susie was grateful for the presence of Union troops everywhere.

June was too busy staring at everything to utter a word since they had started walking. Little Simon seemed mesmerized by all the bustle and activity, staring with frightened eyes when they passed the blackened buildings. He remained silent, gripping his mama's hand more tightly.

"Tired..." Simon finally said plaintively as they started up the hill.

June chuckled. "I imagine you are," she said as she swung him up into her arms. "You've been such a brave boy to walk this far."

Simon beamed. Safe in his mama's arms, he gazed around. "Daddy here?"

June nuzzled his soft cheek. "I don't know," she replied. "But if he is, we're going to find him."

"Uncle Moses, too?" Simon said hopefully.

"I don't know that either," June said. "We're going somewhere we can spend the night," she said confidently, staring at Susie as if to tell her she had better be right.

Susie smiled, hoping she wasn't taking June on a wild goose chase that would end up with them in an area they shouldn't be in. Unsure why, she simply felt compelled to head for Carrie's house. She had breathed easier when she realized the fire had not spread that far. As far as she knew, Carrie may have already left town for the plantation, but still she felt compelled to go there. She had learned to follow her heart in the uncertainty of the last years, and she wasn't going to stop now.

Both Susie and June were breathing hard when they reached the side road lined with tall trees. June stared around her. "Where are we?"

"We're almost there," Susie replied, gazing down the road. The dinner hour had almost everyone inside. The street was eerily quiet as they walked the last remaining distance. Laundry flapped in the breeze and birds sang, while the whistle of the train in the distance reminded them they were in a busy city.

Susie took a deep breath to gather her courage when they reached the familiar brick house. She walked up the stairs and knocked.

The door opened moments later. An elderly black man gazed at her. "May I help you?"

Susie swallowed. "I'm here to see Carrie Borden. Is she in?"

"Who be askin'?"

"I'm Susie." She glanced over at June. "That's June."

The elderly man gazed at them sharply and then smiled unexpectedly. "Do tell? You be Susie and June?" He looked down. "Then this must be Simon."

Susie stared at him. "Yes." She didn't know what else to say.

"You folks come on inside." He smiled broadly. "I'm Micah. There be some people eatin' supper that gonna be right glad to see all of you."

Susie and June stared at each other but followed Micah. They both stopped and gaped when they rounded the corner into the dining room.

"Look who I found on the porch," Micah announced, stepping back.

Pandemonium broke loose.

"Susie!" Carrie yelled.

"June!" Moses bellowed as he jumped up from the table. "Simon!" he yelled, as he swung the little boy up in his arms and grabbed June close.

"June! Susie!" Rose laughed with delight as she hurried forward to wrap both of them in a warm hug. "How in the world did you get here?"

"Girls! Simon! Welcome!" Aunt Abby pushed through to wrap both of them in her embrace.

Susie and June were both rendered speechless.

Susie was the first to find her voice. "What...? How...?

Moses chuckled and guided them both to the table. "We'll answer all your questions, but I have a feeling both of you are hungry."

"Hungry!" Simon called, walking willingly into the chair Carrie pulled out for him. "Who are you?" he asked, reaching out to touch Carrie's face.

"I'm Carrie," she said, smiling through her tears as she stroked his cheek. "I'm very glad to meet you. I've heard a lot about you."

Simon nodded and reached eagerly for a thick chunk of cornbread. "Hungry!" he announced again before he took a big bite.

Laughter erupted in the room.

Rose headed for the stairs. "I have about a million questions, but I need to wake someone up to be a part of this party. He fell asleep early tonight because he played so hard, but he can't miss this."

Moments later, she returned with John wrapped in her arms, his sleepy eyes clearly asking what all the confusion was about. He gazed around until his eyes rested on Simon. His sleepy eyes cleared. "Down, Mama. Down!"

Rose laughed and lowered him to the ground.

"John!" Simon yelled as he dropped his cornbread and slipped from the chair.

The two friends stared at each other with delight and then began to wrestle on the floor, their delighted laughter pealing through the house.

"Boys!" June snorted and fell into Rose's arms. "I missed you so much!" She turned to stare at Susie. "Did you know they would all be here?" she demanded.

Susie could only shake her head in amazement. "I had no idea," she stammered. "I was just hoping Carrie would be here." She stared around. "How...?"

******

Carrie shared a glance with Micah. He nodded and turned into the kitchen.

May's head popped out into the room. "I reckon we gonna need some more food," she announced. "I'll have it right out." She gazed fondly at the two boys wrestling on the floor. "You two want some cookies?" she called.

"Cookies!" John yelled as he grabbed Simon's hand and pulled him into the kitchen.

Laughter rang around the table as stories were shared. Darkness wrapped the house in its embrace as the oil lamps flickered over the joyful faces. Rose was sharing how she had discovered Moses recovering from his wound when there was a knock on the door.

"Micah?" Carrie asked quietly, a smile playing on her lips.

Aunt Abby gazed at her. "Are we expecting anyone?"

"We are now," Carrie replied. "I can't wait to see who it is this time."

Silence fell on the room as they waited to see who Micah would return with. The silence didn't last for long.

"Simon!" June screamed, launching herself from the table.

"June!" Simon boomed, catching her up in his arms and swinging her around.

The door to the kitchen flung open. "Daddy!" Simon hollered, rushing forward on his sturdy legs.

Simon laughed as he swung his son up into his arms and claimed June's lips with a fervent kiss.

He finally raised his head and stared around the room, his smile growing even brighter when he saw Susie. "How...?"

"That seems to be the favorite question tonight," Aunt Abby said with a chuckle. She stood and pulled another chair forward. "Join the party," she invited.

Talk flowed around the table for hours more. Little John was fast asleep in Moses' arms. Simon was snuggled close to his daddy, regularly reaching up to pat his face to convince himself he was real. Finally, the boy closed his eyes, laid his head on his father's shoulder, and fell fast asleep.

Simon was the first to stand. "I hate to break this up, but I have to report back to my unit." He smiled at June's look of disappointment. "Don't worry. Captain Jones said I could have three days off starting tomorrow night." He glanced at Carrie.

"You can stay here," she said promptly. "You two can have Janie and Clifford's old room." She felt a stab of pain as she thought of Janie, but forced herself to focus on the joy of the moment.

"I would love to have Susie in my room," Aunt Abby offered.

Susie finally asked the question that had been burning in her throat all night. She had been afraid to ask, not sure she wanted the answer, but now she had to know. "My daddy?" she said softly. "Has there been any word?"

Carrie smiled. "I was hoping to surprise you, too, but I guess you'll have to know in advance."

"Surprise me? Do you know something?" Susie asked hopefully.

"I'd say so," Rose laughed. "Your daddy escaped Castle Thunder before the city fell. He came here, too.

Carrie hid him for a while, and then found him a safe place down in the black quarter. He's waiting until we all head out to the plantation, and then he's coming with us."

Susie made no attempt to hide her tears. "Daddy..." she whispered. She turned to Carrie. "Thank you." A smile wreathed her face as she wrapped Carrie in a warm hug. "The plantation?"

Carrie grinned. "It's still there. As far as we know, all is well. I'm waiting for Robert to get strong enough to head out, but Moses and Rose will be going there soon." She answered the question in Susie's eyes before she asked it. "And, yes, you can most certainly go out with them!"

"We won't be going out for another week," Moses said. "Captain Jones said the Union troops are going to be marching through Richmond on May first. Simon and I aim to march with them," he said firmly.

"As you should," Carrie said immediately. She looked at Susie. "You are more than welcome to stay here until they leave."

Susie nodded. "Thank you, but I think once my daddy arrives, I'll see if I can stay with him while I look for my husband. We've got a lot of catching up to do," she said.

They were all still talking around the table when June came back in from telling Simon goodbye. A smile lit her face, although her eyes were wet with tears. "I do believe this has been one of the best nights of my life," she declared.

"I could not agree with you more," Carrie replied. "The war kept us all separated for so long. It's such a joy to finally meet you, June."

June smiled. "I know there is so much still to talk about, but I'm wondering if anyone has heard from Matthew."

"He was here until about a week ago," Aunt Abby responded. She gazed around the table. "I was just getting ready, before the excitement, to tell all of you that Matthew sent a telegram. I got it when I was in town earlier."

Carrie leaned forward. "Where is he? Is everything alright?"

Aunt Abby nodded. "His telegram said he has the privilege of heading up the Mississippi River on a steamboat carrying Union prisoners-of-war home. He was getting ready to load when he sent the telegram. He also said the *Inquirer* has directed him to return to Richmond after he reaches Cairo, Illinois to cover what is happening here." She smiled. "He should be home soon."

Chapter Nine

"Peter!" Matthew was relieved beyond words to see his friend sitting amongst a group of prisoners, talking and laughing. It had been two days since he had seen him.

Peter jumped up and came over to clap Matthew on his shoulder. "I wasn't sure we would find each other in this mass of humanity," he said. "You are a sight for sore eyes."

Matthew smiled, but it soon faded away to be replaced by a frown. "I may be the only sight for sore eyes on this boat. The conditions these men are enduring are terrible."

Just then, four men standing several yards away broke into song and dance, causing all the men around them to laugh and cheer.

Peter gazed at them for a minute. "They don't seem to mind the conditions," he replied. "I guess after the prison camps, this isn't so bad."

"It would take a comparison to Andersonville or Cahaba to make the conditions anything but pitiful," Matthew growled. "There is not one army doctor on board for all these sick men. I met a civilian doctor last night who is doing what he can, but obviously he is only scratching the surface of the need."

Peter nodded. "You're right," he said heavily. "I keep trying to focus on how glad all the men are to be going home, but that doesn't mean I'm not aware of the chronic diarrhea that seems to be plaguing almost all of them."

Matthew scowled. "Almost every one of these men is suffering from malnutrition and scurvy. There is no telling how many of the civilians on this boat will get sick from coming into contact with pneumonia, typhoid and dysentery."

"I would argue and say the army was doing the best it can, but I know that's wrong," Peter admitted. "I keep thinking about the almost empty boats that pulled away from the dock in Vicksburg while the *Sultana* was loading."

"Not to mention all these men have to eat is hard tack and raw salt pork or bacon," Matthew snapped. "As far as I'm concerned, this is criminal!"

It was impossible to talk without being overheard, so Matthew wasn't surprised when he felt a hand on his shoulder.

"Don't worry about us," an emaciated soldier said cheerfully. "Things aren't so grand on this old boat, but at least we're headed home and we're officially in the land of the free! We've lived through the worst, and now we're headed home to our families. It might be salt pork right now, but I reckon my wife is going to have a feast when I get home." He glanced down at his skeleton-thin body. "It will take a little while, but she'll put meat back on these bones." He smiled again. "We're going home!"

Matthew stared at him and smiled reluctantly. "I guess you're right," he acknowledged, well aware of what they had lived through. "What's your name, soldier?"

"Joseph Sprake."

"You mind if we talk a little while? I'm a reporter for the *Philadelphia Inquirer*. I would be honored to share your story with the country."

Joseph's skeletal cheeks bloomed in a grin. "Why, of course! I was a guest of Andersonville for almost fourteen months...thirteen months, twenty-four days and twelve hours to be exact," he added. "I reckon I have lots of stories to tell."

Matthew stared at him, somehow managing to hide his dismay, while a wave of admiration and respect rolled through him. Anybody who survived Andersonville for the entire time it was open, deserved to have their story told.

Peter slapped him on the back. "You're going to be busy for a while. I'm going to go find my own stories."

Matthew nodded. "We may not find each other again before we get to Cairo. Take good care of yourself."

"You too, old man." Peter paused. "I hear we are stopping at Memphis in a few hours. They're going to let some of the men off to go into town to celebrate. I'm thinking about joining them so I can send my paper a report. Do you want to go?"

Matthew thought for a moment and then shook his head. "I don't think so. I'm going to stick close to the boat so I can get as many stories as possible. I've interviewed a lot of the men who are too weak to do anything but lie on the floor of the boat. I don't think I want to miss hearing any of their stories."

"Not even to have a break from these conditions?" Peter asked.

Matthew smiled, knowing his friend understood his passion. "I'll survive." His thoughts spun ahead. "Once I get to Cairo, I've been called back to Richmond. May will make sure her cooking wipes away all the memories of this boat ride."

Peter grinned. "See you in Cairo," he called over his shoulder as he walked away.

Matthew turned back to Joseph. "How about if we sit down?" In spite of Joseph's cheerful expression, he could see the deep fatigue and weakness in the young man's eyes.

"I guess that would be a good idea," Joseph agreed, sinking down immediately. His eyes closed in relief for a long moment, before he opened them again. "What do you want to know?"

"Let's start with where you're from and how old you are," Matthew suggested.

"I'm nineteen," Joseph replied. "I left our farm in Ohio when the war started and joined up."

"When the war *started*?" Matthew exclaimed. "You would only have been..."

"Yes," Joseph responded with a smile. "I was only fifteen. Course, the army boys didn't know that. I told them I was eighteen. All three of my brothers signed up right away. I wasn't about to get left behind." Dark shadows flitted through his eyes as the cheerfulness ebbed away to be replaced by deep sorrow. "I'm the only one left. Jake got killed at Bull Run." He managed a weak smile. "At least he didn't have to fight for long. He's probably mad he got killed in the first real battle of the war, but I reckon he was the lucky one."

Matthew waited quietly.

Joseph took a deep breath. "Charles was killed the next year at Seven Pines, when we were trying to take Richmond. I saw him fall. I got to him to pull him back behind the lines for the medics, but he was already gone—shot right through the head." He shrugged his thin shoulders. "At least he didn't suffer like some of those I heard moaning out on the field for hours."

A long moment of silence passed while Joseph stared off into space. When he began to speak again, his voice was low and hoarse. "Adam made it until December of that year. The Rebels got him at the Battle of Fredericksburg."

Matthew grimaced as he remembered.

"You were there?"

"I was there," he admitted. "It was terrible."

"Yes," Joseph agreed. "That's where my fighting days ended, too. I've been a guest of Rebel prisons since then," he added darkly.

"Andersonville has only been open since February of last year," Matthew observed. "Where were you held?"

"Richmond."

Matthew took a deep breath. "Libby Prison?"

"No," Joseph said quietly. "That was too good for the likes of me and my buddies. They took us out to Belle Isle."

Matthew managed to stifle his groan as sympathy flowed through him. Libby had been horrible, but Belle Isle was even worse. He could only imagine how Joseph had suffered through the brutal winter of 1863 with virtually no shelter and hardly any food. "I'm sorry," he said.

Joseph looked at him more closely. "You know something about that place?"

Matthew nodded. He was not interviewing these men to tell his own story, and he had not shared it with anyone else, but he felt Joseph needed to know how completely he understood. "Are you familiar with Rat Dungeon in Libby Prison?"

Joseph nodded. "It's a hell hole," he muttered. "I've talked to some of the men who made it out of there."

"I was there for several months," Matthew admitted.

"When?" Joseph demanded.

"The winter of 1863." He wondered if Joseph would make the connection.

Joseph nodded and his eyes grew wide. "I heard about a journalist fellow who broke out of Libby Prison with some of his buddies, digging a tunnel and making sure lots of the other prisoners knew about it so they could escape, too. You wouldn't be...?"

Matthew nodded.

Joseph stared at him. "Well, if that doesn't beat all! Tell me how you got out of there."

Matthew shook his head. "It's not important now. I'm here to tell *your* story, not mine," he insisted. "I escaped, but you somehow managed to survive two and a half years in conditions that would have killed most men. I want to hear how you did it."

Joseph stared at him for a long moment. "It was something my grandfather used to tell me," he said softly.

Matthew was silent as Joseph closed his eyes.

"My grandfather used to tell me never to say that I couldn't do something, or that something seemed impossible or couldn't be done, no matter how discouraged I got. He told me I'm only limited by what I allow myself to be limited by—my own mind." Joseph smiled. "He told me I am the master of my own reality, and that when I understood that, absolutely anything in the world was possible."

"Your grandfather was a wise man."

"The wisest," Joseph agreed. "Every time I thought I couldn't keep going, I would see my grandfather saying those words. He used to tell me so many times I got sick of it, but I reckon he somehow knew I would need it." He paused again. "I owe my life to my grandfather," he said quietly. "I just hope he's still alive so I can tell him when I get home."

"Does your family know you're still alive?" Matthew asked.

Joseph's grin bloomed again. "They do now! I got a letter off to them about a week ago from Camp Fisk. I haven't heard anything back, but I'll bet big money they'll all be waiting for me when I get off this boat in a few days." His grin widened. "I reckon that is going to be the best day of my life," he said.

Matthew smiled and laid his hand on his arm. "I reckon it will be," he agreed. "Give me your parents' address," he added. "I'll make sure you get a copy of the paper when your story comes out."

Joseph scribbled down his address and lay back on the deck against a column. His face was tight with exhaustion. "I think I'll rest a little while," he murmured before he closed his eyes.

Matthew stared into his young, sunken face, heartbroken that a nineteen-year-old could have such deep wrinkles and pain etched into his face. He hoped his family was ready for his condition when he stepped off the boat, but surely Joseph must know how bad he looked. He had been staring at the mirror images of fellow prisoners for over two years. He shuddered as he imagined what this boy had experienced. He also prayed the rest of Joseph's young life would be full of easier times.

******

Peter strode from the gangplank, and took what felt like his first easy breath in two days. Even though the decks of the *Sultana* were open-air, the crush of twenty-five hundred people—many of them ill—created a stench that permeated every pore in his body. He smiled as he watched hundreds of prisoners pour from the boat to head up the cobblestone wharf to the closest saloon so they could celebrate their freedom. He was sure alcohol was the last thing any of them needed right now, but he couldn't begrudge their desire to escape the boat for a while.

The *Sultana* was being emptied of her hogsheads of sugar and cases of wine. He was glad some of the strain on the engines and boilers was being reduced.

A glance at his watch told him it was 6:30 pm. If he hurried, he should be able to get a telegraph off to his office. He strode through the crowded streets of Memphis, climbing the hills that took him high above the Mississippi River. He knew the city was situated on the

Fourth Chickasaw Bluff, the highest elevation on the east bank of the Mississippi. Protected from the regular floods and raging torrents, by the 1850s it had outlasted all other competition from other river ports, and claimed its title as the "capital" of the mid-South.

Though Tennessee had joined the Confederacy and Memphis had been largely pro-Confederacy, they were also the home state of President Johnson. He was certain Tennessee would be the first to re-enter the Union.

Peter smiled as he strode past the old offices of the *Memphis Appeal* newspaper. In spite of being on a different side of the conflict, he had to admire their determination to exist during the war. During the first year of the war, they had declared they would rather sink their presses at the bottom of the Mississippi than surrender. They loaded their equipment on boxcars and continued to operate as a refugee newspaper. He knew they moved five times to escape capture before finally being seized just ten days earlier. He had heard the news from a colleague in Vicksburg. He celebrated another marker of the war being over, even while feeling sympathy for those who resisted for so long. He could only hope they would use that same energy and determination to rebuild the Union.

There was a long line out of the telegraph office when he arrived. He frowned, but relaxed when he realized he had plenty of time. The *Sultana* was not due to leave again until 11:30.

"Did you hear the news?"

Peter turned to the man who had just joined him in line. "What news?"

"They've killed Booth!"

Peter whistled. The search for Lincoln's killer had taken twelve days, and hundreds of men scouring the countryside. "Where did they find him?"

"Hiding out in a tobacco barn on a farm just south of Port Royal, Virginia," the man sneered.

"Did he surrender?" Peter asked eagerly, knowing just what a crazy search it had been through the Maryland countryside, and across the Rappahannock River.

"Not Booth! The man with him surrendered, but he yelled out that he preferred to come out and fight. The soldiers set the barn on fire," he continued.

"I thought they had orders to take Booth alive?" Peter commented.

"They did. They set the fire to flush him out. One of the soldiers shot him in the neck."

"Why?"

"We don't have those kinds of details yet."

Peter nodded and looked at the man more closely. "What paper do you work for?"

"The *Illinois State Register*," he said. "One newspaperman can always tell another. My name is Crandall Masters. You?"

"Peter Wilcher," he responded with a firm handshake. "Did the bullet kill Booth?"

"Eventually. They dragged him to the porch of the farmhouse. He died three hours later," he said with satisfaction. "I heard he requested his mother be told that he died for his country."

Peter sighed. Booth's passions had led him to be the one to actually assassinate Lincoln, but he knew there were many who sympathized with his feelings and applauded his actions. Booth had been captured and killed, but it would do nothing to alleviate the hard feelings on either side.

Crandall looked at him closely. "Is this really the first you've heard of this?"

Peter nodded. "I just came off the *Sultana* down on the waterfront. I've been on the steamer for the last two days with a load of Union prisoners who are returning home."

"Then you don't know that General Johnston surrendered the last of the Confederate troops today," Crandall said.

That earned a genuine smile from Peter. "Finally! The war has been over since Appomattox, but this finalizes things now that the last standing army has surrendered." He paused. "Did President Johnson honor Sherman's armistice agreement with the Rebels?"

Crandall snorted. "Not a chance! He sent Grant down there to demand the same terms of surrender that Lee received. General Johnston really had no choice but to accept them."

Peter nodded as he stepped up to the counter. It took him just a few moments to send a telegraph telling his editor he had collected many powerful stories from the Union prisoners. He had turned away when he heard his name called.

He turned back to the counter. "Yes?"

"You've got a telegraph here, Mr. Wilcher," the agent said, handing him an envelope.

It took Peter seconds to realize he would not be returning to the *Sultana*. His editor had directed him to travel to Springfield, Illinois to cover Lincoln's final burial. The funeral train was winding its way through New York but would soon head across the Midwest, arriving in Illinois on May third. Peter was to catch the train leaving Memphis the next morning.

He looked up and realized Crandall was just leaving the counter. "Looks like my plans have changed. I head for Springfield in the morning. Do you have a recommendation for a good hotel?"

"I'm staying at the Bell Tavern. It's not fancy, but the food is good."

"That works," Peter replied. "Have you eaten yet? Food on board the *Sultana* is scarce. I'm starving!"

"Let's go," Crandall replied.

Peter gazed off toward the waterfront as they walked down the street toward the tavern. He would have told Matthew of the change in plans if he had any hope of finding him on the crowded steamer. As it was, he knew Matthew was in his element interviewing the soldiers. He would send him a telegraph in the morning that would be waiting for him when he arrived in Cairo with the prisoners. Both of them knew plans could change in a moment's notice. Their paths would cross again.

******

Matthew was deep in conversation when he felt the engines start up again. The last five hours had flown by. He watched as the lights of Memphis receded, but all the steamer did was cross to the other side of the river and dock again.

"What's going on?" one of the soldiers asked.

One of the crew was walking by at that moment. "We're taking on a load of coal," he explained.

Matthew frowned. He had been relieved when the steamer had lost some of its freight in Memphis but now they were putting more on the overloaded vessel. His frown deepened as a cold drizzle began to fall. Many of the men crowding the boats had no blankets to use against the chill night air.

Flashes of lightning split the night air as the *Sultana* started back upriver at 1:00 am. Matthew stared down at the rapidly flowing water, his thoughts restless. Most of the men were sound asleep, but he couldn't relax. Strong spring storms had created flood conditions on the river. The Mississippi was always wide, but the floods had extended the river to more than four miles across. He could see nothing but dark, swirling water when the lightning flashed. Plowing upstream against the raging current had to put more of a strain on the engines and boilers.

Matthew had already given his blanket and coat to a sick soldier he found shivering on the hurricane deck, so he hunched his shoulders against the cold rain and turned his thoughts south to Richmond. The people he cared about most were all in the brick home high above the city streets. It was easy to imagine the warmth and flickering lights, the laughter, the easy conversation. His heart ached with longing, but as he thought of all the stories he would have to tell when he landed, he knew he wouldn't have chosen to be anywhere else. The knowledge helped a little, as cold seeped into his bones.

To keep his mind occupied, he stared out over the steamer from his position on the bow. The pilot house, where the pilot manned the wheel, crowned the steamer's superstructure. Beneath the pilot house were three decks: main, boiler and hurricane. Matthew frowned when he realized the *Sultana's* upper decks were sagging under the mass of passengers. He knew that light, flimsy wood had been used in the construction to help reduce the weight of the boat so they could carry more cargo.

On the main deck lay a battery of four boilers, each measuring eighteen feet in length, and filled with steam and boiling water. Matthew had already located the small patch used to repair the leak before they departed from Vicksburg. With nothing but silence to occupy him, Matthew thought over what he knew about steamers. A boiler on a steamer contained enough energy to hurl the boiler over two miles into the air. The heated water in the boilers had about the same energy as a pound of gunpowder. The idea of them exploding was terrifying.

He pushed that thought away, and continued his examination of the boat. Beneath the boilers was a coal-burning furnace running nearly the breadth of the steamer. Constant firing was necessary to maintain the steam in the boilers. Matthew shuddered when he thought about the other boats on the Mississippi that had caught fire and burned up. As he stared out over the crowded, sagging decks, all he could do was hope the *Sultana* had the ability to reach Cairo.

"Can't sleep?"

Matthew looked up as Joseph settled down next to him. "No. You?"

"Nope. Thinking about getting home in a couple days. I learned to get along without much sleep in prison."

Matthew thought about the long nights of lying sleepless on the cold floors of Libby Prison. "I know what you mean."

"Where are you headed after here?" Joseph asked.

Matthew smiled. "Back to—"

He never finished his sentence, as the world around him exploded into flames, hissing steam and the screams of dying men.

******

At almost 2:00 am, on the morning of April 27, three of the *Sultana*'s four boilers erupted with a volcanic fury that resounded across the countryside.

Chapter Ten

The force of the explosion threw Matthew against the bow railing. He lay gasping for breath as heat and smoke swirled around him. His mind told him there had been an explosion, but the reality was not truly registering... Until the noises began to filter through the madness.

Screams ripped through the night—death cries rising through the air.

Hissing steam provided a backdrop as the decks of the *Sultana* cracked and collapsed from the weight of their human freight.

Matthew's breath choked on a cry as the massive smokestacks toppled and crashed onto the decks, crushing the men who lay in their path.

Flames shot through all of it, outlining the hundreds of bodies strewn around the decks.

The screams were constant and never-ending.

Live coals and splintered timber shot into the night sky like fireworks. Matthew watched in horrified wonder as the pilot house flew into the air and fell into the dark water that now glowed like a lantern, illuminating the bodies already bobbing amid the destruction that was raining down from the sky.

The frantic neighing of horses, the braying of mules and the squeals of terrified hogs added to the cacophony of sound.

Matthew stared in fascinated terror as men, lucky enough to have lived through the blast that hurled them into the frigid water, held on to pieces of wreckage or floundering horses.

He shrank back against the railing as boiler fragments, pipes, bricks and machinery flew through the air with killing speed. He barely dodged a piece of timber that impaled a wide-eyed soldier just yards from his position. Matthew could only be glad the soldier died instantly, his blank eyes staring in his direction before he slumped over on the deck.

Matthew held his fist to his mouth to stop the nausea as bodies and dismembered limbs flew through the air to land in heaps all around him. He bit back a cry as a bloody leg landed inches from his own.

He could do nothing but continue to stare as men, their clothes burned or blown from their bodies, stumbled out of the steamy fog, their skin charred and burned. Their faces gaped in contorted screams as they dived over the railing of the destroyed steamer to escape the flames. His horror grew as he watched them sink beneath the black waters.

His terrified gaze was wrested back to the boat, as the screams of men trapped beneath burning embers rose on the wind and then slowly died away.

Another voice gradually cut through his horror.

"Matthew! Matthew!"

Matthew slowly turned his shocked gaze away from the flames and realized Joseph was lying on the deck a few feet from him, pinned beneath a piece of timber.

"Help me! Please, help me!" Joseph pleaded, his eyes wide with fright and pain.

The look on his face pierced Matthew's shock and disbelief. Muttering both an oath and a prayer, he leapt to his feet, stunned to find he was completely unharmed save for a few minor cuts from flying debris. He rushed to Joseph's side and managed to pry the timber from his chest.

Joseph took several deep breaths as he stared around him wildly. "What happened?" he gasped.

"The boilers blew," Matthew answered. Now that the shock had passed, it was time to help whomever he could. "Stay here," he ordered. "I've got to see what I can do to help."

"I'll come," Joseph gasped.

Matthew would have laughed at the idea of help from the emaciated soldier who had barely survived Andersonville if it hadn't been so heartbreakingly tragic. He took a moment to kneel down in front of him. "You stay here," he ordered more gently. "You've given enough. I will be back," he promised.

When Matthew turned away, he had no idea whether he would be able to keep his promise. He picked his way across the boiler deck until he was stopped by a huge opening. A wild groan escaped his lips when he leaned over to look down. Fire had already erupted in the wreckage of the main deck below, creating the closest thing to hell that he could ever envision.

Mangled, scalded bodies were heaped and piled amid the burning debris. The smells of smoke and burning flesh beat against his face. The cabin was cut in two, with broken planks pointing down into the flames as if inviting them to devour the upper decks. In moments, the planks were bright with fire.

Matthew jumped back, knowing the flames would consume the boat rapidly.

Peter! Where was Peter? Sobs tore at his throat as he realized he stood no chance of finding his friend in the maelstrom surrounding him.

His teeth ground in agony, fear and desperate anger. He and Peter had survived Libby Prison only to die together on a boat in the middle of the Mississippi River. And thousands of men had escaped the horrors of Andersonville and Cahaba to die in the river's cold, raging waters, because men decided to horribly overload a boat when it was completely unnecessary.

Matthew's cold anger broke through the rest of his shock. He gazed around him as the flames turned the night sky a bright red. He had a moment of hope that help would arrive, but dismissed that idea as soon as it entered his mind. They were on their own.

Screams and cries for help continued to fill the air. His years on the battlefield had taught him to distinguish a death cry. He was sure the constant screams surrounding him would never fade in his mind. He was also sure the only escape from certain death was to go into the water, but he couldn't until he had done all he could to help.

He watched as dozens of men rushed past him and flung themselves into the water. Some went in holding pieces of broken timber as their life preservers. Some held chairs or splintered tables. They had grabbed whatever they could find that might serve as a flotation device.

Matthew glanced over the railing and watched what seemed to be hundreds struggling in the water, but he knew they were beyond his ability to save. A quiet voice sounded at his shoulder.

"We must do what we can to help."

Matthew whirled around and stared at the calm-eyed woman behind him. One arm had burns, and her face was pocked with cuts, but her eyes were what held him. In the midst of sheer madness, she gazed at him with utter tranquility. He knew there were staff wives aboard. He also knew there were members of the Christian Commission that had loaded in Vicksburg. He was certain she was a member of the latter.

"We've got to get as many men in the water as we can," she urged. "It is the only thing that will save them."

Her quiet words broke through Matthew's confusion. "You're right," he responded. "I will get pieces of timber for them to use for flotation. You locate the ones we can help, and we'll both get them in the river."

When he heard her call again, Matthew already had a small pile of loose pieces of timber big enough to support a man's weight by an opening blasted in the railing.

He sprang to her side, reaching down to help a soldier to his feet. He chose to ignore the scalded skin and charred hands. "Here we go, soldier," he said gently, lifting him to his feet. "You keep looking," he told the woman as he turned to help the soldier to the railing.

When they stood in front of the railing, he pressed a large piece of timber into the man's hands. "I'm sorry, but this is all I can do. Hold on to the wood as tightly as you can. Help must surely be on the way." He had no way of knowing if he told the truth, but he had experienced the power of hope to save lives many times during the war. He would not send this soldier into the water without hope.

The man nodded bravely, his blue eyes set with determination as he grabbed the wood and slid into the water.

Matthew, not waiting to see what would happen, turned and hurried back. The calm-eyed woman had already located three more survivors. Again, he refused to analyze their injuries. They may die in the water, but at least they had a chance. Staying on the *Sultana* only guaranteed their deaths.

"Help me! Quick!"

Matthew sprang to the woman's side and gazed down at the frightened man trapped under a timber, his brown eyes pleading with them for help.

"I can't get the timber off him," the woman gasped, her chest heaving as she struggled with the thick beam.

Matthew lent his strength to moving the beam, but it didn't budge. He groaned as an end of it burst into flame. He grabbed a piece of metal bar and wedged it next to the man's body, hoping to lift it high enough to slide the soldier out, but it remained stubbornly lodged, the flame licking closer.

The woman sobbed out a prayer as the flames licked to within feet of the terrified soldier's body. She grabbed his hands, and would have stayed there with him if Matthew had not pulled her back.

Matthew held her close as the man's dying shrieks filled the air. He felt nothing but relief when the screams died away, knowing the man would no longer suffer.

"Okay." The woman pushed him away. "I'm all right. We must find others to help."

Matthew knew they were running out of time, but it was more than that. Wordlessly, he pulled the woman over to the opening in the railing and motioned for her to look down.

Tears filled her eyes as she stared down at the boiling mass of humanity. Men fought like demons to stay afloat, using whatever was handy to keep from sinking, even if was another man. "They are drowning each other," she moaned.

Matthew nodded. "Help me gather wood to throw out to them for flotation. We have to try to save them."

She leapt into action, tossing everything Matthew could find out to the men. The wild fighting continued. She finally knelt down and began to call to them. "Please! Please! You must listen to me." Her high voice rang out into the madness.

Matthew saw several men shift their terrorized eyes and fix them on her calm figure.

"You must act like men," she called. "I know you are frightened, but you are doing nothing but assuring your death," she yelled. "Please listen to me!"

Gradually, more of the men quit clawing and fighting as they clung to the pieces of wood Matthew had thrown to them.

"Look around you," the woman called. "Find someone without a piece of wood and get them over to the ropes and chains hanging from the boat. You are soldiers," she added. "You must help your fellow soldiers."

She smiled softly as the soldiers calmed and began to direct other floundering men to grab hold of what was around them.

Matthew glanced behind them and realized they were running out of time. He rushed to where he had last seen Joseph.

"I knew you would come back," Joseph gasped. He had pulled his coat up to shield his face from the gagging smoke. "I don't seem to have the strength to move."

Matthew smiled grimly, snatched Joseph up to throw him over his shoulder and dashed back to the opening. "Hold him!" he ordered, and then darted over to grab a hefty piece of lumber from a pile that had just caught fire. Joseph was sagging in the woman's arms when Matthew made it back.

"Go with him," the woman urged. "He'll never make it without you."

Matthew gazed at Joseph and knew she was right. The odds were that neither one of them would make it through the night, but he had to give the young soldier a chance. He stared down at the woman who had once more leaned over to call to the soldiers who seemed to only be calm when she was talking to them. "Only if you come with me," he said urgently.

The woman hesitated and then nodded. She handed him another piece of lumber and tilted her head toward the opening. "You first," she insisted. "Get in the water so I can hand this soldier down to you. He won't make it otherwise."

Matthew hesitated, torn by something he saw in her eyes, but a glimpse over his shoulder revealed the fire was less than a yard away. He estimated less than twenty minutes had passed since the explosion. The entire boat was now engulfed in flames. Gasping a prayer, he jumped into the water, and turned to catch Joseph as he splashed down right behind him.

"I can't swim!" Joseph gasped.

Matthew stifled a groan and wrapped Joseph's arms around the lumber. "You don't have to swim. You just have to hold on!"

"Jump, lady!"

"Jump! Save yourself!"

Matthew whirled around to see the woman standing where he had left her. She was simply gazing down at the men pleading with her to join them. "Jump!" he called. "It's too late to do more. You must jump!"

The woman shook her head calmly. "I can't swim. I'm afraid I might lose my presence of mind, and be the means of death to some of you."

"What?" Matthew cried. "Jump! I will save you!" His eyes filled with tears of helplessness as she calmly shook her head and stared into his eyes.

He refused to look away as the flames engulfed her body—not wanting her to die without human connection. It was the only gift he had to give her. A scream wrenched from his throat as she folded her arms quietly and burst into flames. Tears wracked his body as he watched her burn.

When he knew she was dead, he stared around numbly. Her death had caused even the most frantic soldier to become quiet. They stared at Matthew.

"Who was she?" one called.

Only then did Matthew realize he had never learned her name.

"Watch out!" one of the men screamed as he turned and began to thrash away from the boat.

Matthew whipped around in time to see both wheelhouses fall away into the water. The flaming wheels landed on a mass of men who had just escaped the inferno.

"The boat is turning!"

Matthew grabbed Joseph and began to pull him away from the boat. It broke his heart as he watched men struggle and sink, but he knew there was no way he could save everyone. He was going to do his best to save this young man on the way home to his family.

"Hang on!" he called. "Kick your legs if you have the energy." A quick look into Joseph's pale, strained face told him not to expect any help. He thought gratefully of his mother's insistence he learn how to swim in the West Virginia lakes he grew up around. He paused long enough to rip off his shoes, and then, gripping the piece of lumber Joseph clung to, he struck out strongly with one arm, pushing through fields of debris until he was at least a hundred yards from the boat.

"They're going to have to jump!"

Matthew's head jerked around to look at the bow of the *Sultana*. What looked to be several hundred men had taken uncertain refuge on the bow while winds drove the flames toward the stern. With the wheelhouses gone, the current had caught the burning boat and swung it around. The flames that had been blown toward the stern by the wind were now licking their way toward the bow.

"Jump!" he hollered, adding his voice to the hundreds of men already in the water. It was their only hope now, though he also knew how many of the men clinging to the bow had critical injuries that would not allow them to swim. He was certain, though, that drowning was preferable to burning to death. "Jump!"

Screams of fear echoed through the air as hundreds of men hit the water at the same time.

Matthew made no effort to fight his tears. He knew the sudden mass of humanity would cause most of the men to drown. As he listened to their screams, he thought of all the stories he had heard in the last two days. The notes he had taken were strapped tightly to his body in an oilcloth pouch. He had no idea if they would survive, or even if he would, but he fervently hoped that someone would find the stories that so desperately needed to be told.

Joseph's moan ripped his attention back to the weak man clinging to the board. Matthew knew his emaciated body made him even more vulnerable to the frigid waters of the flooded Mississippi. If he didn't get him out of the water soon, he would surely die. Gritting his teeth, he struck out in the direction he hoped would lead to land. He knew the river was extremely wide north of Memphis. What he didn't know, was just how much wider the flood waters had made it.

"Cold..." Joseph gasped.

"Just hold on," Matthew replied as he continued to kick and stroke as hard as he could. "I'll get you out of here." The screams of burning men followed him, but he refused to look back again. He had a chance to save at least one of the soldiers who had somehow survived the horrors of the prison camps. Looking back would accomplish nothing. Now he could only look forward.

******

Peter was jolted awake and sat straight up in bed. He listened intently but could hear nothing to indicate what had awakened him. The only sound vibrating through the room was Crandall's gentle snoring. He frowned as he felt his heart pounding in his chest. What was going on? He swung his feet over the edge of the mattress, wincing as the cold floor met them. A cold rain and chill wind had turned the spring day into something that felt more like winter. He felt a moment's sympathy for Matthew huddled on the deck of the *Sultana*, quite sure he would have already given his blanket and coat to one of the unfortunate soldiers.

"What's up?" Crandall's sleepy voice broke the stillness.

"I don't know," Peter admitted. "Something woke me, but I have no idea what it was."

"Go back to sleep," Crandall growled.

Peter knew that was the sensible thing to do, but there was something curling in his stomach that he knew would make sleep impossible. "You go ahead," Peter said instead. "I'm going for a walk."

"What time is it, man?"

Peter reached for his watch. "Two fifteen." He pulled his pants on and reached for his coat. "Go back to sleep."

"Not a chance," Crandall said as he groaned and swung out of bed. "You think after years of being a newspaper reporter that I don't recognize intuition when I see it? I'll be blamed if I'm going to let you get the scoop on whatever is happening in this city."

Peter grinned but couldn't push away the anxiety crawling in his throat.

Moments later, the two men were striding out of the hotel. By unspoken agreement, they both headed for the wharf. In a town like Memphis, if something was going on, it was most likely happening on the waterfront. From their position high above the water on the bluffs, Peter kept his eye on the river. Suddenly, he gasped. "There! Look north!"

Crandall whipped his head around and sucked in his breath. "A boat is on fire," he snapped.

Both men began to run toward the wharf.

Peter's breath came hard as fears swamped his mind. He had no way of knowing the burning boat was the *Sultana*, but he couldn't push the thought away. Images of the crowded steamer accompanied the slap of his feet. Memories of the patched boiler and the concerned crew roared in his head.

Within minutes, they were on the wharf, joining the small group of sailors looking north.

"What boat is it?" Peter called.

They all shook their heads. "We don't know," one replied. "We saw the sky turn red about twenty minutes ago."

Peter's face tightened. "Why aren't you headed up there?" he demanded.

The sailor standing closest shook his head. "Our captain isn't on the gunboat. I tried to convince our first mate to head upriver, but he wouldn't take responsibility. He said most likely the boat was near shore and everyone would get off."

Peter ground his teeth as he looked around frantically for a boat, not at all sure what he would do if he found one.

Crandall put a hand on his arm. "We have to wait," he said quietly. "We don't have a way to do anything. We have to wait," he repeated.

Peter scowled but knew his new friend spoke the truth.

The sailor who had spoken to him turned around. "There's another steamboat, the *Bostonia II,* that is due to dock shortly. They'll be able to help whatever boat is burning."

"Is there another boat that has left since the *Sultana*?" Peter asked, hoping against hope there had been, though he wouldn't wish suffering on anyone.

"No," the sailor admitted reluctantly.

Peter groaned and clenched his fists.

"You know someone on the *Sultana*?"

Peter didn't bother to respond. He couldn't bring himself to acknowledge Matthew might be caught on the burning inferno, and there were no words to describe his feelings about the dozens of men he had interviewed who were convinced all the bad things that could happen had already happened. He thought briefly of their happy faces as they described their anticipated homecomings, but he pushed the vision from his mind. It would do nothing but make him mad. "Could it be the *Bostonia II*?" he asked.

The sailor shook his head. "Not likely," he said.

"But possible?" Peter persisted, holding on to whatever thin thread of hope he could find.

The sailor hesitated and then shrugged. "I guess so."

Peter would take what he could get. "What do we do now?"

The sailor stared toward the bright red glow. "We wait."

Peter glanced at his watch. It was now 2:45 am. He pulled his coat closer against the rain and began to pace the wharf.

******

Matthew fought to control the chattering of his teeth as he pressed forward into the darkness. He could still hear screams and the calls of men floundering around him, but his sole focus was on saving Joseph. He watched numbly as dead bodies floated by, their faces pale in the dark night, their eyes staring blankly.

"Can't make it," Joseph mumbled weakly.

Matthew whipped his head around. "Yes, you can! You can't give up on me," he pleaded, recognizing the blank look spreading across Joseph's face. His thoughts raced as he tried to think of something to say to keep the young man trying. He finally latched on to something Joseph had told him during the interview.

"Remember what your grandfather said." He gasped and dodged the floating carcass of a mule that swept past him, the tail hairs flicking across his face.

"Grandfather?" Joseph muttered.

"Yes. Your grandfather told you never to say that you couldn't do something, or that something seemed impossible, or couldn't be done, no matter how discouraged you got." Matthew was amazed all the words were coming back. "He told you you're only limited by what you allow yourself to be limited by—your own mind."

Matthew was encouraged when Joseph smiled.

"He told me I am the master...of my own reality and...that when I understood that...absolutely anything in the...world was possible." Joseph's voice was weak and broken, but Matthew heard him.

"That's right! You can't give up now, Joseph. You've lasted through the prison camps. A float down the Mississippi is nothing."

Joseph's eyes lost their blankness and took on some semblance of life, however weak. "Why are you saving me?"

Matthew took a breath of relief. "It seemed like the thing to do at the time."

Joseph smiled again and looked back at the burning boat. "There aren't many gonna live through that," he murmured.

Matthew still refused to look. "I don't reckon so, but we are," he said. Even as he spoke the words, he knew he was getting weaker, and as far as he could tell, they were still nowhere near shore. The cold was sapping his energy, but he knew Joseph wasn't strong enough to help. He wasn't sure how long he could continue to propel both of them through the racing current. He began to look around for something in the water that could help them.

A looming shape in the darkness shot hope into him. He reached out just in time to grab the log floating toward him. He rejoiced when he realized how big it was. "Grab hold of the limb," he commanded.

A spark of determination shot into Joseph's eyes. Still holding on to the timber that had carried them so far, he managed to snag one of the branches as it brushed up against him.

Matthew angled his body against another large limb, hoping the weight of his body would slow it down long enough for both of them to crawl on it. "Climb up!"

Joseph tried, but fell back against the timber and could only shake his head in defeat.

Matthew groaned, knowing Joseph was too weak to do more than he was doing. "Hold on," he gasped as he swung himself onto one of the largest limbs and reached down to grab Joseph's shirt. Gritting his teeth, he used all his remaining strength to pull Joseph out of the water onto the log, praying with all his might that the log wouldn't spin and throw them back into the raging current. He positioned Joseph across the log and held him there with one arm while he fought to catch his breath.

"Thank you," Joseph sputtered.

Matthew nodded, knowing the boy's efforts had weakened him even more. "Just lie there," he said, gripping Joseph's arm securely. He realized the instant Joseph went unconscious. Perhaps it was best. Matthew accepted he did not have the strength to pull them both to shore, but at least they were out of the water.

He finally took a moment to look back, feeling a desperate surge of hope when he saw the bright lights of another steamboat approaching the *Sultana*. He realized quickly that the current had already taken them out of reach of help from that quarter, but perhaps it would be in time to save some of the other passengers.

All he could do was pray as he stared out over the black waters, the flaming hull of the *Sultana* growing further away as the current swept them south.

Chapter Eleven

Peter was still pacing when he heard a cry from the river. "What was that?" he yelled, as he leapt to the edge of the wharf, knowing it was too dark to see anything.

Crandall was beside him instantly. "Someone is calling for help," he said urgently, whipping around to summon the sailor. "There is someone out there!" he called.

The sailor nodded and ran for one of the cutters tied up to the wharf. "I heard it, too!"

"Help!"

"Help me!"

A chorus of cries sounded from the river.

"God help them!" Peter groaned, as he turned to the sailor. "May we come with you?" He already knew Crandall was a strong swimmer and familiar with boats. "We can help!" he urged.

The sailor hesitated but finally nodded. "Get in," he said tersely as he untied the boat. "Man the oars," he snapped as three more men jumped to join them.

More calls sounded from the water. One plea came through clearly. "The *Sultana* caught fire! Save us! Please save us!"

Peter groaned, knowing his nightmare had come true. He tried to push thoughts of Matthew from his mind as he put his entire strength into the oars. They had to try to save who they could.

In just minutes, they saw a large piece of wreckage with men clinging to it.

Crandall did a quick count. "There are twelve of them!" he called in triumph.

One of the other men who had jumped on board suddenly quit rowing. "We can't help them!" he cried, his eyes wide with fright. "If we go alongside that raft they will swamp us!"

"Row!" the sailor ordered as he steered the boat toward the survivors. "Row, or prepare to swim for your life yourself!"

Peter watched in admiration as the sailor steered the boat around the wreckage and stopped its forward progress. Within minutes, the boat was full of shaking men. As the last man was crawling over the side of the boat he lost his balance and slipped back into the water with a panicked scream. Peter lunged and caught him by the hair just as he was disappearing under the water.

Crandall leapt to his side and reached down to grab the hapless man's shirt. Together, they hauled him into the boat, where he lay gasping for breath, his thin body shaking violently.

"Get these men to shore!" the sailor ordered.

When they turned back to land, Peter saw a crowd had already gathered on the wharf. The word of the disaster was evidently spreading. When they reached the wharf, hands reached down to pull the soldiers out of the boat and wrap them in blankets. Wagons were waiting to load them.

"We're taking them to the hospital," one man announced. "There are more wagons coming!"

The steamboats still at the wharf began to ring their bells to announce the disaster.

Peter watched the wagon start up the hill and then turned back to his oars. There were men to save.

******

Matthew stared up at the sky as the log moved downstream. One arm gripped a limb on the log, while the other was wrapped around Joseph as he strained to keep his unconscious body out of the water. The boy's shallow breathing told him he was alive, but Matthew knew he hovered close to death.

Matthew could feel the cold seeping into the very core of his being. He struggled to control the shivering, gritting his teeth as his hands and arms began to go numb. He shifted enough to brace one of his feet against a protruding limb. By pushing with all his strength, he managed to relieve a little of the strain from his arms, but he didn't know how much longer he could hold on. His mind floated to Joseph's grandfather. "I am the master of my destiny," he said through chattering teeth. "Anything is possible."

The wind picked up, the cold air slicing into his drenched, weakened body. He struggled to pull Joseph closer. "I am the master of my destiny." Matthew knew his voice was growing weaker. "Anything is possible."

Unbidden, thoughts of Carrie swarmed into his mind. Her dancing green eyes and laughing mouth flooded his thoughts. He tried to push them away, knowing he shouldn't be thinking of another man's wife, but he was too weak to do anything but let thoughts of her offer what comfort they could.

He had loved her since the minute he laid eyes on her. He had been careful to be sure she had no idea, knowing her love for his friend Robert was the most important thing in her life. Still, he had held on to hope. A hope that died when Carrie married Robert. He had learned to be content with her friendship, but he knew he would never love another woman the way he loved Carrie Cromwell. Love that should have brought hope and light, had become nothing but a persistent reminder of a lost opportunity.

For tonight, he would let his imagination warm him. There was no one out on the river to know his thoughts—no one to see inside his heart. He felt a twinge of warmth as he imagined his lips claiming hers. He felt a spark of hope as he imagined her smiling into his eyes and telling him she loved him. He felt strength return to his numb arms as he imagined her warm body pressed against his.

Matthew felt fresh determination when he imagined her grief if she were to receive word of his death. She may not be *in* love with him, but he was quite certain she loved him. He did not want to be the cause of yet more grief for her. She had borne too much, and she was now carrying the burden of Robert's illness. "I am the master of my destiny," he said, his voice stronger this time. "Anything is possible."

The long night passed as corpses swept past him. The cries for help had long since ceased. Matthew knew that anyone still in the water could not have survived, especially men who were already diseased and malnourished. He could only hope that bodies could be recovered, giving some type of closure to families faced with fresh grief.

Matthew felt a spark of hope when daylight began to kiss the horizon, but he also knew his strength was reaching its end. He didn't know how much longer he could hold on. Joseph had not moved even once during the long night, but Matthew refused to give up hope the young man would survive this latest ordeal.

He had passed the night imagining Carrie's love for him. He thought it was just another dream when he heard a distant call.

"Hello...."

Matthew shook his head and stared down the river.

"Hello..."

Suddenly, his heart leapt into his throat. "Help!" he called, groaning when his voice came out as little more than a hoarse croak. He coughed hard and tried again.

"Help!" His cry was weak, but it was stronger. "Please, God," he whispered. "Please..."

He could do nothing but stare as a boat appeared through the early morning mist. He had no arms available to wave. "Help!" he called again, certain his voice could not possibly carry over the sound of the river, waves and wind, but knowing he had to try. "Help!"

"There's one!"

Matthew felt tears prick his eyes when he heard the shout. Had they seen him? "Help!" he called one more time.

Moments later, the boat swung in his direction. "We're coming!" a man hollered.

Matthew stared as the boat drew closer and wedged itself against the log. "Take him first," he gasped as the men reached for Joseph.

"You have to let him go," one of the men said.

Matthew stared back at him. His numb arm had cramped in the position that held Joseph against his body. "I can't," he whispered.

One of the men in the boat rushed forward to work his arm free. Matthew cried out as pain ripped through his body, but he sighed with relief when Joseph was hauled into the boat. Strong hands then reached for him, prying his hand free from the limb and pulling him into the boat.

"Good to see you!" one of the men said.

"Thank you," Matthew whispered. "Thank you." He stared down at Joseph as they wrapped a blanket around him. "Take care of him first." He couldn't miss the look the men exchanged, but his mind refused to accept it. "He needs help," he insisted. "Him first."

The men gazed at him with deep sympathy. Tears welled in Matthew's eyes. "No," he whispered. "No."

One of the men put a hand on his arm. "You tried," he said kindly. "You gave him a chance."

Matthew was not ashamed of the tears streaming down his face. Joseph's family would not have their only surviving son return home. His grandfather would never hear that his words had saved Joseph's life.

The world began to swirl. He had held on all night to a soldier who had probably been dead for a long time. Before he slipped into unconsciousness, Matthew had a brief realization that holding on to Joseph had saved his life.

******

Peter stood on the wharf, gratefully sipping the hot coffee someone had handed him. As the day had dawned, it brought the realization that anyone still in the water was dead. He watched numbly as a boat pulled up with men plucked from trees along the riverbank. Somehow they had clung to the branches—most of them naked after their clothes burned off—while the long night passed.

Crandall stepped from a boat full of men they had pulled from along the bank. Most of them were dead. The rest were close.

Peter blanched, knowing that the line of dead soldiers on the wharf was about to get longer.

Crandall, his face pinched and drawn, stepped up to him. "Any word on Matthew?" he asked quietly, reaching out to claim the hot coffee a woman placed in his hands with a nod of gratitude.

"No," Peter replied, clenching his teeth.

"They're still finding people," Crandall said. "He could be out there."

Peter stared at him, trying to hold on to the hope that had sustained him through the night. Every boatload of soldiers and passengers they picked up could have held Matthew. None of them did.

"The *Bostonia II*?" Crandall asked.

"He wasn't one of the ones they saved," Peter said. "I checked everyone. Most of them are in the hospital getting treatment." He closed his eyes as his mind swarmed with the images of charred flesh and emaciated bodies. He knew that many of the passengers plucked from the river would not live through the day. He could only hope their suffering would end quickly.

Crandall stood silently by his side. After a night of non-ending rescues, there was simply nothing left to say.

One of the women from the Sanitary Commission, a portly blonde-haired woman with kind eyes, stepped up to them with a plate of hot beans and cornbread. "Would you care for something to eat?"

Crandall reached for the plate with a grateful smile, but Peter shook his head. "No, thank you, ma'am."

She eyed him for a moment and then shoved the plate into his hands. "You have to eat," she said crisply, seeming to know sympathy was not what he needed at the moment. "This day is far from over. Letting yourself get weak and hungry isn't going to help anyone." She paused for a moment. "I've been watching you. You've been at it all morning, ever since the first boat went out. You need to eat."

Peter stared at her while her words penetrated his numbness. Finally, he nodded and reached for the fork she held out to him. She was right. The day was not over. He would not stop until he had been to every single place they had taken survivors. It was possible he had been out on the water when Matthew was brought in. He thought of Aunt Abby, Carrie and the rest waiting for his return in Richmond. Peter had to try everything before he sent a telegram about the disaster. "Thank you," he mumbled.

"Thank *you*," the lady responded with a wide smile. "This is a dark day in Memphis history, but it's men like you who have given what little light there is."

Peter gazed after her as he slowly ate the food, appreciating the warmth and strength that spread through his body. The truth of her words pierced his numbness. He had not found Matthew, but he and Crandall had helped pluck more than one hundred men from the swollen river.

"Here comes another boat," someone yelled.

As the skiff drew closer, they could hear a man holler, "We've got one survivor on here! Found him clinging to a log. The fella he was holding didn't make it. He's unconscious, but he's alive."

Peter, more from force of habit acquired during the long morning than by any act of hope, stepped forward to gaze into the boat as it pulled to the wharf. "Matthew!" he cried. Throwing aside his plate of food, he jumped forward and reached out his arms to help haul Matthew's still form up onto the wharf.

Tears filled his eyes as he gazed down at his friend's face, miraculously unburned. "He's still alive?" he asked.

"Yes," one of the men assured him. "His breathing seems pretty good, and there are no burns on his body." He nodded at Joseph's still form. "We found him holding on to this soldier. I don't know how long he's been dead, but we had to pry him out of Matthew's arms."

Peter glanced down, his heart sick with sympathy as he recognized the boy Matthew had been interviewing when he last saw him. "Yes," he murmured. "He would have held on."

A wagon appeared behind him, and he was gently pushed aside. "We have to get him to the hospital," someone said.

Peter nodded. "May I come?"

He saw the doctor begin to refuse and then change his mind. "Come on," he ordered brusquely. "There is room on the wagon seat."

Within a few minutes, they had arrived at Gayoso Hospital, the wagon rattling up the hill as more wagons headed for the waterfront. Frantic activity filled every room and hallway as the medical personnel worked to save lives. Peter winced as he heard the cries of suffering pouring from every room.

A nurse appeared as soon as Matthew was carried in on a stretcher. She pointed toward a bed in the corridor. "It's all we have left," she said apologetically. "At least for now."

Peter realized that without the actual words, she was saying space would be made as patients died. He nodded. "Thank you."

She gazed back down at Matthew's still form. "This one doesn't look so bad," she murmured, laying a hand on his forehead. She jumped back, startled, when Matthew's eyes fluttered open.

Peter grinned with relief and leaned in. "Hey, old man."

Matthew gazed at him for a long moment before his lips twitched. Then he lost consciousness again.

Peter stared at him with dismay. "Will he be okay?"

"Probably," the nurse assured him. "He's suffering from exhaustion, exposure and hypothermia. We'll get him warm and into a room as fast as we can."

"Can I stay with him?" Peter asked.

The nurse nodded. "I'm glad he has a friend here," she said. "Most of these poor souls are all alone."

Peter was glad Matthew had a friend there, too. He would send a telegram to his editor later to let him know he wouldn't be making it to Springfield. He would not leave Memphis until Matthew left the hospital.

Chapter Twelve

Aunt Abby was coming down the stairs when a knock sounded on the door. Micah appeared through the parlor, but she waved him away. "I'll get it," she said cheerfully. "I was just going out on the porch to get some fresh air." She had spent the morning reading to Robert. "It's a beautiful day," she tossed over her shoulder as she opened the door.

"Telegram for Abigail Livingston," the uniformed boy said.

"I am Mrs. Livingston," Aunt Abby said graciously. She reached for the envelope with a smile. "Thank you."

"Have a good day, ma'am," the boy said as he tipped his hat and left the porch.

Carrie came in from the garden, her arms laden with a basket of vegetables. "Good news?" she called.

"I don't know," Aunt Abby responded, wondering at the quickening of her pulse as she gazed at the envelope.

"Only one way to find out," Carrie teased as she handed the basket to May and stepped up beside her. She glanced at Aunt Abby's face more closely. "Is everything all right?" she asked with concern.

Aunt Abby forced a laugh. "I have no reason to suspect otherwise," she said. "I don't know why this telegram has made me uneasy. I suppose four years of war have left me never knowing what to expect. I can't get used to the fact that I no longer have to worry about the people I love most," she added, ripping the envelope open. "Let's see what news there is today."

Moments later, she sank onto the porch swing, staring with wide-eyed shock at the telegram.

Carrie stepped forward, alarmed. "Aunt Abby?"

"It's Matthew..." she whispered.

Carrie snatched the telegram from her hands and began to read. Just then, Rose and Moses stepped up on the porch, their expressions alarmed when they saw Aunt Abby's face.

"Carrie?" Rose asked, sinking down beside Aunt Abby and taking her hand. "What is it?"

Carrie took a deep breath and cleared her throat. "It's a telegram from Peter," she said hoarsely, and began to read. "'*Terrible tragedy on the Sultana.*'"

"The boat Matthew was on?" Moses asked.

Carrie nodded and continued, tears blurring the words on the page. "'*Matthew has survived, but is still hospitalized. I am staying in Memphis until he is released. Will return with him to Richmond.*'"

She gasped and put down the telegram.

"That's all?" Rose asked, her own eyes swimming with tears. "How badly was Matthew hurt? What happened?"

Carrie could only shake her head, her thoughts spinning.

"Peter wrote all he knows," Aunt Abby said, straightening her shoulders as she fought for control. "He probably wanted to wait until he had more news, but was afraid we would hear about the *Sultana* before he could notify us that Matthew survived." Her voice softened. "He's given us all he could give."

Carrie stared out into the bright sunshine. "Didn't you tell me the *Sultana* was carrying a load of prisoners released from the Confederate prisons?"

"Yes," Aunt Abby said sadly. She shook her head. "We can make up all kinds of stories, but without facts we have nothing but theories. Matthew is alive," she said firmly. "And obviously Peter is, too. We will focus on that, and wait to hear more news."

"You're right," Carrie agreed. Her thoughts flew upstairs to where Robert lay in bed. He was alive, too, but his spirit and soul were dead. His emaciated frame had put on a little weight, but he still looked like a man ravaged by four years of war.

When Rose stepped forward to take her hand, Carrie knew her friend was reading her thoughts and harbored the same fears. Matthew was alive, but what kind of shape would he be in when he got back to them?

"Stop it, girls," Aunt Abby snapped.

Carrie jolted and swung her gaze to the older woman. She had never heard her speak that way.

"We don't know anything," Aunt Abby scolded. "I'm scared, too, but dreaming up worst case scenarios will serve no purpose. Peter would not be talking about bringing Matthew home, if he weren't able to withstand a train trip." She rose and grasped Carrie's hands. "He cannot possibly be in Robert's condition," she said firmly, her eyes warm with compassion.

Carrie took a deep breath and forced herself to relax. "You're right," she responded. "Of course you're right." She took a deep breath and allowed hope to replace the despair.

Aunt Abby hugged her close. "Fear is not a bad thing," she said gently. "It's only human to be afraid of what could have happened to Matthew, but allowing it to control your thoughts will serve no purpose. You have to let the fear roll through you and push it aside with faith."

Carrie nodded. She had seen Aunt Abby do that very thing where she was sitting on the swing. "How long did it take you to learn how to do that?" she asked shakily.

Aunt Abby laughed. "Longer than you've been alive, but you three are smarter than me, so I believe you'll conquer it sooner."

Moses swung down off the porch. "I'm going back into town to see what I can find out. Matthew has introduced me to some of his journalist friends from Philadelphia and Baltimore. I know where they are staying."

Aunt Abby nodded. "Thank you," she said gratefully, and then pulled Carrie and Rose down onto the swing. "I believe we'll go back to enjoying the day," she said firmly. "And we'll pray for Matthew," she added, brushing away a tear.

*****

Jeremy reached for his bowl of steaming soup as he cocked his head and listened intently. "I believe I just heard Moses come up on the porch."

Carrie, Rose and Aunt Abby exchanged a long glance as they waited for Moses to join them. They had already filled Jeremy in on the little they knew about the *Sultana*.

Carrie forced herself to breathe evenly, refusing to let thoughts of fear enter her mind. She had spent the afternoon reading to Robert. He had no idea that his best friend had been injured, and she wasn't about to *let* him know. He'd had his fill of death and dying, and had seen far too many men hideously injured. Somehow, she had managed to keep her voice light and cheerful while she was with him. She felt nothing but relief when he had finally slipped off to sleep about an hour before dinner.

May bustled in from the kitchen, and laid down another heaping plate of food as Moses entered the dining room. He smiled his gratitude, but it was a smile that didn't reach his eyes.

Carrie tensed, knowing the news was bad. She reached out her hands and grasped Rose's and Aunt Abby's. "Tell us what you found out," she said quietly.

Moses hesitated.

"The truth is always the best," Aunt Abby said. "I know you want to protect us, but shielding us from the truth will do nothing but ensure we're not ready to deal with it when we finally discover it."

Moses nodded and took a deep breath. "The *Sultana* blew its boilers a couple miles north of Memphis three days ago and then caught fire. The news is all over the North, but chaos here in Richmond has kept it out of the papers."

"How bad?" Aunt Abby asked.

Moses winced. "They estimate about fifteen hundred dead."

Everyone at the table gasped in disbelief. Dust motes floated through the air as a soft breeze stirred the curtains and parted them to allow a shaft of light to pierce the room.

Jeremy was the first to speak. "That's impossible!" he exclaimed. "There's not a steamer on the Mississippi that could handle that many people."

"You're right," Moses agreed heavily. "The fella I talked to said the *Sultana* was cleared for about four hundred. No one seems to know how the boat ended up with so many."

"How many survivors?" Carrie asked, desperately trying to hold on to some hope.

Moses shook his head. "They're not sure. As far as I can tell, they pulled about seven hundred from the water, but many of them have already died from their burns and injuries."

"On top of the fact that they were probably sick and malnourished from their months and years in the prison camps," Carrie said, hot bile rising in her throat as she imagined the scene. She barely bit back a groan as she thought of Matthew.

"Dear God," Aunt Abby managed. "Matthew was so excited to have the opportunity to accompany those men home to their families."

"Most of them will never make it," Moses stated, anger flashing in his eyes.

"Over two thousand passengers?" Jeremy repeated, shaking his head. "That could have only happened through..."

"Greed and bribery?" Moses interjected. "It will take some time for the whole story to come out, but that seems to be the consensus among the reporters."

Rose reached out for her husband's hand, knowing he needed the comfort. "Did you find out any more about Matthew?"

Moses nodded. "He was not injured in the blast, but he stayed on the boat for a long time helping other passengers get off, so they would have a chance for survival."

"That would be Matthew..." Aunt Abby murmured, her eyes shining with pride.

"When they found him on a log floating down the river about seven hours after the blast, he was holding on to a dead soldier. Evidently, it was a soldier he had interviewed. He held on to him all night." Moses' voice got thick. "He didn't know the boy was dead until his rescuers pried him out of his arm."

No one made an attempt to stop the tears streaming down their faces.

"Matthew was frozen and suffering from hypothermia when they rescued him. The reporter I talked to said he thought he was being released tomorrow."

"Peter?" Rose asked.

Moses explained how Peter had escaped being on the boat. "He's been with Matthew since they got him to the hospital. He won't leave him."

Carrie smiled. "They've been through so much together," she said tenderly. "I'm glad Matthew isn't alone."

Moses gazed around the table. "Matthew is going to be okay."

"Peter said he was bringing him back to Richmond," Aunt Abby said. "We'll have a chance to care for him."

Moses nodded. "I imagine that's all he wants right now."

"We'll be ready for him," Carrie said, her voice trembling with both relief and pain. She was so glad Matthew had survived, but she could only imagine the pain of families eagerly awaiting their soldier's return from the prison camps. "It's so unfair," she whispered. "They were so close to home..."

A deep silence dropped over the table again.

Once more, Jeremy was the first to break the silence. "We thought the end of the war would stop the senseless dying," he said, his eyes flashing. "I guess it will never stop."

"No, it will never stop," Aunt Abby agreed, reaching out to touch his shoulder.

"That's hopeful," he muttered.

"It can be," she replied, her eyes gazing into his. "Once you accept that suffering will never cease, you also have the chance to accept that God will never leave you alone in the suffering. Instead, he empowers you to sit in the midst of the suffering and taste the coming joy."

Jeremy stared at her. "You sound like my father."

Aunt Abby smiled. "Thank you for the compliment. I understand your father was a remarkable man."

Jeremy nodded. "He was."

"It's rather depressing to know that suffering will never end," Carrie said slowly.

"Haven't you already learned that in the last four years?" Aunt Abby asked gently.

"Yes, but I suppose I hoped it would end with the war."

Aunt Abby shook her head. "The war didn't cause the suffering. The suffering was caused by people's choices made from greed and fear. Unfortunately, that is the human condition."

"So it never ends?" Rose asked.

"The suffering never ends," Abby responded, "but that doesn't mean you can't taste the coming joy." She gazed around the table. "Nothing lasts forever. The suffering will end and joy will come. And," she added, "the joy will end and suffering will return."

"The circle of life," Jeremy murmured.

"Yes," Aunt Abby agreed. "The suffering is never something we look forward to, but if we can hold on to the fact that joy will return, it becomes much easier to bear."

"I could use some joy right about now," Carrie said.

"Then choose it," Aunt Abby said bluntly, her eyes direct, but kind.

"Choose it?"

"Yes. When hard times hit, the best thing you can do is focus on all the things you have to be grateful for. Like all of us here together after four years of war. Like Robert's still being alive. Like Matthew having survived the explosion. Like Cromwell Plantation not being destroyed in the war." She paused. "I'm sure you can come up with many more."

Carrie flushed and lowered her head. "You're right," she said remorsefully. She raised her head and stared at Aunt Abby. "Do you think I will ever learn how to trust God?"

Aunt Abby jumped up to wrap her in a hug. "Of course you will." She swept her arm across the table. "All of you will. I just happen to have a twenty-five-year head start on you. What's the use of getting older, if some wisdom doesn't come along with the wrinkles?" she asked teasingly.

"Wrinkles?" Carrie snorted. "You're the most beautiful woman I know!"

"Thank you, but I'm not blind about what I see in the mirror." Aunt Abby laughed. "The thing is, it doesn't bother me. I have discovered the more sand that escapes from my hourglass of life, the more clearly I can see what is important."

Rose laughed. "My mama used to tell me that getting old and wrinkled was better than the alternative of death."

"She was right," Aunt Abby said. "Now, no more sadness. We can feel compassion for the families who are dealing with pain, but we can also rejoice that Matthew and Peter are coming home to us."

"And on that note," May announced as the door swung open from where she had obviously been listening, "I gots a hot rhubarb pie waiting for some hungry people."

"Rhubarb pie?" Moses exclaimed. "Can I help you carry it in?"

"What? And have your big hands stealing a piece before it ever gets to the table?" May demanded. "You sit right there, boy. I'll be bringin' this pie in myself!"

Laughter rang around the table as Moses settled back with a chastised look on his face, his eyes dancing with mischief.

The sound of boots on the porch had everyone turning around.

"Are we expecting anyone?" Jeremy asked.

Carrie shook her head and jumped up. "Perhaps it's a messenger with more news of Mathew." She pushed back her chair and walked toward the door. "Coming," she called.

"I certainly hope so. The porch isn't that grand of a place."

Carrie jolted to a stop and stared at the door. "Father?" She raced forward and flung the door open. She fell into his outstretched arms, laughing and crying. "You're home!"

Thomas hugged her tightly and finally pushed her back far enough so he could stare down into her face. "Carrie," he murmured. "I missed you so much!"

"Father," she said, reaching up to stroke his tired face. "I'm so glad you're home. I've missed you every moment and worried about you so much." She hesitated. "Are you home for good? Do you have to leave again?"

Thomas shook his head. "I'm not leaving. We received word that President Johnson had put out an award for the top Confederate officials, but the rest of us are clear to return home. I left Danville as soon as I was sure the information was correct." A brief smile flitted across his face as he gazed around his house. "So, I'm not leaving. Except to go home to the plantation," he added. The smile faded as dark shadows filled his eyes. "If it's still there."

"It's there!" Carried proclaimed gladly. She answered the question in his eyes. "It's *all* still there. There has been no damage."

Thomas gasped as his eyes lit with gladness. "Are you sure? How can you know this?"

Carrie laughed. "It's quite a long story..." When Thomas laughed in return, Carrie's heart surged with gladness. She was sure it had been a long time since he laughed.

"It's always a long story," he said teasingly. He lifted his nose and sniffed. "Do you think May has any of that soup left? I've been dreaming about her vegetable soup for the last month."

May's shining face appeared around the corner. "I just set a bowl down on the table for you. Welcome home!"

Thomas smiled. "Thank you, May," he said gratefully.

He looked back down at Carrie as he pulled off his coat. "I thought I heard voices when I walked up on the porch. Is Jeremy here?" he asked hopefully.

Jeremy appeared around the corner. "In the flesh," he said with a broad grin, stepping forward to shake Thomas' hand and wrap him in a warm embrace. "Welcome home. You were missed."

Thomas cleared his throat as he stepped back. "You have no idea how wonderful it is to be home," he said, his voice thick with emotion.

"You heard more than Jeremy's voice," Carrie said. "We have rather a full house right now." She hoped her father wouldn't feel overwhelmed. "So much has happened in the last month." She knew the rest were giving her this space to welcome her father home.

"The whole world has turned upside down," her father said. "I can only imagine the stories you have to tell.

Let's go in the dining room so I can meet our houseful and hear your stories. And eat May's soup," he added. He paused before he turned. "On one condition, however."

Carrie smiled up at him, knowing by his relaxed tone that it was something good. "And what would that condition be?"

"That as soon as you introduce me, you go out and see a horse that has been whinnying since we reached the Richmond city limits."

Tears flowed again. "Granite," she whispered. "I was afraid to ask."

"Your horse is doing extremely well, young lady. He's put on weight since he won the heart of the innkeeper where I stayed. I'm quite certain she fed him more than she fed me," he said with a smile.

Carrie grabbed his hand and pulled him around the corner. "There's only one person you need to actually meet," she said quickly. "The rest you know."

Thomas hesitated when he entered the dining room and saw Rose and Moses gazing at him, but for only a moment. He smiled, strode forward, took Rose's hands and pulled her to her feet. "Hello, Rose," he said warmly. When she opened her mouth to say something, he put a finger to his lips. "I've waited a long time to say this."

Rose closed her mouth and waited.

Thomas took a deep breath. "I'm so sorry for what my father did to your mother, but I'm just as sorry that I kept you a slave and sent Jeremy away. I did what I thought was the best thing at the time, but I know now that it was wrong." He squeezed her hands. "We have a lot of history to overcome, but I want you to know I'm proud to have you as my half-sister. If even half of what Carrie says is true, you are an amazing woman. I saw you grow up, but I realize I don't know you at all. I want that to change."

Rose gaped at him, her eyes wide with disbelief. Finally, she found her voice. "Carrie said you had changed," she murmured.

Thomas laughed, his lined face relaxing to reveal how handsome he still was. "Yes, that would be putting it mildly," he said.

He swung around to grip Moses' hand. "Hello, Moses." His eyes swept Moses' strong, confident face.

"Hello, sir," Moses said gravely.

Thomas' eyes suddenly filled with tears. "Thank you," he said softly. "Thank you for saving Carrie at the plantation. I so hoped the day would come when I could thank you in person. You saved the most precious thing in the world to me. I will never be able to repay you. And now you're my brother-in-law. Welcome."

Carrie stared at her father, her eyes glazed with joyful tears. Yes, he had already changed, but evidently the month away from home and the end of the war had changed him even more. She knew he would be welcoming to Moses and Rose, but she had not envisioned this warm meeting.

"You're welcome, sir," Moses said, his eyes shining with surprise. "I love your daughter. I would do anything for her."

Carrie stepped forward. "He also saved Robert, Father, but that is a story for later." She turned to where Aunt Abby was sitting quietly, a sheen of happy tears in her eyes. "And this beautiful woman is Abigail Livingston."

Thomas turned his gaze. "Abigail Livingston," he said quietly. Then his eyes widened. "You're Aunt Abby?"

Aunt Abby laughed. "Right with just one guess," she said, rising to extend her hand. "It is such a pleasure to finally meet you, Mr. Cromwell."

"Likewise, Mrs. Livingston, but please call me Thomas. We're all family here."

Aunt Abby smiled. "Certainly, but only if you call me Abby."

Carrie understood when a small shadow appeared in his eyes behind the smile.

So, evidently, did Aunt Abby. "I'm so sorry," she said softly. "I had forgotten for a moment that Abigail was your dear wife's name. I understand it might be painful to call me that."

Thomas shook his head, his smile genuine when it came forth again. "Nonsense, Abby. It's wonderful to have you here." He peered around the room. "Any more surprises?"

Just then, June swung down the stairs singing. She had been sitting with Robert after putting John and Simon down for the night.

"That newest surprise is June," Carrie replied. "She is Moses' sister." She smiled at June. "And this is my father. He just arrived home."

June grinned broadly. "Welcome home, Mr. Cromwell. Carrie has been real worried about you."

Thomas swung around to gaze at Moses for a moment and then turned back to smile at June. "Hello, June. It's wonderful to meet you." He eyed Carrie with a question on his face.

"Robert is upstairs," she said quietly, anticipating his question. "He can't come down because he is still too ill."

"How long?" Thomas asked, his expression saying he had seen far too many consequences of the war.

"He's been here since two days after Appomattox. We found him in the hospital and brought him home." Carrie briefly explained his condition, knowing her father would be aware of how hard this was—a potential repeat of her mother's slow death. She stepped forward and took her father's hand. "Robert is getting stronger physically, but his spirit seems to have shut down."

Thomas nodded. "I understand." His simple words rang through the room, somehow conveying just how much he truly did understand. "He needs the plantation," he said.

Carrie nodded. "You're so right. I'm just waiting for him to get strong enough to move."

"You were going out there on your own?" Thomas asked.

Carrie smiled. "Only if on your own means with Rose, Moses and Aunt Abby."

Thomas stared around the room and sank down in front of his bowl of soup. "I guess it's time to start hearing the stories," he said.

"Don't you be touchin' that soup, Mr. Cromwell," May called. "Y'all done talked so long that it got cold. I'm bringing out some fresh soup right now."

Thomas smiled when she appeared with a hot bowl of soup and a plate of steaming cornbread. "That looks wonderful," he said, inhaling the aroma and closing his eyes in delight when he took the first bite. "I missed you, May," he murmured. Everyone was laughing when he opened his eyes. "I seem to remember a condition," he said, looking at Carrie.

Carrie laughed with delight. "Gladly! You eat dinner. When I get back, we'll have dessert."

"Unless I eat your piece," Moses said playfully.

"You do, and I'll make sure May doesn't feed you for a week!" Carrie threatened. "I have a horse to welcome home!"

May was standing at the door with several carrots when she walked into the kitchen. "I'm thinkin' these will make that ole horse happy."

Carrie laughed and hugged her. "You're the absolute best, May! He will love them." She was singing as she strode out to the barn and laughed when excited whinnies exploded from the interior. She ran the last several yards, flung open the door and wrapped her arms around Granite's solid neck.

Granite's frantic whinnies turned into contented snorts as he nuzzled Carrie's shoulder, his massive gray head bent to receive her embrace.

"I'm so glad you're home," Carrie murmured. "There are no more battles to be fought. You're home."

Granite sighed, seeming to understand what she was saying. He reached one leg out to paw the ground and snorted again before he began to nose her pockets.

Carrie's laughter rang out through the still air as she dug into her pocket and pulled out the carrots. "I'm going to plant a whole garden of carrots just for you," she cried, wiping at the tears in her eyes.

Granite nodded his head solemnly as he munched his carrots, his great eyes never leaving her.

"Well, if I ever wondered if an animal could be in love, I guess I have my answer."

Carrie whirled around. "Aunt Abby, this is Granite!"

"I figured that one out all by myself." Aunt Abby moved forward to stroke Granite's neck. "You two are quite the pair. I've heard so much about him that I just had to come see him for myself." She gazed admiringly at the towering, gray Thoroughbred. "You weren't exaggerating how beautiful he is."

"He's the best horse in the world," Carrie said fervently, throwing her arms around his neck again. "We're going home to the plantation soon, Granite," she promised. "No more being stuck in a stall all the time. Soon you'll be running free again."

Granite snorted loudly.

"I do believe he knows what you're saying," Aunt Abby said.

"Of course he does," Carrie replied. "I don't know why people have decided that humans are the only ones that can understand human talk. Granite knows exactly what I just said. He's probably wondering why I'm not smart enough to understand what *he* just said."

"Oh, I have you covered there," Aunt Abby said lightly. "He said he's glad, he can hardly wait, and it's certainly about time."

Carrie laughed joyfully, gave Granite a final pat, and took Aunt Abby's arm to lead her out of the barn. "I'll be back in the morning," she called over her shoulder. "Get some rest."

Chapter Thirteen

Thomas was just finishing his meal when Carrie and Aunt Abby walked in from the barn. He sighed and settled back in his chair. He let his eyes sweep the simple elegance of his home.

Carrie's heart ached as she glimpsed the lost look in his eyes. She saw the exhaustion lurking there, and the sorrow that was eating at the core of his being. She settled down in the chair beside him. "I'm so glad you're home."

Thomas stopped his perusal of the house and looked down at her. "I'm not home yet," he said simply.

Carrie understood. "Will you keep this house when we return to the plantation?"

Thomas shrugged. "Permanently? I don't know. I have absolutely no desire to remain in politics, so I can't imagine I will need it. For the present time? Now is not the time to sell, so I will keep it. At least as long as I can afford it." He sighed heavily. "I'm afraid I don't have many answers right now," he admitted. "Life as I've always known it is over."

Silence hung over the room. The Old South was indeed dead. Gone were the glory days of huge plantations run by slaves.

"I believe the future can be just as bright," Carrie ventured.

Thomas gazed at her. "Perhaps," he murmured. "All I know right now, is that I have a plantation with no one to work it. It was time for slavery to die, but I don't know if I have enough to buy everything that will be needed and also hire field workers."

Carrie was glad to hear the absence of bitterness in his voice. Her father had indeed changed. She also thought about the cache of gold upstairs. Would it be enough to let her father start over? She knew it was so much more than most Southerners had right now, but it might be far from enough. "The economy is bad, I know."

"Bad?" Thomas snorted. "It's a debacle. Our government issued bonds to finance the war, but the simple truth is the investment from the public never met the demands.   Southern taxes were lower, and we collected them with less efficiency. European investment was insufficient to bridge the gap. Davis' wonderful solution was to continue to print more and more paper money. Inflation increased from sixty percent in 1861 to three hundred percent in 1863, and six hundred percent in 1864. Davis never seemed to grasp the enormity of the problem."

"And now you're left to rectify his mistakes and try to rebuild," Aunt Abby observed.

"Yes," Thomas said dully. "I have some resources, but I fear they are not enough to meet the need."

"But you have the plantation and this house as collateral," Aunt Abby protested. "Surely that will make a difference."

"Will it?" Thomas asked. "I rode through town on the way here," he said, his voice thick with grief. "I saw the destruction from the fires. The business district has been destroyed. All the banks are gone. The focus must first go to rebuilding Richmond."

"But it's also necessary to re-establish agriculture," Aunt Abby argued. "In order to truly rebuild Virginia, there must be job opportunities on the plantations."

Carrie hid her grin when Thomas eyed Aunt Abby more closely. She was quite sure he had never had a financial discussion with a woman his own age.

"You seem to know quite a bit about it," Thomas finally said.

Carrie didn't bother to hide her grin this time. "Aunt Abby is quite a businesswoman," she said proudly. "She owns several factories in Philadelphia. She has also just become an investor in the First Bank of Richmond."

Thomas settled back in his chair and stared at Aunt Abby. "Well," he managed.

Aunt Abby laughed. "I inherited the businesses from my late husband. They have done well." She leaned forward. "I know this is premature, since you have just arrived home, but I feel confident I can arrange financing for the plantation. It was hugely successful in the past. There is no reason it can't be again."

Carrie saw the spark of hope ignite in her father's eyes.

"That would be wonderful," Thomas murmured. "I look forward to the discussion."

"There's something else, Father," Carrie said. She hadn't been sure when she would find the right time to broach the topic she and Moses had discussed, but now seemed to be the perfect opportunity.

When Thomas turned to her, she nodded to Moses. "Go ahead and tell Father what we talked about. He knows you ran the plantation after I kicked Ike Adams off."

Moses shifted and cleared his throat but met Thomas' eyes squarely. "I have an idea that could help get the plantation on its feet again, and also help some people I care deeply about."

Thomas nodded, his eyes fixed on Moses intently. "I'm listening."

Moses straightened his shoulders. "I love farming. It's all I've ever really wanted to do, and I'm good at it," he said confidently.

Thomas nodded. "I saw the figures from the plantation while you were running it. They were quite impressive. What do you have in mind?"

Moses relaxed noticeably. "I headed up a unit in the Union Army, sir. Most of my men were field hands from Southern plantations. They want their freedom, but they also want to work doing what they know best. I propose hiring them to work at Cromwell. They are good men, sir."

Thomas gazed at him. "I don't know how much I can pay them," he responded honestly. "Things are going to be tight until we get a crop in, and it's already late in the year."

"Yes, sir. It's too late for tobacco," Moses responded. "The seedlings should have been started in February. But if we can get started soon, I think we can still get a good crop of oats and wheat in. Then next year, we put the tobacco back in. We'll have this winter to work the fields and get them ready." He paused. "We'll figure out how much you can pay the men now, and then we can give them a percentage of the crops once they are sold."

"And you believe they'll be okay with that?" Thomas asked, disbelief warring with hope on his face.

"They will be if I am," Moses said firmly.

"And you'll run everything?" Thomas asked.

"With your permission, sir."

Thomas frowned. "You've got to stop saying that," he said abruptly.

"Excuse me?" Moses was clearly confused.

Thomas smiled. "You are my brother-in-law. You may act as my overseer, but you are still my brother-in-law. You must call me Thomas."

Moses smiled. "That might take a little getting used to, but I'll do my best." He paused. "I have my own conditions."

Thomas eyed him. "And they would be?"

"One, I won't be called an overseer." His eyes were dark with memories. "That's not a word any of us take too kindly to. I prefer to be called a manager."

Thomas nodded. "Of course. I'm sorry. I wasn't thinking."

Moses shook his head. "No reason to apologize. There have been a lot of changes. There are going to be a lot more. It's going to take a while for everyone to get used to them."

"Yes."

"The other thing is that I won't be able to start working until I go find my mama and sister."

"Where are they?"

Moses shook his head. "I don't know. The last I knew, they were on a plantation a couple hours north of the city on the James, but I have no idea if they are still there. I have to try," he said a little desperately.

"I remember them," Thomas said softly. "All of you were separated the day I bought you." His voice was thick with regret. "I am so sorry."

"Thank you," Moses replied, knowing there was no way Thomas could truly understand the pain he had endured when they had been ripped apart on the auction block. It was enough that he was sorry.

"Take as long as you need," Thomas said. "When you return, you can come out to the plantation with your men."

Moses turned to Rose and Carrie. "I want to leave tomorrow," he said. "Now that Mr. Cromwell—I mean Thomas—has returned, you will be safe here, Rose. When they go out to the plantation, you can go with them."

Rose nodded quickly. "Of course. You must go find your family."

Moses hesitated, and then asked Thomas the other question on his mind. "Do you know how other plantation owners are feeling about rebuilding their plantations?"

Thomas frowned. "Like you said, it's going to take a while for everyone to get used to the changes. Right now, I think people are floundering. There is a lot of fear and uncertainty. Many of the plantations are destroyed. It will take years for them to ever produce again. The ones that are workable..." He shrugged his shoulders and hesitated a long moment.

"The truth is always best," Aunt Abby said gently.

Thomas gazed at her for a moment and swung his eyes back to Moses. "Too many plantation owners don't see a reason for things to change," he said flatly.

"We're free now," Moses protested.

"Yes, but you're still a slave to them," Thomas said honestly. "A piece of paper doesn't change more than a hundred years of belief and conditioning." He paused and then pushed on. "I believe they will make it as hard on the freed slaves as possible. They want to be able to treat them the same way, no matter what the law says."

"Which is why military governments are being set up," Aunt Abby observed. "And why the Freedmen's Bureau is being established. Someone has to stand up for the rights of the freed slaves."

"You're right," Thomas admitted heavily. "But don't expect anything to be easy," he warned.

"If you go against the tide, things will be rough for you, too," Aunt Abby said quietly.

"You sound as if you speak from experience," Thomas replied. "Yes, things will probably be rough, but I'm prepared for that. I lived for too long doing what I was taught to believe was the right thing to do. I've come out of it with nothing but regrets. I'm going to do it differently this time," he said.

"You're an extraordinary man," Aunt Abby responded, watching him thoughtfully.

"Far from it," Thomas said. "Anything that is extraordinary about me right now is all because of my daughter, who was able to love her father when he was a short-sighted idiot."

"You have never been any such thing!" Carrie protested.

Thomas smiled. "I appreciate how much you love me, but in the end, each of us is ultimately responsible for our beliefs and our actions. I am listening to men every day who insist blacks have to continue to be treated like slaves because they have been taught they simply cannot live on their own."

Aunt Abby snorted.

Thomas laughed. "I agree completely, but the difficulty is going to be that people do not generally want to challenge their own belief systems, because it means change has to happen, and people aren't comfortable with change. I was lucky enough to have Carrie continue to hold the truth out to me, but it was still ultimately my choice to change what I believed."

"Then we must hold the truth out to people," Moses stated. "And we must do it for as long as it takes."

"We're ready to do that, Thomas," Rose said quietly. "I'm sure there are plenty of the freed slaves who believe everything is going to be a picnic now that they are free, and they believe the federal government is going to take care of them, but there are plenty of us who know that's not true. Just as you are responsible for your beliefs and actions, so are we."

Thomas regarded her closely. "You were always a smart one," he finally said.

Laughter rang through the room, lightening the atmosphere. The rhubarb pie had long been demolished, and the air wafting into the room had taken on the nip of early spring.

Jeremy cleared his throat. "As long as we're talking about the cost of standing up for our beliefs..."

The others turned to face him.

"What is it?" Carrie asked.

"Well, it seems the word has spread about me being mulatto," he said lightly, only his eyes showing his concern. "I've been let go from my job," he admitted.

"They fired you?" Thomas exclaimed. "You're the best financial analyst in the city!"

"Not anymore," Jeremy responded. His smile was weak, but his voice was firm when he continued. "I don't regret it."

"What will you do now?" Aunt Abby asked gently.

Jeremy shrugged. "I don't know what I will do in the future, but as soon as Moses and Rose head out to the plantation, I'm going with them."

"Out to Cromwell?" Thomas exclaimed. "That is wonderful news!"

"I've known my twin less than three weeks. We've still got lots of catching up to do. And," he added, "I'd like to see where I was born, and discover that part of my heritage."

Thomas smiled. "Whatever the reason, I'm simply glad you're coming. I believe you'll love it."

"Aunt Abby is coming out for a while, too," Carrie added.

"Only if my being there won't be an imposition," Aunt Abby said quickly. "Now that you are home, you may find you don't want a houseful of people."

"The people sitting around this table are not people," Thomas said. "They are family." He looked at her warmly. "You've been family to Carrie for a long time. That makes you family to me, too. You're always welcome."

Aunt Abby flushed with pleasure. "Thank you. I do so love Southern hospitality," she added playfully.

"Can I tell him about the factory?" Carrie asked eagerly.

Aunt Abby laughed and nodded.

Carrie turned back to her father. "Aunt Abby has bought the land that three of the burned warehouses stood on. She is going to build a clothing factory here in Richmond to provide good jobs for the freed slaves." She smiled at the surprised look on her father's face. "The site is almost cleared and all the bricks clean."

"Quite an undertaking," Thomas murmured.

Aunt Abby smiled. "It will take a while to get the factory operating, but I'm going to do everything I can to help rebuild your city and establish equality for the blacks." She paused. "I have promised myself that all Lincoln did would not be in vain. It's going to take everyone standing up to do their part."

Thomas nodded sadly. "Lincoln's death was yet another devastating blow to our country."

"You believe that?" Aunt Abby asked.

"Absolutely," Thomas said. "We may have spent the war on opposite sides, but Lincoln was an extraordinary leader. I believe the pains of reconstruction are going to be much greater under President Johnson, but only time will tell."

Carrie was struck by the deep fatigue in his voice. She stood and pushed back from the table. "I think it's time to call it a night," she said. "You rode in from Danville today, and we've been talking for hours. You must be exhausted."

Thomas looked at her gratefully. "You're right. I could use a good night's sleep."

"And tomorrow is a big day for Moses, as well," Carrie added. "He has to report in the morning to march with the Union troops through Richmond."

A wave of sorrow crossed Thomas' face, but he smiled and nodded. "Yes, I'd heard that was tomorrow." He hesitated. "I hope you don't mind if I don't attend."

Moses' eyes softened. "You are handling so much," he replied. "There is no reason you should be glad about the loss of everything you fought for four years to hold on to. Accepting it is one thing, having it paraded in front of you is another."

Thomas nodded. "Thank you for understanding." He kissed Carrie and headed for the stairs. "Goodnight, everyone."

******

The crackling of brush in the distance had Robert on full alert. He tensed, his hands locked tightly around the barrel of his rifle as he waited, searching the black night with his eyes. He craned to hear what might be coming toward him, but now only the chorus of crickets and frogs rose up around him. Slowly, very slowly, he relaxed.

And then the woods exploded with gunfire and wild yelling. He heard the screams of his men all around him as the gunfire reached its target. He gasped and looked frantically toward the woods, firing, but knowing his bullets were missing their mark.

When the firing ended, the wild laughing began. He gasped as the woods rang with taunting, hideous laughter. He shrank back as the trees leaned in, parting their limbs to reveal his position. His breath came in short gasps as he saw his men lying all around him, their eyes open and blank in death. Then, as one, they all turned to stare at him—accusing, blaming...

He was relieved when he heard the final gunshot, and felt the bullet rip through his heart. He stared down in fascination as blood spread across his chest, drenching his shirt.

And then the laughter began again. Only now, the laughter was coming from his men. Eyes still wide with death stared at him as the laughter rolled forth—mocking, accusing, blaming...

Robert screamed—a silent scream no one could hear—and he jolted awake to stare into the black emptiness of his room.

"It was a dream, Robert. Just a dream."

Robert stared up as the soothing voice replaced the laughter. He recognized Carrie, but the recognition brought no peace. His turmoil was the same awake, as it was asleep. He saw the concern in her eyes, but he couldn't find the energy to care. There was nothing left to care about. His life was over. His life would never be more than hideous dreams, and endless guilt and remorse for all the lost lives.

"Sleep," Carrie said soothingly.

Robert willingly closed his eyes, not wanting to look at the reminder of all he had lost. He would not sleep, but he would lose himself in the darkness...

Chapter Fourteen

The morning air was crisp and clear when Moses stepped out onto the porch, dressed proudly in his Union blues. The sun was climbing over the horizon, turning puffy clouds into a panorama of purple and gold. As he watched, a great shaft of light pierced the clouds with radiant rays that seemed to dance in the easy breeze.

"Rather spectacular, isn't it?"

Moses spun around. "I didn't see you there."

Thomas smiled. "I wanted to see a sunrise over my city. It's putting on quite a show."

Moses nodded. "That it is." He settled down on the top stair and leaned back against the post. "You look rested."

"Sleeping in your own bed will do that," Thomas said. His gaze turned to the east. "I'll rest even better when I'm home."

"I can only imagine how hard it's been to be away all these years."

Thomas frowned. "Not at first. I was so glad to be gone, because every breath there was a memory of my beloved wife. I thought I would never want to call it home again. I was quite content here in the city."

Moses gazed at him, astounded he was having an early morning conversation with the man who had bought him just four years before. He had no trouble feeling his equal, but becoming comfortable with it was probably going to take a while. "What changed that?"

Thomas stared off at the sunrise, the shafts of light falling on his face and gleaming in his blue eyes. "I didn't really feel that way until I had to flee Richmond, and go to Danville. It was so hard to leave behind everything I had worked for, knowing it would all be gone when I returned." He frowned. "I certainly never thought I would return to find the city burned, but I fully expected the Richmond I had always known would be no more."

Moses nodded and waited quietly for him to continue.

"When I thought about coming back, all I wanted to do was go home to the plantation. The memories of my wife will always be difficult, but they become filled with more joy as the years pass." He smiled. "We had many wonderful years together." His eyes grew thoughtful. "I finally realized Cromwell Plantation is my true home. I've spent my life building it. Carrie grew up there. My heart has always been there—I just had to hide it for a while." He paused for a long moment. "There is still so much to be done," he said. "Probably more than I know, because I've not cared for the last four years, but it will give me something to do for the rest of my life."

Moses watched him, seeing the hope come to life in his eyes, knowing he was watching a man who had given his all and now simply wanted peace. "It's a wonderful place," he said. "I will do all I can to help you rebuild it."

Thomas smiled. "Thank you," he said simply, and then looked off toward the city. "I believe you have somewhere to be," he said.

Moses nodded. "Yes." There was no need to say more. Thomas knew where he was going. He was also quite sure he would hear the sound of a fifty thousand-man army marching through his city. But he would do it from the sanctuary of his porch.

******

Moses and Simon took their places in the seemingly endless line of Union infantry. The sun was now well over the horizon, but it was still early. The air was celebratory, but quiet held them as each man contemplated the price that had been paid to bring them to this moment.

Moses sighed as he thought of all the friends he had lost, but none of them had hit him harder than Pompey. The elderly man was both a friend and a father figure—a long-time slave who had leapt at the chance to join the fight to end slavery. Memories of the long talks they had around campfires filled his mind. The pain of watching him run forward into a cornfield and fall under a barrage of bullets was still raw in his mind and heart.

When the music signaling the beginning of the march sounded, Moses lifted his head high. He would march for his country. He would march for freedom. Mostly, he would march in memory of all the men, both black and white, who gave their lives to hold their country together.

No one had any clue what the beginning of war would mean. Certainly, no one could have known that it would last four years, and result in nearly a million men dead or wounded. Moses frowned when he wondered how many of the wounded would die in the months and years to come from their injuries. Just because the war was over, it didn't mean the suffering had ended.

"It's not a day for frowning, Moses," Simon said as they began to march forward, breezes fluttering the United States flags lining the road into Richmond.

Moses shook off his sorrowful thoughts. "You're right," he agreed. "It's just making me think of everyone we lost."

Simon nodded. "We paid a huge price, that's for certain, but there ain't a man who signed up to fight who didn't know he might have to pay it. I'd be willing to bet they're all watching us, cheering us on to take advantage of the freedom we have now." He looked thoughtful. "We think we're free, but they're the ones who really be free."

Moses stared at him, realizing exactly how right he was. He was able to smile as he thought of Pompey gazing down at him. He could almost hear him saying to straighten his shoulders and march like a *real* soldier. "You're right," he agreed. "We've still got to fight for our freedom. They'll never have theirs taken away."

It took all day for the Union forces to march through the conquered capital. Most of them would be marching on to Washington, DC and then be released from the army to go home and continue their lives.

Moses' men would be staying behind to bolster the forces maintaining order in Richmond. The massive chest wound Moses had suffered before the end of the war had ended his fighting days, and for that, he could feel nothing but relief. By the time he got back from looking for his mama and sister, the rest of his men would be released from duty. The powers that be understood it would take white soldiers to maintain order and create equality for the blacks. The continued presence of black troops would do nothing but add to the tension building in Richmond.

But today was a day for celebrating. Moses shook off any remaining dark thoughts as he marched proudly with the conquering army. There was not one white face in the sea of black that lined the parade route. Cries of joy and gratitude rang in his ears with every step he took.

The pain of all he had lost faded away as he gazed into the happy faces surrounding him. True, there was still a heavy price to be paid for freedom, but the people lining Broad Street would never have imagined a short time ago that they would be free on the streets of Richmond, Virginia to create a new life for themselves.

******

Moses knew the tromp of feet would still be heard for a long time as he and his men peeled away from the marching column when they reached the northern edge of Richmond.

"You're heading out of the city?"

Moses looked up as Captain Jones, his commanding officer, rode up to him. "Yes, sir."

"I hope you find your family, Moses."

Moses nodded. "I'll find them," he said confidently. "I don't know how long it will take me, but if my mama and Sadie are out there, I will find them." He had nothing but deep respect and appreciation for his captain. It had been Captain Jones who had arranged for him to take time off to find June and bring her to the contraband camp. He smiled as he remembered his terror when June went into labor, having Simon right there in the woods beside the road. But all had turned out well.

"I wish you the best," Captain Jones replied.

"Will you be here when I return, sir?" Moses asked, suddenly realizing his captain might have orders to go elsewhere.

"I don't know," Captain Jones admitted. He smiled. "To tell you the truth, I have tendered my resignation from the army."

Moses whistled. "You've served for a long time."

"Twenty years. It's enough."

Moses gazed at him. "It's been a rough four years, sir."

Captain Jones nodded. "It has, indeed. I think I've got enough gray hair and wrinkles to prove it."

He spoke lightly, but Moses saw the fatigue and darkness lurking in his eyes. "What will you do next, sir?"

"I don't know," he replied. "Probably as little as possible for a while. I'll spend time with my wife and kids and then figure out what comes next."

"You deserve nothing but great things," Moses said warmly. He stepped forward and held out his hand. "Thank you for everything, sir."

Captain Jones gripped his hand firmly, holding it for a long moment. "I thank you, as well," he finally said. "I've depended on your leadership and your good sense. You've taught me many things." He hesitated. "You're a natural leader, Moses. Your people are going to need leadership from their own in the years to come."

Moses frowned. "I appreciate the compliment, sir, but all I want to do is farm." He explained briefly his plan to take his unit out to Cromwell Plantation and bring it back to life.

Captain Jones listened intently. "Cromwell Plantation, eh? That's quite a place." He stared off at the horizon for a moment and then swung his gaze back. "Is Carrie Borden going back out there?"

"As soon as her husband is well enough to move. He's still very ill. Her father has also arrived home. He returned last night. Everyone will be going out together."

Captain Jones nodded. "Tell her to contact me when they're ready to go," he said suddenly.

"Excuse me?"

"It's fairly safe in the city now, but we haven't been able to bring the entire countryside under control. There are too many desperate people out there who wouldn't hesitate to accost someone of obvious means. It won't be safe for her and her father. My resignation won't be effective for a few months. I will send a unit of my men with them when they are ready to go."

Moses gazed at him with appreciation. "Thank you, sir," he managed, knowing that it wasn't enough.

Captain Jones smiled. "I might just join the unit myself. Perhaps I'll discover how Mrs. Borden managed to escape with that giant, gray Thoroughbred of hers."

Moses laughed. "I wouldn't count on it, sir."

Captain Jones eyed him more closely. "You know the answer, don't you?"

Moses said nothing but laughter danced in his eyes.

"I could order you to tell me."

"But you won't," Moses replied, his voice confident.

Captain Jones scowled but his eyes brightened. "You're right. I won't." He waved his hand. "Go on and find your mama."

Moses nodded and turned away. He had already told Simon goodbye. He knew his friend would keep an eye on everyone on the hill.

Suddenly, his gaze sharpened. "Jeremy!" he called as he hurried over to where he sat on a wagon seat. "What are you doing here?" His heart quickened. "What's wrong?" he asked.

Jeremy smiled and shook his head. "Not a thing."

Moses was confused. "Then what are you doing here?"

Jeremy answered with a question of his own. "How are you planning on bringing your mama and Sadie home?"

Moses shook his head. "I don't know," he admitted. "I haven't thought that far." He was embarrassed to acknowledge that was true. Did he really think his mama and Sadie were going to walk back to Richmond with him? Carrie had offered him Granite, but he had refused, not willing to separate them again.

"That's what Thomas figured," Jeremy replied.

"Thomas?"

"Yes. We were talking about it this morning." Jeremy's expression grew more serious. "He feels responsible for separating your family."

Moses said nothing, as it was true.

"He also told me it was dangerous for you to be out on the roads by yourself right now."

Moses frowned and began to protest.

Jeremy held up his hand. "There is nothing but chaos in the South right now. No one has figured out what to do with all the freed slaves traveling on the road."

Moses shook his head. "That's not going to stop me from going," he said.

"Of course it's not!" Jeremy exclaimed. "That's why I'm going with you. In this wagon," he added.

Moses stared at him. "What?" A smile spread across his face. "Thomas sent this wagon for us to use? And you're going with me?"

"That's right." Jeremy leaned forward. "Accept the gift, Moses. Thomas feels terrible, and needs a way to help make it right. This will never make up for separating your family, but he can at least make it easier for you. And for your mama and Sadie," he added. "Besides, I'm unemployed at the moment, so I have plenty of time to make it out to the plantation."

"Not to mention that having a white man with me will make things easier," Moses said wryly, though he was wise enough to appreciate the logic of Thomas' solution.

"We don't have to tell anyone I'm really your black wife's twin," Jeremy replied ruefully. "What they don't know won't hurt them."

Moses laughed. "I'm all for keeping people in the dark," he said, climbing into the wagon seat. "Let's roll," he said, his heart beating faster as he realized he truly was on his way to find his mama and Sadie. The added benefit of a wagon, and Jeremy for company, only made it better.

******

Moses took deep breaths of the fresh spring air as they began to roll out of the city. The horse pulling the wagon, a solid-looking bay, held his head proudly and moved at a good pace. Once they left the charred remains of the business district behind, the beleaguered city still showed some of its old grandeur. The houses were faded, fences were broken, and shutters hung from their hinges, but children were once more playing in the streets under the shade of brilliant dogwoods, their creamy white blooms standing in stark contrast. Colorful azaleas lined the foundations of homes that seemed to be waiting for a new beginning.

Moses smiled at Jeremy. "This trip is going to be a lot different than I envisioned."

Jeremy smiled back at him. "It will also happen a lot faster than you thought."

Moses nodded, looked at him more closely, and then started laughing. "Which is part of the reason Thomas sent you and the wagon. He wants me back out on Cromwell to start putting in crops as soon as possible."

Jeremy smiled again. "He is a businessman who is trying to do the right thing. But, yes, he is eager to get things moving again."

Moses nodded. "I am, too," he admitted. "I want to start building the life I dreamed about during all the years of slavery, and during the years I've been fighting. It's time." He thought back to his daddy, and the price he paid when he tried to escape to build the life he dreamed of. His dream ended with him dangling from a rope. Moses was determined to create the life for his mama and sisters that his daddy had envisioned for them.

******

What started with the feeling of a grand adventure faded into a constant panorama of the stark reality of war as they headed west from Richmond. Everywhere they looked, they saw destruction. Houses and barns were burned. Fields were scorched and fences torn away, their ties littering the ground. Railroad tracks were torn up in twisted masses. Fields that should have sported the fresh green of new crops lay brown and barren. Bridges were gone. Only Jeremy's knowledge of the roads enabled them to find alternate routes that kept them moving forward.

"My God," Moses said, gazing around. "How do you come back from something like this?"

"It's worse further up in the Shenandoah," Jeremy responded. "Most of this is General Sheridan's work. My understanding is that he had orders to destroy the Virginia Central Railroad and the James River Canal, while Lee was bombarding Petersburg."

"He did his job well," Moses said. Now that the war was over, it was impossible not to look at everything with an eye to rebuilding. He thought of Cromwell Plantation as he stared over the barren fields. "It's going to take a long time for things to return to normal," he finally said.

Jeremy nodded. "Yes, it will, but the people of Virginia are resilient."

"They will have to be."

"Just as the people of Georgia will have to be, to rebuild after Sherman wreaked his destruction down there." Jeremy sighed. "It's the cost of war." He scowled. "The war should never have been fought, but it was. Now the South has no choice but to rebuild. It will take a long time, but it can be done. It *must* be done," he added fiercely.

Moses thought about Jeremy's lost position with the government. "You feel helpless not to be a part of it," he observed.

Jeremy sat quietly for a long moment and then shrugged his shoulders. "Not helpless exactly. I know I could have made a difference as a financial analyst, but only if they would have listened," he admitted. "I tried to warn Virginia not to follow in the footsteps of the Confederacy in regard to how they handled their currency, but..."

"They wouldn't listen," Moses finished.

"No one wanted to acknowledge we were fighting a losing battle from the very beginning," Jeremy said heavily. He frowned as the remnants of another scorched barn appeared as they rounded a curve. "The rebuilding is going to be as painful as the war," he predicted. "Maybe more so. It's certainly going to last longer."

"Do you have confidence it can happen?" Moses asked.

Jeremy was quiet again for a long while.

Moses waited, knowing he was pulling together his thoughts. Though he'd certainly had many opportunities to talk with Jeremy in the last several weeks, he was glad they were taking this trip together so he could get to know him better. He smiled knowing Rose was probably very jealous right now, though he also knew she was glad he wasn't alone.

Finally Jeremy spoke. "The South will rebuild, but not without a lot of bitterness and anger. The men who started this war still believe their cause was just and right. They have been beaten in battle, but that hasn't changed the feelings that started the war in the first place."

"Will it ever end?" Moses asked. "Or will they continue to fight the war in a different way?"

Jeremy gazed at him. "That's the question to be answered." He paused. "It's common for Southerners to romanticize tragedy. They started a war they had no chance to win, but if they can convince themselves and the rest of the world that they were the victims in unjust aggression, they may feel they can salvage their pride."

"That didn't work so well before," Moses observed.

"They were asking for money and support then," Jeremy reminded him. "Now they are looking for sympathy."

"To what end?" Moses was puzzled.

Jeremy shrugged. "They've lost everything. If they can somehow salvage their pride, they can continue to protest that the war was wrong in the first place."

"So it never ends," Moses said heavily.

"It depends on how the next few years go," Jeremy answered. "If Lincoln were still alive, I would feel much more optimistic. I know he would have made sure that blacks' rights were enforced, and that the freed slaves had a fair opportunity to build new lives."

"And you don't believe President Johnson will do that?"

"I've been studying everything I can get my hands on," Jeremy began.

Moses interrupted. "I thought you were a *financial* analyst."

Jeremy smiled. "I am, but that means understanding the forces that control the finances. So far, President Johnson is looking like he's going to be tough on the South, and make sure they adhere to the terms of surrender."

"You sound like you doubt that will continue."

"Let's just say it would be out of character based on what I've learned so far," Jeremy responded. "President Johnson is a Southerner who was a slave owner. That can never be forgotten. He fought to maintain the Union, but he fought equally hard to maintain slavery. Only time will tell what he does now."

Moses leaned forward and stared into the distance. "What is that?" he asked tensely. He saw clouds of dust and heard frantic yells, but he couldn't tell what was going on.

Jeremy continued to drive forward.

Moses' lips tightened in fury when they got close enough to see. A group of what looked to be former slaves had been surrounded by a group of white men on horseback. Their tattered uniforms identified them as former Confederate soldiers.

"Where you niggers think you're going?" one yelled.

Moses saw the stark terror on the faces staring up at the horsemen. He opened his mouth to say something, but Jeremy put a hand on his arm.

"Don't."

"We can't just do nothing!" Moses protested.

Jeremy kept his hand on his arm. "They're not doing anything but scaring them right now," he said. "The two of us won't be able to stop them. If we challenge them, they may hurt them just to prove they can."

"And what if they decide to hurt them anyway?" Moses asked angrily.

"You headed into the big city?" another one of the men yelled. "You think you're going to find your big opportunity?" he sneered.

The group continued to stare at the horsemen silently.

"Just wait," Jeremy urged. "If they try to hurt them, of course we'll step in to try to stop them."

Moses clenched his fists and teeth as he stared at the scene playing out before him.

The veterans continued to taunt the band of freed slaves, spinning their horses around them in circles until the dust caked their faces and covered their clothes. They finally seemed to tire of their fun.

"Let's get out of here!" one of them, a thin man with straggly black hair and sallow skin, finally yelled. "These people are so stupid they can't even talk. They'll get to Richmond and find out soon enough that no one wants them there either."

Whooping and hollering, the men on horseback wheeled and galloped off.

Moses watched them with disgust. He was also aware of a feeling of gratitude that Thomas had insisted on Jeremy and the wagon.

Jeremy drew the wagon up next to the group. "You people okay?"

They simply stared at him, fright still shining from their eyes.

Moses stepped off of the wagon. "It's all right," he said. "You're safe now."

"Until the next group comes along," one of the men ventured. "Dey ain't the first that come after us."

Moses scowled. "If you keep moving you can be in the city before dark."

"Where should we go?" the spokesman asked. "You know anythin' about Richmond?"

"Enough," Moses responded. "Listen carefully, because you don't want to go into the wrong area." He told them the route to take to get to the black quarter. "If you don't get there before dark," he cautioned, "stay in the woods until tomorrow morning."

"So Richmond ain't no better?" one tired looking woman asked as she held tightly to the hand of her little girl.

"It is better," Moses assured her, "but it's not safe in certain areas at night."

"I thought the army be there to take care of things?"

"They are, but they can't be everywhere at one time. Once you get to the black quarter, you need to find one of the churches. Tell them Moses Samuels sent you."

The man opened his eyes wide. "You be someone important?"

Moses shrugged. "Not really, but I've made it a point to know everyone down there. Until recently, I was a Union soldier."

The frightened looks turned to excited smiles.

"So we gonna find us some good jobs?" the woman asked. "Does the army got food for us?" She stared down at her little girl. "We ain't had much to eat since we done set off from the plantation."

Moses sighed. He'd heard this story hundreds of times in the last weeks. "They'll help you," he assured them, "but you'll have to find work. It won't be easy because the city is filling up, but you'll have to keep looking. The government won't always be there. It's up to all of us to make the most of the freedom we've been given."

The man who had spoken first scowled. "What you know about being a slave?" he sneered. "You and your fancy talkin'."

Moses eyed him. "I was a slave for the first twenty-two years of my life. I have the lashes to prove it. When I got a chance to escape, I took it. When I got the chance to learn to read, I took it. When I got the chance to learn how to speak correctly, I took it, because I want to take advantage of my freedom, and I want things to be different for my family."

His gaze swept the group that had lost their suspicious looks. "Nobody can change the fact that you were slaves and had years stolen from you. But only you can change what comes next. If you sit around waiting for things to be handed to you, your life won't be much different. When you get to Richmond, go to school. Learn how to read and write. It will make the rest of your life a lot easier."

Moses looked at the sun sinking toward the horizon and knew they needed to keep moving. They would also need to find a safe place before it got dark. "I wish you the best," he said, and turned to climb back into the wagon.

"Thank you, Mr. Moses Samuels!" one of the women called out.

Moses waved his hand as Jeremy moved the horse forward.

"That was something," Jeremy finally said. "Rose told me you're a natural leader, but I haven't had a chance to see you in action before now."

Moses shrugged, thinking about what Captain Jones had said. "I just want to be a farmer."

Jeremy laughed. "I reckon you learned a long time ago that what we want and what we actually get aren't usually the same thing."

Moses stared at him, not wanting to think about it, but also not able to deny the glow of satisfaction he felt when he had been able to help that group. "I did the leadership thing in the army," he finally said. "I'm done."

Jeremy moved the horse into a brisk trot. "We can sleep in the wagon tonight. May threw in some blankets and a huge basket of food."

Moses smiled, looking at the back of the wagon for the first time. "Bless May's heart," he said gladly. "I'm starving."

Chapter Fifteen

Carrie was standing on the porch when her father walked out with two mugs of steaming coffee in his hands.

"Want some?" Thomas offered.

Carrie smiled and reached for a mug gratefully. "After three years of drinking cups of liquid that didn't remotely resemble coffee, it is still such a joy to drink the real thing."

Thomas nodded. "I'm grateful our stores are filling up with product again, even if they are ridiculously expensive." He took a big sip and stared out over the city. "You're sure this is what you want to do?"

Carrie nodded. "I've thought it through a hundred times. Robert is not getting any stronger here. He's already lost all interest in living, and every day seems to take him a little further from me. The only time he speaks is during the hideous nightmares he has every night. He's closing down," she said desperately.

"Are you sure he can manage the trip out to the plantation?"

Carrie shook her head. "No, I'm not," she admitted, "but I am quite sure he will die here if I don't get him out of the city. I have to take the chance." She turned to her father. "Do you think I'm wrong?"

"No," Thomas said firmly. "Hope is so often the only thing that keeps us alive. I fear this house has become nothing but a symbol of despair for Robert because of the memories it holds from the war. He can't get away from them. I believe you're doing the right thing."

Carrie leaned against him, so grateful for his strength. Her father had been home only a week, but already his eyes were brighter. The reality that they were leaving for the plantation in just an hour had brought a glow to his face that she hadn't seen in years. "You're really glad to be going home?"

"Yes," Thomas said gratefully. "I truly never believed I could feel the plantation was home again, but it's all I want now."

"You won't miss your work here in Richmond?"

Thomas shook his head. "I've had enough of politics to last a lifetime." His face creased with thought. "This country will only reunite when people stop seeking the Republican answer, or the Democratic answer. The only one that counts is the *right* answer. It's just not important who is to blame for the past. I find I simply want to live my life taking responsibility for my part of the future."

"I couldn't agree more," Aunt Abby said fervently as she stepped out on the porch to join them. "I couldn't help overhearing the last thing you said. I can only pray more people on both sides of this equation will make the same decision."

"Don't hold your breath," Thomas replied, but then smiled. "Good morning, Abby."

"Good morning!" she said brightly as she slipped an arm through Carrie's. "I can't believe that after all the years of hearing about your wonderful plantation, I'm actually going to get to see it for myself."

Carrie grinned, visions of racing across the fields on Granite filling her mind, and blanking out all other concerns. "You're going to love it!" Suddenly, she couldn't wait to get on the road. "Do you think Micah is almost done packing the wagon?"

Aunt Abby nodded. "As long as he can get it all in. May keeps handing him baskets of food." Amusement danced in her eyes.

"We'll be out there this afternoon," Thomas protested. "We don't need that much food."

"May is determined that no one will have a moment of hunger," Aunt Abby replied. "When I suggested she might be overdoing it, she waved a spoon at me and told me to get out of her kitchen. That's when I decided the front porch was safer."

Carrie and Thomas laughed with her, and then Thomas grew thoughtful. "I'm very lucky to have those two. I still feel badly about leaving them here at the house without a salary."

"Don't," Carrie said, repeating what she had already said to her father before. "They talked about this before you even came home. You are leaving them with a home and a garden that will supply their needs. It will give them time to figure out how they want to live their future. When they want to do something else, they know they can tell you. By that time, you may know more about what you want to do with the house."

"It just feels so odd," Thomas murmured.

"Life is going to feel odd for a long time," Aunt Abby agreed. "Nothing is as it used to be."

"For you either?" Thomas asked.

"It's almost like the circle of life," Aunt Abby admitted. "My family is here in Virginia. I never thought I would return here—certainly not to open a factory."

"Your family must be very proud of you," Thomas said.

Aunt Abby sighed. "One could hope," she replied, "but they have never understood my independence and my determination to run my husband's business. They told me I was bringing disgrace to the family name."

"They can't still feel that way!" Thomas exclaimed.

Carrie saw the shadow fall over Aunt Abby's eyes. "The letter that came yesterday," she said. "It was from your family?"

Aunt Abby gazed at her and nodded. "You would think by the time I reached middle-age, that I would no longer care about my family's impressions of me, but I find it still stings," she admitted, her forced laugh not reaching her eyes. "They told me I am doing nothing but bringing further disgrace to the family name by bringing evil Northern money down here. Losing the war was bad enough, but now my kind and I are coming down to rub their noses in it."

Carrie reached for her hand. "I'm so sorry."

Aunt Abby took a deep breath and shook her head. "Don't be. I've been hearing this for years. I have made the decision each time to live my life. How they feel about me is not my responsibility."

"Now I know why you and Carrie get along so well," Thomas said blandly.

Aunt Abby laughed merrily. "We *are* very much alike." She looked up at Thomas, shading her eyes from the sun. "Does that bother you?" she asked.

Thomas shook his head immediately. "Not at all. After years of living with Carrie, I find submissive women quite boring!" He held out his arm. "Care to join me for breakfast, Abby?"

Aunt Abby smiled up at him. "Why, I would be delighted, Thomas."

Carrie gazed after them as they walked into the house. She had turned to join them when the sound of horses caused her to spin back around. She shaded her eyes from the sun as she peered down the road. When the riders got close enough, her eyes widened with surprise and she stepped off the porch to walk to the gate. "Hello, Captain Jones," she called. "What are you doing here?"

Captain Jones smiled and vaulted off his horse to stand beside her. "I've come to do Moses a favor."

Carrie stiffened. "Have you heard from him?" Moses and Jeremy had been gone a week. There had been no word. They hadn't expected any, as Southern communication lines were still very poor, but perhaps they had gotten word through.

"No," Captain Jones replied. "Moses asked me a favor before he left. I heard from Simon last night that you and your family are leaving for the plantation today."

"That's true," Carrie confirmed, wondering what that had to do with his presence.

"I'm going with you," Captain Jones stated. He waved his arm toward the seven men that were with him. "All of us are."

Carrie was speechless. She stared at him for a long moment before she found her voice. "Why?" she finally asked.

His face grew serious. "Moses told me you were all going back out. The plantation is safe, but the roads out there are not. He was worried about what could happen to all of you, especially with an invalid to care for. He asked me if some of the unit could accompany you for protection."

Carrie absorbed the news quietly; suddenly very glad Moses had made the request. "And you are coming, too, Captain? I would think you have much more important things to do."

Captain Jones nodded his head. "Perhaps, but I'm still hoping I'll find the answer to how you got away from me on Granite three years ago."

Carrie smiled demurely. "It will take more than an escort to the plantation to learn that secret."

Captain Jones laughed. "Moses told me I didn't have a chance," he admitted. "When Simon told me you were going out today, I simply decided it was a wonderful day for a ride in the country. I hope you will not turn us away."

Carrie smiled. "I am an independent woman," she replied, "not a fool. Thank you for your offer. I accept gladly."

Captain Jones nodded. "My men and I will be around back."

"I will send some food out. We are almost ready to go, or I would invite you in for breakfast."

"Food won't be necessary," Captain Jones replied. "We all ate just before we rode out."

"That may be," Carrie responded, "but if y'all don't eat some of the food our housekeeper keeps loading in the wagon, there will be no room for my husband."

"Then, in the spirit of sacrifice, we will partake," Captain Jones said, laughter lighting his eyes.

Carrie grinned. "Who would have ever guessed I would like you so much?" she murmured. "Especially since one of your men put a bullet in my shoulder."

Captain Jones nodded. "I will always regret that." He shook his head. "I will never forget the image of you streaking across that field under the moonlight. I can close my eyes and still see you jumping that fence. And bareback!" He looked at her with undisguised admiration. "How is that horse of yours?"

"You'll see for yourself shortly," Carrie replied. "I'm riding him to the plantation."

******

Everyone was just entering the parlor when a knock sounded on the door.

"Who now?" Carrie asked.

Micah appeared a moment later. "There is a letter, Miss Carrie."

Carrie reached for the envelope, opened it, and scanned the contents. "It's from Matthew!" she exclaimed.

"What does it say?" Aunt Abby asked eagerly.

Carrie smiled and began to read.

> *Dear Richmond Family,*
> *I know you are aware of the disaster on the Sultana. They have just released me from the hospital. They kept me longer than I felt necessary, but it also gave me time to think. I have resigned from the newspaper. I have seen enough tragedy and death to last a lifetime. I am going first to Philadelphia, and then I'm coming to Virginia. I hope I will be welcome on the plantation for a while until I figure out what steps I wish to take next. Since most of the people I consider family are going to be at Cromwell, I would like to join you.*
> *I will wait for your reply.*
> *With deep fondness,*
> *Matthew.*

"Of course he's welcome at Cromwell," Thomas said instantly. He shook his head. "He's endured so much..."

"I will send a response immediately," Carrie said, jumping up and rushing over to the desk in the parlor.

Minutes later, she handed an envelope to Micah. "Please mail this as soon as we are gone."

"Yessum. Mr. Matthew gonna know he's got a home waitin for him," Micah said, his voice rough with emotion.

"Yes, he will," Aunt Abby said. She glanced at Thomas. "Do you feel your plantation is becoming a haven?"

"I sincerely hope so," Thomas responded. "It's always been a haven for me. It will be wonderful to see it full of life again."

Just then, Captain Jones appeared in the doorway from the kitchen. "I don't mean to interrupt," he said, "but May said you might need some help getting Mr. Borden into the wagon. I have two men ready to carry a stretcher up to his room."

Carrie smiled brightly. "That would be wonderful. With Moses and Jeremy gone, I wasn't sure how we were going to pull it off. Please have your men come in. I will take them upstairs.

******

With Robert safely in the wagon, Carrie went back upstairs to walk through the house with her father to make sure they had everything they would need. When she was certain they were alone, she turned to him. "Is the gold in the wagon?" she asked quietly. They had agreed that no one else would know about it.

Thomas nodded. "It's in a box beneath the platform we built for Robert's bed."

Carrie nodded, relieved she was no longer responsible for keeping it safe. She knew every one of her father's plans revolved around the gold. It was all he had left of the massive fortune he owned before the war. "Will it be enough?" she asked.

Thomas shrugged. "It will have to be." He put an arm around her waist. "My grandfather came over here and started with nothing but a piece of land and hope. He managed to build something substantial. It's my responsibility to care for it. Whatever it takes, that is what I will do. What we have is what we have. It will simply have to be enough."

Carrie nodded thoughtfully. "There has always been *enough*. Even when things were really rough during the war, there was always enough. It wasn't what we were used to, and it wasn't what we wanted, but it was always enough." She paused. "I guess it's all in how you look at it."

Thomas nodded. "The plantation may never be what it used to be, but that won't matter. It will be enough..."

"Because we will choose to *let* it be enough," Carrie finished for him, turning to give him a big hug. "Was it hard to reconcile yourself to losing your wealth, Father?"

Thomas gazed at her. "Until last year it was," he replied. "Until you walked in one frigid night with a box full of severed and frozen hands and feet. Not until then, did I truly understand the price our boys were paying to attempt to preserve a lifestyle most of them had never experienced. That was the night it ceased to be important."

Carrie winced as she remembered that night, but smiled when she thought of the wagons of shoes, gloves and clothing they had then collected from Richmond residents to take to the troops in the trenches guarding the city. "We helped a lot of men," she murmured.

"Yes, but it was really only a drop in the bucket," Thomas said. "I'm determined to rebuild the plantation, but I also want to help others rebuild their lives."

"You are. You're providing an opportunity for a lot of men and their families."

Thomas nodded. "I'm glad for that, but..."

"But what, Father?"

Thomas stared out the window into the backyard, where the wagon and everyone waited. "I don't know," he finally said. "I'm going home. That's all I can think of right now. I'm going to let the future unfold as it will."

******

"Did you get word to Eddie?" Carrie asked Micah again.

Micah stared down at her. "Now, Miss Carrie, you done knows that I did. How many times you gonna ask me that?"

Carrie flushed. "I'm sorry, Micah. I just don't understand where he is. Surely he is eager to reunite with the rest of his children."

"Somethin' be holdin' him up, Miss Carrie."

Carrie couldn't miss the worried look in his eyes. "Micah, do you know something?" she demanded. "Something you're not telling me?"

Micah shrugged. "There be plenty of trouble in the city, Miss Carrie. You know that."

Carrie remained silent as she stared down the road, willing Eddie and Susie to appear.

"Just give it a few more minutes," June urged. "I talked to Susie a couple days ago. They were planning on going out with us."

Carrie looked at Robert lying in the wagon. He was comfortable enough, but she was aware the sun was climbing rapidly. If they didn't leave soon, they wouldn't get to the plantation before dark. Captain Jones had made it clear that would be a bad idea. "Ten minutes," she said reluctantly, and then she went into the stables to prepare Granite.

Captain Jones was standing at the horse's stall, his arms crossed over the door, talking quietly. Granite had stretched his nose out to be rubbed.

"He likes you."

"He knows an admirer when he sees one. He's as beautiful as ever. He needs to put on a little more weight, but that shouldn't take long once he gets on Cromwell grass again."

Carrie nodded. "That's what I'm counting on." She slipped into his stall and quickly saddled and bridled him.

"No sidesaddle?" Captain Jones asked, lifting an eyebrow.

Carrie smiled. "I've become rather accustomed to going against convention, Captain Jones. I find the sidesaddle constricting and limiting," she explained. "I had always ridden that way, though, until I escaped on Granite." She grinned. "The freedom of riding astride was exhilarating. I'll never go back to sidesaddle." She lifted her long skirt just enough to reveal the breeches she wore beneath it. "I'm not willing to totally defy all Southern traditions yet, but you can be sure that when I'm at home on the plantation, this is how I will ride. Long skirts are nothing but a hindrance."

Captain Jones grinned in return. "You would like my sister. Perhaps the similarities are why I like you so much."

"Oh?"

"Susan rides in breeches and is one of the finest horsewomen I know. I've told her about your daring jump over the fence bareback. She was quite impressed."

"I look forward to meeting her," Carrie said. "I'm afraid I'm the only one I know who is thumbing their nose quite so defiantly at Southern tradition."

"Someone must always lead the way," Captain Jones observed.

"Do people have a difficult time with your sister?"

"Certainly in the beginning," he acknowledged. "Once she started out-jumping everyone on the courses in Pennsylvania, they quit complaining—or at least they kept quiet about it. Now they just complain because they can't win against her."

Carrie laughed. "I would indeed enjoy meeting your sister." She opened the door and led Granite out into the sunlight.

"Here they come!" June called.

Carrie sighed with relief and smiled brightly when she saw Eddie and Susie striding toward her.

"I's so sorry, Miss Carrie," Eddie puffed as he hurried up. "I..."

"There will be time for explanations on the way," Captain Jones interrupted. "We've got to get going if we're to reach the plantation before dark."

Thomas nodded. "It's time to go," he said crisply. He smiled down at Eddie and Susie. "I'm Thomas Cromwell," he said. "I'm glad you've made it on time." He motioned for them to join the rest of the group in the wagon.

Carrie swung into the saddle and looked down at Rose. "Is Robert all right?"

"He's resting comfortably," Rose assured her. "He has enough blankets under and around him to protect him from anything."

Carrie hoped so. She knew the road conditions out to the plantation were going to be horrible. There was nothing she could do about it, though. Robert was going to slowly die if he stayed here in the city.

She eyed the wagon. She was glad her father had gotten a large one with a team of two horses to pull it. It was loaded to the brim with people and supplies, but everyone looked excited and happy. She led the way out of the gate on Granite, waving goodbye to Micah and May. "Let's go home!" she called.

******

Excited chatter fell away to stunned silence as the wagon rolled out of the city limits, and moved into the country. Most of them had not been out of the city for the last two years. There was hardly a living thing in sight. Trees had been cut, fields razed, houses and barns burned. Occasionally, they would round a curve and see a home peeking through the woods, but every one seemed deserted and forlorn.

Carrie swallowed to keep from being sick when they passed whitened bones or hastily built graves that failed to cover remains.

"My God," she finally whispered, turning to exchange a long look with her father.

Thomas' face was white and drawn as the wagon rolled forward. "Virginia has been destroyed," he said hoarsely.

Aunt Abby put a hand on his arm and gazed at him with sympathy. "And it can be rebuilt," she said softly.

He turned to stare at her, but only shook his head. "From this?" He looked around wildly. "This is too much. There is nothing left."

"There are people," Aunt Abby said. "People built it in the first place. They will build it again."

Carrie watched her father. He had changed his feelings about slavery, but she knew he was thinking about the reality that slave labor had built the South. What would happen now that there were no more slaves?

Aunt Abby read his thoughts as well. "People built it, Thomas," she said. "Not slaves. People."

Thomas turned his head to look at her.

"The freed slaves are people," Aunt Abby said as she held his gaze. "This is their home, too. They want to rebuild what it used to be, but they want to do it on their own terms. They want to do it as free people."

Thomas turned his head toward the men riding with Captain Jones. "You're some of Moses' men," he said.

"Yes, sir," one replied, riding closer to the wagon. "I'm Simon."

"June's husband?"

"Yes, sir."

"Are you one of the men who wants to work on the plantation?"

"Yes, sir."

"Is Mrs. Livingston right?

"Yes, sir, Mr. Cromwell. The war has made a mess of things, but we all"—his hand swept to include the men riding with him—"want to help put it back together."

"As free men?"

"Yes, sir," Simon said firmly. "We want a chance to do what we know how to do, while we take care of ourselves and our families."

Thomas eyed him. "You know tobacco?"

"All of us do," Simon replied. "We all come from tobacco plantations." He lifted his head proudly. "We're good," he said confidently. "We can make Cromwell successful again."

Thomas gazed at him for a long moment and then nodded. "Thank you," he said simply. "I will pay you all I can, and then we'll share in the profits." He paused for a moment. "Captain Jones said you were just accompanying us to the plantation and then going back to the city."

"Yes, sir."

"Why? Why aren't you staying if you're planning to work?"

Simon hesitated. "Moses said he thought you would be more comfortable if he was there before we all came out. We plan on coming out when he gets back with his family."

Thomas reached a quick decision. "You'll have to return to the city to get your things, but I would like it if you would come back immediately. We've already lost enough planting time. I'll be in charge of things until Moses gets back." He turned to Captain Jones. "Is that okay with you, Captain?"

"Yes. The men know they are free to go. They have served their country well. More troops are coming in to

Richmond to take their place in a couple days. They may leave then."

Thomas nodded briskly. "I'm assuming all the men will bring their families, as well?"

Simon looked at him. "With your permission, sir. At least until we have a chance to get some land of our own and build homes."

"Of course." Thomas thought for a moment. "The only lodging I have is down in the slave quarters," he said apologetically.

"That will be fine, Mr. Cromwell," Simon responded "We know it's going to take a while for things to be anything close to normal. We'll all figure things out as we move forward."

"I'll meet with you in a week and we'll discuss wages," Thomas continued. "That will give me enough time to figure costs for supplies and equipment. I have no idea what is left, or what is still usable."

Simon nodded. "That will be fine," he said again easily.

"You're being very trusting," Thomas said suddenly.

Simon smiled. "You're Carrie's daddy."

Thomas took a deep breath and looked at Carrie. "And once again my daughter paves the way for me," he murmured.

Carrie shook her head. "You have paved your own road, Father."

"She's right," Aunt Abby added. "There are many plantation owners in the South who are going to fight all the changes. You are doing your best to adapt to them and be fair to everyone." Her voice was thick with admiration.

"We've got a long road ahead of us," Thomas said heavily. "Even if the plantation is in good shape, the Southern economy is terrible. We can grow crops, but we have to find buyers, and we also have to find ways to transport it. Entire railroad systems have been destroyed." He took a deep breath and straightened his shoulders. "But it will be enough," he said firmly. "We will work with what we have, and it will be *enough*."

Carrie smiled brightly when his eyes met hers. Love pulsed through her as she gazed at the man who was her father. She didn't believe she had ever been more proud of him than she was right that minute.

******

Silence fell on the group once more as they continued.

Carrie watched Robert carefully. The road was as deeply rutted as she feared it would be, but he seemed to be oblivious. He had not opened his eyes once, the entire time they had been traveling. She didn't know if he was sleeping, unconscious, or simply not willing to open them, but there was nothing she could do about it now. She had made the decision to take him to the plantation. Now they just had to get him there.

The destruction was tearing at her, but it was the men they passed on the way that left her truly brokenhearted. The road was full of thin, blank-eyed men walking slowly, many of them with crutches or canes. Some still had bandages wrapped around their heads. They were missing arms and legs—more evidence of the consequences of the last four years. She wanted to stop and help each one, but knew that wasn't possible.

She also knew what they really needed, was something she couldn't give them. They needed hope. She winced as she wondered how many of them suffered from the same nightmares Robert did. She wondered how many had nothing to return to.

"They rip your heart out," Captain Jones said quietly.

Carrie turned, appreciating the sincere sympathy in his eyes. He had fought hard for the North, but now that the war was over, he had chosen compassion. "Yes, they do," she agreed. "I want to help them."

"How?"

"I don't know," Carrie admitted. "These men need medical help. There are so many of them. I don't know how they are going to get treatment, especially when they get back out on their farms." She frowned. "I'm afraid many of them are going to die from their wounds. The fighting may be over, but they will carry these injuries for the rest of their lives."

"We have the same situation in the North," Captain Jones said, but then he hesitated. "But not the same," he acknowledged slowly.

Carrie shook her head. "No, not the same. The North has resources to help them. I'm afraid these men are going to be another casualty of a war that should never have been fought." Tears filled her eyes. "I'll find a way to help them," she murmured, forgetting for a moment that Captain Jones was beside her. "I will find a way..."

"If anyone can, it will be you, Mrs. Borden."

Carrie turned her eyes to another group of hopeless-looking men huddled on the side of the road. *Yes, she would find a way to help them.*

She turned to the wagon. "Does anyone know what is happening with Chimborazo now?" she asked. "The last I knew, it was being used to treat Union soldiers." The remaining Confederate soldiers had been moved to other hospitals in the city. Surely, all those men would soon be returning home. Couldn't the hospital be used to treat veterans who still had life-threatening injuries and illness?

"Yessum," Eddie replied. "I heard tell they's gonna turn it into a school."

Carrie stared at him, envisioning the acres of buildings and white tents. "A school?"

"Yessum," he said eagerly. "I hear they's gonna make it a school for all the freed slaves, so's they can learn how to read and write."

"That's wonderful!" Rose exclaimed, her eyes as bright as her smile.

"Yes, it is," Carrie agreed, but her mind was still racing to figure out a way to help. She couldn't be a doctor yet, but that didn't mean she couldn't help. She just had to come up with a way.

"You'll figure it out," Captain Jones said.

"Excuse me?" Carrie asked.

"You're figuring out a way to help those men," he said quietly. "If you really want to, you'll come up with a way."

Carrie smiled, touched by his sensitivity. "Thank you," she said softly. "I don't know that I've ever really thanked you adequately."

"For?"

"Saving our plantation," she said. "I know your orders were to destroy it. Why didn't you?"

Captain Jones looked uncomfortable. "I couldn't," he finally said. "The image of you jumping that fence on Granite...I'd never seen such courage. You reminded me so much of my sister. I knew that someone else might come through and destroy it, but it wasn't going to be me."

"I heard your men that night when I was hiding in the woods. You took a big risk of losing their respect."

Captain Jones shrugged and grinned slightly. "What's the good of leadership if you don't get to call the shots sometimes?" His voice grew more serious. "Our goal was to win the war, not randomly destroy things because we could. I tried my best not to lose sight of the fact that we were still countrymen, and would someday have to work together to rebuild what we were fighting over."

"The reason you're coming out here with us now," Carrie observed.

"It's the right thing to do."

"We're almost there!" Rose cried.

Carrie's head jerked up. She'd been so intent on watching the men, and then on her conversation with Captain Jones, that she had lost track of where they were. She caught her breath when they passed the very same hidden trail she had used to escape the plantation three years earlier. Her heart pounded as they turned down the drive between the brick pillars that were miraculously still in place. Captain Jones had sent out a unit a month ago to ensure the house was still standing, but what if something had happened since then? Just because the war was over didn't mean the destruction had stopped.

A quick glance at her father's tense face told her they were sharing the same thoughts.

Granite snorted and began to dance lightly down the drive. Carrie couldn't hold on to her fearful thoughts in the face of his obvious joy. "We're almost home, boy," she laughed. "You can feel it, can't you?"

Granite snorted again and bobbed his head.

Everyone laughed, but the wagon quickly grew silent as they all stared ahead.

Carrie held her breath as they reached the final curve and rounded it.

Chapter Sixteen

A joyous laugh bubbled in Carrie's throat as the familiar house rose up before them. "We're home!" she cried.

Thomas' laughter mingled with hers as he stared at the three-story mansion. It had a soft air of neglect. Its once-gleaming white paint no longer gleamed, but its columns still spoke of strength and pride. He could tell, even from a distance, that the windows were sparkling and clean, sending back shafts of the dying sun as it sank toward the horizon.

"Oh, Carrie..." Aunt Abby murmured. "I expected it to be beautiful, but I didn't anticipate it would be so magnificent."

Rose stared at the house with wide eyes. "I didn't know how I would feel about coming back after so many years."

Carrie knew Rose was remembering the years of slavery, the death of her mother and the fear of their escape. "It's your home now," she said softly. "For however long you and Moses want it to be."

"So many memories," Rose murmured. She smiled brightly. "It's good to be back. It's as beautiful as I remembered."

"My goodness!" June exclaimed. "I've seen some plantations in my days as a slave, but I don't believe I've ever seen a place like this one." Her voice reflected her overwhelmed eyes.

The only two in the wagon that remained silent were Eddie and Susie. Their eyes were locked on the house, their faces tight with anticipation.

Carrie understood. Would Opal and the rest of their family still be there? She wanted to race ahead on Granite, but she held back, wanting to share the homecoming with her father. Suddenly, the door opened and someone stepped out on the porch, shading their eyes to see who was coming. Carrie's face exploded with a smile, and she cried out the exact same time as Rose did.

"Sam! Sam!"

The figure moved slowly to the edge of the porch and peered harder.

Carrie couldn't stand it. She released Granite into a gallop and covered the last hundred yards in moments. "Sam!"

The old man, his ebony face lined and weathered, his eyes still sharp, straightened his bent body as his face wreathed into a broad smile. "Carrie girl? That be you for real, Carrie girl?"

Carrie laughed, vaulted off Granite and raced up the stairs into the arms he held out. "You're safe!" she cried. "You're still here! I was so afraid you would be gone."

Sam shook his head. "I done told you I's be here when you got back," he said simply, as he patted her shoulder. "Who else be with you?" he asked.

Carrie realized his elderly eyes couldn't see as far as they used to. "Come see for yourself!" she said excitedly, taking his elbow and helping him down the stairs, a little alarmed when he didn't insist he could do it himself. Sam had indeed gotten older.

Rose was the first out of the wagon when it pulled to a stop. "Sam!"

Sam made no attempt to hide the tears in his eyes as he caught her close. After a long moment, he held her away to stare down into her eyes. "Rose girl?" he whispered. "I'd given up hope of ever seeing you again." He pulled her back into a tight embrace, looked over her shoulder, and suddenly stiffened to attention and pushed her away gently. "Welcome home, Master Cromwell," he said gravely.

Thomas smiled and leapt from the wagon. "Hello, Sam." He reached out to shake his hand.

Sam stared at it for a long moment, before he slowly reached out and shook it firmly, an odd look on his face. "Never shook hands with a white man before," he said.

"Things have changed," Thomas said. "You are now a free man. Please call me Mr. Cromwell. I find I never want someone to call me 'Master' again."

"Yes sir," Sam agreed faintly. "That mights take a bit of gettin' used to," he murmured, his eyes shining with pride. "I's real glad you be home, Mr. Cromwell," he said. "We done took real good care of eberthin'."

Thomas nodded. "I'm sure you have, Sam."

Susie stepped forward. "Hello, Sam."

Sam's smile, if possible, grew even wider. "Susie! What..." He looked over her shoulder and stopped talking, his face twisted with emotion. "Is that...?"

Susie nodded and reached behind her to pull Eddie forward. "Sam, this is my father, Eddie."

Sam stared at him. "For real? You for real be Eddie?" Eddie nodded, his eyes staring past Sam up to the house. "Are they still here, Sam? My kids? Opal? Are they still here?"

Sam opened his mouth to answer just as the door swung open.

"What in the world is going on out—" The question dropped away as Opal stared down at the group on the porch. "Good Lawd!" she screamed as she stepped out. The first person her eyes rested on was Eddie. Her hands flew up to grab her mouth, and then slipped away as she screamed again. "Eddie! Eddie!" She launched herself forward and wrapped him in her arms. "You're alive! You're alive!"

Eddie was laughing as he nodded his head, his thin face lit with joy. Then he stepped back. "Opal...My kids?"

Opal saw Susie, laughed even harder, and reached her hand out. Holding both of them tightly, she looked around at the group and said, "I hope y'all won't mind if I take care of somethin' real important right now."

Carrie, a beaming smile on her face, nodded. "Go find those kids," she insisted.

Moments later, shrieks coming from behind the house confirmed Eddie and Susie had indeed found Carl, Amber and Sadie.

"I don't believe I've ever experienced a more satisfying homecoming," Aunt Abby said, emotion thickening her voice.

Sam raised his eyebrows as he looked at Carrie. "And this must be your Aunt Abby," he said.

Carrie stared at him. "How could you know that?"

"You done tole me she be the kindest person you ever knew. Them eyes are the kindest eyes I eber did see. Couldn't be nobody else," he said simply as he reached out to take the hand Aunt Abby had extended to him. "Welcome to Cromwell Plantation, Aunt Abby."

Rose laughed with Carrie. "And now you know why we couldn't ever get away with anything when we were growing up here," she said playfully.

Sam snorted. "You two girls got away with more den a body had a right to!" His eyes glowed with love and pride. "It does my heart good to see you back together again."

His eyes lit on June. "Anybody gonna tell me who this pretty girl be? And these two fine young'uns peering over the wagon?"

Rose smiled. "This is Moses' sister June and her son, Simon." Then she nodded her head to the soldiers with Captain Jones. "And that fella who is almost as big as Moses is her husband, Simon."

Sam shouted with joy! "Moses done found them!" he hollered. "He came through here on his way, but I neber did hear what happened."

June smiled. "He found us, Sam. It's a joy to meet you."

Simon swung off his horse and shook Sam's hand. "It's a pleasure to meet you, Sam."

Sam eyed all the soldiers. "Somethin' I should know?" Then his eyes widened as he stared at Captain Jones. "Ain't you..." he asked, his face instantly becoming suspicious.

Captain Jones swung down from his horse so he could look Sam in the eye. "Yes, Sam, I'm the same man who came to the plantation at the beginning of the war."

"The same man who did *not* destroy it," Carrie said firmly. "He is a friend, Sam. He and some of Moses' old unit rode out with us, to make sure we stayed safe. All of these men are going to be working on the plantation to bring it back to life. We're home, Sam!"

"Good Lawd," Sam finally managed. "I done had me some happy days in my life, but I don't reckon none of them match up to this one." Sam's grin faltered as he looked over at little John peering over the wagon. He turned and stared hard at Rose. "Rose girl?"

Rose nodded, her face glowing. "This is John, Sam. We named him for my daddy."

Sam had tears streaming down his face when he stepped forward and took John's hand with something akin to reverence. "Hello, John," he said gently.

"Hi, Sam," John lisped, his eyes watching him solemnly. "Mama told me 'bout you."

Sam laughed. "Well, you just wait, because I got stories to tell on your mama," he announced.

Rose groaned and rolled her eyes.

Sam turned to Rose and took her hands. "My Rose girl is a mama," he murmured. "Your mama would be so proud."

Rose smiled and glanced in the direction of Sarah's grave. "I believe she is," she answered softly.

Just then, Opal and Eddie came around the house with the four kids in tow, all of them laughing and talking.

Opal stepped forward. "I don't have food for everyone, but Eddie tells me you have baskets in the wagon."

"Enough for an army," Carrie declared.

"Well, I just pulled a whole bunch of rhubarb pies out of the stove."

Eddie grinned. "Opal makes the best pies in the world!" he declared.

"I'm glad May isn't around to hear you say that," Rose replied teasingly.

Carrie grinned, her heart almost bursting with happiness. "Opal, we'll help you put everything out on the table inside," she said. "We'll have a huge buffet for everyone." She looked at Captain Jones. "Will you please bring Robert inside? I'll show you where to put him, and then we would like all of you to join us for some supper."

Sam frowned and stepped closer to the wagon. "I's didn't even see Mr. Robert in there." He turned back and looked at Carrie, his eyes troubled. "What be wrong with him?"

"Nothing being back on the plantation won't take care of," Carrie said firmly. She'd been dismayed that he'd not opened his eyes once during the reunion, but she was determined to hold on to her belief that being on

Cromwell would restore him to her. "I'll tell you more about it later. Is the blue room available?"

When Sam nodded, she led the way into the house as the men carrying the stretcher followed her.

******

Aunt Abby found Rose in the backyard staring off into the woods. "Rose?" she asked.

Rose turned to smile at her, but her eyes were far away. She said nothing as she slipped an arm around Aunt Abby's waist.

They stood that way for a long time, simply breathing in the soft air of a late spring afternoon. Pink and white dogwoods bloomed profusely, while purple lilacs perfumed the air. Happy chatter wafted out through the open windows of the house that seemed to glow with joy now that its family had returned.

Aunt Abby smiled as Granite played and cavorted in the pasture, his head and tail lifted high. "That is one happy horse," she said, her eyes shining with pleasure.

Rose nodded. "It's been years since he's been free of a stall or corral."

"Or not being shot at," Aunt Abby said reflectively. She took a deep breath. "It's hard to believe there was a war when you're out here."

Rose nodded. "It's a miracle it survived." She frowned. "Edmund Ruffin wasn't so fortunate."

Aunt Abby strained to remember where she had heard that name. "He was rather a rabid secessionist, wasn't he?"

Rose nodded. "Yes. He was also a brilliant agriculturalist. His discovery of marl as a fertilizer saved the tobacco farms in this region." She frowned. "His plantation was completely destroyed. They even salted his fields so he couldn't farm again."

"Oh my," Aunt Abby murmured. "How could it possibly do any good to destroy someone? No matter what he has done..."

"I'm sure the Union soldiers would call it justice," Rose said ruefully. "The only thing I'm sure of is it has guaranteed his enmity."

Aunt Abby nodded and continued to gaze around. "Could I meet your mama?" she said.

Rose smiled softly, took her hand, and led her into the woods to the very same spot she had been staring at. It took them just a few minutes of meandering down a barely visible path, to reach a small clearing in the woods ringed by dogwoods. Rose dropped to her knees in front of the simple stones that marked the graves for both her mama and daddy.

"I'm back, Mama," she whispered, tears gleaming in her eyes as she reached out to touch the stone. "I'm free—just like we dreamed about. I'm a teacher now, and I have a little boy. His name is John, just like you, Daddy." Her voice thickened. "There is never a day that passes that I don't think about you."

Rose reached up and took Aunt Abby's hand. "I want you to meet Aunt Abby. She's the second most amazing woman I have ever known. Y'all would have loved each other."

"Thank you," Aunt Abby whispered. She walked over to pick a bouquet of wild bluets and glowing pink trillium. She returned and laid them on the ground in front of Sarah's stone and then knelt with Rose.

"You would be so proud of your daughter. She means the world to me—both her and Moses. And little John? He's the spitting image of Moses. Rose is a fine teacher, Sarah, just like you knew she would be. More importantly, she's one of the most beautiful human beings I've ever had the pleasure to know." Aunt Abby paused. "I so wish I could have known you, but I almost feel I do because I know Rose. I suspect she is becoming more like you with every day that passes."

A solemn silence fell over the clearing. A gentle breeze ruffled the tender, young leaves. The setting sun cast a golden glow over everything as birds chirped and sang, an occasional owl hooting its announcement of the coming night.

Rose finally stood, her face and eyes peaceful. "Thank you," she whispered as she took Aunt Abby's hand. "We have to get back before dark. I don't know these woods well enough to navigate them."

"Not like you did the woods where you had your secret school?"

Rose smiled. "I could walk those paths with my eyes closed." Her face took on another faraway look. "I wonder where everyone is. I never heard from anyone again after I got word they made it safely to Canada."

"Freedom means people can reconnect," Aunt Abby replied. "I believe you'll get answers in time."

Rose nodded. "Maybe, but if not, it's enough to know they were free long before a piece of paper said they were."

"Are you okay, Rose?"

Rose turned to gaze at Aunt Abby, not even asking how she knew her heart was in turmoil. "I have no right not to be," she replied.

Aunt Abby cocked a brow and waited.

Rose searched for words. "I'm glad to be here," she began. "I want to support Moses' dream of being a farmer, and this is a good place for John." She paused, knowing Aunt Abby would remain silent. "I'm glad to be here for Carrie," she added, "and it feels a lot like coming home, only better, because now I'm free." She lapsed into silence.

"But..." Aunt Abby finally prompted.

Rose smiled. "But I feel like I'm going backwards," she admitted. "Life in the contraband camp was hard because I was separated from Moses and Carrie, but I loved every minute of teaching. I woke up every day knowing I was going to make a difference." She sighed. "I can close my eyes and see all those faces smiling back at me. I can see the joy when they learned to read, when they figured out how to write. I had the joy of knowing I was preparing someone else to be free."

"And you feel like that's gone," Aunt Abby observed.

"It is," Rose said, trying to keep the sorrow from closing her throat.

"Really?"

Rose frowned now, and turned to stare at Aunt Abby. "What are you trying to say?"

"You're a teacher," Aunt Abby said. "You don't need a school building to teach, but if you want one, why don't you build one?"

Rose started to laugh but then stared at her wordlessly, an idea struggling to free itself from her sorrowful thoughts.

"All you need are people who want to learn," Aunt Abby continued. She paused a moment. "How many kids are about to be on the plantation?"

Rose thought about Eddie's kids and all the children Moses' men would bring with them. "A lot," she admitted. Her mind began to spin as she thought about the neighboring plantations that would need black labor, and the families that would be a part of it. Suddenly, her eyes grew wide. "Aunt Abby..." she said breathlessly.

Aunt Abby laughed. "Now you're seeing the picture," she replied, a broad smile on her face.

"I can start a school right here!" Rose exclaimed.

"And I'll make sure you have all the supplies you need," Aunt Abby said, her eyes dancing with delight. "One letter will have boxes here as soon as you need them."

Rose clapped her hands together sharply, grinning as the sound vibrated through the trees. "And I don't have to do it in secret," she said, almost in awe.

"Never again," Aunt Abby assured her. *"Never again."*

******

Thomas, standing by the fireplace, enjoyed the warmth that started to ward off the night air as he stared around his crowded parlor. Captain Jones' men spilled out onto the porch, laughing and talking easily. He watched as Eddie laughed with Sam, and he smiled when Carrie leaned down to hug Carl, Eddie's youngest, who was now ten years old, and looked like a heavier version of his daddy.

Aunt Abby, who had just strolled into the house, walked over to stand beside him. "You look like a man deep in thought."

Thomas gazed down at her. "Care to go for a walk?"

"I would love to," she replied.

Dusk had fallen when they walked away from the house, skirting the boxwoods that lined the driveway. Granite walked over to have his head scratched and then they moved on, silence falling between them like a comfortable glove.

Thomas felt himself relaxing more and more as they moved toward the barren fields bordered by trees sporting soft green leaves. "Spring is my favorite time of the year," he finally murmured.

"Mine, too," Aunt Abby agreed, thankful for the warmth of her cloak as she pulled it close.

"Are you cold?"

She shook her head. "Not at all. I feel perfect." She gazed around. "I don't know that I've seen a more beautiful place."

Thomas frowned. "It's not what it was." He straightened his shoulders. "But it will be." He reached down to pick up a handful of soil and let it run through his fingers. "The war years have been good for the fields. It's given them time to rest and gather renewed vigor. Next year's tobacco crop will be a good one," he predicted.

"How large is the plantation?"

"Twenty-five hundred acres." Thomas waved his arm. "Everything you can see and more. It's bounded by the James River and by the main road that leads into Richmond." He frowned. "We won't be able to put all of it back in crops for a while. They're simply won't be enough workers because I can't pay them yet, but the time will come when we'll produce what we used to," he said with determination.

Aunt Abby smiled. "I believe that."

Thomas shook his head. "I still can't believe what Opal and the kids have done," he said in disbelief.

Aunt Abby looked at him. "I must have missed that. What did they do?"

Thomas smiled. "I think you were out with Rose. Opal and the kids found some cows and pigs running free in the woods a couple years ago. When the last group of soldiers came through, they managed to hide them before they got here. They had built a pen way back in the woods." He veered off down a road behind the barn. "She said they're back here."

After a few minutes of steady walking, they came out upon a series of pens and sheds. "Well, will you look at that!" Thomas exclaimed. He leaned on the fence and stared at a dozen small calves tottering and playing, while what seemed to be a small army of piglets suckled at their sow's teats.

"Look at them!" Aunt Abby walked forward and held out her hand to a young calf sticking his head through the fence, staring at them with a comical expression. "I'd say you have the beginning of quite a herd."

Thomas nodded. "I do, indeed. It will be enough to keep everyone fed. I'll buy some more, but this is quite a foundation." He glanced around, his expression sad this time.

"What is it, Thomas?"

He hesitated. "I have so much to be grateful for, but it hurts my heart every time I look out into the pasture and see only Granite. I had some of the finest horses in Virginia before the war. I already knew they would all be gone, but I can't get used to seeing empty fields."

"You'll change that," Aunt Abby said with confidence, knowing intuitively that sympathy wasn't what he needed.

Thomas stared at her and laughed. "You're right," he said. "I will change that." He walked away from the pens and continued on down a road through the fields. "It's getting dark," he mused. "Do you mind?"

Aunt Abby looked up at the stars, reveling in the sense of openness. "Not at all. It's been so long since I've been free of the confines of a city. This is simply splendid."

"Did you grow up on a plantation?"

"Yes. My father's home is not as grand as this, but it's beautiful. He has five hundred acres near the Shenandoah Valley." She hesitated. "He was a hard man. I left as soon as I had the opportunity."

"That's not easy for a Southern lady," Thomas commented. "Carrie's independence was frowned upon. I imagine yours was more so."

"Let's just say I'm used to doing things my way," Aunt Abby said demurely.

Thomas laughed and tucked her hand in his arm. They continued to walk, letting silence fall between them again. Frogs and crickets filled the night air as a breeze blew strong enough to keep any spring mosquitoes at bay.

They turned around and began to walk back before Thomas broke the silence. "Tell me more about your plans in Richmond," he invited.

Aunt Abby began by telling him the vow she made to Lincoln as his funeral train rolled by. "I believe building factories is the way I can best contribute. It's what I know best."

"How long do you think it will take to build them?"

Aunt Abby shrugged. "At least six months. Then I have to equip them and train the workers. I suspect it will be close to a year before we're in full operation, but if I can speed things up, I certainly will."

"And you're planning on hiring only black workers?"

Aunt Abby shook her head. "Not at all. I want my factories to begin the integration of society. Factories in the North have blacks and whites working side by side."

"And you believe that can happen down here?"

"By the tone of your voice, you don't believe that is possible."

Thomas shook his head and pressed her hand. "Not at all. Oh, I used to believe that, but I don't anymore." He hesitated. "I just believe it will be very difficult."

Aunt Abby smiled. "I've always believed life is a daring adventure or nothing at all."

Thomas looked down at her. "You are quite unusual."

"So I've been told." Aunt Abby paused for a long moment as she stared out over the fields glowing in the moonlight. "My grandmother was quite unusual as well. While her daughter, my mother, was trying to teach me to be a good plantation wife, my grandmother was telling me not to let anyone mandate my future but me. She warned me it would be very difficult because so many would be threatened, but that I was the only one who should make choices for my life."

"Your mother must have loved that," Thomas said wryly.

Aunt Abby laughed. "She never knew. It was Mamaw's and my secret. She told me that if Mama knew we talked about such things, we would never see each other again. I adored my grandmother, so I never said a thing. I just lived my life as I wanted." She grew silent. "When Mamaw died, I thought my heart would break. I was only eighteen, but I was gone the next week."

"How?" Thomas asked with astonishment, turning to stare down at her.

Aunt Abby shrugged. "I just left. I told one of our slaves I had a trip to make into town. When I got there, I told him he would no longer be needed, handed him a letter to give to my parents, and I left on the next train for Philadelphia."

"That must have been *quite* the adventure," Thomas commented.

Aunt Abby laughed. "I had absolutely no idea what I had gotten myself into," she admitted. "Thankfully, I met my husband very soon after arriving. He was untraditional enough not to be appalled by a young lady on her own. I think I would have loved him just for that, but we shared so much in common. I loved him almost from the day we met. My parents washed their hands of me when I married. My husband gave me security, but he also respected my need for freedom and independence. I believe we made a perfect couple."

"What happened to him?

"He died in an outbreak of cholera," she said sadly. "At least he didn't suffer long." She took a deep breath. "He talked to me about his businesses, but I had no idea how to run them. It took me a while, but I figured it out." Her voice became reflective. "When Charles was dying, he found enough strength to tell me something that carried me through."

Thomas waited quietly.

"He told me I would hit a lot of brick walls in running the business, but the walls would be there for a reason. They weren't there to keep me out. They would be there to give me a chance to show how badly I wanted something—that they only stop people who don't want it badly enough." Aunt Abby paused. "I decided that night that I wouldn't let anything stop me."

"And you haven't," Thomas said admiringly.

"I've had help," Aunt Abby said. "Men who stood by me, when most turned away. People, like Matthew, who offered protection when I was in danger. People who gave me a chance, when others refused to acknowledge me."

"None of us ever accomplished something of greatness alone," Thomas agreed. "I used to think I did...until I realized it was really my slaves who built the plantation. I thought it was me, because I believed them to be my property," he said regretfully.

"And now you know the truth," Aunt Abby said gently.

"Yes," Thomas murmured. "I have much to make up for."

"How long do you plan to beat yourself up?" Aunt Abby asked.

"Excuse me?" Thomas stopped walking and turned to her.

"Did you honestly believe you were doing the right thing when you were a slave owner?"

Thomas stared at her in the darkness. "Yes," he replied slowly, "but that didn't make it right."

"Of course not, but you were not intentionally inflicting harm. I learned a long time ago that no great accomplishment can flourish out of guilt or fear. The only valid plans for the future can be made by those who have the capacity for living now," Aunt Abby stated. "All of us, if we are human, have done things we are not proud of, or that we wish we could undo. We can wallow in the guilt, or we can simply live the best we can in the present."

Thomas let her words sink into his heart and mind. He turned and started walking with her again, feeling the breeze on his face as it ruffled his hair. And as he walked, the truth filtered through. "I'm making myself feel guilty almost as a way of feeling better about the mistakes I made."

Aunt Abby remained quiet.

Thomas knew she was letting him think it through. He felt a moment of gratitude before he ruthlessly examined his thoughts. "I'm wasting valuable energy by focusing on the wrong things," he realized. "I can't go back and change the fact I was a slave owner. I can only live the life I believe in now."

Aunt Abby smiled. "Carrie told me you were an extraordinarily smart man. She was right."

Thomas chuckled as they arrived at the bottom of the steps. Laughter still rang from the house. "It's so good to see the house alive again," he said, his eyes bright with pleasure. He looked down. "Thank you so much for your company. And thank you for helping me clarify my thinking."

"It was my pleasure, Thomas," Aunt Abby assured him.

******

Carrie tapped lightly on the door to Aunt Abby's room. She answered with a soft, rose-colored robe wrapped around her waist, her hair still mussed from sleep. "I know it's early, but I was wondering if I could entice you into a ride."

"Both of us on Granite?"

Carrie laughed quietly. "Captain Jones isn't heading back to Richmond until after lunch. He's enjoying the plantation. He agreed to let you borrow his horse."

Aunt Abby's eyes lit with pleasure. "In that case, I would love to! Give me just a few minutes."

"Meet me in the stables," Carrie said. "Opal fixed us some ham and biscuits to take with us." She pulled out the hand she was hiding behind her back and presented a hot cup of coffee. "I thought this would help," she said teasingly.

Aunt Abby reached for it. "Blessings, my child," she murmured, closing her eyes as she took a sip. Her eyes sprang back open as she smiled over the rim of the cup. "I'll be right with you."

"Sidesaddle?" Carrie asked.

Aunt Abby grinned. "Are you kidding?" She nodded at the breeches Carrie was wearing. "You look absolutely wonderful *and* comfortable. Do you have more of those?"

"Philadelphia society would be mortified," Carrie said with mock horror.

"All the more reason!"

Carrie reached for the pair of breeches she had laid on the chair beside the door. "I was hoping you would feel that way," she replied. "You'll have a much better chance of keeping up with me."

Aunt Abby snorted. "I haven't been in a saddle for years, so I'm going to be sore all over tomorrow, but don't you worry about me keeping up," she challenged.

Carrie laughed. "I'm seeing a side of you I never suspected."

"Prepare yourself for surprises, my dear," Aunt Abby said demurely.

Carrie was still laughing when she let herself out the front door, stopping onto the porch and letting the splendor of the early morning wash over her. She had always been mesmerized by the mornings, but after years of being trapped in the city, the sensation of freshness and openness was almost overwhelming. She closed her eyes and took deep breaths. The aromas of fresh grass and lilacs flowed over her. Listening carefully in the early morning stillness, she could hear bees buzzing as birds welcomed the new day. A snort and whinny in the distance broke through her contemplation. She smiled with anticipation as she ran lightly down the stairs.

Carrie was waiting; both horses bridled and saddled, when Abby strode up to the stables, a warm coat of her father's over breeches tucked into riding boots that must have been her mother's.

Aunt Abby's words confirmed it. "Your father saw me on the way out. He insisted that I wear your mother's boots. They're almost brand new."

"Mother seldom rode. I only saw her on a horse twice. The boots are old, but they're certainly not used." She glanced at Aunt Abby's breeches. "How did Father take your attire?"

Aunt Abby shrugged as she lifted an eyebrow. "He just looked at me over his coffee cup, and told me to have a good time with his non-traditional daughter."

Their laughter pealed through the air as they led their horses over to the mounting block. Within moments, they were headed out to the fields at a brisk trot.

Carrie was impressed with Aunt Abby's seat in the saddle. "I had no idea you rode, until Father mentioned it last night."

"Since I was a child," Aunt Abby responded. She told Carrie about her grandmother. "Her teaching me to ride was another of our secrets. My mother was quite intimidating. I think Mamaw was afraid of her, but only afraid of her ending our relationship. She was determined I would have a chance to live to my potential."

"The reason you have given that same chance to so many others," Carrie said quietly. "You've certainly done that for me. Also for Rose and Moses. I'm sure there are countless others."

"Whatever I have given, has come back to me a thousand-fold," Aunt Abby responded warmly. She looked out over the fields. "It must be absolutely breathtaking when the tobacco crop is ready to be harvested."

"Nothing like it," Carrie agreed. She grinned. "Ready to do more than trot?"

Aunt Abby smiled in return and leaned forward, calling out in delight as the big sorrel gelding she was riding broke into a gallop. "Catch me if you can!" she called over her shoulder.

Carrie laughed, waited a few moments to give her a lead, and then gave Granite his head. She felt pure joy explode in her horse as he settled into a dead run, his long legs devouring the ground. She made no attempt to slow him as he raced past Aunt Abby's mount, making it seem the sorrel was running in place.

Carrie let him run, knowing he had earned it after years of hardship and deprivation. She would have come back to the plantation for Granite if nothing else. She tossed her head as she felt her braid come loose and fall down her back. The rush of freedom flowed through her body, breaking the chains of sorrow and pain that had wrapped themselves around her heart.

Granite slowed as he neared the woods. Carrie turned him and rode back to meet Aunt Abby.

"Goodness," Aunt Abby said with a laugh. "He passed us like we were standing still!"

Carrie laughed. "I even gave you a lead."

"How kind... I'm not sure I noticed."

Carrie laughed harder and headed toward a break in the trees. "I have something to share with you." She was quite sure Aunt Abby knew where they were headed, but she followed Carrie in silence.

Carrie took deep breaths of the fragrant air as they rode forward, the ground carpeted with the vibrant colors of trillium and other wildflowers. She pointed out the wild columbine and the soft purple of the Virginia cowslip trying to hide beneath the fresh new fern fronds. She picked her way around fallen limbs and tree trunks blocking the almost non-existent path, sure of where they were going.

She dismounted in silence when she reached her destination. With Granite tied to a branch, she walked slowly to the edge of the river, her heart surging with an emotion so strong she could barely breathe.

Aunt Abby remained silent as she slipped up beside Carrie and put an arm around her waist.

They stood that way for a long time. Carrie felt the rest of the burden of the war years fall away as she watched the James River rushing by, the waves catching the sun in a glistening tumble of water and sparkles. Each rushing wave seemed to tear away a chunk of heaviness, and send it hurling down the river. Finally, feeling washed clean, she rested her head on Aunt Abby's shoulder.

"It's a magical place," Aunt Abby said softly. "I feel like years were just swept from my heart."

Carrie nodded and stared into her eyes. "That's exactly what I feel," she whispered. "It's been so long," she murmured.

"Thank you for sharing your place with me."

"I've wanted to for so long. I knew you would understand."

Aunt Abby nodded. "You can feel it." She gazed around and walked over to settle on the log Carrie had spent so many hours contemplating life upon when she was younger. "It is a sanctuary."

"That it is," Carrie agreed. She settled down on the log to join her. "I was sitting right here when I finally understood slavery was wrong."

"Then it is indeed a sanctuary," Aunt Abby said with a smile. "You learned to listen to the voice of God here."

******

Carrie and Aunt Abby sat quietly for a long time. Neither felt the need to interrupt the silence that wrapped them in its peace.

Fish broke the surface of the James, leaping up to grab bugs before they landed with a splash. Brightly colored cardinals and blue jays mingled with sparrows and chickadees as they danced through the trees. Squirrels chattered as they raced up and down the tree trunks, springing from one limb to another.

Aunt Abby tapped Carrie's leg and tilted her head silently toward a scene nearby.

Carrie smiled as a doe and a tiny fawn, still tottering on newborn legs, crept into the clearing. The doe froze when it caught sight of them but slowly relaxed, seeming to know there was no threat. The pair slowly picked their way through the clearing and merged into the woods once again.

"Beautiful," Aunt Abby whispered.

Carrie smiled but her heart was simply too full to speak. She suspected it would take a long time for the beauty and freedom of the plantation to completely wipe away the remnants of pain and suffering from the years in Richmond, but each special moment healed her heart a little more.

"How is Robert?" Aunt Abby finally asked.

Carrie sighed, hating to have reality intrude on her peace, but acknowledging one of the reasons she had brought Aunt Abby here was because she wanted to talk about her husband. "No different," she admitted. "I don't see any change at all."

"How are you handling it?"

Carrie frowned. "What do you mean? I guess I was hoping bringing him out here would create a miracle."

"And it still might," Aunt Abby said quietly, "but I'm asking how *you* are handling your husband's illness." She held up a hand when Carrie opened her mouth. "I already know how badly you want Robert to get better. I already know you're doing everything you can."

Carrie was confused. "Then what are you asking me?"

Aunt Abby took her hand. "Carrie, you have been married for two years. Most of that time, your husband was fighting, or in England. You've had so little time together. Now, when the war has finally ended, your husband is critically ill. So the question is; how are *you* doing?"

Carrie shook her head. "How should I be doing?" she asked. "All I can think about is getting Robert well."

"Then you're a better woman than I am," Aunt Abby said bluntly.

Carrie stared at her. "I'm afraid I don't understand."

"You, my dear girl, need to let yourself count," Aunt Abby said firmly. "Carrie, you are a vibrant young woman. I'm assuming you've had sexual relations with your husband?"

Carrie flushed but nodded. "Of course," she murmured.

"And isn't it hard to accept that part of your life seems to be over?" Aunt Abby pressed.

Carrie turned a brighter red, but managed to look Aunt Abby in the eyes. "Yes," she said softly, "but I try not to think about it."

"I'm aware that is the standard way of dealing with things," Aunt Abby replied gently, "but you still think about it, don't you?"

Carrie nodded reluctantly. "I'm afraid it makes me seem very selfish."

Aunt Abby snorted. "It makes you nothing but human, my dear."

"But there's nothing I can do about it," Carrie protested. "What good does it do to think about it?" She turned to stare blindly out over the water, turmoil raging in her heart.

Aunt Abby gently gripped Carrie's chin and turned her head, forcing Carrie to look at her. "Pretending you don't have the feelings will do you no good. They will keep churning in you anyway. I believe it's more about acknowledging you have them and accepting that, for right now, you can't have what you want. It does not mean, however," she added, "that you won't have it again."

"I'm afraid to hope for that," Carrie said. She managed a small smile. "I've never had a conversation like this with anyone," she admitted.

Aunt Abby laughed. "If we're going to be modern, non-traditional women, then we need to be able to talk about sex." She sobered. "My husband was ill for the last two years of his life. It was so difficult to have that part of my life end. My love for him didn't change, but that doesn't mean I had everything I wanted."

Carrie stared at her. "That's how I feel, too. What did you do?"

"I learned how to give my desires to God. I didn't try to pretend I wasn't having them. I didn't tell myself I was selfish for being human." Aunt Abby paused. "And I did what I could..."

"What do you mean?"

"When was the last time you slept in the same bed with Robert?"

"I haven't wanted to disturb his sleep," she replied defensively.

"So instead you have deprived both of you of physical closeness and intimacy," Aunt Abby observed, her eyes kind.

Carrie looked down and back again. "I guess I never thought about it that way."

"It won't hurt Robert to sleep with him, will it?"

"No."

"Would it make you feel better, too?"

Carrie closed her eyes and thought of at least being able to snuggle up to her husband, even if he was no longer the strong, robust man she had married. To feel him close... To lay her head on his shoulder...

"Don't bother to answer," Aunt Abby said. "It's written all over your face."

Carrie opened her eyes and smiled. "I think tonight is going to be a good night."

"For both of you," Aunt Abby predicted. "Even if Robert doesn't respond in any way, the knowledge you are there is still getting through to him." She smiled. "Even when my husband was ill, he always wanted me there."

Carrie nodded. "Are you hungry?" she said suddenly. If she was going to have a conversation like this with someone, she could only imagine it being with Aunt Abby, but now she wanted to think about something else. She jumped up and went to Granite, pulling off the saddlebags. "I'm ready for some breakfast."

Aunt Abby played along. "I'm starving!" she announced. "I hope you have a lot of ham and biscuits!"

Chapter Seventeen

"This is it," Moses said, struggling to tamp down his excitement. There had been too many disappointments in the last twelve days.

It had taken them a week to reach the plantation he thought his mama and Sadie had been sold to. When they reached it, they found the place abandoned, but for one elderly man in the slave quarters. He told them his old owner had sold off all his stock right after the war began and had gone into the city. The owner let him stay because he had no value left. He'd lived out the war by tending a small garden and a pen of livestock. He'd been astonished to discover he was free, but he still didn't plan on leaving unless he had to.

Careful questioning had revealed Moses' mama and Sadie had been sold to another plantation owner further up the river. It had taken a couple days to figure out where it was and another two days to travel there. They'd been gone much longer than Moses had hoped, but he was determined not to give up until he found them.

Moses stared at the weathered sign attached to the dilapidated fence, most sections sagging to the ground. He refused to put words to what he was thinking.

Jeremy did it for him. "It looks deserted," he said quietly.

"Only one way to find out," Moses said shortly, knowing Jeremy was trying to prepare him for more disappointment. "I'm sorry," he said immediately.

"No need to apologize," Jeremy responded. "You've been waiting for this a long time."

Moses nodded, unsure how to say what he was thinking. Yes, he had been waiting for this day for a long time. He so wanted to see his mama and Sadie again. But it was more than that. He had carried the feeling of responsibility for so long. His mind flashed to the day he watched his daddy hang limply from the noose in the clearing, the flames from the bonfire licking at his feet. Moses knew then that he was the man of the family. It was up to him to take care of things. He had labored under the burden for so long. He had suffered so much when he was helpless to keep his family from being ripped apart. Finding his mama and Sadie would fulfill his responsibility. He hoped it would release something in him.

Jeremy turned the wagon down the overgrown, rutted road. They sat silently as the mid-afternoon sun beat down upon them. The only sounds were buzzing insects, chirping birds and the jangle of their horse's harness.

Moses knew Jeremy understood his feelings. Even if the hunt for his family was unsuccessful, he would always treasure these days with his brother-in-law that had brought them so close. No topic of conversation had been off-limits. They had forged a bond that would not have been possible without this time together.

Moses was silent when they rounded a curve and found the burned-out hull of a plantation home. Knowing they were in the path of the Shenandoah Valley destruction, he had anticipated this. Most of the places they passed had been burned.

Jeremy turned the wagon down another narrow road. The Union Army had not burned slave quarters. They tried to talk all the slaves into leaving, but they made sure any that remained behind would have a place to live.

Moses held his breath as they broke out into another clearing ringed by wooden cabins. A quick glance didn't reveal life, but that didn't mean anything. "Hello!" he called loudly.

The only response was more explosive chatter of squirrels.

Jeremy pulled the wagon to a stop and they both stepped down.

"Hello!" Moses called again, his hands clenched tightly as he battled the disappointment rising in his stomach like bile. He would not give up hope.

Jeremy gazed around and began to walk rapidly. "There's a garden back here, Moses," he called.

Moses joined him, looking down at the carefully tended garden. The rows were laid out perfectly and were clear of weeds. "Someone has to be here," he said hopefully. "Hello!" he called again. Only silence echoed back.

He stared around again, noticing that one of the cabins had a different air than the rest of them. He walked over to inspect it more carefully. "Jeremy, there is a rope here for a clothesline," he said excitedly. Something stirred in him...

"It could be anyone," Jeremy cautioned.

Moses nodded but the stirring continued. "I'm feeling something," he murmured, as he stared out into the woods. "It's like I can feel my mama." Five years had not diminished the vision of her strong, loving face. He could still picture her piercing eyes that could always see into his heart.

He stepped out into the clearing, cupped his mouth, and hollered. "Mama! Sadie!"

A sudden rustling in the woods behind him made him spin around.

"Moses?" A bent figure stepped from the woods. "That really be you, boy?"

"Mama!" Moses ran forward and grabbed her in a hug, quickly alarmed by how fragile she felt. He bit back his dismay when he felt how thin she was.

"Moses..." his mama whispered. "I knew you would come." She turned around and called into the woods. "It be safe, Sadie! You's can come on out!"

Moses gasped as Sadie limped from the woods, her eyes wide as she stared at him. She'd been twelve when they were separated. Now she was a beautiful, seventeen-year-old woman.

Sadie was the first to break the silence. "Sho 'nuff took yo time gettin' here!"

Moses laughed out loud and grabbed her up in an embrace. Suddenly, both of them were crying and laughing, their joy ringing through the woods.

Jeremy stood to the side and watched them quietly, a wide smile on his face.

Moses finally stepped back from Sadie. "Why were you two hiding in the woods?" he asked.

Sadie cocked her head. "We tell ya, buts you gots to tell us when you done started talkin' so fancy?"

Moses smiled. "We've got lots of talking to do. I promise to tell you everything." He turned to his mama. "Why were you hiding?"

"We been hidin' for the last year or so," she replied. "Eber since dem soldiers came through and burnt eberthin'." Her eyes darkened. "They's took de rest of Master Jake's slaves wid dem. But not us," she said firmly. "No sirree, dey not take us."

"Why not?"

"I already knew you gonna have a right hard time findin' us," his mama said. "Weren't gonna make it no harder." Her eyes shone with pride. "I known you would find us, Moses. I known you would come get us. I aimed to be here when you did. Ain't no soldier gonna take us away."

Moses stared at her. "Have you and Sadie been here all alone for the last year?"

"Sho 'nuff!" Sadie said. "We been doin' just fine. I's gettin' a little tired of what we's eatin', but it ain't so bad," she said. "They's burned the house, but they didn't touch nothin' in the basement. The Jakes left most of it behin' when dey ran away. We figured we would help ourselves."

"We didn't want to do no wrong," his mama said anxiously. "You think we did wrong, Moses?"

Moses grinned. "I think you're the two smartest females I know," he replied. "Well, next to my wife, of course."

His mama peered into his face. "Yo' wife?"

"Prettiest, smartest woman you ever laid eyes on," Moses said proudly. "I also have a son."

His mama gasped. "My boy done got a boy?"

"Yes. You're a grandmama," Moses said. "Actually you have two grandbabies."

"You done got two fine babies?" his mama asked, her voice almost breathless.

"No..."

"What you talkin' 'bout, boy?" his mama demanded. Then her eyes grew wide and her lips began to tremble. "June?" she managed to whisper.

Sadie grabbed his arm. "You done found June?"

Moses laughed as he nodded his head. "I found her two years ago," he admitted. He told them briefly how his captain had given him a break to go find her. "I knew I couldn't make it up this far, so I had to settle for finding June."

"And she have a baby?"

"His name is Simon," Moses said. "She was so anxious to have it; she had him right on the side of the road in some bushes while I was helping her escape."

His mama laughed, wiping away her tears. "Dat girl was always sho 'nuff in a hurry to do eberthin'!"

Sadie turned around to stare at Jeremy. "Who dis be, Moses?"

Moses smiled and took Jeremy's arm to pull him forward. "This is my brother-in-law, Jeremy Anthony. Jeremy, I'd like you to meet my mama. Her name is Annie. And this is my sister, Sadie.

"It's wonderful to meet both of you," Jeremy said warmly.

Silence fell on the clearing. Sadie was the first to speak. "Dat be a white man," she finally said. "You done marry a white woman, Moses?" Her voice was disbelieving.

Moses laughed. "No. That's quite a story, too. I told you we had a lot of talking to do."

******

The sun was sinking down below the horizon before any of them took a long breath. Stories had flown through the golden afternoon, wiping away the pain of the long years of separation.

Moses stood up, stretching his long legs. "We'll have lots of days to talk. Jeremy and I will sleep in the wagon tonight, and we'll leave in the morning."

"How long it gonna take us to get down south?" Sadie asked, her voice trembling with eagerness. "I sho 'nuff ready to leave dis place!" she announced.

"It should take us about seven days," Jeremy said.

"And you's gonna be our old owner?" Annie asked.

Jeremy smiled. "Only if someone stops us. Moses and I decided to play that little game on the way up. We let people think he is my devoted slave who couldn't bear to be parted from his master, even though he's free."

Sadie snorted.

"My sentiments exactly," Jeremy said with a grin. "It got us out of some tight spots, though. We decided we could be right, or we could do what needed to be done to find you. We'll go back to fighting for equality when everyone is safe on Cromwell."

"Whateber you say, Masser Anthony," Sadie said demurely.

Jeremy laughed. "You didn't tell me your sister was so spirited."

"Who knew?" Moses asked, staring at her. "She was only twelve when I last saw her." He shook his head with amusement.

Sadie tossed her head. "It's only my leg that don't work," she reminded him. "Not my brain."

"And certainly not your mouth," her mama said, pride shining in her eyes. "It done be a real good thin' we be free now. I think Sadie wouldn't have made such a good slave."

Moses laughed again and then sobered. "I wish Daddy could see us all now."

A solemn silence fell on the clearing as they thought of Sam, and of all the slaves who had gone before them, paying a mighty price that had resulted in their freedom.

"I think your daddy knows," Annie said softly. "Dere ain't a day dat goes by, dat I don't talk to your daddy about his chilun. I think he be right here wid us..."

******

"You done lived in dis house, Moses?" Sadie stared up at Thomas' huge brick home. Her eyes had been wide as saucers ever since they reached the outskirts of Richmond, but now they were practically bulging. "And you wasn't no slave?"

Moses shook his head. "No." He had told them the whole story of his relationship with the Cromwells, but Sadie was having a difficult time accepting it as truth. He understood why. She had no point of reference to imagine any relationship between a black and white except as slave and owner. That would change, but it would take time.

Micah opened the door and stepped out on the porch. "Well, ain't y'all a sight for sore eyes," he called. "What you doin' back in Richmond?"

Moses grinned and jumped from the wagon. "I've got some very special people I want you to meet, Micah." He made the introductions quickly.

"You said you was goin' to find them, Moses," Micah said admiringly. "I reckon you did." He held the door open and beckoned to them. "Y'all come on inside, Miss Annie and Miss Sadie. May just pulled some cookies out of the stove. I figured she and I would eat them all, but I reckon I'm willin' to share with Moses' family."

Everyone laughed, but Annie hung back at the bottom of the stairs.

Moses turned back to her. "What's wrong, Mama?"

Annie stared up at the house. "I ain't neber walked in de front door of a white man's house," she said fearfully. "I don't aim to start now. Where de back door be?"

Moses took her arm. "I know it's going to take some getting used to, but things are different now. You're free, but it's more than that. The Cromwells are family," he said soothingly. He could tell by the frightened look in her eyes that she wasn't convinced. "Mama, don't you trust me?"

Annie looked at him then, obviously absorbing strength from what she saw in his eyes. She nodded slowly. "I do trust you, Moses, but..." She stared at Micah. "You be a slave here?"

"No, ma'am," Micah said promptly. "I sho 'nuff used to be, but I's be free now."

"Then what you still be doin' here?" Annie asked suspiciously.

Micah straightened himself proudly. "Mr. Cromwell told us we could leave. May and I decided not to. At least for now. We like it here. We have all the food we need, and we gots a fine house to live in all by ourselves." He grinned, his white teeth flashing against his dark face. "Why would I want to go and leave somethin' like that?"

"You go in and out the front door?" Annie asked.

"No, ma'am," Micah answered honestly. "But that's because I work here. You be comp'ny!" He held the door open and beckoned to her again. "Things ain't like they used to be, Miss Annie. You hold your head up high and walk through this door. You're comp'ny!"

Annie stared up at him and then lifted her head high. "Thank you, Micah," she said graciously, her eyes full of wonder as they all walked into the foyer.

May bustled out of the kitchen, her face flushed from the heat of the stove. She stopped short when she saw the group in the foyer, but her face flashed into a grin when she identified Moses and Jeremy. "Welcome home!" she called. "I didn't know you two was comin'. Don't you know you's supposed to let a body know?"

Moses made the introductions again. "We weren't sure we were going to stop," he explained. "Mama is getting tired after so many days in the wagon. We decided soft beds and some of your good cooking would get us the rest of the way to the plantation."

"Hmph." May sniffed and gazed at Annie. "That boy of yours always known how to get his way?"

Annie smiled, relaxing even more. "Eber since he was old 'nuff to talk," she agreed. "My man used to say our boy had a golden tongue."

"He was right," May agreed. She waved her hand toward the parlor. "Y'all go right on in there. I'll bring out some cookies and lemonade."

Annie moved toward the kitchen. "I'll help," she offered.

May stepped in front of the door. "I'll be happy to let you in my kitchen sometime," she said firmly, "but right now you are guests of the Cromwells." She smiled and pointed toward the parlor. "Go act like guests," she commanded.

Annie acquiesced, a look of wonder on her face. "Guests in a white man's house," she murmured, her eyes shining. "I reckon things are really a-changin'."

Jeremy pulled Moses to the side. "I'm going into town to get the news," he said quietly.

Moses nodded gratefully. He, too, had seen the increased tension on the faces of the black people they passed. He saw the fear shining from their eyes, and he could feel the strain in the air. He was glad his mama felt safe at the Cromwells, but he knew all was not well.

******

Annie sat back in her chair with a sigh. "A body could get used to eatin' like this eberday," she said.

Moses smiled. "I'm going to make sure you have a place where you and Sadie can eat like this every day, Mama. It may take me a little while, but I'll make it happen," he promised.

"You also gonna decide to tell me what's botherin' you?" she asked casually. She laughed when Moses stared at her. "You think I didn't see you and Jeremy whisper together when he got back? You think I couldn't see how your eyes got all tense after the two of you talked?" She smiled, but her eyes were serious. "It may have been five years since I done seen you, but that don't mean a mama forgets her boy—even one that grows up to be a giant."

Moses took her hand. "I don't want you to worry, Mama."

Annie laughed and raised her eyebrows at May, who had come in with a hot pot of coffee. "Ain't that just like a man," she scoffed. "Dey ain't no good at hidin' things anyway, and then dey think we're too stupid to see what's dere."

"I don't think you're stupid," Moses protested.

"Good," Annie replied serenely. "Then why don't you quit playin' your little game, and tell me what's going on? Me and Sadie been takin' care of ourself a long time. A little truth ain't gonna kill us."

May chuckled as she set the coffee down. "I do like your mama, Moses," she said decisively. "You and Mr. Jeremy done look worried ever since he done got back. Since I'm sure it's trouble for the black folk, I do believe me and Micah will listen in, iffen you don't mind?"

Moses looked at Jeremy and shrugged. "I told you they would know," he muttered.

Jeremy nodded. "You were right." He took a deep breath and turned to everyone. "There's trouble," he admitted.

"Boy, life be about trouble," Annie said. "What kind of trouble there be now?"

"The white folks here in Richmond are afraid of how many freed slaves are pouring into the city."

"They just be lookin' for a living," May protested. "They's free now!"

Jeremy nodded. "That's true, but the city doesn't know what to do with them. It was already overpopulated. It's getting worse. The freed slaves are coming because they believe there is opportunity, but there aren't enough jobs for everyone."

"What dey expect dem to do?" Sadie demanded. "They's free now."

"I heard a lot of talk," Jeremy responded. "I may have lost my job, but I'm still white, so it's easy for me to listen."

"Handy," Micah commented laconically.

Jeremy chuckled and then continued, his eyes worried. "The plantation owners are afraid they won't have any labor to put their new crops in, if all the freed slaves come to Richmond."

"Seems to me if they's givin' out jobs with pay dat plenty of us will want to work," Annie observed. Then her voice sharpened. "You still ain't tellin' us what's really goin' on. You tellin' us what it be about, but you ain't saying what kind of trouble there be."

Moses shrugged. "She was always smarter than me," he said. "Tell them what is going on, Jeremy."

Jeremy hesitated and looked around the table. "The military came through and arrested hundreds of blacks for vagrancy. They took them outside the city limits and told them to not come back."

"What?" Micah exclaimed. "They's can't do that to free men!"

Jeremy frowned. "I'm afraid laws are being made up as they go," he admitted. "The North is convinced the only way to revive the Southern economy is to rebuild agriculture. They're also convinced that reviving the economy is the only way to keep everyone down here from starving, and also make their job easier."

"That seems 'bout right," Micah agreed. "Mr. Cromwell talked about how bad the economy is. You worked with all that money stuff, Mr. Jeremy. Don't you think they be right?"

Jeremy sighed. "I agree with the fact that the Southern economy needs to be rebuilt..."

"But they's wantin' to force all the freed slaves back out to de plantations," Annie said.

Jeremy exchanged a long look with Moses. "You did say she was smarter than you," he murmured. He turned to Annie. "Yes, ma'am," he agreed reluctantly. "That's their plan. The army is issuing stringent orders to stop the influx of freed slaves into the cities." He took a deep breath. "I learned today that the army is banning any more freed slaves from coming into Richmond."

"Anybody?" May gasped.

Jeremy shrugged. "The order says anyone seeking employment, family members, or protection against violence."

Silence fell over the table.

"I reckon that be everybody," Micah growled. "They can do dat, Mr. Jeremy? What about us bein' free?"

Jeremy shook his head. "Everything is a mess right now, Micah. I don't think what they're doing is right, but I'm not sure what I would advise them to do differently. Richmond can't support the number of people here now. Letting more in will only make it worse for those who are already here—both white and black."

"But where are the free people gonna work?" May asked. "How they gonna survive now?"

Jeremy spoke carefully. "They are trying to get the freed slaves to go back to work on the plantations."

"You mean dey gonna make 'em," Sadie said flatly. "Just like dey still be slaves."

Moses opened his mouth to protest, but closed it again. His sister was speaking the truth.

"They'll have to be paid," Jeremy said, spreading out his hands. "There are no easy answers," he admitted. "The North wanted the slaves to be free, but they have no real idea how to help them live as free people. Before the war started, there were over two million slaves in the South. The Southern economy has been destroyed by the war, and now there are two million more people who need to have jobs and survive."

Annie nodded. "It's a problem, sho 'nuff," she agreed. "I reckon there be a bunch of us dat don't want to go back and work on another plantation, 'cause it be just like slavery again. In fact, I 'magine there be a bunch that don't want to work at all. Dey's just want to be taken care of now."

Jeremy stared at her with admiration. "Yes, ma'am, that seems to be the crux of it."

"What the plantation owners gonna do to make it right?" she demanded. "If dey be wantin' us to come back to work, what dey gonna do to make it right?"

Jeremy hesitated. "The problem is that so many of the plantation owners lost everything in the war," he admitted. "They still have their land, but they have no money."

"So's dey want all their old slaves to come back and work for nothin'?" Sadie asked. "How dat be any diff'nt from slavery?"

Moses jumped into the conversation. "Thomas has the same problem. We've worked out a plan where he will pay us what he can, and then we'll get a percentage of the crop when it comes in."

Annie nodded. "That sounds like it might work with someone like Mr. Cromwell, but what about owners that don't tell the truth about what dey make? What's to keep them from lyin' and not payin' when the season is done?"

Jeremy smiled tightly. "You do have a way of getting to the core of an issue," he replied. "We quite simply don't have the answers to all those questions yet."

"Ain't gonna be fun findin' them," Annie said. "Gonna be a lot of anger and wrong thin's done on both sides."

Moses stared at her, knowing she was right. "At least you and Sadie will be safe out on the plantation," he said gratefully, confident he was speaking the truth.

His mama gazed at him, her eyes knowing. "Trouble done have a way of findin' even the ones who do the right thing," she said matter-of-factly, "but I believe it be the best place for now."

Moses took a deep breath, suddenly very glad they were going to be leaving the city in the morning. He looked at both May and Micah.

"Don't you be worryin' none about us," Micah said reassuringly. "We knows where to stay out of, and you won't find us on the streets after dark."

Jeremy frowned. "I'm not sure that will be good enough," he muttered.

"We're staying right here," May said firmly. "This been our home all through the war. They's gonna round up the ones who are new, but they ain't gonna bother with us. We're going to stay right here takin' care of Mr. Cromwell's house. If things change, we'll figure it out." She smiled. "That's part of being free, Moses. Freedom don't mean things are going to be easy. It means we get to make our own decisions. This be the first time I've gotten to make my own decisions. This is the decision I'm making. I'll live with what happens."

Moses nodded. "You're right," he said slowly, the truth of her words sinking in. "We all have to live with the consequences of our actions."

Jeremy nodded. "My father used to tell me that the life I'm living right now, is the direct result of every decision I've ever made." He smiled slightly. "I didn't like that very much, especially when I wasn't happy with the life I was living, but I knew he was right." He gazed at all of them. "All of you have had the right to make your own decisions taken away. Your lives were a result of other people's decisions. It won't always be easy, but May is right."

"And you be only part right," Annie said gently. "Slavery took away our right to make certain decisions, but it didn't get to take how we feel or how we think. That be up to us eber time."

Moses thought about Rose's mama. "Sarah used to say that people could make her live like a slave, but they couldn't make her a slave inside, and they couldn't make her hate."

Annie nodded. "She be right. Ain't nobody can control what be inside of you."

Chapter Eighteen

Janie stepped outside into the warm sunshine, trying to find pleasure in the soft rays filtering down through the mighty arms of the oak tree shading their back porch. She listened carefully to the songs sung by cardinals and the grating calls of the blue jays, but they had lost their ability to make her smile. Her attention was caught by a pair of young raccoons staring down at her, but she found no joy. She had almost gotten used to the ever-present unhappiness, but the numbness slowly spreading through her was causing her alarm. Some part of her told her she should care about *something*, but she couldn't seem to identify what that might be.

"Janie!"

She sighed, carefully reconstructing her calm mask, and stepped back into the house. "Yes, Clifford?"

Clifford glared at her, lifting his eyebrows as he took in her slightly disheveled appearance. "Are you ill?" he asked somewhat contemptuously.

Janie shook her head. She hadn't found the energy to care about how she looked that morning.

"I certainly hope you will not embarrass me in front of my friends tonight by appearing like that," he said.

Again Janie shook her head, not bothering to speak. Clifford would find fault with whatever came out of her mouth, so she simply spoke less and less. What was the point?

"There is something we must discuss," Clifford said sharply.

Janie gazed at him, waiting for his latest proclamation. She could tell by the angry glint in his eyes that he was displeased with her again.

Clifford reached in his coat pocket and pulled out a packet of letters.

Janie stiffened, but she held her tongue.

"I thought I told you there was to be no communication with Carrie Borden," he snapped. He didn't bother to wait for a reply. He seemed to know she had nothing left in her to fight him with. He managed a tight smile. "Did you really think I didn't know you were trying to send her letters?"

Janie stared at the floor, her heart racing. Clifford must be holding every letter she had tried to send Carrie since they had arrived. Why had he waited until now to inform her? She tried to find anger for their housekeeper, but she knew Wanda must be as frightened of Clifford as she was. She could feel nothing but compassion for the tiny black woman who came most days to help her keep the house to Clifford's exacting standards.

"Especially now, Carrie Borden can do nothing but hurt us," Clifford said contemptuously. He pulled himself up and lifted his head even higher than the arrogant position he always seemed to maintain. "I have been asked to take a leading role in the Democratic Party here in Raleigh," he announced. "It would do nothing but harm my chances if the party were to know my wife is a nigger lover who has friends like Carrie Borden."

Janie supposed she should say something, but the black cloud of depression weighing her down also held her tongue. All she could do was feel a longing for Carrie, and try to block the images of their years of working and laughing together from her mind. The only bright spot she could find was the understanding of why Carrie had never responded to her letters. She was sure Clifford had another packet of letters Carrie had sent.

Clifford stared at her for a long moment, his anger growing. "You have nothing to say? After all I do for you?"

Janie looked at him, unable to formulate a response, though some part of her knew her silence was only making things worse. She focused on keeping her hands from trembling.

Clifford cursed and took a step toward her. He whirled away and slammed his fist on the kitchen counter. "What good are you as a wife?" he growled. "I thought losing an arm would be the worst thing that could happen to me, but having to put up with a brainless whit for a wife is far worse."

When Janie remained silent, he turned to leave. "I will be back with very important men after work," he said tersely. "Do something with yourself by then, or I will be quite unhappy." With those words, he marched out, slamming the front door as he departed.

Janie remained rooted in the kitchen, wondering what else he could do to show his unhappiness. He had already sucked every bit of life from her with his bitter tirades and humiliation. Embarrassed by the nightmares he still had, he had long ago banished her from his bedroom, but she could still hear the moans coming from his room at night. She knew she should feel nothing but compassion, but there was a part of her that took pleasure in his miserable nights, because in some small way, it made up for her ongoing miserable days.

When she had any energy at all, her thoughts focused on just why Clifford had wanted to marry her—why he had brought her to Raleigh. The end of the war had either radically changed him, or simply released the monster he had been before the war. She may never know the truth, but it didn't really matter. The results were the same. Her life had become one long nightmare that never ended.

She wondered sometimes why her family never came to call, or why they never inquired as to why she never came to visit. She could only imagine Clifford had some kind of hold over them, just as he seemed to have over so many men in Raleigh who treated him with kid gloves, obviously afraid of him.

******

Janie was still standing in the kitchen, in the exact same spot, when Wanda came bustling in thirty minutes later.

Wanda took one look at her and clucked sympathetically. "Mrs. Saunders! What you be standing here in the kitchen for?" She put a hand on her arm and looked up into her face. "You be sick, Mrs. Saunders?"

Janie shook her head. "No," she said faintly, finding some degree of pleasure in the fact that her voice still worked. "I won't send any more letters through you," she said softly.

Wanda tightened her lips, sorrow shining from her eyes. "I be real sorry. I tried to send dem letters."

Janie felt a stirring of compassion. "It's okay," she said more firmly. "I should have known Mr. Saunders wouldn't let them be mailed."

"That Carrie Borden be a good friend of yours?"

Janie nodded, tears pooling in her eyes. "A very good friend," she said quietly. "She is the most remarkable, loving woman I have ever known."

Wanda gazed at her. "I know it ain't my place to be askin', so it be okay if you don't want to be telling, but why Mr. Saunders not want you to write her?"

Janie started to remain silent, but a flickering flame of defiance that had somehow not been stamped out flared in her. "Carrie Borden is a threat to his politics because she firmly believes in the equality of blacks, and is doing everything she can to make sure that happens. We worked together all through the war to help make that a reality."

"Do tell..." Wanda responded, her eyes big as saucers. "But..."

Janie decided to answer the question that remained unspoken. "But why did I marry Mr. Saunders?" she asked, her laugh a bitter bark. "I ask myself that every day. He wasn't like this when I married him, Wanda."

Suddenly, she was desperate to talk to someone. The seclusion Clifford had forced on her since arriving in Raleigh was close to destroying her, but somewhere deep from within the recesses of her heart, she heard a voice saying she was making choices. She was allowing Clifford to destroy her. What if she simply made another choice? What if she *refused* to let him destroy her? One of the last things Carrie said to her in Richmond rose up in her mind. *I can't expect anyone else to have respect for me, if I don't have it for myself first...*

"I see..." Wanda murmured.

Janie's laugh was real this time. She took Wanda's arm and led her to a chair by the table. "I'm sorry," she apologized. "I know you're in a terrible position, but I want you to know it stops today. You're only here to be our housekeeper. I'll not ask you to do anything I can't do myself."

Wanda gazed at her, her dark eyes soft with sympathy and understanding. "You're a fine woman, Mrs. Saunders. Don't let nobody take that from you."

Janie nodded. "He came close," she admitted.

Wanda hesitated. "What you gonna do?"

Jamie opened her mouth, but there was nothing in her brain to create words. "I have no idea," she admitted, but for the first time she saw more than a black hole, and her lungs were free to breathe again. "But I will," she said confidently. "I've got to be smart about it." Her brain raced as she thought through options.

Wanda reached forward and laid her ebony hand over Janie's.

Janie stared at it, realizing it was the first human contact she had felt since leaving Richmond. She put her other hand over Wanda's. "Thank you. You've made me remember I'm not alone, and I'm not helpless."

******

Janie was appropriately attired when Clifford arrived home that night in the company of six other men. He glanced at her briefly before he headed for his study. She appeared with drinks and hors d' oeuvres moments later. She smiled around at the men, hiding her flash of satisfaction when she saw the pleased look on Clifford's face, and then she left, being sure not to pull the door all the way closed behind her.

When she stepped into her hiding place in the darkened guest room, she held her breath, hoping Clifford wouldn't close the door. The rumble of men's voices continued, their words floating clearly to her position. Janie didn't know what she expected to learn, but she was quite sure any future plans would require as much information as possible.

"President Davis has been moved," one man commented.

Janie frowned. *Moved? What had happened to the Confederate president?* She had wondered what the Union response would be to the man who led the rebellion.

"It's been almost three weeks since they captured him down in Georgia," another said. "I guess they were trying to figure out what to do with him."

"I heard he's at Fortress Monroe."

"Yes," Clifford responded, his strong voice rising easily above the rest. "My understanding is that they have shackled him with leg irons and he is allowed no visitors."

Janie had not supported the war, but she felt sympathy for the Confederate president and his family. She wondered how they had caught him.

"It was all over for Davis when President Johnson put a hundred thousand dollar reward on his head. It was only a matter of time. I heard he was going to hide out down on one of the Florida Keys."

"He didn't make it," Clifford said casually.

"You don't sound bothered by our venerable leader being in custody," one of the men observed.

"Why should I?" Clifford asked. "I hated Lincoln, but he was a much better leader and politician than Davis was. If the roles had been reversed, I think we would have won the war. As it is, we have to face the consequences of defeat."

Janie could hear him begin to pace. Only Clifford had that strong, determined tread. She could envision him striding back and forth in front of the brick fireplace.

"We have been left a mess here in North Carolina," he began. "Thousands of men who once held positions of power, authority and influence are now destitute. Their plantations have been destroyed, or their businesses have failed because of the economy. Worthless currency has caused record numbers of foreclosures," he said.

"Not to mention the cost of all the slaves going free," another man said bitterly. "I figure it totals millions of dollars lost in capital investment."

"What's even worse is that the slaves don't want to work on the plantations anymore," another added.

"And we've lost more than thirty thousand men from North Carolina in the war," another growled. "It's even more who were severely wounded or disabled. They can't go back to work."

Janie frowned at those words, but the thought of all the women who had stepped up to support their families during the war and were even now continuing that role, made her feel stronger. Women everywhere were facing challenging times. Hiding in the dark, she straightened her shoulders and lifted her chin. Something had shifted in her that day. She would continue to let Clifford think he was controlling her, but the time would come when she would make her move. The plan was beginning to take shape in her mind.

"We're the only ones who can fix things in our state," Clifford said. "We can continue to growl about what has happened, or we can start changing things."

Janie pursed her lips. She agreed with Clifford's words, but she was quite sure his intention was completely different from any she felt.

"Our political system is in shambles," Clifford continued. "Both the state and local governments collapsed this year."

"We know all that," one man interrupted. "I thought you said you had news for us?"

Janie smiled, imagining the look of fury in Clifford's eyes at the interruption, but she also knew his ability to hide his feelings when he found it advantageous.

"So I did," Clifford said smoothly, just a hint of frost in his voice. "We all know General Sherman left General Schofield in charge of the state when our troops surrendered a month ago." He paused for a moment for dramatic effect before he finished. "That all changed today. President Johnson issued two proclamations. I received notice just as I was leaving my office."

Janie leaned forward.

"The first one Johnson issued is the Amnesty Proclamation. He has offered a pardon to all Southerners, except those in positions of leadership and extreme wealth. They have to swear an oath of loyalty to the United States and the Constitution. In return, they will retain all their property except for the slaves."

"And for those of us who retain any leadership or wealth? What about us? I thought Lincoln's plan was to include everyone."

"It was," Clifford responded. "Our new President Johnson is a lifelong supporter of small farmers and the lower classes in general. He decided to specifically exclude the wealthy classes from the proclamation."

Janie could hear his voice tighten in frustration. Clifford was not wealthy, but she could tell by his voice that he had been excluded from amnesty.

"The president's idea of wealth is quite different from mine," Clifford continued. "Anyone who has taxable property over twenty thousand dollars is not included. There is another long list of exclusions that you can read about in the paper tomorrow, but everyone in this room has taxable property over that amount."

One man snorted. "Perhaps before the war," he protested. "It hardly has that value now."

"According to the government, it does," Clifford responded. "Here's where it gets ridiculous. If we want to be pardoned, we have to make a special application to President Johnson. If he chooses, he will pardon us."

"For fighting for what was rightfully ours?" a man shouted angrily. "We may have lost this war, but that doesn't mean we were wrong!"

"Perhaps," Clifford said thoughtfully, "but I believe there is a part of Johnson that is trying to help us."

"How do you figure that?"

"Because of the second proclamation," Clifford replied. "Johnson has made William Holden the provisional governor of North Carolina."

"How can that be good? Holden has been a Unionist all along. He'll go along with whatever Johnson wants."

"I hope so, because what Johnson wants is a state convention in the fall to restore North Carolina to the Union," Clifford answered. "We'll have to repeal the Ordinance of Secession and ratify the Thirteenth Amendment that made the slaves free."

"What's good about that? We all knew that has to happen."

"Because the convention is going to provide for the election of a new governor, state legislature and US congressman." Clifford paused. "We will reestablish civil government in the state."

A long silence fell on the room as the men pondered his words.

"You mean a civil government of our own choosing?" a man asked, his voice eager but disbelieving. "I didn't think Congress was willing for that to happen until they had punished us long enough."

"Congress isn't in session," Clifford said, rich satisfaction in his voice. "They won't be again until December. My sources tell me President Johnson is moving quickly to create his own kind of reconstruction."

"When is the convention?" another asked.

"It's set to convene on October second," Clifford responded.

Another silence fell on the room while Janie processed what she was hearing. What kind of man was President Johnson? She knew very little about him.

"We've got to move quickly," Clifford said, his voice ringing through the room. "This is our chance to create the North Carolina we all want to live in."

"With the slaves all freed?" one man asked skeptically. "I never thought I'd live to see the day that Negroes are walking around the streets, like they have a right to be there."

"That's why we have to move quickly," Clifford said decisively. "The Negroes may be free, but they still live in the South. We've got to take control of the government so that we can take control of everything."

Janie's lips tightened. Clifford had changed from niggers to Negroes because he didn't want to risk offending these important men, but she knew his heart was full of hatred.

"We've got until October to make sure the Democrats win all the seats and take the governorship," Clifford continued.

"And which position are you running for?"

Janie listened carefully as the shrewd question hung in the air. All of the men listening to her husband were well aware he had brought them there to make an announcement.

"I'm running for a seat in the state legislature," Clifford said confidently. "I believe I can win our district. I promise I'll do everything I can to get the nigg—*Negroes* back out on the plantations so our economy can be revived."

Janie's mouth tightened, knowing what her life would be like if Clifford won that seat. She was already nothing more than a necessary prop to be treated with disdain and humiliation in private, while he pretended to treat her with respect when men came to the house.

"And then the Congress?" a man asked.

Janie could envision the flush of pleasure on Clifford's face.

"If being in that position could improve our fine state, then I would be honored to be considered," Clifford said carefully.

Janie held back her snort and decided it was time to disappear into the kitchen. If she were discovered listening, the rest of the men would simply be puzzled that she had an interest in political talk. Women were gaining more prominence in the North for speaking out about equal rights, but Southern gentlemen had absolutely no comprehension of why women would even *want* such a thing. In spite of the fact the war had destroyed the old Southern civilization, it hadn't yet dawned on most of the men that it was women who had held the South together for four years, and that everything had changed now, because women had changed how they saw themselves.

Clifford, on the other hand, would be furious if he found her skulking around. Janie held her breath as she slipped past the door soundlessly, not breathing easily again until she was perched on the steps of the back porch. As she sat, she let the conversation run over in her mind. And she made plans.

******

"Still no word from Janie?" Aunt Abby asked.

Carrie shook her head, her green eyes worried. "No. I know mail service is not back to normal, but she's been gone for almost two months. I've sent letters every week." She took a deep breath and stared out over the pasture where Granite grazed, his sleek body no longer showing the years of deprivation. "I'm worried about her," she admitted. "I wish I knew what I could do."

"Just be here when she needs you," Aunt Abby said quietly.

Carrie searched her eyes. "You believe she's in trouble?"

"I believe her life has become very difficult," Aunt Abby said carefully. "I also know Janie is a strong and resourceful young woman. I saw that, in spite of the brief time we had together."

Carrie's attention was diverted by a call. She shaded her eyes and looked down the road toward the fields. She grinned as she saw her father and Moses walking together, waving for her attention. "I don't think I'll ever take that sight for granted," she said softly.

"As well you shouldn't," Aunt Abby agreed. "It's taken hundreds of years and a disastrous war to make that happen. It should never be taken for granted."

"By either blacks *or* whites," Rose said, stepping out onto the porch. "Freedom is something that has to be cherished and built on." She waved a hand at Moses. "It's so easy for people to forget the price they paid for something. It's also easy to forget what freedom is."

"And what is it?" Aunt Abby asked.

Rose closed her eyes for a moment and then gazed directly into Aunt Abby's. "Freedom isn't just casting off the chains of slavery. It's about living in a way that respects and enhances the freedom of others," she said thoughtfully. "I believe that being free makes me morally responsible for everything I do."

Carrie laid her hand on Rose's arm. "You've been doing some deep thinking."

Rose nodded. "I'll soon have my own school for free black children. I want to teach them more than how to read and write. I want to help teach them how to live, and I want them to become proud of who they are and where they have come from."

"And you will," Aunt Abby said firmly. She waved at Thomas and Moses. "Hello," she called.

Carrie grinned as her father strode up the stairs, thrilled to see the flushed excitement on his tanned face. She had seen him come alive in the month since they had returned to the plantation. His blue eyes sparkled with life again and years seemed to have dropped away. He was up early every day, going out into the fields to work with the men. She would have been astonished, if she hadn't already seen the changes growing in her father during the years of the war. She knew he was determined to rebuild Cromwell Plantation.

"Hello," Thomas called back. "The last field was planted today," he announced proudly.

"Congratulations!" Aunt Abby cried.

"All in oats and wheat?" Carrie asked.

Thomas shook his head. "We decided to take a risk and plant fifty acres in tobacco. If we have an early frost this year, it will have been in vain," he admitted with a casual shrug.

"But if we have a late frost," Moses added, "we'll be one of the few plantations who can take tobacco to market. The profit margin will be quite high," he added. "The men were all willing to take a risk."

Annie walked out on the porch, her face streaked with flour. "You two need to get a move on," she scolded. "Me, Opal and Sadie done have dinner ready. Do you want it hot?" she demanded.

Moses chuckled. "Didn't take you long to start getting real bossy, Mama," he said teasingly.

"Didn't take you long to forget I runs my own kitchen," Annie retorted, her eyes gleaming with love and pride. "Ain't no war gonna change that!"

Thomas chuckled and continued up the stairs. "We'll be right in," he promised.

Rose took Moses' arm as he moved into the house. "I'm worried about Carrie," she said softly when they got out of hearing range.

Moses glanced down sharply. "What's wrong?"

"She seems to be giving up hope in Robert." Rose paused. "I'm seeing the same look in her eyes that I saw when her mama laid up there in that very room and died."

Moses frowned. "What can we do?"

"I don't know," Rose said helplessly. "Carrie is doing everything she knows to do, but Robert just lies there day after day." She took a deep breath. "I'm angry at him," she admitted. "I don't think there is a thing wrong with his body. He just seems to have given up on living. It's not fair to Carrie."

Moses gave her a thoughtful look. "You have no idea what he went through, Rose. Union soldiers certainly faced challenges, but we always had food and clothing. We were never cold. We were never without shelter. We never lived for months on green apples and raw corn. Battle was terrible, but I used to watch the Rebels and wonder how in the world they kept going."

"Well, he needs to use some of that spirit now," Rose retorted.

"I think Robert is empty," he said slowly. "I've seen it in the eyes of lots of other Rebel soldiers. The war is over, but they can't find a big enough reason to move beyond the darkness that is filling them. They've given up."

"But we have to *do* something," Rose pleaded. "I can't stand seeing that look in Carrie's eyes. She's borne so many burdens for so long. She made sure we were free. She gave me back Jeremy. We have to *do* something."

"I'll do anything in the world for Carrie," Moses said quietly. "You tell me what to do, and I'll do it."

Rose gripped his hand and nodded. "I know you will," she said softly, "but that's the problem. I have no idea of what we *can* do."

"We'll keep watching," Moses promised. "If we think of something, we'll do it."

Rose nodded, her expression saying she was far from satisfied, but aware there was nothing else to be done. She decided to change the subject. "How are the houses coming?"

Moses smiled, his eyes bright with excitement. "They finished another one last night. They are tearing down three slave quarters for each house they are building. They're simple, but they're much better than anything they have ever lived in. In another month, they should have homes for everyone. Once they're done, they'll take a break and go back to the contraband camp for their families. It's helped to know all of them are safe while they are building everything."

Rose smiled. She had been down to the old quarters several days earlier, and seen the tiny cabin her mother had lived in torn apart. She was quite sure Sarah was smiling with delight to see another relic of slavery demolished and used to build something better.

"Your mama and Sadie seem happy," Rose said.

Moses smiled again. "They are," he agreed. "Living in our old cabin is like living in a palace for them. Mama sings while she's in the kitchen, and my sister Sadie has become good friends with Eddie's daughter Sadie. Those two have become inseparable. I never thought I would see my little sister smile like that again," he said softly.

"Sadie Lou is teaching Sadie how to read."

"Sadie Lou?"

Rose smiled. "They decided having the same name was too confusing, so they added on to Eddie's daughter's name."

Moses nodded. "Sadie didn't tell me she's learning how to read."

"She wants to surprise you," Rose admitted. "So do me a favor and act surprised."

Moses chuckled. "I promise. Right now, I just want some of that food Mama was talking about."

******

Carrie waited until dinner had been served before she cleared her throat. "I'd like to talk to all of you about something," she said hesitantly. "Actually..." she swung her eyes to Moses. "I need to talk with just Moses at first."

The table fell silent. Everyone seemed to sense that whatever Carrie had to talk about was important.

Moses swung his gaze to Carrie. "What is it?"

"I wanted to ask you about the family that saved Robert after the battle at Antietam."

"What do you want to know?"

Carrie felt a little foolish, but desperation drove her. "Who were they?"

"Hasn't Robert told you about them?"

"Yes," Carrie admitted, "but I never learned where they live."

Moses took a deep breath and gazed into her eyes. "Why are you asking, Carrie? Tell me straight out."

Chapter Nineteen

Carrie managed a small smile. "You could always see straight through me." She sighed and squared her shoulders. "I want to go find them."

"Gabe and Polly? Why?" Moses' eyes were wide with surprise.

"Because they brought Robert back to life once before," Carrie blurted, all her fears shining in her eyes. "Actually, I know it was little Amber that brought him back to life," she corrected. She twisted the napkin in her hands, and looked around the table at everyone. "Robert is dying. I know the signs. Nothing I do reaches him. The darkness in his heart is swallowing him. I don't want him to die," she cried.

No one spoke for a long moment. Annie and Opal, bringing in a platter of cookies, remained frozen by the door to the kitchen.

"And you think Amber can help bring him back to life?" Aunt Abby asked gently.

"I don't know," Carrie whispered, tears welling in her eyes. She brushed them away impatiently. "But I don't know anything else to try." She gave a tiny moan. "I watched my mama die this way. If I have a chance to save Robert, I have to try."

"I understand," Aunt Abby replied.

"Do you? Do you really?" Carrie whispered. "You don't think I'm crazy?"

"I think you're a woman very much in love with her husband," Aunt Abby replied firmly. "I believe Robert is a lucky man."

"As do I," her father agreed. "What do we have to do?"

Carrie made no attempt to stop the tears from rolling down her face. "Thank you," she murmured. "I know it might not work..."

"But you'll have done everything you could to save him," Moses finished for her. "When do we leave?"

Carrie gasped and reached out to grab his hand. "You'll come with me?"

"You'll have a real hard time finding them without me," Moses said with a chuckle. Then he sobered. "You'll have a real hard time finding them *with* me," he admitted. "I hardly remember that night, Carrie, but I'll do anything in the world for you. You should know that by now. When do we leave?" he repeated.

Carrie turned to her father. "Is it really all right if I take Moses? With the crops all in..." Her voice trailed off.

Thomas nodded. "With the crops all in, this is the perfect time. The men are working together well, and Simon can handle things if I can't be here for some reason. Moses is not needed to get the cabins finished, and the gardens are almost in. I'd say this is the perfect time," he said gently. "You go find them, and see if you can get them to come back here." He paused. "If they agree, they can live in Ike Adams' old house."

When Rose stiffened, Thomas put a hand on her arm and patted it gently. "I can't think of anything more fitting than putting black conductors for the Underground Railroad into Ike Adams' house. Can you?"

Rose chuckled reluctantly.

"I thought about burning it to the ground," Thomas admitted, "but then I figured it would be much better to use it for redemption. Ike Adams was a sick man, but he's gone now. He can't ever hurt anyone again."

"Use it for redemption," Rose whispered. This time when she smiled it was genuine. "I like it."

"And you don't mind if I take your husband away?" Carrie asked.

"I'll miss him every minute he's gone," Rose admitted easily, "but if him going will give you Robert back, I will do nothing but rejoice."

Carrie gazed around the table. "Thank you all," she said softly.

"Do you want me to go along?" Jeremy asked. "I'd be more than happy to."

Carrie shook her head. "Thank you for offering, but no. I overheard you and Aunt Abby talking. I know you've made plans to go and check on the progress of the factory. I want you to do that. Moses and I will be fine."

"He makes a good houseboy," Jeremy said, his eyes laughing.

"Why, yessum, Miss Carrie, I be right willin' to keeps you safe whiles you be travelin'," Moses drawled. "I done know hows to make sure we don't get in no trouble while we travel through the big, bad South."

The table erupted with laughter.

"You know," Rose said when the laughter died away, "it's going to take a long time before we can act like we're free, isn't it?" Her serious question hung in the air.

Aunt Abby was the one to answer. "Yes," she replied honestly. "At least now you have the freedom to fight for it. Just remember you're not the only one fighting. Women all over this country are fighting for equal rights. They want to vote. They want to have their voices heard. In any society, there are people who will have to fight for their rights. It's only when people give up that right that society truly fails."

"I wish no one had to fight," Rose murmured.

"I, too, wish for Utopia, but accepting that it is nothing but a figment of my imagination makes it easier to deal with the fact I don't live there," Aunt Abby replied.

"Utopia?" Annie asked, her eyes puzzled. "What dat be?"

Aunt Abby laughed. "There was a man named Sir Thomas More who wrote a book in 1516 called *Utopia*. It was about a fictional community that was nearly perfect."

"Hmph!" Annie snorted. "Ain't no such thing. Nots as long as they be people livin' in it," she declared. "Ain't no human perfect, so theys can't be nothin' like no perfect place."

"And that is the truth," Aunt Abby agreed. "We can all strive to make our world better, but as long as it's full of people dealing with human nature, it will never be perfect."

"And on that cheerful note," Opal muttered, "here is a platter of cookies. My arm is about to fall off holding them."

Carrie reached for a cookie and took a big bite. "Sugar makes everything better," she agreed, her eyes shining. She looked at Moses. "It's Monday. Can we leave in two days?"

"I'll be ready, Carrie," Moses promised. "I'll do my best to help you find Gabe and Polly, and their kids."

******

Eddie was waiting for Opal in the kitchen when she came back in from delivering the cookies, his lanky form leaning against the butcher block cutting table. "Hi, Opal."

Opal smiled shyly and ducked her head, annoyed with herself for feeling uncomfortable. She had lived with Eddie and Fannie for more than a year in Richmond. Never once had she felt nervous around her cousin's husband. She forced herself to lift her head and smile naturally. "Hello, Eddie. You need something?"

"Just to see if you're done for the night." Eddie hesitated when he looked around and saw the unwashed pots still in the tub. "Or maybe if you could take a little break."

"Something wrong with one of the kids?" Opal asked sharply, reaching behind her to untie her apron.

Eddie shook his head, looking uncomfortable himself. "I ain't doing this right," he muttered. He stood straight and looked her in the eye. "I'd like to take you for a walk, Opal."

Opal stared at him, something fluttering in her stomach. "A walk?" she echoed faintly, jumping when Annie shoved the door to the kitchen open.

Eddie turned to Annie. "It be all right if I take Opal out for a little while?"

"Before the kitchen be clean?" Annie asked. "What you thinkin'?"

"I'm thinkin' I'd like to take Opal to see the sunset over the river."

Opal's eyes grew wide, but she remained silent, unable to think of even one word to say.

Annie eyed Eddie closely. "Sure be a right nice night," she finally said. "I reckon I can finish up in here." She waved a hand at Opal. "Get on with you den," she ordered. "Just plan on me not bein' the first in the kitchen in the mornin'," she growled, her eyes dancing.

Opal managed to nod, and then followed Eddie down the stairs into the backyard. She remained silent as he led the way through the woods, holding back limbs so they wouldn't hit her in the face. When they broke out onto the trail, he moved back to walk beside her, but he seemed content to not talk. Opal was too busy trying to analyze what was happening in her heart, to care if they were saying anything or not.

"Sure is a nice night," Eddie finally said.

"Sho 'nuff is," Opal agreed, relaxing enough to feel the warm breeze and smell the wisteria perfuming the air. She gazed up at the cascading purple blooms hanging from the vines climbing the trees toward the sky. She smiled as she took a deep breath, letting the rich fragrance wash over it. "Sho 'nuff is," she repeated softly as she caught the look in Eddie's eyes.

Nothing more was said until they broke out onto the banks of the river. Opal sucked her breath in as she gazed out at the thick cumulus clouds piled on the horizon. She watched as they shifted from glistening white, to a glowing pink, to a brilliant orange, and then gasped when they were shot through with glorious purple, as the rays of the sun sent shimmering shafts through the canvas. A stiff breeze kicked up white caps on the river, each one reflecting the riotous colors of the sunset as they danced their way out of sight.

"I'm not sure I've ever seen something so beautiful," Opal murmured. As she thought about it, she realized that was true. During her years on Cromwell as a slave, no one had thought of going to watch sunsets. They were too busy working. Her time in Richmond kept her confined to the black quarter or the factory. In the three years she'd been back on the plantation, it never crossed her mind to watch a sunset. "Thank you," she murmured softly.

"If I get my wish, it may not be somethin' you can see that much," Eddie responded.

Opal watched until the dying sun carried the colors below the horizon before she turned to Eddie. "What you be talking about?" she demanded.

"I ain't planning on staying down South," Eddie began hesitantly.

Opal waited, knowing from the pounding in her heart that something important was about to happen.

"I know there prob'ly be hard things in the North, but I don't reckon they's gonna be as hard as they gonna be down here. I's planning on leaving the South, Opal."

Opal stiffened but nodded. She had fallen in love with Eddie's kids like they were her own, but she'd always known they were not really hers. She'd known the day might come when they would leave. "I understand," she replied, determined not to shed a single tear as she held his gaze. "What you planning on doing?"

"That depends," Eddie replied, a strange look on his face.

"Depends on what?" Opal demanded. She'd always known Eddie wasn't one for a lot of talking, but the idea of losing the children made her want to rip the words from his throat, not patiently pry them out.

"On whether you gonna come with us," Eddie replied.

Opal stared at him, again unable to find any words. "You want me to come, so I can help take care of the kids?"

Eddie shook his head. "I want you to come as my wife."

Opal gasped and looked around for something to sit on, sinking down gratefully on a boulder as she stared up at him. "What you say?"

Eddie smiled and knelt down in front of her, his eyes soft. "I won't never forget Fannie," he said, his eyes glistening for a moment before he took her hand, "but I also never met another woman as fine as her until I met you, Opal. You was just my Fannie's cousin for a long time, but I don't look at you that way no more."

Opal locked her gaze with his. "You don't?" she whispered, her heart beginning to dance joyfully. She had been stomping on her feelings ever since Eddie arrived in that wagon. She had been scolding herself as she watched him play with his kids, or help Sam around the house. She loved his kind eyes and his strong heart. Telling herself a hundred times a day that he was her deceased cousin's husband, had done nothing to temper the building feelings.

"I don't," Eddie answered. "Do you think you could ever love me?" he asked uncertainly.

Opal's heart exploded with joy as she reached out her hands to cup his face. "You might better ask if I could ever learn to *stop* loving you. I'm afraid that answer would have to be no."

Eddie sucked in his breath and moved forward to take Opal in his arms. "I love you, Opal," he murmured.

They remained silent for a long time, the sun sinking lower and lower until the sky began to turn a cobalt blue. After the years of loneliness, neither one wanted the embrace to end.

Opal finally pulled back but slipped her hand into Eddie's. "Where are you figuring on going?"

"Depends."

Opal grinned. "Do you ever use a lot of words?"

Eddie smiled back as he shrugged. "Not less I have to."

Opal nodded. "Then I reckon I'll have to do enough talking for the both of us."

"Shouldn't have too much trouble with that," Eddie said matter-of-factly.

Opal snorted but kept grinning. Happiness was exploding in her heart. She was just going to let the wonder of it sink in. "So what does it depend on?"

"On where you want to have your restaurant."

Opal became very still and finally looked up at him. "My restaurant?" she whispered.

"You still want to have your own?"

The happiness grew as Opal nodded her head. "I sho 'nuff do!" she exclaimed. She closed her eyes to think. "I'm thinkin' Philadelphia would be a good place," she said slowly. "Rose and Moses have told me a lot about it. I know things ain't perfect for black folks there, but they told me about other black restaurants."

Eddie nodded. "I've heard it can get real cold up there," he warned.

Opal shrugged. "Ain't no place perfect. The weather might get real cold, but I think the kids will have an easier time growing up there."

"You really love them kids, don't you?"

"Like they were my own," Opal said firmly. "Nothing in the world would make me happier than to be your wife and to keep on being their mama."

Eddie gripped her hand and began to lead her back to the house. "Let's go tell the kids."

******

Gabe slammed open the door to the cabin.

Polly jumped back from the fireplace, where she was stirring a big pot of soup. "Land sakes, Gabe. You about scared the life out of me!"

"Better me din them other scoundrels," he growled.

Polly took a deep breath and pulled the pot off the hook over the fire, placing it on the table. She glanced at Amber and Clint. Both had stopped their studies as soon as their daddy burst into the house. "Is it time?" she asked.

Gabe nodded his head in frustration. "I think it be best," he growled.

Nine-year-old Amber got up from the table and walked over to stand in front of her daddy. "Is it time for us to go away now, Daddy?" Her eyes were full of a sweet trust.

Gabe ground his teeth, but kept his face calm as he knelt down in front of her. "I'm afraid it be, honey."

"How long are we gonna be gone?"

Polly strode forward, knowing the innocent question had no answer. "We don't know, Amber," she said briskly, determined to keep all fear from her voice. "We're just going to go on an adventure and see how long it lasts."

Clint snorted but said nothing. Polly shot him a look of gratitude, knowing he was keeping silent not to increase Amber's fear.

Amber swung her gaze around to her seventeen-year-old brother, who had grown even taller than his daddy. She walked over, crawled onto his lap, and cupped his face in her hands. "Don't worry, Clint," she said soothingly. "You don't need to hide nothing. I know we aren't really going on an adventure."

"How you...?" Gabe started.

Amber looked at him. "I heard you and Mama talking one night when you thought I was sleeping," she confessed. "Don't worry, Daddy. I'm not scared."

Polly stared at her, trying to calm the pounding in her own heart. "You're not?" she asked.

Amber shook her head. "Not a bit. I know you and Daddy will keep me and Clint safe. Then we'll come back to our house."

"How can you be so sure?" Gabe growled, not sure if he was angry or thankful that he was asking this question of his nine-year-old daughter.

"We done had things to be scared about before," Amber answered. "Like when Robert came." Her eyes grew soft with the memories. "Having Robert here scared both of you real bad, but look how good it turned out."

"I guess that be true," Gabe admitted.

"And look how many people we helped by being conductors for that Underground Railroad," she continued earnestly.

Polly sucked in her breath.

Amber laughed brightly. "Did you think I didn't know about that, Mama? You told me and Clint they was just people coming to visit, but I knew back then that wasn't true. I figured it out later when..."

"When you heard them talking," Clint finished for her, pride in his voice.

Amber nodded. "That's right. I learn a lot by listening."

"I'll say," Polly muttered. There was nothing but pride shining in her eyes.

"So where are we going for our adventure?" Amber asked.

Laughter rolled through the cabin as the anger and fear fell off Gabe's heart and mind. He took a deep breath and settled down at the table, waiting until everyone joined him. "We're going to go back into the woods for a while," he said. "I don't know for sure how much danger we're in, but we're not going to take any chances."

"I thought the slave owners were just apprenticing their old slaves' children?" Clint asked. He knew about the state constitutional amendment that passed after Maryland abolished slavery the year before. Slave owners, not knowing how they would run their plantations, decided to enact a pre-war statute that allowed local courts to apprentice black children, even over the objections of their parents.

Gabe shrugged his shoulders. "That's what I thought," he replied, "but I'm hearin' different things. The courts are tellin' black parents they can't have their young'uns back 'cause they ain't got the means to take care of them."

Polly snorted. "How they gonna have the means when they just got free?"

"It's nothing but a way for slavery to keep goin'!" Clint growled.

"Are they comin' after children like us?" Amber asked, bravely trying to control the fear in her voice.

Gabe turned to her and put his hand under her chin, tilting her face so their eyes could meet. "They're not going to get you, Amber," he promised. "Ain't no one taking you and Clint."

Amber took a slow breath, staring into her daddy's eyes. "Okay, Daddy," she finally said. "I believe you. When we leaving?"

"Today."

Polly gasped. *"Today?"*

Gabe nodded. "I heard about some white men roamin' around the country, when I was over at Lee's this morning. He ain't sure what they be up to, but he pretty sure it ain't to no good. If them plantation owners want black children, we couldn't stop them if they come here." He had a brief vision of being beaten or shot if he tried to stop them, knowing they would take the kids anyway. "They could be figurin' they would get a lot of work done before the courts would make them give our kids back..." He knew he didn't need to finish that thought.

Polly nodded and sprang into action. "Clint, you go harness the horses and bring the wagon around front. Amber, you go upstairs and pull down all our bedding. Gabe, you and Clint load up whatever you think we'll need. I'll make sure we have plenty of food for a while." She paused. "If we need more, you can maybe sneak back in at night and get us something."

Everyone sprang into action. Within one hour, they were rolling along a barely discernible road through the woods. People who lived in the area knew about it, but someone skulking around for children to apprentice would never find it. Gabe wasn't taking any chances, however. He had scouted out an area a few weeks ago when he'd heard the first rumblings of trouble. Nothing would keep him from taking care of his family.

Chapter Twenty

Carrie tensed as Moses turned the wagon down the road leading to Sharpsburg, Maryland. "We're almost there?"

Moses nodded. Memories pounded him as they moved down the picturesque road that still bore the scars of the battle almost three years earlier. Trees sporting bright green stood side by side with splintered trunks and patches of barren ground. All he had to do was close his eyes to see the piles of dead and hideously wounded bodies. He gritted his teeth and continued to drive forward.

Carrie put a hand on his arm. "This is terribly difficult for you," she murmured.

Moses didn't bother to deny it. "It would have been just fine if I never saw this place again," he muttered. He shook his head heavily. "I hate for you to see it, Carrie."

"But it's been almost three years," she protested.

Moses said nothing. He had seen other old battlefields. The passage of time seemed to do nothing but reveal more of the horror, as rain and erosion washed away the efforts to bury the casualties of the war.

"Moses!" Carrie gasped, her face white as she pointed toward a field they were passing. "Are those...?"

Moses nodded grimly, staring at the bleached bones sticking up from the ground. Toothless skulls gaped up at them. His mind flew back to the night he had spent seemingly endless hours carrying wounded Union soldiers from the field. He bit back a groan as he remembered having to leave the ones deemed too far beyond help. He still had nightmares of their eyes beseeching him for help, before they dulled into complete hopelessness and then closed to accept the death that was hovering over their heads.

Carrie moved closer to him on the wagon seat and took his hand. She wasn't sure if it was to give or receive comfort. "I'm sorry you have to come back here."

Moses remained silent, gripped by the memories. He wasn't embarrassed when his hands trembled. He hoped he would never become immune to the horrors of battle and death.

Carrie gripped his hand more tightly, certain now who needed the comfort. She could only imagine what had happened here, but Moses had lived it. He had told her very little about the night he found Robert and Granite.

Nothing more was said as Moses drove slowly, trying to piece together the battle so he could identify exactly where he would have been. The Battle of Antietam happened before black troops were able to fight. He served that night as help for the medics. In the bright light of day, with fields and woods trying to cover up the terrible memories, it was difficult to figure out where he had been and where he had gone.

As they drove along with Carrie's hand offering comfort and strength, Moses was able to analyze the battlefield without the pounding of his heart making it impossible to think. Somehow, he separated the landscape from the human faces.

It began to come back.

"They charged through that cornfield there," he muttered. He shook his head to free himself from the memories of thousands falling with the cornstalks, forcing them into the background again as he took deep breaths. "The Rebel soldiers were coming at us from the woods over there." He pointed slightly southwest. "They had crossed over the Potomac River. It was the first battle of the war that was fought on Northern soil," he said almost matter-of-factly.

Carrie continued to hold his hand, but she didn't interrupt. She knew it would help him get through the day if he could detach from some of the emotion and see it through his mind.

Moses pulled the wagon to a stop and stood on the running board to get a better view. The horses snorted, but they stood calmly. Carrie was glad for the blinders Moses had insisted on for the team. She was quite sure the sight of the bones mixed with the smell that remained in the air, would have completely spooked them. She was certain the road being empty was not an accident. Even with the sun shining brightly, she could feel death in the air.

Finally, Moses sat back down and raised his hands to move the horses forward. "There's a road that leads away from those woods. I'm pretty sure that's the one we marched in on before the battle. I would have passed Gabe and Polly's house then. The only thing we can do is try to retrace the route."

Carrie nodded, a sudden peace filling her. "We're going to find it, Moses." She smiled, confidence joining the peace. "We're going to find it."

It had taken them five days of steady travel to reach Sharpsburg. Two days of it had been on muddy roads through a misty rain, but they simply wrapped their oilcloths more tightly around them and pressed forward. They had stopped every night at an inn. It was difficult for Carrie to go inside when Moses was forced to sleep outside in the wagon, but he convinced her they would be safer if he was out there alone—painting a vivid picture of what white men would do to him if they found her in the wagon with him. The best Carrie could do was bring a hot breakfast out to him every morning. They would drive until they found a stream where he could wash up, and then they'd continue to press forward. The five days had brought them, if possible, even closer.

Moses' gaze sharpened as they reached the far side of the cornfield and turned to travel along the edge of the woods. He slowed when he reached an area strewn with stacked logs and timber. "They haven't cleared it yet," he murmured.

Carrie waited.

Moses stared at the field for a long moment and pointed. "That's where I found Robert," he stated hoarsely.

Carrie took a deep breath. "Hobbs told me he built a barricade of logs to keep Robert from being hit by any more bullets."

"That's how I found him," Moses said. "The wall of logs caught my attention. If they hadn't..." He shook his head.

Carrie shuddered, realizing how close she had come to losing Robert, but clamped her lips together tightly.

She felt like she was just as close—only this time, his soul, not his body, had been pierced and shattered. "Let's go find Gabe and Polly," she said. She felt Moses' hand relax as they turned away from the battlefield and began to move further into the woods, away from the grisly remains and reminders.

Miles passed beneath the wagon wheels. Carrie drew in a deep breath of appreciation. "It's beautiful," she said as she gazed out over lush fields vibrant with corn and tobacco. "It's like the war never happened here."

"It happened," Moses stated. "You can't see all the men and boys who will never return here." He stiffened and pulled the horses in.

"Moses?"

"I think..." he said slowly, and then continued to look around. "There is something familiar here," he said as he gazed up a wooded road intersecting the main one they were on.

"If you were marching through, why would you have gone up a side road?"

Moses shrugged. "My commanding officer at the time told me the fella in the house at the end of the road was a conductor for the Underground Railroad. He sent me up to find out if he had any information about Lee's movements."

"Did he?"

"No. He just wished us luck and went back inside."

"That was all the contact you had with him?" Carrie asked with astonishment. "And yet you brought Robert back here?"

"I agree it was crazy," Moses said easily. "I also couldn't deny how strongly I felt it was the right thing to do." He kept staring at the road and turned the team to follow it. "I've got the same kind of feeling now," he muttered. "If it's the wrong road, we'll come back and keep going."

Carrie nodded and peered down the road, silently praying they were about to find Gabe and Polly.

******

Amber walked over and crawled into her daddy's lap, watching as her mama cooked some rabbit over the fire. "This adventure sure is lasting a long time, Daddy."

"Not so long," Gabe replied. "We've only been out here a week." He hoped Amber couldn't feel his frustration. He was sure they were safe, but he was equally sure he had absolutely no idea of what was going on. Were the white men still out there looking for black children to enslave as apprentices? Was their house safe? Would they have a home to return to when the *adventure* was over?

Polly walked over to him and settled down. "I think it's time you go back for some more supplies," she said calmly.

Gabe stared into her face, knowing she was aware of the turmoil raging in him. "You reckon?" he asked, gratitude sweeping through him.

"Yes. We need some more cornmeal out of the root cellar. And I need me some more lard."

"You gonna find out what's going on, Daddy?" Clint asked.

Gabe knew his restlessness was growing as well. His son had made him proud by making sure they had a steady supply of cooking wood and water, and he had devised clever traps to keep them in wild rabbit, but Gabe also knew his son was anxious to get back home to his books. In spite of all that was on his mind, he chuckled.

"What you laughing at, Daddy?" Amber asked.

"Just thinkin' about how much Clint wants to get back to them books." He shook his head in wonder. "I can remember the day he thought learning was just for white kids."

Amber smiled brightly. "Robert changed all that!"

Gabe nodded. "That he did," he agreed.

"He made both of us want to learn everything we can," she continued. "It's just that Clint spends most of his time learning about horses."

"Well, of course I do," Clint responded. "I'm going to spend my life working with them. I figure I should know all I can."

Gabe nodded, glad Clint didn't know how much he had to sacrifice to buy them books about horses for him. "You already know more than anybody else," he said proudly.

Clint shrugged. "I want to be ready when Robert contacts me." His eyes said much more than his casual voice revealed.

"We ain't heard from Robert since he left," Amber said sadly.

"You know there ain't no letters coming through from the South," Polly scolded, though she admitted she had secretly hoped for something since the war ended. For all she knew, Robert was dead. They had saved him, but he could have fallen in another battle.

Gabe polished off his last piece of cornbread and stood. "I reckon I'll go on. I'll be back before dark," he promised. Clint didn't offer to join him, though he saw the desire shining in the boy's eyes. He knew he had to take care of his mama and sister.

******

Carrie leaned forward anxiously as the wagon rounded the final bend in the road and came out into a bright clearing. "Is this it?" she asked eagerly.

"I'll be," Moses said in wonder as he gazed around. "This is it! It's just like I remembered."

Carrie gazed around at the immaculate clearing that contained a small, sturdily-built cabin and a small barn. She smiled as she heard the chickens cackling in their coop and the pigs snorting in their pen. "Someone is still living here," she said with relief.

"Hello!" Moses called. Silence echoed back to them, even after he called two more times. "They must be gone for the day," he said.

Carrie bit back her disappointment. "I guess I couldn't expect them to be here waiting for us," she said casually.

Moses looked at her knowingly. "Expecting isn't the same as wanting," he observed.

Carrie smiled, grateful he knew her so well. "No, it's certainly not." She gazed around the clearing. "Do you think it's okay if we wait under that tree in the shade?"

She reached behind her to pull out the basket she'd had the innkeeper fill that morning. "Want some lunch?"

"The answer to both those questions is yes," Moses responded with a quick grin. "Did you talk that grouchy cook out of some chicken this morning?"

"You doubt my persuasive abilities?" Carrie asked, cocking an eyebrow at him.

"Not even for a moment," Moses assured her. "I was only giving you something to boast about."

Laughing easily, they spread a blanket under the tree and settled down to enjoy their lunch, forcing the grisly remains of the morning from their thoughts.

******

Gabe left the wagon a good quarter of a mile from the house, tied the horses to a tree to make sure they didn't wander, and then made his way quietly through the woods. If there was going to be a surprise, he wanted to be the one causing it. He smiled when he saw the outline of the cabin still standing, but stopped short as he approached the rear of his home and heard laughter.

Coming to a standstill, his mind raced through his options. He finally decided that while running back to their camping spot would make him feel safer, it wouldn't give them any information. He knew no one would find the rest of his family without him leading the way. He wanted some answers.

Picking his way silently, he walked far enough from the cabin to be out of earshot, swung south, and began to walk rapidly. Ten minutes later, he was approaching a small hill that looked over the clearing that housed his cabin. He crept up the hill quietly, crawled behind a large boulder, and peered around its protective bulk.

His eyes widened as he identified a man and a woman on a blanket beneath one of his trees. A *white* woman. And a *black* man. He listened carefully, but he couldn't catch anything they were saying. He could tell they were talking and laughing, but a north-blowing breeze carried their words away.

"If that don't beat all," he muttered. "A white woman and a black man. What they be doing?"

He couldn't imagine a white woman coming after his children. Suddenly, his eyes narrowed. He peered around the boulder again. The man was walking over to get something from the wagon. Gabe stared at him, his mind racing. How many men could be that big? His mind raced back to an unsuspected knock on his door three years ago in the middle of the night.

Making a decision, he slid back down the hill and circled his property again, knowing he could creep up behind the barn without being heard. He was going to be careful, but something pounding in his heart told him the two in his clearing did not represent danger.

Twenty minutes later, he slid in behind the barn, biting back a groan when he realized the sounds from the chickens and pigs were covering most of the conversation. He had to content himself with brief snatches.

"What happens if they're not back before dark?"

"I sure hope Gabe and Polly still live here."

Gabe laid back and tried to work it through. He knew he had never told his name to the giant black man who questioned them before the battle, nor when he left Robert with them. How could he know their names?

More time passed while he tried to decide what to do. Eventually he stood, deciding to simply go with his gut. Everything in him told him it would be all right. He'd survived so many years as a conductor of the Underground Railroad by learning to trust his gut. There was no reason to stop now.

******

Carrie jumped to her feet when Gabe materialized from the woods.

"Hello, ma'am. There be something I can do for you?"

"Hello!" Carrie responded. "Are you Gabe?"

"I reckon that depends on who be askin'," he replied evenly.

Moses swung around when he heard Carrie's voice. A few strides had him back at her side. "It's you," he said with relief.

Gabe stared at Moses. "Yes." He figured it was best to just wait and see what they had to say.

Carrie smiled and moved forward. "I'm so glad to be able to thank you in person," she said softly.

Gabe continued to look at her. "Thank me for what?"

Carrie held her smile. She understood the wariness in his eyes and voice. All Gabe knew was that a strange white woman was at his house with a black man he barely knew. "I want to thank you for saving my husband. I'm Carrie Borden."

Gabe's eyes widened as he moved forward. "Robert's Carrie?" he asked in astonishment.

Carrie laughed. "Yes!" She reached out to grip his hand. "Thank you for saving my husband and sending him back to me."

Gabe relaxed as he stared at his hand engulfed in hers. "Robert said you was real different..."

"That would be putting it mildly," Moses said, reaching out to offer his hand as well. He answered the question he knew was in Gabe's mind. "You can trust her, Gabe."

Gabe shook Moses' hand but continued to stare at Carrie. "What you doing here, Mrs. Borden? I can't imagine you just be passin' through."

Carrie smiled. "That's rather a long story," she admitted. She glanced at the cabin. "When will the rest of your family be home? I'm so eager to meet them."

Gabe hesitated but once again he trusted his gut. "We're hiding out in the woods," he said. "Ain't so safe for black children around here right now."

Moses frowned and looked around. "What's wrong?"

Gabe glanced at Carrie. "I reckon that's a long story, too," he said mildly. He made a quick decision. "I can take you to them if you want." He saw Carrie's quick nod but continued. "It will be a little rough. There won't be no bed for you, Mrs. Borden."

Carrie smiled again. "I tell you what," she replied. "You quit calling me Mrs. Borden, and I'll be happy to sleep in our wagon. My name is Carrie."

Gabe glanced at Moses, received an unspoken message, and nodded. "All right, Carrie," he agreed. Then he looked back at Moses. "Since you're here, could we load some supplies into your wagon? It be a lot easier den carryin' everythin' back to mine."

A short time later, they had arrived at Gabe's wagon. Now they were following him through the thick woods. By unspoken agreement, everyone was waiting until they arrived at their destination to talk.

One hour later, they broke out into the campsite.

Gabe wasn't alarmed when he saw it empty. He figured his family had identified the sounds of two wagons. Uncertain of what that meant, Clint would have taken them further back into the woods to the cave they had discovered. He also knew Clint would be watching. He waved his hand as he pulled the wagon to a halt. "You can bring 'em back, Clint," he called. "It's safe."

Polly, Amber and Clint emerged from the woods, their eyes wide with questions as they stared at Carrie and Moses.

Amber pulled away from her mother and raced forward. She stopped in front of Moses and stared up at him. "You be the man who brung Robert to us, ain't you?"

Moses knelt in front of her. "Yes, I am. And you're Amber."

"I sho 'nuff am! You here to tell me about Robert? I think about him most every day, 'specially when I go back to my secret place. I reckon Robert be one of the best friends I ever had," Amber said excitedly. She pulled at Moses' hand. "Does Robert be okay?"

Carrie knelt down now and looked into Amber's eyes. "Robert told me so much about you," she said quietly. "Now I understand why he loved you so much."

Amber pulled away from Moses and turned to look at Carrie. "Who are you?"

"I'm Carrie."

Amber stared at her hard and a brilliant smile exploded on her face. "You're Robert's Carrie?"

"Yes, I am." Carrie forced back her tears of emotion as she took Amber's hand. "Robert loves you so much."

Amber nodded, her eyes gleaming. "Me and Robert done love each other," she said matter-of-factly. "Now, you gonna tell me how he's doing?"

Carrie smiled. Robert had told her Amber could see straight through any pretense. He had been right. "Could I meet the rest of your family first?" She waited for Amber's nod, and then turned to Polly and Clint. She loved both of them immediately, drawn in by their warm faces and direct eyes.

"Thank you," she said huskily, taking both of their hands. "You're the reason my husband is alive. He's told me so much about all of you." She turned to Clint. "And I have you to thank for saving Granite."

"Granite is okay?" Clint asked anxiously.

"The war was tough on him, but he's back on our plantation as fat and sassy as ever," Carrie assured him.

"Husband?" Polly asked. "So Robert done married you?"

Carrie nodded. "Just after he returned from your home."

"He ain't doing so good," Polly said flatly. "Ain't that why you're here on your own?"

Carrie nodded again, almost relieved to get right to it. "No, he's not doing very well," she admitted. "He's very ill."

"Robert's sick again!" Amber cried. "What be wrong with him?"

Polly took Carrie's hand and led her over to the fire, pushing her down onto a log gently. "Must have taken a lot of days to get here," she said kindly.

Carrie nodded, suddenly feeling the strain of the last week.

"Must have wanted to get here real bad," Polly said. She nodded at Clint. "Get Carrie and Moses some of that soup I made this morning," she ordered, holding her hand up when Carrie started to speak. "You sit there until you get some food in you."

Carrie smiled and waited quietly. Now that they had found Gabe and Polly, she could wait until she had food to make her request. She had thought about it before, but now, sitting here in this wooded clearing, she fully realized how crazy her request was going to sound. She bit back a sigh. She had come this far. She had no choice but to tell them why she was here.

The only sounds were of the birds and crickets as they ate the bowls of soup Clint handed them. Carrie could see the questions boiling behind Clint's piercing eyes, but she had a feeling no one in this family stood up against their tiny mama very often.

"So why don't you tell us what's wrong with Robert?" Polly asked when Carrie took her last bite. "We have lots of things to talk about, but I reckon that's the most important."

Carrie took comfort from her kind eyes. She could imagine her holding Robert up...feeding him spoonful's of soup...wiping his face...wrapping his legs in warm cloths so he would walk again. She took a deep breath, knowing she had made the right decision to come. "Robert came home from the war very sick," she began. She told the entire story, wanting to gloss over some of the details because Amber was listening, but sensing Polly and Gabe needed to hear it all.

"So Robert's spirit has just withered up," Polly said when she was finished.

Carrie nodded. "Yes."

"Do Robert's legs still work?" Amber asked.

Carrie nodded, hoping she was right. He had not stood since they brought him home, but she had no reason to think he couldn't.

"And it's just his heart be sick?" Amber pressed.

Carrie nodded, knowing that somehow this nine-year-old little girl understood.

Amber stood and walked to where Gabe was sitting, listening quietly. "We got to go to Robert, Daddy," she said earnestly.

Gabe exchanged a look with Polly and started to open his mouth. Amber held her hand up. "Don't say no, Daddy. I got to go to Robert. He needs me." She spun around and stared at Carrie. "Ain't that why you're here? Because you believe I can make Robert better?"

Carrie stared at her, not sure how to answer. She finally nodded, her eyes pleading with Gabe and Polly to understand. "I didn't know what else to do," she admitted, her voice breaking as the reality of what she was asking them to do sank in.

Silence settled over the clearing. "That's a lot to think about," Gabe finally said, his voice startling the squirrels into increased chattering.

Carrie nodded again but had no idea what to say.

Moses was the first one to break the silence. "You said you were hiding back here in the woods? Why?"

Carrie was grateful for something to take attention away from her crazy request, but part of her silently screamed for an answer. She clasped her hands tightly as she forced herself to listen.

Gabe explained what was going on with the enforced apprenticeship program.

His explanation shocked Carrie out of her thoughts. "That's nothing but a different kind of slavery!" she said angrily. "It's wrong!"

"That's what we figure," Polly replied, "but we also know there are a lot of strong feelings in people right now. Them plantation owners are scared they gonna lose all their help."

"Meaning they lose their precious plantations," Clint snorted. "I have two friends who got taken back to their old plantations to work. Their folks been trying to get them back, but they can't."

Carrie stared around the fire. "There has to be a way to stop this!"

Gabe shrugged. "I hope so, Carrie, but for right now I just aim to keep my kids safe. And keep me alive to provide for them," he added.

"We ain't gonna let Gabe fight for his kids," Polly said firmly. "They'll kill him and take the kids anyway."

Carrie wished she could refute the statement, but knew it was probably true.

"I think we can help you," Moses said.

Even Carrie turned to gaze at him.

"You can't keep hiding here in the woods forever," he said. "We've got a house waiting for you down at the plantation if you'll come back with us." He briefly described Ike Adams' house. "It's not fancy, but it's big enough for all of you." He looked at Gabe. "You handy with a hammer?"

"I reckon I be. I built our cabin."

"Then we'll hire you to help with the new school we're building. My wife, Rose, is going to be the teacher." Moses looked at Polly next. "That soup was delicious. Are you good in a kitchen?"

Polly nodded, though her eyes said why she'd been there before.

Moses knew she and Gabe had spent years in slavery before escaping. "We can hire you to help as much as you want to." He took a moment to make things clearer. "I've been hired by Carrie's father to make Cromwell Plantation profitable again."

"You're the overseer?" Gabe questioned.

Moses frowned. "That word will never be used on Cromwell Plantation again," he said. "I'm the manager. A group of the men from my old military unit are working with me. Right now, they are building homes for their families. We've planted all the crops for the season— that's the reason I could get away to come with Carrie."

He turned to Clint now. "I understand you love horses."

Clint nodded eagerly.

"There aren't any horses on the plantation now, but it's part of our plan. Robert will need help when he's better."

"What about Oak Meadows?" Clint asked. "Robert told me all about his place in the Shenandoah Valley."

Carrie was the one to answer. "We don't know what is going to happen with Oak Meadows right now, Clint, but I think you'll love Cromwell Plantation. We had a lot of beautiful horses before the war." She suddenly realized what a perfect solution Moses was proposing.

"Horses are horses," he agreed. "I'll work with Robert wherever he is." He smiled, his eyes revealing his excitement. "It don't hurt none that Granite is there."

Carrie realized with a sudden rush of emotion how much Robert meant to this boy, who had initially been so angry when a white slave owner had been dropped into their life. "Thank you," she murmured.

"And me?" Amber demanded. "What about me?"

Carrie turned to her with a smile and took her hand. "And you and I will work together to make Robert better."

"It won't take much," Amber announced.

"Is that right?"

"You need to make sure I got lots of books. I'm gonna curl up with Robert and read to him," she said. "That's what I did before."

When Carrie looked into her glowing eyes full of confidence and compassion, she could almost believe it would be that easy. And who was to say it wouldn't be?

"You got a house for us?" Gabe asked slowly, his eyes revealing how fast his mind was working.

"Yes," Moses assured him. "It's furnished, and we can build whatever else you need. You can leave your house just like it is. It will be waiting here for you when the courts figure out this ridiculous apprenticeship program. I know things are crazy right now, but I don't believe it will always be that way."

Gabe eyed him. "You and me both know it's gonna be crazy for a good long while," he said somberly.

Moses gazed at him, not bothering to refute what he was saying. "We've all got to figure out ways to live until it's not so hard," he finally said.

"Yes," Gabe agreed, "I reckon that's the truth." A long silence passed as Gabe stared into the flames. Then he turned and gazed at Polly. Slowly, he nodded his head. "I reckon we're going to Virginia," he announced.

Chapter Twenty-One

Thomas lounged in his rocker on the porch, relaxing after a long day riding the fields. He took a slow sip of his iced tea as he gazed out over the fields in the distance, thrilled with the bright green spreading as far as he could see. The long, warm days were making the oat and wheat grow quickly. A trip through the fifty acres of tobacco proved his prediction that the fields having rested during the war was going to produce a bountiful crop. If the weather cooperated, the plantation would take a big step toward recovery.

His eyes shifted to the pasture, and he frowned a bit as he looked at Granite. He knew the Thoroughbred was thrilled to be back on the plantation, but it bothered Thomas that he was alone in the pasture. Horses were herd animals. They weren't meant to live in solitude, but it was too soon to add more livestock.

"It's far too lovely a day for frowning."

Thomas smiled when Abby walked out onto the porch and settled down in the rocker next to his. "You're absolutely right. Just minutes ago, I was thinking about how wonderfully the plantation is doing."

"What caused the frown?"

"Watching Granite out in the field alone. When Carrie is here it doesn't bother me so much, but I don't believe herd animals should be alone."

"Why not put one of the cows in with him?" Abby asked, laughing when Thomas gave her an amused look. "Why not? It may not be a horse, but at least it's another living being. I've seen stranger pairs."

"Such as?"

Abby closed her eyes as a strong memory swept through her. "We always had two horses on our plantation, but during a very bitter winter one of them died. The one left behind was inconsolable, but my father said we couldn't get another one until spring. Right after that, one of our sheep became very ill and needed to be inside. Some cows had to be brought in as well, so I decided to put the sheep in with our remaining horse."

"A sheep?" Thomas murmured.

"A sheep," Abby said. "They became the closest of friends. Even after the sheep got better, and we got another horse, the sheep stayed with her friend. Whenever you looked out in the field, it would be the three of them."

"It's worth a try," he replied. "I'll have one of the kids move a cow into the pasture tomorrow." His face grew more thoughtful. "Are you happy here, Abby?"

"I love the plantation."

Thomas paused and looked deep into her eyes. "But are you happy here?"

Abby looked at him for a long moment, knowing he was asking more than he was saying. "I truly love the plantation," she repeated, "but it wouldn't be enough for me all the time. I've become a certified city woman with a passion for business. This has been a wonderful reprieve, and I'm not eager to leave just yet, but the time will come when I'll want to return to Richmond. They should be done clearing the factory site in the next few weeks. I have work to do."

"Yes," Thomas murmured. "Will you join me for a walk?"

Abby rose immediately, wondering what was on Thomas' mind. "Of course."

Thomas tucked her hand in the crook of his arm, but remained silent as they moved down the lane between the boxwoods and passed through the grove of magnolias near the east wing of the house. He still said nothing as they meandered down a well-maintained trail that brought them out on the far side of the horse pasture.

Abby was content to merely walk along, taking deep breaths of the fragrant air and enjoying the soft, warm breeze on her skin. She smiled with appreciation when they finally broke out on the bank of the James River. "How beautiful," she murmured. The late afternoon sun glimmered on the tranquil surface of the river. Swallows swept low over the water to feast on mosquitoes and bugs. "Every time I see this river, it seems to show a different face."

"That it does," Thomas agreed. "I've lived here my entire life, but I never grow tired of the river."

"It would be impossible," Aunt Abby said, settling down on the log Thomas led her to. She looked him directly in the eye. "Why are we here, Thomas?"

"Can't I just take a beautiful woman for a walk?" Thomas parried.

"You most certainly can, but that's not what you're doing," Aunt Abby replied. "There's something you want to tell me that you didn't feel comfortable talking about at the house." Her eyes sharpened. "Did you hear news from Carrie?"

"No," Thomas said quickly. "I haven't heard anything since the telegram arrived three days ago telling us they were on the way home with Gabe and his family. I expect they will arrive tomorrow."

Aunt Abby relaxed, watching as a blue heron skimmed the surface of the water, its long legs stretched out behind it. "Do you know their wingspan is almost seven feet across?" she asked.

Thomas chuckled. "A city woman who knows the wingspan of a blue heron?" he teased. "You are quite an unusual woman."

"My grandmother gave me a thirst for knowledge very early," she replied easily. "We studied all kinds of things. I found it was a habit I continued, because I love knowledge."

"And do you believe knowledge is power?"

Abby cocked her head. "No," she said thoughtfully. "I've learned over the years that knowledge on its own is nothing. I've also discovered, however, that the *application* of useful knowledge is very powerful indeed."

Thomas chuckled again. "And you like being powerful."

Abby raised an eyebrow. "Does that disturb you?"

"Certainly not. I find it makes me love you even more."

Abby took a deep breath. "Excuse me?"

Thomas laughed. "This wasn't quite the way I envisioned telling you this, but then I hadn't determined *anything* about how I was going to talk to you. I simply decided to bring you to my favorite place on the plantation since I was a boy. I was hoping something brilliant would come to me."

Abby couldn't think of a thing to say, but she was intensely aware of a warm feeling spreading through her body. "I see..." she finally murmured.

Thomas sat down next to her on the log. "Obviously, I have no idea how to tell you I'm wildly in love with you. I've heard so much about Carrie's Aunt Abby over the last several years. The moment I laid eyes on you, I knew why she loved you so much. What I didn't expect was my own immediate attraction to you. The last weeks have done nothing but make my feelings grow stronger."

Thomas paused, but Abby just continued to listen, her gray eyes fixed on his. He wished he could read her thoughts, but for once they were not running rampant across her face. He took a deep breath and continued. "The last few years have taught me that nothing lasts forever. They've also taught me to take advantage of every moment of joy, because life also holds so many moments of sorrow. You can't escape the sorrow, but too many people don't latch on to the joy."

The shrill cry of a hawk split the evening air as the frogs began their nightly chorus.

"Aren't you going to say anything?"

"Not yet," Abby said lightly, but what was shining in her eyes gave him the courage to continue.

"I've thought so much about what I want since I arrived back on the plantation," Thomas continued. "When my wife died, all I wanted to do was escape Cromwell and go to Richmond. When the war ended, all I wanted was to leave the city and return home to rebuild." He took a deep breath. "It's so good to be back home..."

"But it's not enough," Abby observed.

Thomas smiled slightly. "No, it's not. And I'm not even going to ask you how you know that. I've learned those gray eyes never miss a thing." He smiled as a fish jumped out of the water and landed with a splash. "I love it here with all my heart, and it's been exactly what I've needed, but I believe there is so much more I'm meant to be doing. I no longer have a taste for politics, but I am discovering a growing passion to rebuild my state."

"How?"

Thomas shrugged. "That remains to be seen. It also remains to be seen if I share the next season of my life with someone."

"Someone who fell in love with you the first day, and has been wondering ever since how she was going to explain to your daughter what had happened?"

Thomas sucked in his breath sharply and turned to grasp her hands. "You mean it, Abby?"

"You should know by now I don't say things I don't mean," she chided.

Thomas laughed. "That I do." He put his hands on her shoulders and stared into her eyes. "I just want to look at you," he murmured. "I never believed I would love again. To be loved in return by such an extraordinary woman is almost more than I can comprehend."

Abby smiled and raised her hand to rest it on his cheek. "I've lived alone for so many years. I had determined that was going to be my lot in life and I found so many ways to make peace with that, but after a few days with you, Thomas, I knew I would never have peace with it again."

Thomas grasped her hand and pulled her close. "I love you, Abigail Livingston," he said tenderly. "Will you do me the great honor of becoming my wife?"

Abby laughed, tears glistening in her eyes. "Only if you don't make me wait a long time, Thomas Cromwell," she responded joyfully. "If nothing else, the war taught me not to take anything for granted, and to make the most of every moment."

"We will marry soon," Thomas promised as he claimed her lips.

When he raised his head, he couldn't take his eyes off her face. "Could we marry tomorrow?" he asked hopefully.

Abby laughed, feeling like a girl again. "I think your daughter might have something to say about that."

Thomas interpreted the sudden look in her eyes. "My daughter," he said, "is going to be the happiest woman in the world when she hears the news. She loved her mother, but she has thought of you as her mother since the first summer you met. I know you are aware of how much she loves you, but I'm not quite sure you fully comprehend how much you *mean* to her."

"I know that Carrie is the daughter I always dreamed of having," Abby said softly. "To join my life with such an amazing man, and also have Carrie part of the package, is more than I ever hoped for."

Thomas shifted so he could pull her tightly into his arms as they gazed out over the river. The setting sun had turned the water from a rich blue to a shimmering gold. Fireflies flitted through the trees along the banks, glimmering like dancing stars in the rich, leafy canopies. Whippoorwills sang into the night as owls joined their hooting to the orchestra.

"It's amazing to think we will always have this to come home to," Abby said with a sigh. She turned to Thomas and laid her hand on his face. "I would love it if we could build the factory together."

Thomas looked at her for a long moment. "I don't know much about the factory business."

"Perhaps not," Abby said casually, "but you are an astute businessman, and you are wonderful with people. You also know what we are going to be up against here in the South."

"I may be a hindrance," Thomas said hesitantly. "There may be a lack of trust because I served in the Virginia government during the war."

"And you may also be the perfect example of a man who is adjusting to changes in the South as we fight for equality," Abby replied calmly.

Thomas chuckled. "This seems to be something you've thought about."

"Let's just say that I spent some evenings alone with my fantasies of a perfect life."

Thomas laughed loudly and kissed her again. "I can't believe I'm so lucky!" He pulled Abby to her feet and swung her around the beach in a slow waltz. "Did Carrie ever happen to mention I love to dance?"

"That *might* have been part of my fantasy," Abby murmured as she wrapped her arms around him and lost herself in his warmth.

******

Early the next morning, Granite's frantic neighing announced Carrie's arrival, even before they heard the wagon wheels.

Everyone was waiting on the porch when the wagon pulled to a stop.

Thomas was the first to step forward. "Welcome to Cromwell Plantation," he said warmly, reaching forward to grasp Gabe's hand, as Moses swung Polly down from the wagon.

Clint and Amber both jumped down and stood with their heads back, gaping at the house. "This be your house?" Amber gasped.

Thomas nodded and stooped down in front of her. "It is," he said. "Do you like it?"

"I think it's the prettiest house I ever did see!" Amber replied. "Are you Carrie's daddy?"

"I am. And I bet you're Amber."

"Yes, sir. I be Amber." She looked up at the house again. "Where is Robert?" she demanded. She turned to Carrie. "Robert be needing me," she said.

Rose stepped forward. "You two go ahead. I'll take care of getting everyone settled."

Carrie opened her mouth to protest, but Aunt Abby walked up and put her arm around her waist. "We'll take care of everyone," she assured her.

Carrie nodded her thanks and looked at Aunt Abby more carefully. "You look very happy," she murmured. "Has something happened?"

Aunt Abby smiled. "Go up to Robert. We'll talk later."

Carrie felt the urge to press for more information, but Amber tugged at her arm.

"You need to take me to Robert," she said again, her eyes glowing with intensity.

Carrie gripped the girl's hand, waved to the group, and walked in the door. "He's upstairs," she said, leading Amber up to the landing, aware her young eyes were wide as saucers as she looked around the house.

"Robert sure do have a beautiful house to be sick in," Amber announced.

When Carrie reached the door to the bedroom, she knelt down and forced Amber to look at her. She had done her best to prepare the little girl, but she didn't know how Amber would handle Robert's appearance. He didn't look even remotely like the man she had waved goodbye to two years earlier. "Amber..."

Amber sighed and reached up to pat Carrie's face. "I know you be scared for me to see Robert, but you don't need to be. I know he's been real sick, and I know he don't look good. That don't change how I feel about him," she insisted. "You came all the way up to our home to get me so I could be *with* him, not stand out here in the hall," she said.

Carrie was torn between amusement and amazement as she looked in Amber's glowing eyes.

"As long as the books I asked for are in his room, I got everything I need," Amber announced.

Carrie took a deep breath and opened the door, glad the windows were open as she had directed. At least Robert's room didn't smell like a hospital ward. A breeze blew in through the screened windows, bringing in the fragrance of early summer. Fresh flowers filled a vase on his nightstand, which also held a heavy load of the books Amber had requested.

Amber hung back as Carrie walked over to Robert. "Hello, dear," she said gently.

If Robert heard her, he didn't acknowledge it. His eyes remained closed, but the change in his breathing told her he was awake. Her sigh was a mixture of sorrow and frustration. She was aware of Amber watching them with almost terrifying intensity. Carrie hoped she had not brought the cheerful, believing little girl all this way just to have her heart crushed.

"Robert, I have someone here to see you," she said, wondering how she was going to tell him.

"Hi, Robert!" Amber said brightly, moving past Carrie to clamber up onto the bed. "I knows you be awake, Robert. You used to play that game at home, too. Don't you know I knew it every time you was playing?" She patted Robert's cheek gently. "You ain't got nothing to be afraid of, Robert. I'm here to take care of you now."

Robert stiffened and slowly opened his eyes, confusion and disbelief racing across his face. "Amber?" he croaked.

Amber laughed with delight. "That's right, Robert. It's me! Carrie came all the way to get us."

"Us?" Robert managed, swinging his eyes to Carrie's face.

"All of us," Amber continued. "Daddy and Mama be here. Clint, too!" She reached forward to hug Robert and then snuggled in next to his side and reached for one of the books.

"You can go on downstairs now, Carrie. Me and Robert gonna be just fine."

Carrie stared at them, unsure what to do. She could tell Robert was confused, but there was also something in his face she hadn't seen in a long time. When she finally recognized it as the first glimmerings of hope, she felt a jolt of her own hope that had been lying dormant.

Amber smiled at her sweetly and looked down at the book in her hands. She frowned when she looked at it, but then gazed up at Robert. "This book gonna have some big words I don't know," she confided. "You'll have to help me with them. You can do that, can't you, Robert?" she demanded.

Carrie felt another surge of hope when she saw him nod slowly, his eyes fixed on Amber's face. Carrie was smiling when she pulled the door closed.

******

Thomas was alone on the porch when Carrie walked downstairs, humming lightly. "Where is everyone?" she asked.

"They've all gone to get Gabe and Polly settled," Thomas responded.

Carrie started to nod but caught something in his eyes. "*All* of them?"

"All of them," he confirmed. "They should be back by lunch."

"I see," Carrie murmured, gazing into her father's eyes.

Thomas chuckled. "I told her you would see right through it."

Carrie stared at him now. "See right through it? What is going on?" She felt no alarm because her father's eyes were so peaceful, but she could tell he was hiding something.

"I wanted to talk to you alone," he admitted. "I suggested to Abby that she talk everyone into helping Gabe's family get settled."

Carrie settled down in the rocking chair and waited.

Thomas walked to the edge of the porch and stared out over the pasture. Granite was pressed up against the fence, waiting for Carrie to come out to see him, but he had to talk to her first. He just wasn't sure how to start the conversation.

"Aunt Abby says it's best to say things straight out," Carrie suggested in an amused tone.

"Yes, that sounds like her," Thomas said. "That's one of the reasons I love her."

Carrie nodded, and then suddenly gasped. "What did you say?"

Thomas smiled and moved over to sit down in the chair next to hers. "I said, I love Abby," he stated. "I've asked her to marry me. Do you mind?"

Carrie could only stare at him, the words swirling through her mind. "Aunt Abby? You're marrying Aunt Abby?"

"I am. Do you mind?" Thomas repeated, suddenly anxious. "I've loved her from the first day I met her," he admitted. "Being out here together has been wonderful. I talked to her last night, and she has agreed to be my wife."

Carrie heard the words as if from a tunnel.

"Carrie?"

The words coming from her father's mouth finally congealed in Carrie's mind. "You're marrying Aunt Abby?" Joyous laughter rang from her throat. "I do believe that's the most wonderful news I've ever heard!" She jumped up and pulled her father to his feet, throwing her arms around him. "Congratulations, Father. You are about to marry the most amazing woman in the world!"

Thomas joined in her laughter as they held each other. "Thank you, Carrie," he managed.

"*Thank you*? How could you not know I would be deliriously happy? For both of us," she said joyfully. Suddenly, she frowned.

"What is it?"

Carrie chose her words carefully. "I have no problem at all believing Aunt Abby has fallen in love with my dashing, handsome, charming father. I'm having a harder time seeing her happy living on the plantation." She looked at her father apologetically. "I could be wrong."

"You're absolutely right," Thomas said. "That's why we're moving back to Richmond."

Carrie gasped and reached behind her for the rocker as she sank back down. "Perhaps you should tell me everything."

Thomas told her of their decision to return to Richmond to build the factory together.

"You'll be happy there?" Carrie asked.

Thomas nodded. "The plantation will always be my home, but I want to be involved in rebuilding Virginia. Moses doesn't need me here to run the plantation. He proved that years ago. I know it will be in good hands."

"How soon will you be married?" Carrie asked, her heart pounding with anticipation.

"The middle of July."

"Six weeks?" Carrie gasped. "There is so much to do!"

"Not so much," Thomas disagreed. "Both of us have been married before. We don't need a fancy ceremony. We've both learned to savor the joys of life when they come. We don't want to wait."

"Of course you don't," Carrie agreed, her eyes dancing with delight. "But you absolutely will not keep me from making it a grand celebration," she said firmly. "If six weeks is what I have, it's what I have. I'll handle everything."

"Abby said that's how you would respond," Thomas replied with a chuckle.

"You have an advantage now, Father."

"And what would that be?" he asked in amusement.

"You now have a way to understand your hard-headed daughter, because you are about to marry an older version of her. Abby will always know what I am thinking and feeling because we're so much alike."

"Score one for the men of the Cromwell family!" Thomas said dramatically. "We need all the help we can get."

Carrie froze, her head lifting as she listened intently. "Father!"

"What is it?" Thomas asked, suddenly panicked.

Carrie smiled and pressed her hand to his arm. "Listen!"

Thomas stood quietly, hearing nothing but a soft murmur coming from the window over their heads. And then he heard what had made Carrie freeze. A broad smile covered his face as the sound wafted through the window again, lifted gently on a breeze that knew it carried a precious cargo.

Robert *laughed*.

******

Carrie was waiting on the porch when the wagon rolled back up.

"They're all settled," Aunt Abby called as everyone unloaded. "I believe they'll be quite comfortable in the house."

"I believe they will," Carrie agreed, and then she clapped her hands together loudly. "I have an announcement to make," she said, stepping to the front door to call Sam, Opal and Eddie out onto the porch.

She waited until everyone had assembled, then walked down the stairs to take Aunt Abby's hand. She led her onto the porch to stand beside her father. Carrie turned back to the group with a huge smile on her face. "I would like to announce that my father is going to marry Abigail Livingston on July fifteenth!"

Clapping and cheers broke out as the group surged up onto the porch to shake hands and give hugs.

Aunt Abby finally broke away from the group and took Carrie's hand. "Come with me," she said firmly, leading her down the stairs and out to the pasture fence where Granite was waiting to rub his head against Carrie in greeting.

"Hello, boy!" Carrie laughed, wrapping her arms around his neck. "I missed you, too." She lowered her voice to a whisper. "I want you to meet your new almost grandmother," she said.

"*Grand*mother?" Aunt Abby echoed in a choked voice. She laughed so hard she doubled over, gasping for breath. When she finally straightened, she grasped Carrie's hands. "I know I don't have to ask you if you're okay with this. I can see it all over your face. Thank you."

Carrie threw her arms around Aunt Abby. "You can't possibly know how happy I am right now," she said. "I have thought of you as my mother from the first summer I was with you. I loved my own mother, but you gave me something no one ever had—someone who totally understands me." She held up her hand when Abby started to speak. "You have encouraged me, challenged me, and made me believe I could do anything. There have been so many times I have wished for someone to come along who would be worthy of your love—someone who would love you the way you deserved to be loved."

Aunt Abby stared at her. "I had no idea," she finally said.

Carrie smiled. "I can hardly wait to see you marry my father!" she exclaimed. "Of course, part of it is purely selfish, because now I have the assurance we will always be a part of each other's lives."

"As if there was any doubt," Aunt Abby snorted.

"Perhaps not, but it will certainly be handy to have you both in the same place," Carrie said smugly. "And now, perhaps we should join the party," she continued. "Opal and Annie are fixing a very special celebratory dinner. We're going to have a grand picnic on the lawn so that everyone can attend."

"Oh, Carrie," Aunt Abby murmured. "I never thought I would have a family again. Now..." Her voice thickened as she looked toward the porch where Thomas was standing, smiling as he watched them. "I have Thomas. I have you. I have Rose, and Moses, and John. And Jeremy..."

"All blood-related," Carrie said softly. "You are marrying into quite a colorful family," she teased.

"I can't imagine anything more wonderful!" Aunt Abby said happily.

Carrie started toward the house and then stopped. "What should I call you now? I can't exactly call you Aunt Abby. And Rose and Moses can't call their half-brother's wife their aunt," she murmured.

"I've thought about that already."

"And...?"

"I think everyone should just call me Abby." She laid a hand on Carrie's face. "I'll be your friend...I'll be your mother...I'll be your partner in flaunting tradition," she added with a laugh. "We are going to have a most wonderful time!"

"I do believe you're right...Abby," Carrie said, suddenly throwing her head back in another joyful laugh. "Let's go have a party!"

******

There was not a crumb of food left on the tables when the sun sank behind the trees. Amber, finally convinced she must let Robert get some rest, had played so hard she was now sleeping contentedly in her father's lap. She and ten-year-old Carl had immediately become friends, running around the yard with shouting laughter. There was some confusion about another child with the same name as Eddie's thirteen-year-old daughter, Amber. Eddie solved it by insisting they call his little girl by his nickname for her—Sunny.

Gabe was deep in conversation with Eddie, and Polly had bonded instantly with Annie and Opal.

Eddie stood and walked to the center of the yard. "I reckon I gots an announcement of my own," he said solemnly.

"I was wondering how long we would have to wait," Abby said.

"What you be knowin'?" Eddie asked with wide eyes.

"Only that I can tell someone with a secret when I see one," Abby replied. "Also that I can recognize someone in love when I see them," she teased, a broad smile on her face.

Carrie turned to gaze at Eddie. "In love? What have I missed?"

Eddie grinned shyly, and stepped over to pull Opal to her feet. "Miss Abby be right. Opal and me are getting married."

He waited until the cries of congratulations faded away and then held up his hand again. "But that ain't all," he said, his eyes shining with determination. "We's won't be here much longer. Me and Opal be taking the kids up to Philadelphia to start a restaurant," he announced proudly.

"That's wonderful!" Abby cried. "Opal, you're such a fabulous cook. I know it will be a success."

"We're sure hoping so," Opal said shyly, her eyes shining with excitement.

"May I invest?" Abby asked.

Carrie wanted to leap up and hug her. No one had asked how Eddie and Opal were going to *start* a restaurant, but she knew it had been on everyone's mind.

"Invest?" Opal asked.

"Why, yes," Abby answered casually. "I've been wanting to invest in some black businesses in Philadelphia, but it's important to be careful. Not everyone has what it takes to succeed in business. I pride myself on being an astute businesswoman. I believe investing in your restaurant would be a wise business decision."

Carrie exchanged a look with her father, knowing he was thinking the same thing she was. Abby was offering to help in a way that preserved Eddie and Opal's pride and self-respect.

Eddie nodded slowly. "We would like that, Miss Abby. We'll make you proud."

"Oh, I'm absolutely sure of that," Abby responded. "We'll figure things out in the next few days."

"We're planning on leaving in a couple weeks," Eddie said. "We want to get there and get things established during the summer."

Abby nodded again. "If you don't already have a place in mind, I have some suggestions for where a restaurant may be most successful."

"We'd welcome any of your help," Opal replied, her eyes shining.

Moses' little sister Sadie stood suddenly. "I'm going with them," she announced.

Moses and Annie looked up with startled expressions on their faces.

"What's that you're sayin', girl?" Annie asked sharply.

"Mama, I know you be happy here on the plantation," Sadie said earnestly, "but it ain't what I want. I'm almost eighteen. I done been a slave on a plantation all my life. Whether I'm free or a slave, it still feels the same to me. I want to go north and live in Philadelphia with Eddie and the rest," she said firmly. She turned to Moses. "Please tell Mama I'll be okay."

Moses turned to Eddie with a question on his face.

"She's welcome to come with us," Eddie assured him. "She done tole me what she wanted, but I tole her she have to talk to you and her mama. She and my Sadie Lou be close as sisters. We'll take good care of her."

Moses turned to his mama and waited quietly, understanding the mix of pride and sorrow on her face.

Annie nodded slowly. "I done had you all these years, Sadie. I knows you have a heart and mind too big for a plantation. I'll miss you somethin' fierce, but I reckons you should go to Philadelphia."

Sadie gave a cry of gladness and flung herself in Annie's arms. "Thank you, Mama!"

Carrie watched quietly.

"What are you thinking?" Rose asked, leaning closer to hear what she said.

Carrie looked at her with a smile. "Just thinking about how things always change. Life is nothing but change..." She looked toward the woods. "And I'm thinking about something your mama told me during one of the countless times I was afraid of the future. She asked me how I could possibly know what I was capable of, if I didn't embrace the unknown." Her eyes misted over. "Her words gave me the courage to move forward."

"All of life is an unknown," Rose agreed. "Even when I think I know where I'm going, suddenly the road shifts and I'm going in a different direction. The only way I can make sense of it is to plunge down the new road and make the most of it."

Carrie narrowed her eyes. "Has something in your road shifted?"

Rose laughed and pressed her hand. "I'm glad I like it that you can see right through all my secrets. Otherwise, you would be quite annoying."

Carrie smiled but waited quietly.

Rose took a deep breath and stood to her feet. "Eddie and Opal aren't the only ones with an announcement," she said.

Chapter Twenty-Two

Moses smiled and moved to stand next to Rose, his eyes glowing.

"Moses and I are going to have another baby," Rose announced, quickly holding up her hand to stop the congratulations. "I've also decided to start a school right here. Thomas has agreed to donate some land out on the main road, and the American Missionary Association has agreed to send supplies. The school will be ready before the end of the summer. I'll teach all the kids and adults on Cromwell, but it will also be open to everyone on the other nearby plantations. My goal is to make sure every black person has an education," she said.

Carrie jumped up and grabbed her in a tight hug. "I'm so excited for you," she said. "And so very proud! And at least this time I get to see you pregnant!" she laughed.

"One more," Jeremy said, standing beside Rose. "As long as everyone is telling their plans, I guess it's my turn."

"You're leaving, aren't you?" Rose asked sadly.

Jeremy nodded. "Yes, but I'm not going far," he assured her as he turned to everyone. "Thomas and Abby have asked me to run business operations for the new factory. I have accepted. I'll be moving into the city in the next few weeks to oversee the building of the new factory, but I'll be back for the wedding," he said.

Rose joined in on the congratulations, but Jeremy pulled her aside as soon as things settled down. "What's wrong?"

Rose frowned. "I'm sorry. I don't mean to spoil your happiness."

"You're not spoiling anything, but I know when something is bothering you." He led her over to the edge of the woods. "Talk to me."

"I'm worried about you," Rose admitted. "You were already fired from your job. What if people decide to make it hard for you?"

"Then I'll be one of many," Jeremy said quietly as he took her hand. "I've thought about it, Rose. Whatever is going to happen is going to happen. I can't run from trouble any more than you and Moses can."

Rose opened her mouth to say that wasn't true, but closed it again. Jeremy had made the decision not to deny his black heritage. All she could do was stand with him. "I understand," she said softly. "I'm proud of you. The new factory is going to make such a difference for so many people."

Jeremy's eyes glowed with excitement. "Yes, I believe it will. Change is coming, Rose, whether people want it or not. My father used to tell me that change is hard for people because they overestimate the value of what they have, and they underestimate the value of what they may gain by changing."

"And they almost always hate the messenger of change," Rose said ruefully. "Even if the change is a good one, people seldom are appreciated when they are introducing a new order of things."

"You're one to talk," Jeremy stated. "Do you think the white people in this area are going to embrace a school for blacks on the main road?"

Rose shrugged. "They'll have to get used to it," she said bluntly. "So we're both doing the same thing," she acknowledged. "I still get to worry about you."

"And I get to worry about *you*," Jeremy responded playfully. His eyes became serious. "All we can do is walk the path we are given to walk. You'll be creating ripples of change in one area. I'll be creating ripples in another. Hopefully, the time will come when all the ripples join together to create a world better than the one we are living in."

******

Thomas found Moses standing next to the big oak tree staring out over the fields. "Is everything all right?" he asked quietly.

Moses nodded and took a deep breath. "Just trying to settle everything in my mind," he replied. "There are a lot of changes happening all at the same time."

"Does that bother you?"

Moses shook his head firmly. "No. All of life is about embracing change. Sometimes you just have to take a moment to let your heart catch up with all of them."

Thomas smiled. "Has it caught up enough to take on another one?"

"What do you have on your mind?" Moses asked.

"Care to join me for a walk?"

Moses fell into step beside Thomas, catching Rose's eye and nodding to let her know everything was all right. He remained silent, choosing to let Thomas take the lead to reveal what he wanted to talk about.

Thomas waited until they had walked well into the fields. He stopped on the raised road of oyster shells and looked out over the undulating green of the oat and wheat sprouts.

"They've grown a lot in the two weeks I've been gone," Moses said, his heart surging with joy as he looked at the evidence of all their hard labor. "You're going to have a good crop."

"*We're* going to have a good crop," Thomas corrected him. He swung around to look into Moses' eyes. "You know I'm going to be going into Richmond when Abby and I marry. We'll build the factory together. I'll always come back, but, at least for now, Richmond is going to be my home."

Moses nodded but continued to wait quietly.

"The plantation is going to be left in your hands," Thomas said.

Again, Moses nodded.

"Does that bother you?"

Moses smiled now. "Should it? The better question might be; does it bother you?"

"Not a bit," Thomas said. "You're a competent farmer, you understand how to care for the land, and you're a capable leader. I couldn't leave Cromwell Plantation in better hands."

"I'll take care of it like it was my own," Moses assured him.

"That's good, because half of it will be."

Moses took a step back now and stared at Thomas. "What?"

Thomas smiled. "That's what I brought you out here to talk about. I want you to take over complete management of Cromwell Plantation in exchange for half-ownership."

Moses stared at him, unable to find a single word in his head that would make sense, if it were to come out of his mouth.

"There will be a lot of things to take into consideration, but we'll figure them all out. The first one is that neither of us can sell our half to anyone else, and if you ever decide to leave, your half will revert back to me."

Moses could still only look at him, trying to make sense out of what Thomas was saying.

"You are a competent farmer," Thomas continued, "but you will need training in business and management practices. Carrie handled the books before. I will want you to do that now. I will use the next six weeks to mentor and train you, and then I will be close enough to give you help moving forward."

The words began to seep through Moses' brain, but the best he could do was begin to smile.

"Should I assume your smile means you are pleased?" Thomas teased, his blue eyes dancing with fun.

"You can assume that," Moses said, grateful he still remembered how to talk. He took a deep breath. "That's a big decision, Thomas."

"Yes, it is," Thomas agreed. "You can be sure it was not one I made lightly. The world is changing. *I* am changing. My life is changing." He paused. "The plantation will always be in my family, but I will not be here to oversee it. Carrie is here for now, but I know the time will come when she will follow her passion to be a doctor."

"I hope so," Moses murmured.

"It's just a matter of time," Thomas said. "Robert is going to get better. When he does, I know he will encourage Carrie to follow her dream."

Moses frowned. "Why not Robert?" he asked. "He grew up on a plantation. He knows how to run them. He's your son-in-law."

Thomas nodded thoughtfully. "That's true," he agreed, "but Robert is not a farmer. He is a horseman. I hope the day comes when Cromwell once more has a strong lineage of horses, but that will remain separate from the plantation itself. My hope is, when that time comes, you and Robert will be able to work together," he added. "But that will be a choice you will have to make." He turned to gaze out over the fields. "Abby has told me of the history you and Robert share. You've had a chance to deal with it, but is it true Robert still has no idea it was your father who killed his father when you were boys?"

"It's true," Moses said heavily. "I had hoped to talk with him after the war, but his illness has made that impossible."

"Yes," Thomas murmured. "We're going to let time play it out. My gut tells me everything will be okay, but Robert still owns Oak Meadows. When he is well, he may decide to return there."

"Does Carrie know?"

Thomas nodded. "Yes. I told her today after I told her about marrying Abby." He answered the question in Moses' eyes. "She's thrilled."

Moses finally allowed the smile dancing in his heart to explode on his face. "You won't be sorry, Thomas," he said.

"I already know that, Moses, or I wouldn't have made the decision," Thomas replied, an answering smile on his face. Then he sobered. "I also realize things may change for you. If they do, we'll talk it out and determine a solution."

"Change for me?"

"Rose is like Carrie," Thomas stated. "She has huge dreams. Right now, she is choosing to be content teaching at a school here on the plantation, but do you really think that will satisfy her forever?"

Moses blew out his breath. "No."

"Abby has helped me understand a lot of things. Our country is changing, especially for women. Or maybe I should say that women are changing."

"*Have* changed," Moses stated.

"You're right," Thomas admitted. "I fought it for a long time, but having Carrie as a daughter has made me face things most Southern men are not willing to even think about. More and more women are going to go to college. They are going to want careers." He paused. "They want freedom to vote and have a voice in the United States."

"That's a ways down the road for me and Rose," Moses said, "but I'm in complete agreement that women should be able to vote." He reached down and picked up a handful of oyster shells from the roadbed, watching as they dribbled through his massive fingers. "I know Rose won't be content here forever," he admitted. "But since she's about to have another baby..."

"You're hoping she'll be all right with staying here for a while."

Moses tossed down the rest of the shells and looked Thomas in the eye. "Rose and I have been apart far more than we have been together over the last four years. The same is true for Robert and Carrie. All I want is time to be with my wife and have a family. But that doesn't mean I don't want my wife to have everything she wants—just like she wants the same for me." He turned to stare out over the fields again. "Running this plantation is everything I've ever wanted, but that isn't more important than Rose having what she wants, too."

Thomas put his hand on Moses' shoulder. "You'll figure it out because you love each other," he said firmly. "Both of you are going to have to bend. Learning to bend almost *broke* me," he said ruefully. "I'm counting on you being smarter than me."

"Me, too," Moses said wryly.

Thomas laughed. "Just be willing to change. I could never have guessed the roads I have gone down in the last four years. I can't say the journey was always fun, but I'm grateful for the destination." He paused, a wide smile on his face. "All I know is that, at this very moment, I have made an agreement for you to become the co-owner of Cromwell Plantation. I don't know about you, but that's plenty to keep my brain cells occupied for a while."

Moses shook off his thoughts about Rose as he let Thomas' words sink in. "I do believe I would like to go talk to my wife," he said, a wide grin splitting his face.

******

Abby was waiting at the foot of the stairs when Carrie came down with the breakfast tray. "How is Robert this morning?"

Carrie smiled. "Peaceful," she said. "Absolutely peaceful." She had a look of wonder on her face. "I wasn't sure I would ever see him this way again. He and Amber have read two books already." She glanced down at the tray. "And he ate a full breakfast," she murmured, raising shining eyes to Abby's face. "I do believe my husband is going to get well," she whispered.

Abby stepped forward to give her a warm hug. "Your determination to bring Amber here has made all the difference."

Carrie stared at her. "Yes...but I was so frightened that it wouldn't work. I almost didn't do it."

"But you did," Abby said gently. "My grandmother asked me one time to think about who the happier woman would be—one who braved the storm of life and truly lived, or one who stayed securely on shore and merely existed."

"I already know how you answered."

"Yes," Abby mused. "Her words gave me the courage to leave home, but there have been other times I've forgotten my answer and decided to stay on shore. I've always regretted not taking risks. I hope I've learned to never do that again, but life can be scary. It's easy to want to hunker down where you believe it's safe."

Carrie listened carefully. "I have a feeling all of life is nothing but taking one risk after the other."

"At least it's never boring," Aunt Abby said lightly.

"Do you feel you're taking a risk by marrying my father?"

Abby looked at Carrie closely and smiled. "Any time you choose to love, you risk not being loved in return. You risk pain and you risk failure. But..." She laid her hand on Carrie's cheek. "...the risk must be taken, because the greatest hazard in life is to risk nothing."

Carrie took a deep breath and nodded. "You're right," she said softly.

"Why are you thinking about this so much?"

Carrie held her gaze. "Because if Robert doesn't get better, I have nothing else to try. I keep thinking about things that will bring him back to life. I know he thinks constantly about Oak Meadows. He talks about it during his dreams."

"And if he gets well and wants to go back to Oak Meadows?"

Carrie flushed. "Sometimes I wish you couldn't see through me quite so easily." She shook her head. "But I wouldn't want it any other way." She walked over to the open front door and stared out over the pastures. "I don't know," she answered. "I don't know that it would bother me. Father doesn't need me here anymore. And I..." Her voice trailed off.

"Have you been reading the medical books Dr. Strikener sent?"

"Every night. I am learning so much. The advances in medicine during the last four years have been astounding."

"And your desire to become a doctor is growing more intense," Abby finished for her.

"Yes." Carrie knew it would be pointless to deny it. "I'm content for now, but..."

"You're thinking it will be helpful to spend your time worrying about what is going to happen, or not happen," Abby said bluntly.

Carrie stared at her and then laughed. "And *that* is such a pointless way to destroy an otherwise glorious day."

"One could look at it that way," Abby murmured, her eyes shining with empathy. She took hold of Carrie's hands. "I don't know how the path of your life is going to unfold any more than I know how my own path will unfold. All I know for certain is that I can trust God to walk it with me. I also know that if I spend more time listening than I do talking; I'll figure it out as I go along. I believe you will, too, Carrie."

The sound of carriage wheels had them gazing down the road.

"We're not expecting anyone," Carrie said as she walked out to the end of the porch. She shaded her eyes so she could see against the glare of the sun. Suddenly, she let out a whoop of joy and dashed down the stairs. "It's Matthew!" she called over her shoulder.

Abby, Rose, Jeremy, Opal, Sam and Annie had joined the welcoming party by the time Matthew brought his carriage to a halt.

Carrie breathed a sigh of relief when Matthew jumped out of the carriage with a smile. Whatever had happened on the *Sultana* had not left a visible injury. He looked like his old self. "Matthew!" she cried as she launched herself into his arms. "You're finally here!"

"And staying for a while, unless your father gets tired of me and kicks me out."

Carrie looked closer and saw the strain in his eyes that went with his tired voice. "You will never be kicked out," she said. "Father has been as anxious as I have been for you to arrive."

Abby stepped forward to wrap Matthew in a warm hug. "My dear boy," she murmured. "It is so wonderful to see you."

Matthew grinned and hugged her back. "I'm surprised you're still here," he admitted. "I thought you would be back in the city by now."

"I prefer to wait until Thomas can join me," Abby said lightly. "I find I want to start my new life in Richmond with my new husband by my side." Her eyes danced with fun.

"What?" Matthew exclaimed as he looked at Carrie.

Carrie laughed. "It's true! Father and Abby are getting married on July fifteenth, and then they will be leaving the plantation to build the factory."

"Well..."

Rose launched herself forward. "You can hear all about the love affair later," she proclaimed as she kissed him on the cheek. "I think the woman who is about to be a mama again should have gotten the first hug."

Matthew laughed loudly. "Congratulations! Another baby to join little John? I bet Moses is about to pop with pride."

"About more than that," Rose murmured, pulling away with a teasing grin. "But I'll let him tell you the rest of the news."

Matthew glanced up at the porch then. "Sam! Opal! It's good to see both of you." He shook Sam's hand and gave Opal a hug. "I've spent a lot of time thinking about your pies, Opal." He looked hopefully toward the kitchen.

"I got some strawberry pies about to come out," Opal assured him, "but it's a good thing you got here now. I's leaving in a few days to head to Philadelphia. I'm gettin' married to my Eddie, and going north to start my very own restaurant!"

"Good for you!" Matthew cried. He bent down to look at Annie. "I don't believe we've met," he said cordially.

"Nope, but I done been hearing a whole lot about you from my boy," Annie responded.

Matthew gazed at her and his eyes grew wide. He looked back at Rose, breaking into laughter again when she nodded her head. "You're Annie? You're Moses' mama?"

"I sho 'nuff be!"

"He found you," Matthew whispered. "He's been talking about finding you ever since I've known him."

"Found both me and Sadie," Annie announced proudly. "You go sit down on that chair over there," she commanded. "I'll be bringing you out some ham biscuits and tea to go with that strawberry pie Opal is dishing up."

"I have died and gone to heaven," Matthew murmured as he followed orders.

"You learn quickly," Jeremy said, walking over to shake hands. "Everyone has realized it's easier to do whatever Annie says."

"Moses came by his order-giving honestly, eh?" Matthew asked with a wide smile. He gazed at Jeremy. "So, what's your—"

Suddenly, a head popped out of the window above them. "How am I supposed to read to Robert if all of you be making so much noise? I need you to be a little quieter!"

Matthew stared up as the little head disappeared again. "And that would be?"

Carrie laughed. "That would be Amber. She came from Maryland with her parents and brother."

Matthew's eyes grew even wider. "The family that took care of Robert after he was shot?"

"The same," Carrie assured him. "Amber has taken over Robert's care."

"And...?"

Carrie could tell Matthew wanted to ask so many questions, but was afraid how she would respond if the answers weren't good ones. "She is working wonders," Carrie assured him happily. "Robert is sitting up and talking, reading books, eating full meals..."

"Is he—"

"Walking yet? Not yet, but I'm sure Amber will know when it's time."

Amber's head popped out again. "You got that right, Carrie. Now why don't alls of you go inside and leave us in peace!"

"Mercy," Matthew murmured, his eyes dancing with laughter. "I hope the women get the vote soon. I have a feeling Amber should be running for something important."

Everyone laughed as they moved into the house. Annie bustled out of the kitchen with a platter full of food. "I thought I done tole you to stay in that rocker," she snapped.

"Yes, ma'am, you did," Matthew said hastily, "but Amber told us we were making too much noise."

Annie scowled. "I declare...that little girl done think she runs all of us."

Jeremy grinned. "She *does* run all of us!" He indicated toward the back of the house. "How about if we take this party into the backyard?

******

"I'm afraid I have some bad news, Carrie," Matthew said once they had settled down in chairs in the backyard.

"What is it?" she asked quietly, glad everyone she loved most was with her to hear it. Still, she braced herself for whatever was about to take a piece of her heart.

"Robert's mother and aunt have both passed away."

"*Both* of them!" Carrie gasped. "When?"

"His aunt passed away right before the war ended. His mother, not wanting to be on the plantation alone, went into Charlottesville. She caught pneumonia and passed away in May."

Tears filled Carrie's eyes. She knew how much Robert had wanted to see his mother and aunt again.

"I knew Robert would want news about them, so I went through there on my way here," Matthew explained. "One of his neighbors told me what had happened."

"Thank you," Carrie said softly. "Oak Meadows?"

"It is fine," Matthew said.

"Because of you," Carrie murmured. "Thank you," she said again. She took a deep breath. "I will not tell him now," she said. "He needs to be stronger."

Abby nodded when Carrie looked at her for affirmation. "He will have to be told, but certainly not right now."

Silence fell on the group. The only sounds were the buzzing of bees as they flitted from flower to flower along the edge of the yard. Even the birds and squirrels were silent, lulled into complacency by the summer heat.

Abby was the first to break the silence. "Will you tell us about the *Sultana*?" she asked softly, her heart squeezing with pain when she saw the look on Matthew's face.

"I can't," he finally said in a broken voice. "I wrote a series of stories for the *Philadelphia Inquirer* before I resigned, and I've brought them with me. It's just..."

"Too difficult to talk about," Abby said gently as she laid a hand on his arm. "I understand."

"Perhaps..." Matthew murmured.

"Perhaps you will feel like talking about it someday, and perhaps you won't," Abby finished for him. "It doesn't matter. The only thing important is that you are here with us."

The haunted look finally faded from Matthew's face, but the shadow of loss lurked in his eyes. "It's good to be here," he managed.

Carrie's heart ached for him, but she knew only time could heal the memories and scars. All of them had read the most recent newspaper accounts of the accident, but there hadn't been a lot of information. No one seemed to want to talk about the deadliest maritime disaster in United States history. She could almost understand. The country wanted to celebrate the end of the war, and mourn the death of their beloved president. There just didn't seem to be enough emotional energy to handle more.

"Is that horse pulling your carriage any good under a saddle?" Carrie asked suddenly, knowing Matthew would benefit from a hard ride.

"I'm told he is," Matthew replied. A smile flitted across his mouth, though his eyes remained somber.

"I'm taking Granite out for a ride. Has the war made you too soft to keep up?" she challenged, knowing competition would light the fire in her friend. She laughed when Matthew's eyes sparked.

"Soft?" he scoffed. "How about if I agree to take it easy on you?"

"You do that," Carrie said loftily. "Granite and I will just let you wonder what is happening when a gray blur flies past you."

******

Abby smiled when she watched Matthew and Carrie return from the barn, both of them relaxed and laughing. She was sure Carrie had taken Matthew down to her place by the river to let him take advantage of its healing qualities.

Thomas came to stand beside her. "Does Carrie have any idea Matthew is in love with her?" he asked quietly.

"No," Abby said sharply. "How did you know?"

"It's not so hard to read his eyes," Thomas answered. "I've known for a long time. Just as I've known he would never say anything because of Robert."

"Matthew is a man of honor," Abby said with quiet pride. "Carrie is lucky to have two men who love her so much."

Thomas glanced up and lowered his voice even more, but still the anger snapped through. "If Robert loves her so much, he needs to get out of that bed."

Abby looked at him quickly. "You're angry?"

"I'm trying to not be, but it's hard. She is giving everything she has to him. I'm not sure he's doing the same." He took a deep breath. "I ache for what Robert went through, but I ache for Carrie as well. I'm sure there are plenty of times she has wanted to curl up and quit living, but she has always found a way to press through."

"Women are stronger than men, you know," Abby said.

"Your voice is teasing," Thomas observed, "but your eyes tell me you mean that."

"Why else would God have chosen women to bear children?" Abby said. "The world would be quite under-populated if the job had been left up to men."

Thomas snorted with laughter. "I would like to refute that logic, but I'm afraid I can't."

Abby smiled. "Give Robert a little more time. I believe he is going to come out of this, and that when he does, he is going to be the strong, loving husband Carrie deserves. He will feel badly enough about how he fell apart. He won't need anyone to tell him he fell short."

"Especially not his father-in-law," Thomas said ruefully, squeezing her hand with gratitude before he stepped to the edge of the porch. "Hello, you two. Just how badly did Granite and Carrie put you in your place, Matthew?"

Matthew grimaced. "It wasn't pretty. You need to get some horses out here that can give that Thoroughbred some competition, Thomas. He's getting too cocky. I swear I heard him laughing when he flew past."

"That was me," Carrie said smugly.

Thomas laughed and hugged Matthew warmly. "It's good to have you here, my boy."

"Not half as good as it is to be here," Matthew responded fervently.

"You're welcome for as long as you want to stay," Thomas replied. "I find I rather like Cromwell Plantation acting as a hotel. Especially—"

"Especially when the visitors bring news from the outside," Abby finished for him. "I have so many questions for you, Matthew."

"Let's dig into them," Matthew said, smiling when Rose and Moses moved out onto the porch. He jumped up and gave Moses an exuberant embrace. "So you're going to be a father again? Congratulations!"

"You are also looking at the new co-owner of Cromwell Plantation," Thomas informed him. "Abby and I are moving back into Richmond after the wedding to build the factory. Moses will be in charge out here."

Matthew grinned, but Abby caught something in his eyes that made her tense. "What is it, Matthew?"

"Nothing. I think it's wonderful Moses will be running the plantation," he protested. "No one could do a better job."

Moses stared into his eyes. "Abby is right. Something is bothering you. You know better than to think you can hide something from us," he chided. "What is it?"

"I'm afraid there will be trouble," Matthew admitted.

"Why?" Thomas demanded.

"Because you're doing things differently than your neighbors are doing them, or want to do them. They are going to be threatened."

"Not my problem," Thomas said sternly.

"Until it *becomes* your problem," Matthew persisted.

Chapter Twenty-Three

Thomas took a deep breath. "Why don't you tell us what's going on?"

"Southern planters believe their prosperity and their survival depend upon their ability to command labor," Matthew began. "The conflict is growing as the freed slaves seek to control their lives, while the plantation owners attempt to re-create a disciplined labor force."

"Meaning they are trying to make things as much like slavery as possible," Moses said bluntly. "They're okay with calling it something different, as long as things don't really change."

Matthew nodded heavily. "I'm afraid that's true. Many have decided they have no hope for the future. They are leaving."

Thomas nodded. "Many of the men I knew through the government have left Virginia and abandoned their homes."

"To do what?" Carrie asked, realizing this was the first time her father had been willing to talk about this.

Thomas shrugged. "Some have gone to the North to start over. Others have left for Europe. Many of them are attempting to reestablish themselves as planters in Mexico or Brazil."

"*South America!*?" Carrie asked.

"They're trying to find a place where they can continue to live the life they have always lived," Thomas explained.

"And why not you?" Matthew asked.

"I had too much to come back for," Thomas said as his gaze settled on Carrie and then shifted to take in Jeremy, Rose and Moses. "But that doesn't mean I wasn't scared. I realized I may lose my plantation like so many others have, but Moses showed me another way."

"Are you paying the men?" Matthew asked.

"Of course," Thomas said. He glanced at Carrie. "I still had some resources after the war—some gold bullion I had hidden away. I have converted it into US currency to pay the men and buy seed."

"The men have agreed to a monthly wage," Moses said, "knowing they will receive a fair percentage of the crop profits after harvest. They all know they will make much more that way, than if they were to settle for just wages."

"And you'll pay them a percentage of the true value of the crop?" Matthew pressed.

"Of course," Thomas said sharply. "Do you doubt my integrity?"

"Not a bit," Matthew said immediately. "But that is where the problem is."

Thomas shook his head. "I'm afraid I don't understand."

"I saw the fields today," Matthew said. "The crops are in and looking good. Do you anticipate a profitable crop this year?"

"It will be an extremely profitable crop," Moses said confidently.

"And the men will be paid well? And they are also receiving housing? With the freedom to grow gardens, and raise livestock for food?"

"Of course," Thomas said impatiently.

"What do you think will happen when other freed slaves without those benefits learn what is happening on Cromwell?" Matthew asked next, his gaze locked on Thomas.

Thomas frowned, his eyes saying he had made the connection. "I see..." he murmured.

Moses frowned with him. "You're saying other freed slaves will leave wherever they are working, to come here because they will get a better deal?"

"Wouldn't you?" Matthew demanded.

Moses slowly nodded. "I suppose so."

"And if you were the plantation owner who was watching your labor disappear, knowing you wouldn't have a crop this year because of it, who would you be angry at?"

Thomas nodded. "I get it," he said. "My doing the right thing is making it more difficult for them to do the wrong thing. As long as I'm treating my workers fairly, they will be forced to match what I'm doing, and they don't want to."

"That would be putting it mildly," Matthew replied. "Plantation owners are developing labor contracts that are nothing more than a substitute for slavery. Their excuse is that the black man is basically lazy and incapable of self-care."

Moses snorted.

"It's an old belief that has no part in this new country," Thomas said wearily. "I have had this conversation with planter after planter. None of them want to change their thoughts on it."

"They're terrified of losing whatever they still have after the destruction of the war," Abby said quietly. "Most of them are financially destitute."

"It's poor business," Thomas said. "Even if they choose to harbor their old beliefs, it's good sense to make restoring the plantations a beneficial thing for everyone involved. They need workers. The freed slaves need income and a way to create their own autonomy. It can work for everyone."

"I wish more shared your feelings," Matthew said, "but the labor contracts prove they don't."

"What labor contracts?" Moses asked.

Matthew scowled. "They're terrible," he stated flatly. "Planters are using labor contracts to reestablish their authority over every aspect of their workers' lives. They prescribe gang labor from sunup to sundown, as well as complete subservience to the planter's will." He took a deep breath. "Many of them prohibit the workers from leaving the plantation or having visitors. When I was coming through Kentucky, I read a newspaper that said the former slaves must be taught that they are free, but free only to labor."

"That's preposterous!" Carrie cried.

"Surely they are finding that difficult to enforce," Abby added in protest, her gray eyes flashing with anger.

"Yes," Matthew agreed. "Many slaves are leaving the plantations, but they are not finding better situations, because the planters seem to have come to one mind on this."

"Which makes me even more of a threat," Thomas observed.

"Yes," Matthew said heavily.

"You're concerned about Moses being out here without me," Thomas observed.

Matthew hesitated and shrugged. "I could be completely wrong," he replied.

"Or completely right," Thomas said wearily as he gazed at Moses.

"We're going to be fine," Moses said, his face hardening into lines of determination. "It's really not that difficult. The freed slaves simply want freedom to live their lives. If the planters were to quit insisting things remain the same, and instead treated their workers with respect and appreciation, the South could be rebuilt."

"And I wish every single one of them would listen to you," Abby said fervently. "Unfortunately, fear overrules one's ability to listen to reason, especially if there is no desire to change."

"What is President Johnson doing about this?" Thomas asked. "I haven't heard a lot, but his initial moves indicated he wants to assure the freed slaves their rights. He must be planning to use the military governments to control the situation."

Matthew frowned again. "I'm afraid our President Johnson has revealed his true self in the last few weeks," he said angrily.

Abby sighed. "Then your suspicions were correct."

"Unfortunately, yes." Everyone waited quietly for him to continue. "In the weeks following the assassination, Johnson said enough of the right things to indicate he believed in black suffrage and their right to political equality."

"But he doesn't?" Rose asked.

"President Johnson is a rather unique man," Matthew replied. "The Radical Republicans in Congress believe military governments should run the Southern states until reconstruction is complete—including true freedom for the former slaves." He paused. "President Johnson believes that individual traitors should be punished severely, but since the Constitution does not allow a state to leave the Union, legally none of the Confederate states actually seceded. Therefore, they did not give up their right to govern their own affairs. Each state should decide what to do about what he calls the *'black problem.'* "

Shocked silence met his statement.

Abby was the first to find her voice. "To say they had no right to secede, therefore they could not, is like saying that because a person doesn't have a right to commit murder, they cannot." Her voice rose indignantly. "People do commit murder. And the South *did* secede and raise four years of war against the North. That was certainly a situation the writers of the Constitution did not foresee."

Matthew spread his hands. "You already know I agree. I'm just the bearer of bad news."

"You're right," Aunt Abby said quickly. "Please go on. It's best if we know the truth."

"President Johnson is a very prejudiced man. He believes it is up to white men to govern and manage the South now. He has already called for a convention in North Carolina for them to choose their own government."

"So the same men who got North Carolina into the war, will be the ones to attempt to rebuild it?" Carrie asked. "How can that be right? How can that rebuild a society fair to everyone?"

"President Johnson has taken steps to make it clear he has his own ideas of Reconstruction. While the Republicans in Congress have demanded any state's recognition of reunion has to include the blacks right to vote, Johnson has already extended recognition to Arkansas, Louisiana, Tennessee and Virginia."

"Here?" Thomas asked, startled. "I didn't know."

"It's been very recent," Matthew explained. "Johnson is making it clear he has his own view of Reconstruction. He is moving as quickly as possible."

"What about Congress?" Carrie demanded. "Why aren't they stopping him?"

"The full Congress is not back in session until December," Matthew replied heavily.

"So he just gets to run rampant until then?" Rose demanded. "How is that right?"

"It's totally wrong," Matthew replied. "It's also totally legal." He held up a hand before anyone said more. "I have many friends who are Radical Republicans. I went through Washington, DC and spoke with them. They are already making plans to block Johnson once they are back in session, but"—he sighed—"they agree he can do a lot of harm before then."

"And once things are put in place, it will be more difficult to change it," Abby said sadly.

"So we do what we can," Thomas said. "The last five years have taught me that politics become a black hole of unreasoning passion that pulls people into chaos. The war is over, but that doesn't mean the passions that sparked it have been put out. I rather suspect it has flamed them even higher."

"That's encouraging," Carrie muttered.

"It can be," Thomas responded. "Politicians are always going to create havoc, but that doesn't mean we cannot continue to create change simply by doing the right thing. Every right step we take will create a ripple of change that will touch other situations and other people. Our running Cromwell with integrity will make some people angry. It will make other people choose to follow our example, because the results will speak for themselves." He took a deep breath and continued in a calm voice. "Some people will resent our factory..."

"Others will view it as an example to emulate because they will see the results of the profits," Abby said. Her eyes glowed with pride. "I do believe I love you even more than I did a few minutes ago, Thomas Cromwell."

Thomas reached for Abby's hand and met Matthew's gaze. "I appreciate the warning, but we will simply continue to do the right thing. I'll trust God with the rest."

Matthew nodded, a broad smile on his face. "I was hoping that would be how you would react."

Thomas settled back and reached for his glass of lemonade. "So what's next for you, Matthew?"

Matthew shrugged. "I don't know," he admitted. "I know I'm tired of running all over the country covering one disaster after another. That's the reason I resigned from the *Philadelphia Inquirer*. It's been my life for so long that I feel rather like a fish out of water, but each day I find I like it more and more. I can't continue like this forever, but I've got time to decide what my next steps will be. I'm choosing to believe I'll recognize them when I see them."

"I'm certain you will," Abby said warmly. "I'm sure whatever it is will be a wonderful adventure."

******

Janie had no need to hide to overhear the conversation taking place in Clifford's study; the heat had forced him to leave the windows open. The voices from his office flowed out to where she was cutting flowers. She knew Clifford had been furious when he arrived home, but she had escaped his wrath because he had not arrived alone. He merely nodded at her curtly and disappeared into his study. One man with him— someone she had not seen before—had the grace to look embarrassed as he nodded at her courteously. Janie merely smiled, relieved she didn't have to talk to Clifford.

If possible, he was becoming even more volatile. It was as if it took every bit of his self-control to act the successful businessman during the day, such that when he came home, he vented all his frustration and anger on Janie. There were times she wanted to ask him what good he thought it would do, or what purpose it served to make her feel less than human, but she was wise enough to remain silent. And, in fact, she felt no need to confront him. She had simply stopped listening.

Janie smiled softly to herself as she deadheaded flowers, and cut enough hollyhocks to fill the tall vases she had scattered throughout the house. It had taken her time, but she had become quite adept at detaching from Clifford's anger and vehement words. Oh, she stood there as he spewed out his venom, but most of the time the words could no longer pierce the shield she had placed around her heart and mind.

Not only could she block Clifford out, she had a *plan...*

"Louisiana has the right idea," Clifford shouted, his voice assaulting her over the flowers.

Janie pulled her thoughts back, reminded she needed to learn everything she could about her husband's activities.

"I asked Anthony Simmons here tonight to tell us how Louisiana is handling the freed slaves."

Janie continued to cut flowers while she listened intently.

"Louisiana knows how to handle the niggers," Anthony said bluntly. "I was down there recently. They govern by the pistol, the rifle and the whip. They know as long as there are black people in that state, they must use force to remind them who is boss. The niggers squawk about being free, but I don't see anyone coming in to stop it."

Janie stiffened in disbelief.

"President Johnson has already recognized Louisiana's re-entry into the Union. He's letting things play out the way people in Louisiana want them to play out."

"What about the Freedmen's Bureau?" one man asked sharply.

"What about them?' Anthony scoffed. "They make some noise, but there are far too few to make much of a difference. Oh, they're passing out food, clothing and medical help, but they don't have the ability to stop what is happening. And I don't think President Johnson is giving them a lot of support. He won't come right out and say they aren't needed because it will hurt him politically, but he's not doing anything about Louisiana justice either."

"I heard a lot of black people are ending up dead in Louisiana," Clifford drawled.

"That's true," Anthony replied casually. "They figure about a thousand have already been taken care of. Those who aren't killed are beaten so badly they quit thinking about demanding their rights," he added.

Janie gasped, tears filling her eyes as she imagined the pain and sorrow of people who had been so excited about their promised freedom. Her mind flew to Carrie and the rest. Were they okay? Had Rose and Moses been harmed? What about Micah and May? Were Sam and Opal safe? Eddie? Not knowing was driving her crazy.

She bit her lip to hold back her emotions, and then she tightened her lips and forced herself to continue to listen.

"We've got to do the same here in North Carolina," Clifford stated. "If we don't get things under control now, it's going to get even worse."

Janie heard him slap his hand against the table.

"One of those nigger soldiers had the audacity to greet me this morning," he growled. "I went straight to his commanding officer, and told him I would not allow such insolence. I explained to him that in North Carolina, a black was only to speak when he was spoken to first."

"And how did he respond?" Anthony asked.

"He told me I should get used to things being different," Clifford snapped.

Janie could feel his anger filling the air with a thick heaviness that weighed on her heart.

"It will do no good to go to the Northern authorities," Anthony told him. "They are the ones who created this debacle. It is up to us to resolve it. The only way to regain control is to remind the niggers every chance we get that *we* are the ones in control. Their little dreams of freedom and equality will fade away when they fully realize the price they will be forced to pay."

"But they *are* free," another man protested. "There's nothing we can do to change that now."

"You're right that we can't change the amendment abolishing slavery," Anthony agreed, his cold voice freezing Janie's heart, "but there is no way the government can offer protection to two million freed slaves. We controlled the slaves with fear before—there is no reason we can't continue to do that. We just need to be a little more subversive in our efforts. Keeping our methods hidden will make them no less effective."

Janie shuddered as she walked slowly to the house. She'd heard all she needed to hear.

******

Janie smoothed her hair to make sure she looked presentable enough to satisfy Clifford, and carried a fresh tray of mint juleps into the office, being sure to keep her eyes down. It was best that her husband not catch even a whiff of the nervous excitement causing her heart to pound.

"Gentlemen," she said softly when she opened the door. "I thought you could do with a bit more refreshment."

Talk ceased when she entered the room.

"Thank you, Mrs. Saunders," one of the men said smoothly.

It took all of Janie's self-control not to stare him in the face and announce he was a bigoted idiot, but she kept her eyes down and simply nodded. She backed out of the study slowly and headed straight to her room, closing the door behind her.

Janie stood in the center of the room, taking deep breaths to control her nervousness. Now that the time was here, she wondered if she had the courage to put her plan into action.

"Janie!"

Janie gasped as Clifford strode into her bedroom, his face twisted with anger. He closed the door carefully behind him. She had been so sure he would be too involved with the other men to leave the study. Had he somehow discovered her plans? She fought to remain calm.

"Yes, Clifford?" she asked quietly, putting her hands behind her back to control their trembling.

"I distinctly told you this morning that I wanted chess pie for our visitors tonight. Can I not trust you to do even the simplest things?" he growled, advancing until he stood directly in front of her, his eyes boring into hers.

Janie hid her distress by keeping her gaze direct. How could she have forgotten the pies? "Of course I haven't forgotten," she said quietly. "I thought the men would prefer to have their drinks before a dessert. I planned on bringing them in shortly."

Clifford stared at her. His eyes told her he knew she was lying, but he was also aware of a houseful of men that he had to maintain appearances for. She fought to control her quivering, as she saw a look different from any she had seen before come over his face. The rage in his eyes turned them coal black. Suddenly, she was very much afraid of what Clifford might do.

"I think the men in Louisiana have it right," he finally muttered, his eyes taking on a strange light she hadn't seen before, as his face twisted with fury.

Janie sensed the danger even before Clifford raised his one arm and slapped her hard across the face. She gave a soft cry and stumbled back, grabbing the post of her bed to keep herself from falling.

"Shut up!" Clifford snapped. "You are a useless woman, but it seems I am stuck with you. I have been patient for as long as I intend to be patient." He raised his hand to strike her again and then seemed to think better of it.

Janie struggled to control her trembling, knowing the presence of the other men was the only thing standing between her and more violence. She resisted reaching up to touch her burning cheek and eye.

Clifford glared at her for a long moment and smiled slightly, his eyes gleaming. "I do believe we will finally come to an understanding," he hissed. "You will do what I say, when I say it. Are we clear?"

Janie nodded quickly. "I will bring the pie in right now," she whispered.

Clifford nodded and then paused, seeming to realize his slap had left a burning mark across her face. "You look terrible," he snapped. "Forget the pie. Just don't let me lay eyes on you for the rest of the night."

Janie nodded again. That was an easy promise to make.

"We will continue this discussion in the morning," Clifford growled, before he spun around and left the room.

Janie waited until she heard his footsteps recede. When she heard the door to his office close, she sank down on her bed and covered her face with her hands, allowing the tears to come.

But only for a moment.

She shook her head, wiped away her tears, and sprang into action. She had already made the decision to activate her plans that night. Clifford's attack only made her more determined.

She knew the men would be in Clifford's study until late in the evening. She could only hope his usual routine of retiring directly to his bedroom would continue. It was the only way she would have time. Without allowing herself to think anymore, knowing thought would produce fearful inaction, Janie moved swiftly to her bureau.

It took only moments to gather the few things she was taking, along with the stash of bills she had been hiding away, praying she wouldn't be discovered every time she took a little of Clifford's money. It was such a small amount each time that it hadn't alerted him, but the little bits over the weeks added up to what she hoped was enough.

She didn't want to appear like a woman traveling any distance, so she stuffed her few things in a soft bag, gave thanks it was too warm to need a coat, and moved carefully to the door of her bedroom. She opened it carefully and listened, praying she would hear anything necessary over the frightened pounding of her heart. Fighting to control her trembling, she crept past the study door, holding her breath so she could hear if there was any movement. She allowed herself to take a deep breath when she reached the kitchen, but she kept walking, allowing herself to move more quickly now.

Janie breathed a sigh of relief when she realized dusk had shadowed their yard. Clifford couldn't see out the back, but she didn't want daylight to broadcast her activities. People might see a woman walking alone, but they would have no idea it was Clifford's wife, because he had not allowed her to meet any of her neighbors. They would wonder about a woman out alone at night, but no one would be able to identify her. She refused to allow her fears of what could happen to a solitary woman to rise to the surface. This was her chance for freedom. She could let nothing deter her. She shuddered when she envisioned Clifford's reaction if he caught her before she could get far enough away. She tightened her jaw and walked swiftly through the backyard, coming out onto a road that headed into town.

Now that Janie was free of the house, she walked as quickly as she dared. Her heart was screaming at her to run, but she knew running would draw too much attention. All she knew was that she was headed to the railroad station. She had no idea of the schedule, and no idea of the cost now that the war was over, but she knew it was her only chance to get away. She took deep breaths to control her panic as she moved down the darkening roads, grateful they were almost deserted at night. She knew that made her more vulnerable, but it also made her less noticeable. She stayed as close to the trees along the side of the road as she could, hoping they would help obscure her presence.

Janie took a deep breath when she passed Durham Road. It would take only a few minutes to reach her parents' house, but her instincts told her it would not be a haven. She would find a way to get word to them when she was safe.

Sweat, both from nervousness and the heat, ran in rivulets down her body when she finally reached the station. Her heart sped again when she saw it was almost empty, but she strode forward purposefully. If anyone was watching her, they would believe she knew what she was doing. Janie took a deep breath and stepped up to the counter.

"Hello, ma'am," the weary looking man at the ticket counter said. "What can I do for you?"

"I have just received word my mother has taken gravely ill in Richmond," Janie said crisply. "I must get there as quickly as possible. When is the next train?"

The counterman looked at her more sharply. "Are you going to travel to Richmond alone, Miss..."

"Mrs. Edward Maxwell," Janie said clearly, forcing herself to appear calm and controlled. "And, yes, I will be traveling alone. My husband is already there. He was on his way home from an important trip to Washington, DC and stopped in to check on my mother. He is the one who sent the telegram." Janie allowed her voice to grow sharper. "Her condition is most critical. When is the next train to Richmond? I simply have no time to waste."

Just as Janie hoped, the name of a prominent Raleigh businessman had done the trick. Her belief that a railroad ticket seller would not have reason to know him personally had been correct. She watched the man's eyes change from suspicious to solicitous.

"Yes, ma'am, Mrs. Maxwell. I'm so sorry to hear about your mother." He consulted the schedule. "It's unusual for a train to depart this late, and I'm afraid there won't be any amenities, but there is a special freight leaving for Richmond tonight with medical supplies for the Union hospital there."

"I'll take it," Janie said quickly, her heart pounding wildly while she resisted the urge to peer over her shoulder.

"Are you sure?" he questioned. "There will be one car with seats, but there won't be a dining car."

"That is not a problem at all," Janie assured him haughtily. "I simply must get to my mother." Now she had to pray she had enough money. "What will the cost be?" she asked, reaching casually into her bag.

"It's not a regular train," the man muttered, consulting his schedule. "It's usually twenty dollars, but that doesn't seem fair." He stared at the schedule. "I'll sell you a ticket for fifteen dollars."

"Fine," Janie replied, reaching into her bag and pulling out fifteen of the twenty-five dollar bills she had managed to stash away. "When does the train leave?"

"One hour," the counterman answered, taking her money and handing her a ticket. "I hope your mother recovers."

"I'm just praying I get there in time," Janie said as she calmly took her ticket and gave him a grateful smile.

"You can wait here in the waiting room," the man offered.

Janie looked at the room glowing with lantern light and decided the dark station platform would be a better waiting place. "Thank you," she said graciously, "but I prefer the evening air." Now that she had her ticket, she was beginning to relax.

Huddled on the platform bench, Janie struggled to remain calm, jumping every time she heard a noise or saw a movement. Clifford could not possibly know her plans, but she still expected him to materialize from the shadows at any moment.

She almost sobbed with relief when she heard the train chugging down the track. She was standing next to the passenger car when it slid to a stop.

"Evening, ma'am," the porter drawled. "I reckon you might be the only person on the train tonight," he said apologetically. "This one ain't really a passenger train. We're taking supplies up to Richmond."

"That's quite all right," Janie responded, trying to hide her delight as she explained about her sick mother in Richmond. "It's necessary I arrive as soon as possible."

"I reckon you'll get there sure enough," the porter assured her. He settled her with a blanket and pillow before he walked away. "I'll be back through to check on you, but if you're sleeping, I won't disturb you."

Janie nodded, quite sure her pounding heart wouldn't allow for sleep. She sat tensely, waiting for Clifford to burst through the doors before the train departed.

Tears rolled down her face when the train finally pulled out of the station, and began to roll north toward Richmond. It was too late to undo her actions. Now, she would simply have to live with the consequences. A smile spread across her face as the wheels picked up speed. Every rotation seemed to cry *freedom... freedom... freedom...*

Chapter Twenty-Four

Janie was trembling with exhaustion and hunger when the train arrived in Richmond the next morning. She also felt a wild freedom when she stepped from the train, gloriously happy to see the crowded streets, and the few burned buildings that had not yet been cleared away. *Richmond!* Everything she saw reminded her she was no longer with Clifford. She was free! Deep breathing helped her feel stronger.

She looked around for a carriage to take her to Carrie's house but realized she should save her money. She had no way of knowing if anyone was still there. If not, she was going to have to care for herself until she could decide what to do. Ten dollars would not last long.

Her stomach grumbled as the smells of food wafted from the houses she passed, but she simply straightened her shoulders and continued to walk. The presence of Union soldiers made her feel safe on the crowded streets. Surely she would come to no harm in broad daylight. She relaxed as she strolled along, amazed with how far Richmond had come in clearing away the burned buildings. There was no new construction yet, but she was sure it would follow quickly.

Janie forced her mind off her fatigue and hunger as the sun climbed higher in the sky. She was aware her clothing was rumpled and stained from the long train trip, but there was nothing she could do about that now. Strange looks from fellow pedestrians told her Clifford's slap had probably resulted in colorful marks on her face, but no one stopped her or questioned her. She exulted in the anonymity after being a prisoner in her own home for so long.

Sweat was rolling off her face as she climbed the hill to Carrie's house. She thought longingly of Spencer's carriage, but firmed her lips and grasped her bag more tightly. She and Carrie had fought through much more fatigue and pain than this during the long years of the war.

Janie took a deep breath as she crested the hill and turned down the final road. For the first time, she allowed herself to seriously consider that the house may be empty. Surely everyone would be back on the plantation by now, but perhaps Micah and May were still there and could help her get word to Carrie. She knew it was a weak plan, but it was the only one she had been able to devise with her limited options.

Janie walked more slowly as she neared the brick house, terrified she had come all this way for nothing. She was trembling again as she climbed the porch stairs and knocked on the door.

Tears of relief filled her eyes when Micah appeared.

"Miss Janie!" he exclaimed. "Miss Janie, what you be doing here?"

"Hello, Micah," Janie said softly.

Micah's eyes narrowed as he reached out a hand and pulled her into the house. "I know a woman in trouble when I sees one," he growled. "May!" he called. "Get on out here!"

May bustled out of the kitchen, her face softening with compassion as soon as she saw Janie. She hurried over and wrapped her arms around the quivering woman. "Miss Janie. You be all right, honey?"

"No," Janie managed to whisper. "Except I think I may be all right now that I'm here."

"That be the truth, sho 'nuff," Micah said gruffly. "Mr. Clifford ain't with you, is he?"

"No," was all Janie could manage to say.

May tilted Janie's chin up so their eyes could meet. "You be safe here, Miss Janie. I's glad you came home."

Janie smiled a quivering smile that made her lips tremble. "*Home.* That sounds nice."

May looked at her more closely. "How long it been since you done ate something, Miss Janie?"

Janie frowned, trying to remember. "I'm not sure..."

"You take Miss Janie into the parlor," May snapped. "I'll bring you out somethin' in a few minutes."

Janie gratefully allowed Micah to lead her to a chair by the window. "Is anyone else here?" she asked hopefully.

"No, ma'am," Micah replied softly. "Ever'body done be out on the plantation."

Janie nodded, her throat clogging with tears again. "I can't stay here," she whispered. "This is the first place Clifford will look for me."

"He know you here right now?" Micah asked.

"No," Janie admitted, "but he'll figure this is where I came."

"Ain't your folks live in Raleigh?" Micah asked. "Why ain't they helping you?"

Janie shook her head, too humiliated to admit her parents were under Clifford's control.

"It don't matter none," Micah said quickly. "I's real glad you came here. It was the right thing to do. I know you can't stay, but we'll figure out a way to get you out to the plantation," he vowed.

May arrived with a tray full of ham biscuits and iced tea. "I'll have something better for dinner," she said. "This was all I had that was ready."

"It's wonderful," Janie replied, pushing away her sadness that everyone was gone. She had to eat if she was going to think of what to do next.

While she ate, Micah and May told her everything they knew. Janie smiled happily when they told her of Moses coming through with his mama and sister. "He found them!"

"Yes, Miss Janie," Micah said. "Mr. Matthew came through here about a week ago. He done headed out to the plantation, too."

Janie frowned when she saw the look on his face. "Is something wrong with Matthew?" she asked.

Micah exchanged a look with May. "You done been reading the news, Miss Janie?"

Janie shook her head slowly, realizing she hadn't seen a paper since she left Richmond. "No," she said sadly. "What did I miss?"

"There be a real big explosion on a steamboat Mr. Matthew was on," Micah said gravely.

"Was he hurt?" Janie gasped.

"No, Miss Janie," May assured her. "Leastways, his body weren't hurt none. I can't say the same about his soul. He looked right lost when he got here."

"It must have been terrible," Janie said softly.

"Lost close to two thousand," Micah said.

"Two thousand people?" she gasped. "On one boat? How is that possible?"

"We got some papers here you can read, Miss Janie," May assured her, "but you'll probably only get the real story from Mr. Matthew."

"How can I get out to the plantation?" she murmured.

"How 'bout we get Spencer up here to take you?" Micah asked.

"I'm afraid I don't have enough to pay him," she said hesitantly.

Micah snorted. "Mr. Cromwell done left me some money to take care of things around here. I reckon I would lose my job if I didn't use it to get you out to the plantation," he stated firmly.

A sudden rumble of carriage wheels in the distance made Janie gasp. She ran to the window and peered out from behind the curtains. "I think someone is coming," she cried, too frightened to realize the carriage could be visiting *any* of the houses on the road.

Micah stepped up next to her. "I'll take care of it, Miss Janie," he said quietly. "You go on up to Miss Carrie's old room. You'll be safe up there."

Janie could have kissed him for not suggesting she go to the room she had shared with Clifford. She hesitated, but May strode forward and took her arm.

"You's going upstairs, Miss Janie," she said firmly. "Ain't nobody gonna know you be here," she assured her.

Janie brushed away tears as May led her up the stairs. "I'm sorry I'm so frightened," she whispered.

"From the looks of your face, I'd say you got reason to be scared," May growled, her eyes sparkling with anger. "Mr. Clifford ain't never gonna lay another hand on you if I got anythin' to say about it."

Janie prayed May would not have to face Clifford's anger. She knew what he would do to her. She suddenly realized she had made a terrible mistake coming here. All she had done was put her friends in danger. What had she been thinking?

May pushed her down on Carrie's bed. "You wait here," she ordered. "Me and Micah will done take care of things."

Janie fought the urge to cry out when May left the room. It would do nothing but increase the danger for them if Clifford heard her and knew she was in the house. She crawled onto Carrie's bed and huddled up against the headboard, too terrified to think.

All she could do was tremble uncontrollably when she heard footsteps running up the stairs. Clifford had found her! She gazed wildly at the window, wondering if she would survive a jump—a part of her realizing she hoped she wouldn't. The courage that had gotten her here had drained away.

"Janie!"

Janie gasped with relief and began to sob when Jeremy rushed through the door, his face white with concern. "Jeremy!" she cried.

Jeremy pulled her tight into his arms and held her while she sobbed. "You're safe," he murmured. "You're safe."

Janie finally took a deep breath and pulled back to stare at him, understanding when his eyes sparkled with temper. A brief look in Carrie's mirror had confirmed her face didn't look good. "What are you doing here?"

"Obviously rescuing you," Jeremy said. He took a deep breath. "Did Clifford do this to you?"

Janie nodded, her face flaming with humiliation as she looked away.

Jeremy turned her face back to his. "I'm so sorry, but you have nothing to be ashamed of," he said softly. "Does he know you're here?"

"No, but he will suspect it." Janie's voice quavered. "I don't want to make trouble for anyone," she choked out. "I just didn't know what else to do."

"You did the exact right thing," Jeremy assured her.

"I really must leave here," Janie insisted. "It won't be safe for Micah and May if he comes here and suspects they are hiding me."

Jeremy frowned. "He knows Micah and May. Why would he want to hurt them?"

"He has changed," Janie said, telling him of the conversation the night before in his office and, more hesitantly, about his hitting her. "That is the first time he has struck me," she said, "but I had already decided to leave."

"Because he has been verbally abusing you," Jeremy said flatly. "Carrie told me how frightened she has been for you. She is worried sick. Why haven't you written?"

"I have!" Janie exclaimed, explaining that the letters had never been allowed to leave Raleigh.

"So you've been a prisoner," Jeremy said.

Janie nodded her head in shame. "Yes," she whispered.

"Don't!" Jeremy said sharply.

Janie's head jerked up.

"Don't keep giving him power over you. You know what he did was wrong, don't you?"

Janie nodded, her eyes still downcast. "Yes."

"You know it took great courage to escape him, don't you?" Jeremy continued, his voice more gentle.

Janie looked up at him, relaxing when she saw his warm smile. "I *was* rather clever," she replied, a tentative smile flitting across her lips.

"How did you do it?"

Janie told him.

"Mrs. Edward Maxwell?" Jeremy hooted with laughter. "That was brilliant!"

Janie smiled but twisted her hands, anxiety still knotting her stomach. "He will come here, Jeremy," she said again.

"Yes, but I highly doubt he will come today. We will leave for the plantation tomorrow."

Hope burst forth in Janie's heart. "Really? We're going to the plantation tomorrow?" She knew Clifford might follow her there as well, but it wouldn't be as easy.

Jeremy nodded. "I'm here to take care of some things for Abby. I was going to stay, but I agree with you that it will be best to leave Richmond." He told her briefly of the plans to build the factory, and also of the impending marriage between Abby and Thomas.

"How wonderful," Janie exclaimed, forgetting her fear for a moment. "Carrie must be so happy! And Robert? Is he better?"

Jeremy nodded but stood. "We'll talk tomorrow on the way out to the plantation. If we're to leave so quickly, there is much I must do."

He walked to the top of the stairs and beckoned Micah to join them. "Janie and I will leave for the plantation in the morning." He made no mention of Janie's fear that Clifford might harm him and May. Clifford had no way of knowing who might still be in the house. In spite of the man's growing anger, Jeremy didn't think he would risk confronting Thomas, or Moses, or himself. Men who beat their wives were basically cowards who ruled by fear. Clifford knew he would have no power here, but Jeremy also knew that wouldn't alleviate Janie's fears.

Jeremy turned back to Janie. "I suspect you are hungry and tired," he said kindly. "Micah will alert you if Clifford comes, but I truly believe you're safe here today. Tomorrow is going to be a long day. I suggest you get some sleep and eat some of May's cooking." He stepped aside as May strode into the room with a pan of cool water.

"You two men get on out of here," she ordered, her eyes softening when she settled down next to Janie. "I's going to clean Miss Janie up some so she can get some rest."

"Rest, Janie," Jeremy said. "It may be after dinner when I return. We'll leave right after breakfast in the morning."

He turned back to May. "Could we eat early? Around seven o'clock?" He waited for her nod, gave Janie another gentle smile, and then strode from the room purposefully.

******

"It's time, Robert," Amber said firmly. "You and I both know it's time."

Robert gazed at the little girl, bemused by her calm assurance but also aware she was right. The knowledge both encouraged him and shamed him. As he had felt the strength returning to his body, his shame over what he had put Carrie through grew. There were days he truly wished he had just withered up and died, but there were other days when he had hope for the future again.

"Robert?" Amber stood in front of him, her tiny fists planted firmly on her hips. "It's time."

Robert blew out his breath, his heart swelling with love as he looked at Amber's determined face and shining eyes. She had curled up with him in bed every day for the last month. She said she was reading to him, but he had to interpret many of the words for her—even ones he suspected she already knew. As his brain came back to life, and as his soul responded to her quick laughter and unconditional love, his body began to chafe against his continued inactivity. As laughter, talk and the sounds of the plantation filtered in through the window, he felt a yearning to be a part of it. He knew it was nothing but fear that was keeping him from moving forward.

Robert nodded slowly. "Okay," he said. The very act of saying the simple word seemed to blow a fresh breeze through his soul. He could feel the solid wall of fear dissolving and crumbling away as he made the choice for life.

"Okay," he said more firmly, reaching out his hand.

A bright smile exploded on Amber's face as she reached forward to take his hand.

Robert was a little in awe of the power he felt pulsing in her tiny hand.

Amber nodded, a light smile playing over her lips. "Auntie JoBelle tells me I have the healing touch," she confided.

Robert smiled when he thought of the tall, statuesque woman who had convinced Polly he could walk again, after his wounds at Antietam had left him paralyzed. She had suggested the warm rags and leg movements that resulted in what he believed was a miracle. It didn't matter that she was as surprised as anyone when he actually walked again. It had been her belief that made it possible. "I think she's right," he managed.

"It ain't gonna be as hard as you think, Robert," Amber said confidently.

"I haven't walked in almost three months," Robert reminded her.

"Nope, you ain't, but you been moving them legs for the last month," Amber reminded him with a grin. "Don't worry. I ain't told anyone our secret."

He had allowed Amber to move his legs, exactly as she helped her mama do two years earlier, but he wouldn't let her tell anyone. Robert hadn't wanted to build Carrie's hopes only to dash them again. His wild wavering from hope to despair was painful enough, but he refused to create any more dark shadows in his wife's beautiful eyes.

"My mama says I can't think my way out of being scared," Amber said. "I have to go ahead and do the thing I'm scared of."

Robert was suddenly curious. "What are you afraid of, Amber?"

Amber regarded him solemnly. "I'm afraid I can't get you to walk again," she admitted. "Carrie loves you a right lot, Robert. She came all the way up home to get us and bring us back here. That's a powerful lot of love."

Robert's heart swelled with emotion. Amber was right. He wasn't going to *think* his way into walking. He grasped her hand tightly and swung his legs over the side of the bed. He knew Amber couldn't support his weight, so he asked her to put a sturdy chair beside the bed. He took a deep breath, grasped the back of the chair, and pushed up with his arms.

He stood.

"You did it!" Amber cheered, clapping her hand over her mouth, and running to peer out the window to make sure no one else had heard her. "The coast is clear," she whispered dramatically, her eyes sparkling with fun.

Robert chuckled and sucked in his breath, realizing his legs felt weak, but they were definitely working. He stood there a few moments and then forced his legs to move, walking to the end of the bed. He grabbed the bedpost when he felt his legs quiver, but they continued to support him. A broad smile exploded on his face. He knew all he needed was time.

Amber grinned with him. "I done told Moses that we would fix you up, just like we did that night when he brought you to us."

It took Robert a moment to understand what she had said. He turned questioning eyes to her, just as she slapped her hand across her mouth again.

"I wasn't supposed to say nothing about that," Amber cried. "I forgot for a bit!" Her eyes were wide with distress. "I told Carrie I was real good at keeping secrets. Now I done told you about it."

Robert eased back and sat on the bed, his mind racing. "What are you talking about?"

Amber shook her head. "I wasn't supposed to say nothing!"

"But you did," Robert said gently. "Why don't you go ahead and finish?" He knew he shouldn't press Amber to reveal a secret she had sworn not to tell, but suddenly he had to know. "Moses saved me at Antietam? How?"

Amber shrugged reluctantly. "I only knows he found you out on that battlefield. You was about dead. He found Granite, too. He didn't know what else to do with you since you was fighting for the other side, so he brought you to us. He told us to take care of you for Carrie. That was all we knew," she insisted. "We didn't even know his name until he brought Carrie back to find us."

Robert's forehead creased in confusion. "But why wouldn't they want me to know?"

Amber shook her head. Now that she had revealed her secret, she seemed eager to help him. "I don't know, Robert. I heard them talking about it one night when we was coming here. Carrie said there was more you needed to know, but that she wanted to tell you all at one time." She frowned. "I guess I messed it up," she said sadly. "I'm sorry."

"Don't be," Robert responded quickly. "Maybe it's best I know, so that I'm not caught completely by surprise."

"Could you maybe *act* like you're surprised?" Amber asked hopefully.

Robert laughed and nodded. Suddenly, he was eager to enter the land of the living again. He reached for the back of the chair again and stood, willing strength into his legs.

******

Janie laughed with delight when she saw Spencer sitting in the carriage in front of the house the next morning. "Spencer!"

"How do, Miss Janie," Spencer responded, a broad smile lighting his face. "It be real good to see you again."

When he didn't ask about Clifford, Janie knew Jeremy had already spoken to him. She was grateful she didn't have to talk about it. In spite of her fears, she had slept soundly in Carrie's bed, and May had already shoved enough food in her to make up for many weeks of not being able to swallow a bite.

"I hear we be headin' out to Cromwell Plantation," Spencer said. "I be right glad to finally see that place after hearing so much about it."

"It's even more beautiful than you can imagine," Janie said. In spite of her determination not to, she peered down the road, expecting Clifford to appear at any moment.

"Why don't you climb on in, Miss Janie?" Spencer said. He looked around. "Ain't you got a bag?"

Janie shook her head. She knew Carrie would let her borrow some clothes until she could get more of her own, though how she was going to earn money to do that, she had no idea. Panic welled in her again as the grim reality of her situation taunted her. She swallowed hard as feelings of shame and stupidity swamped her.

"Don't be listening to them voices," Spencer advised softly.

Janie stared at him.

"I recognize that look," he said. "My daddy used to beat on my mama. He beat on her with his words, and he beat on her with his fists. It got to where Mama just disappeared into her pain. She tried to escape sometimes, but the feelings he done put into her made her too ashamed," Spencer growled. "My mama done folded up and died when I turned fifteen."

Janie laid a hand on his arm. "I'm so sorry."

Spencer nodded and gripped her hand tightly with his own. "I'm telling you this 'cause you escaped. You done did the hard part. Them words Clifford put in your head ain't nothin' but lies. You be one of the finest women I know, Miss Janie. Mr. Clifford ain't worth nothing. You remember that!"

Janie's eyes flooded with tears. "Thank you," she whispered. She reached up to touch his cheek. "Thank you so much..."

Jeremy finished strapping bags into the back and swung up next to them. "Let's go, Spencer. They are expecting us. We should be right on time."

"Who is expecting us?" Janie asked, breathing easier as they drew further away from the house. Clifford might come looking, but it was going to be much more difficult to find her.

"That's what I didn't have time to tell you yesterday," Jeremy answered. "I came to Richmond partly to handle some things for the factory, and partly to take care of an investment Abby has made."

"A rather *large* investment," Spencer chuckled.

"I think I would rather you see it for yourself," Jeremy said as he looked at Janie, his eyes dancing with fun. "I'll even let you have first choice."

Janie stared at him. "First choice of *what*?"

Chapter Twenty-Five

Robert was sitting up in bed when Carrie brought lunch to him. She stared at him, encouraged by the light in his eyes. "Hello, dear," she said lightly.

"Can you forgive me?" Robert asked hoarsely.

Carrie placed the tray down and settled beside him on the bed. Though there had been no intimacy, she had slept with Robert every night since her conversation with Abby by the river. It seemed to give him comfort, and it had done much to lessen the ache in her own heart. "Forgive you?"

Robert nodded. "I never understood people who could give up on life," he said slowly. "I never understood a level of pain that made them close their hearts and minds to anything and everything. I thought it was a sign of weakness."

"And now you don't?"

Robert shrugged. "I suppose I still think it's a sign of weakness, but I also have a better understanding of how pain can suck the life from you. People can get to the point where they can't endure one more thing. Rather than risk more pain, they simply shut down."

"Like you have," Carrie said gently.

Robert flushed with embarrassment and raised his eyes. "Yes," he replied. "Like I have."

"And now?" Carrie asked, tempering her hope with caution. She had felt hope before, making it all the more difficult when Robert simply slid back into the darkness.

"And now I want to join the living again," Robert said. "I also hope you can forgive me."

Carrie shook her head. "There is nothing to forgive you *for*," she said quickly.

"You and I both know that's not true," Robert said firmly.

"You were not responsible for becoming so ill," Carrie insisted.

"No, I wasn't," Robert agreed, "but I made a choice every time I kept my eyes closed when you were in the room. Or every time I refused to speak to you, or to anyone. I made a choice when I wouldn't eat. I chose to escape into sleep and oblivion."

Carrie gazed into his eyes burdened with regret. "I forgive you," she said. She had released her resentment months ago, and he didn't need the burden of regret as he struggled to become strong again.

"Can you really?" Robert persisted. "I know how very difficult it's been for you. You thought life would be better when the war ended, but suddenly you were saddled with a husband who had no desire to live. I know you came out to the plantation for me. You went to Maryland to bring Amber back..."

"Which was evidently the best decision I have ever made," Carrie said gladly, joy beginning to spark in her heart. "That little girl is a miracle worker."

Robert nodded. "I'm truly sorry, Carrie. It will take me time to get my strength back, but I want to be your husband again."

Carrie gazed into his eyes for a long moment. Satisfied with what she saw there, a brilliant smile exploded on her face. "Then I suggest you start by kissing your wife," she commanded.

Long moments later, Robert held her back and stared into her green eyes. "I don't know how I ended up the luckiest man in the world, but I will never again let you down."

Carrie shook her head. "We can't promise each other that, because we don't know what the future will hold. I may be the one to let you down, or life may throw something so terrible at us, that we both will want to give up." She took a deep breath. "I think the most we can reasonably commit to is that we will never walk away from the other, no matter how dark it gets. I made you that promise when we married, Robert. I'm making it again."

Robert smiled, his eyes shining with moisture as he clasped her hands. "And I make the same promise to you," he murmured. "I intend to spend the rest of my life letting you know how much I love you."

"Then I will be the happiest woman in the world," Carrie breathed as she crawled onto the bed beside him and settled back against his chest, her head resting on his shoulder.

They spent the next hours talking. Carrie held nothing back, believing Robert could handle it. She told him about his mother and aunt, comforting him when he cried. She told him about Janie's leaving with Clifford and all the fears she had for her friend.

"You've heard nothing from her at all?" Robert asked sharply. "And you're afraid Clifford will hurt her?"

Carrie took a deep breath and nodded. "He was not the same man when he left here."

Robert shook his head. "The war may be over, but the ramifications will continue for a long time," he said quietly.

"I know," Carrie agreed. She told him of seeing all the veterans on the road, when they had come out to the plantation. "I have to find a way to help them," she said softly. "I'm not sure how..."

"I know you'll find a way," Robert assured her.

Carrie glanced up and then burrowed her head into his shoulder, finally letting the tears come. "I have missed you so much," she whispered. "So very much..."

Robert held her tightly, stroking her hair, and letting her cry until the tears had run their course. "How about if we watch Granite in the pasture for a minute?"

Carrie stiffened. "Watch Granite in the pasture? How...?"

Robert moved her aside and swung his legs over the edge of the bed. "I believe the proper term for it is walking," he teased, his face tight with concentration as he rose to stand upright.

Carrie held her breath and watched as he stood and slowly walked to the window. She was at his side in a flash, breathing in the warm air as it flowed over them. "There is a storm coming," she said, joy exploding through every fiber of her being that she was actually *standing* next to the man she loved.

"I would say we could go outside on the porch to watch it, but I'm afraid it will take a few days to get my strength back," Robert said regretfully.

"How about if you had help?" Carrie asked. "I just saw Father and Moses return from the fields. I know they could get you down easily."

"*Moses*," Robert murmured. He turned Carrie's head to meet his eyes. "I'm supposed to be keeping a secret, but I have so many questions exploding in my head."

"Amber told you about Moses saving you at Antietam," Carrie guessed. "I shouldn't have asked a nine-year-old girl to keep such a big secret."

Robert frowned. "Why *is* it such a big secret? Amber said she overheard you saying there was more to the story, but she didn't know what it was."

Carrie nodded and took a deep breath. "It's not my story to tell, Robert. How about if you get some rest, and I'll send Moses up after dinner?"

"Not even a hint?"

"Not even a hint," Carrie said firmly.

******

Moses stood at the bottom of the stairs, forcing himself to breathe evenly. He knew this day would come. He had also accepted that no matter when it actually came, he would probably not feel ready for it. Unfortunately, he had been right.

Rose slipped beside him and wrapped her arm around his waist. "Just speak from your heart," she said gently. "You'll find the right words."

Moses gazed at her, wishing he had the same confidence. Finally he nodded, squared his shoulders, and walked up the stairs.

Robert was sitting in a chair by the window when he entered the room. Moses understood he didn't want the vulnerability of being in bed when they talked. "Hello, Robert."

Robert smiled, his brow creased with curiosity. "Hello, Moses. I understand there are things we need to talk about. Why don't you pull up another chair?"

Moses nodded, glad to have something to do to delay the conversation even for a moment. He had played this over in his head at least a thousand times, but no scenario ever felt right. He carried the chair over to the window and sat down, gazing out at Granite grazing in the pasture.

"You've definitely got my curiosity aroused," Robert finally said.

Moses nodded again, but still he was silent as he searched for a way to begin.

"While you figure out how to say what you obviously have no idea how to say, I want to thank you for saving my life at Antietam," Robert said. "I'm surprised you saved me," he added.

Moses looked up then, seeing an opening. "Me, too," he said bluntly, "but I'm glad I did."

"Why did you? I'm pretty sure you knew how I felt about slaves and black people at that point in my life."

"I did it for Carrie," Moses said softly. "What I thought about you was irrelevant. Carrie loved you. I couldn't have lived with myself if I hadn't tried to save both you and Granite."

"Especially Granite," Robert said wryly. "I guess I should be glad you took me along for the ride."

Moses laughed then, realizing that no matter what the outcome of the conversation, right now it was just two men talking. "It's time to get this all out," he stated firmly. "Secrets always have a way of coming out when you least want them to."

"Secrets?"

Moses nodded and took a deep breath. "I've imagined this conversation so many times, but I've never figured out a good way to tell you that it was my daddy who killed your daddy."

Once he had said the words, they seemed to hang in the air, supported by the breeze and the dust motes dancing in the sun.

Robert stiffened and sucked in his breath. "What?" He hardly recognized his own voice. "What are you talking about?"

"I was eleven years old when my daddy tried to escape the plantation we were on. He got caught, along with a lot of others. They decided my daddy was one of the leaders, and decided to make an example of him by hanging him." Moses paused, trying to keep his voice calm as the memories threatened to swallow him. "I overheard some men talking on the porch of my plantation, so I knew what they were going to do. I didn't want my daddy to die alone, so I snuck out into the woods to watch." His voice thickened as telling the story took him back in time.

He could feel the blackberry bush stabbing him as it pulled him into its embrace to hide him. He could see the flames roaring from the bonfire. He could hear the angry shouts of men. He could see the broken body of his daddy being prodded into the clearing with pitchforks.

Robert waited, watching him closely.

"They had broken both of my daddy's arms. They didn't think he could do anything, so they untied his hands before they took him to the platform where the noose was." Moses faltered as vivid images flashed through his mind.

He could see his daddy's lips tighten. He saw the determined look that said his daddy was going to do something important. He could see the knife waving in the firelight as Master Borden threatened to cut him up before they hanged him.

"It was *my* father who was going to cut him before they hanged him," Robert said heavily, regret mixed with a lingering anger from what he had witnessed so many years before. He thought he had released all the anger, but the vivid images pouring into his mind had his heart and gut tightening like a vise.

Moses gasped. Had he said his thoughts out loud? "How could you...?"

"I was there, too," Robert said.

Moses could only stare at him.

"I saw the whole thing. I overheard some of the men talking, and decided to do the same thing you did. I followed them and hid away in the woods."

"So you saw...?"

Robert nodded grimly. "I saw your daddy lunge off that platform and kill my father."

Moses stiffened with anger but didn't have time to get a word out.

"I also saw my father threaten to cut him with the knife," Robert added in a voice full of regret. "I know your father did the only thing he could do. I also know I would have done the same thing if the roles had been reversed," he added. Saying those words—knowing the truth of them—released the last vestiges of anger, and filled him with peace.

Moses sat back in his chair and gazed at Robert while a stiff breeze blew through the room. "Both of us lost something precious that night," he finally said softly. He felt peace flow through him as the wind swept over his hot face.

"Yes. And it also set both of us on a course we didn't have a lot of control over," Robert said. "Both of us hated because of things other people did. We hated because we were taught to hate." He took a deep breath. "Moses, you had more reason to hate than I did."

Moses nodded slowly. "Yes, I suppose you're right, but that doesn't diminish the pain of a boy watching his father be murdered."

"For either of us," Robert said. A long silence fell over the room. "You knew all this when you saved me," he said slowly.

"Yes."

"And you knew I killed the little boy on my plantation the year before the war started."

Moses tightened, forcing the image out of his mind as soon as it sprang up, because he knew Robert was a different man. "Yes."

"And still you saved me," Robert said in wonder. "You took me to a black family that totally changed my life." He reached out a hand and gripped Moses' arm tightly. "Thank you," he whispered, tears springing to his eyes.

"You're welcome," Moses said, shaking his head. "I've imagined this moment a lot of times. I never thought it would be like this."

Robert smiled. "There has been enough hatred and violence for a lifetime. It still amazes me that God has forgiven me for all the things I have done. How can I not forgive others? Especially a man who tried to escape a horrible situation and got caught?" He held Moses' gaze. "The truth is, my father would have done terrible things to your father if he hadn't killed him. It was a horrible thing, but I determined a couple years ago that I was no longer going to let the past define me."

The sound of laughter drifted up through the window. It caught on the breeze and swirled through the room in a dance.

Robert smiled again. "This is what matters now. *Today.* Laughter. Friends. Family. I think only God could have reunited two boys who watched something so terrible. Only God could have brought you here to Cromwell Plantation, and intersected our paths in Antietam. You're an amazing man, Moses. Thank you for all you've done for Carrie."

Moses' smile came easily now. "You're welcome," he replied. "And I do believe you're right about only God being able to turn all this around," he murmured, his heart light now that the secret was out in the open.

Robert heard a sound in the distance and turned to look out the window. The sun had set, but the day was still bright. He saw a cloud of dust in the distance and a large mass that seemed to be moving. "What in the world?" he muttered.

Moses turned to look out the window too, straining his eyes to determine what was coming. "Your guess is as good as mine," he finally said. "Whatever it is, it seems to be big."

"Were we expecting anyone today?" Robert asked, his eyes on the road.

Moses shook his head. "Not that I know of." He was suddenly anxious to go downstairs and see what was going on. Carrie and Rose had just stepped out on the porch. Their faces said they weren't expecting anyone either. "I think I'll go down."

"Will you help me?" Robert asked suddenly. "I can walk again, but I'm afraid I'm rather weak."

Moses grinned, knowing how happy Carrie would be when Robert walked out on the porch. "Certainly." He wrapped one arm around Robert's waist, stunned at how frail he was.

Robert interpreted the look on his face. "I know it's bad," he admitted, "but I'll get strong again quickly."

Moses nodded. "Just be warned that my mama will be pouring food into you every chance she gets."

"Your mama?" Robert had heard Moses had gone to get his mother and sister, but Carrie hadn't told him anymore.

"Her name is Annie. She is cooking now that Opal is gone."

Robert's eyes were sad. "My father killed her husband," he finally said. "Can she forgive me?"

"She already has," Moses said quickly. "Like you said, there has been enough hatred and violence. The country is starting over, and so are all of us. None of us needs to carry the baggage of the past with us. There are plenty of people in this country determined to do just that. We don't need to add to their numbers. There will be enough trouble as it is."

Robert nodded and leaned into Moses when they reached the stairs.

"Just take them slow," Moses said. "You don't need to worry about falling."

Robert smiled. "I believe you," he said, his legs trembling from the exertion of walking. He paused. "I'd like it if we could be friends, Moses. In addition to all the personal connections, I understand Thomas has made you half-owner of Cromwell Plantation."

Moses shot a look at him as they slowly descended the stairs. "Does that bother you?"

"Not a bit. I can't think of many things I would rather *not* do than run a tobacco plantation," he said ruefully. "My passion has been and always will be horses."

"We'll be friends," Moses said firmly as they reached the bottom of the stairs. He could feel the trembling in Robert's body. "Want to take a break?"

"Yes," Robert responded with a smile, "but I would prefer it to in be the rocking chair out on the porch."

Moses chuckled and walked with him across the parlor.

******

"Robert!" Carrie cried. "You're downstairs!" Her eyes were wide with wonder. "How...?"

"Moses helped me. We had a very good talk." Robert looked down the road. "Does anyone know who is coming?"

"No idea," Carrie murmured, her eyes shining with joy as she exchanged a glance with Moses and then stepped close to her husband. She wrapped her arm around his waist and gently lowered him into the rocker.

"It's so good to see you downstairs," Rose said, handing him a glass of lemonade and a plate of cookies. "Annie is determined to make all of us heavy. I'm so glad you're here to share these."

Robert smiled. "Thank you, Rose." He took a deep breath. "You have a rather remarkable husband," he said.

"That I do," Rose responded easily. "I'm so glad you're feeling stronger. Clint will be very excited to see you out of bed."

Robert smiled. "Where is he?"

"Out in the barn I'm sure. He has oiled Granite's tack so many times it's probably about to wear out!" Carrie said with a grin. "He's ridden Granite a few times. I've never seen such joy on anyone's face."

"He loves that horse," Robert murmured. "And he has a gift."

"He's determined that the two of you are going to work with horses together," Carrie responded. "Now all we have to do is get some horses," she continued with a chuckle. "I told him it would be a while."

Just then, Thomas and Abby joined them on the porch.

"Hello, Father. Look who decided to join us."

Thomas smiled and stepped forward to shake Robert's hand warmly. "Welcome back to the land of the living, my boy!"

Robert winced. "You and I both know it's about time."

"I know it's easy to judge something you've never experienced," Thomas said evenly. "I'm simply glad you're doing better. And just in time."

"Just in time?" Robert asked. "What do you mean?"

Thomas nodded his head toward the dark mass that was drawing closer. It had gotten just dark enough to be unable to determine what it was.

"Do you know who is coming?" Carrie demanded.

Thomas shrugged, a mysterious smile on his lips.

"Abby?" Carrie demanded. She looked more closely and realized Abby's eyes were shining with excitement. "Who is coming?"

"You're about to find out," Abby murmured as she moved close to the edge of the porch. She turned to Robert and bent down to give him a warm kiss on the forehead. "Welcome back," she whispered. "I'd say the timing is perfect."

Rose suddenly leaned forward and peered hard. "There are horses coming!" she cried.

Carrie stepped up beside her. "*Horses*?"

Suddenly, Clint bolted from the barn and waved wildly at the house. "They're here, Aunt Abby! They're here!"

Abby smiled broadly and waved back. "I see that," she called joyfully. "Are you ready for them?"

Clint ran all the way from the barn and skidded to a stop at the bottom of the stairs, his eyes gleaming. "Yes, ma'am! Every stall is cleaned and ready. I've got feed and hay in all of them, and everyone has fresh water."

"And I thought you were just cleaning tack," Carrie said in wonder, her eyes growing wider as the horses drew closer. "Look at them!" she cried. She whirled around to stare at Abby. "You did this?"

Abby shrugged. "I've always wanted to invest in horses. Now seemed the perfect time, since my husband-to-be owns a plantation," she said with a bright smile. "I asked your father to help me, but in the end we both bowed to Clint's expertise."

"Clint?" Robert asked, disbelief on his face as he watched the string of horses parading down the drive.

"I been studying ever since you left us, Robert," Clint said earnestly. "I knew Virginia was real big into Thoroughbreds like Granite, so I studied all the bloodlines."

Robert stared at him, and then swung his gaze back to the horses. "You studied the bloodlines?" he echoed.

"That's right," Clint said eagerly. "I knew just what Aunt Abby should buy when she decided she wanted to."

Robert swung his gaze to Abby, trying to make sense of what he was seeing.

Abby smiled gently and moved over to crouch beside him. "I knew you would get better. I also know how wonderful you are with horses. Between you and Clint, I believe you can be wildly successful. You proved that at Oak Meadows." She shrugged casually. "I've always wanted to invest in horses, and this was my chance. I'll be keeping just a small percentage interest, however. It will be enough to see them prancing in the pastures every time Thomas and I return."

Robert gripped her hand tightly and struggled for words, knowing this amazing woman had just handed him his new chance of doing what he loved best. He had assumed it would be several years before he could begin to rebuild a stable. To see his new life trotting down the road toward him was almost overwhelming. He blinked back tears. "Thank you," he finally managed, his throat tight with tears of gratitude.

******

Suddenly the horses were close enough to see who was leading the string.

"Jeremy!" Carrie cried as she rushed off the porch. "You're supposed to be in Richmond with the factory."

Abby came to stand beside her. "Jeremy? What is wrong?"

Jeremy smiled easily. "I wouldn't say there was anything *wrong*," he replied. "I encountered a situation that demanded I return to the plantation at once. I decided to go ahead and bring the horses with me since I was coming."

"A situation?" Abby asked with a frown. "What situation?"

Jeremy dismounted from the stunning bay Thoroughbred he was riding and took Carrie's hand. "Janie is in the carriage coming up behind me," he said softly.

"Janie?" Carrie cried. "Is...?"

"No, Clifford is not with her," Jeremy stated. "She needs you."

Tears sprang to Carrie's eyes. "He hurt her?"

"Yes," Jeremy answered, anger making his eyes glitter. "She escaped. When I got to Richmond, she was there in the house. She just arrived yesterday morning but was terrified to stay there." His gaze swung to Abby. "I did what I could yesterday afternoon for the factory, but I will have to return."

"The factory is completely unimportant," Abby said firmly. "Carrie, you go meet Janie. Clint will get the horses settled. The rest of us will be waiting inside."

Carrie smiled her gratitude, knowing Janie would need some time with her before she had to see everyone else.

The porch was empty, and Clint and Jeremy were almost to the barn with the horses when Spencer drove up in the carriage. Carrie gave him a warm smile, but had to bite back her moan when she saw the bruises, shame and distress on Janie's face. "Janie!" She climbed into the carriage and pulled Janie into her arms.

Janie began to sob, wrapping her arms around Carrie tightly.

Carrie held her close, letting her cry. *"Janie... Janie..."* she whispered, anger and sorrow mingling in her mind and heart.

Finally, Janie's tears stopped. "Carrie..."

"Shh..." Carrie wiped her tears with her sleeve and stroked her hair. "You're home. You're home, Janie. That's what matters now."

Janie sighed and managed a small, pitiful smile. *"Home...*You have no idea how wonderful that sounds." The smile disappeared as a frightened frown took its place. "I'm afraid I shouldn't have come," she whispered. "Clifford will come after me."

"I almost hope so," Carrie responded fiercely. "I'd like to see him get some of what he has been dishing out. There are several here who would like to make sure he does."

Janie chuckled. "I can't believe you can make me laugh," she said in a broken voice that deepened with distress. "Oh, Carrie, it was...it was awful. I should have listened to you that last day. I shouldn't have gone with him. This is my fault!"

"Nonsense," Carrie said. "The only person to blame is Clifford. You were trying to live up to your marriage vows." She turned Janie's face so she could gaze into her friend's eyes, her own eyes filling with tears when she saw the bruises and swelling. "Oh, Janie... I'm so, so sorry."

"You gave me the courage to leave," Janie said softly. "One day when it was especially bad, I remembered you telling me that no one would have respect for me unless I had it for myself first. I thought about that, and realized I was letting Clifford destroy who I was." She swallowed. "That was the day I started planning my escape."

Carrie closed her eyes against the image of Janie scared and entrapped in her own home. "How did you get away?"

Both of them were laughing by the time Janie finished her story. "I almost wish I could have seen his face the next morning when he discovered I was gone," Janie said. Then her face clouded over again. "He's a dangerous man, Carrie. He's not the same person he was, even when we left Richmond. Every day he seemed to get harder and angrier." She took a deep breath. "And horrible things are happening to the freed slaves in the country. *Horrible* things..."

Carrie bit back the questions flooding her mind. "You're safe here," she said instead. She glanced at the house. "Are you ready to go in?"

Janie nodded. "I appreciate everyone giving me a chance to talk to you." Her eyes filled with tears again. "It's so good to be home."

Carrie wrapped her in a warm hug again and then turned to Spencer. "It's so good to see you again, Spencer. Please come in and have some dinner with us. You'll spend the night before you go back in the morning."

Spencer's eyes widened. "You want me to come eat in the house?"

"Yes," Carrie assured him. "We all live as a family here. We would be honored if you would join us."

Spencer nodded slowly. "I'll come in and eat, but I reckon I'll head down to the quarters to sleep." His face revealed that he couldn't even imagine sleeping in the big house.

Carrie smiled. "The quarters were knocked down. The men working on the plantation have built new cabins for themselves and their families, who are arriving in a week or so. I'm afraid you're stuck with the big house."

Spencer stared up at the white mansion, his black eyes glowing with a mixture of apprehension, excitement and pride. "Yessum," he finally said. "I reckon I be real grateful."

Chapter Twenty-Six

Janie kept her eyes down as they walked into the house. Her throat was tight from shame and embarrassment, and she didn't think she could look anyone else in the eye. She had a wild thought of bolting from the house and fleeing into the countryside, but as quickly as the idea came, it departed. There was nowhere else to run.

"You lift your head up high, Miss Janie," Spencer scolded under his breath. "You ain't got no reason to be ashamed. You *escaped* that monster, Miss Janie. Feeling shame is just giving him power. You hold your head up real high."

Janie gazed into his eyes for a long moment, and felt the truth of his words sweep through her shame. When they rounded the corner into the parlor, she was ready.

Abby was the first to reach her. "Welcome home, Janie." She gazed long and hard into her eyes.

Without saying a word, Abby's message filtered through to Janie's heart. In the eyes of the older woman, was the message that all women had to fight for the right to feel freedom and pride.

Abby wrapped her tightly in her arms and finally whispered, "I'm so proud of you."

Janie felt awe enter her heart. Abby knew nothing of her story for the last three months, but still she offered her unconditional love and belief. For the first time, she understood the power of being a woman—of being part of a community of women determined to live with dignity. Suddenly, she *knew* she would never be alone, and that it was not *possible* to be alone when she had friends who so totally understood her.

One by one, everyone welcomed her home, making it clear she made the right choice to run to them. She knew Carrie would welcome her, but she was a little stunned by the complete welcome and acceptance of everyone in the house.

Robert was the last to approach her. Janie's eyes filled with tears when she saw him walking. She also saw the lines of fatigue, but it was the strength and determination in his eyes that told her he would be himself again.

Robert took her hands in his and peered into her eyes. "Don't be ashamed of losing yourself in darkness for a time," he said softly. "We all do. Just know that the things you have learned in the darkness will be used to shed light into others' darkness. Nothing is ever wasted, Janie. It will take a while, but you'll understand in time."

Janie absorbed his words, knowing that Robert, perhaps more than anyone, understood what she was feeling. She threw her arms around him, allowing the tears to come again. "Thank you. I'm so glad you're better."

Finally she looked around. "Where is Matthew?" she asked. "I thought he was here."

"He is," Thomas said gravely. "I imagine he's down by the river."

"Is he okay?" Janie asked. "Micah and May gave me the papers about the accident on the *Sultana*." She shuddered. "It must have been horrible."

"More horrible than I think any of us fully realize," Thomas agreed.

"Matthew will be okay," Abby said. "He came to the right place to heal. Just as you have, Janie."

Carrie realized exactly why all of them were on the plantation. They had just come through four years of horror and pain. Four years of mistakes and experiences that could have broken them. They had all survived, but their hearts and souls bore the scars. In order to move forward into what life held for them, there had to be healing first. "We're all here to heal," she said softly.

"I reckon you be right, Miss Carrie," Annie said, balancing a tray of biscuits she was carrying in from the kitchen. "This war done been a hard thing for everyone. Slavery done been a hard thing for everyone. Every person here gots to make the decision to move on. It ain't gonna happen without some effort, though. Ever'body in this room gots to rise up, and decide no matter how hard it be, they's not gonna let the past get the best of them.

They's got to decide they's just gonna move on with life. Being here on the plantation is done givin' ever'body a chance to do just that."

"You are so right, Annie," Abby said fervently. "We've all entered a brand new season of our life, but none of us is walking through it alone, because we have each other."

Janie grinned, the reality of her freedom sweeping through her like the wind blown by a storm. "Is it almost time to eat?" she asked hopefully.

Laughter erupted, breaking through the heaviness and casting it into a place that couldn't touch any of them.

"It sho 'nuff is, Miss Janie," Annie said. "By the way, I be Moses' mama."

Janie rushed forward and caught the surprised woman in a huge embrace. "I know. I'm so very happy to meet you."

"You's gonna knock these biscuits out o' my hand," Annie scolded, her eyes shining with pleasure. "I's be real glad to meet you, too, Miss Janie. Now you's go sit down at the table, and I'll bring the food out."

******

Abby was at Robert's side as soon as the meal was finished. "Would you like to join me in checking on our horses?" she asked lightly

Robert glanced at Carrie. "I guess that depends on whether my doctor gives me permission."

Carrie searched his face. "This is the first day you've been up, Robert. Are you sure you feel like it? The horses will be there in the morning."

"I'm tired," he admitted, "but I won't be able to sleep a wink until I've had a good look at what came down the drive. I'll just lay awake all night thinking about them. I was too stunned when they arrived to really see them, but I have vivid memory of sheer wonder when Clint took them to the barn." He glanced at Abby. "She may not want me to go see them because she's afraid Granite has just been handed some stiff competition." Robert's eyes danced with fun.

"In your dreams!" Carrie protested with a laugh, thrilled that her husband could tease again. "We'll all go look at them. I want to explain to Granite that he is still the king of Cromwell Plantation."

Carrie motioned to Moses. "Could you please help Robert out to the stable?"

Matthew walked in through the door just then, a bright smile exploding on his face when he saw Robert. He strode forward and gripped his hand. "It's about time you crawled out of that bed. I was beginning to feel you were being plain inhospitable."

"Heaven forbid," Robert said with a hearty laugh, gripping Matthew's hand. Carrie had told him everything she knew of the *Sultana*. "It's good to see you, old man." He could see beyond the smile to the dark shadows lurking in Matthew's eyes. He thought about what Annie had said about everyone being on the plantation to heal. She was right. "Care to help me out to the barn? Moses has already done his duty today."

Robert saw the look Matthew and Moses exchanged. "And, yes, he told me. There are no more secrets waiting to surprise everyone." He correctly interpreted the look in Matthew's eyes. "The past is the past. It has nothing to do with who either of us has become."

Matthew grinned and then caught sight of Janie in the parlor. He turned to Carrie with a question in his eyes.

"Go say hello," Carrie urged quietly. "I'll explain everything out in the barn."

Matthew walked over and caught Janie in a warm embrace. "Welcome home, Janie. Now that you're here, we're truly a family again."

Janie smiled. "I understand we have both had a rather harrowing couple of months," she said softly. "It's good to see you, Matthew. I would have been so disappointed if you hadn't been here."

"You're stuck with me for a while," he said, not quite able to pull off the casual tone he was trying to adopt.

"Same with me," Janie replied. "It seems as if I have a life to re-create."

Matthew nodded. "Me, too. I'd say we're in the perfect place for that to happen."

Janie glanced over his shoulder and smiled. "Robert is looking rather impatient, and he keeps staring at the barn. Are you needed?"

"That I am. We'll talk later."

"I'll look forward to it," Janie replied.

******

Robert walked slowly to the barn, relishing the feel of the evening air on his skin. The frogs had already begun their nightly chorus and owls were hooting their private messages. He was grateful for Matthew's supporting arm and even more grateful when his friend deposited him in a chair at the barn door. Lanterns hung from pegs on the wall, making the barn glow with warmth. He took a deep breath, glad beyond words to be back in his world of horses. The smell of manure, hay, feed and saddle oil were perfume to him.

"Are you ready, Clint?" Abby called.

Clint appeared immediately, pure joy shining from his eyes. "Yes, ma'am!" He grinned at Robert. "You done got some of the finest horses I've ever seen."

"You *have* some of the finest horses I've ever seen," Robert corrected with a smile. "If you're going to be running my stables, Clint, you need to speak correctly. Thomas tells me you know more about horses than anyone he's ever met, so I know you're brilliant. You don't want the world to judge you because of how you speak."

Clint ducked his head for a moment and then looked up with a new confidence in his eyes. "You have some of the finest horses I've ever seen, Robert."

"Then let's see them," Robert said, a broad smile on his face. "I'm not up for walking around the barn yet, so I'd appreciate it if you would bring them out one at a time."

"Yes, sir! Aunt Abby done told me... I mean...Aunt Abby asked me if I would get all of them ready for a private parade." He grimaced. "It's gonna take time to remember to speak right all the time, Robert."

"You're right. Just keep working on it, and I promise not to correct you every time you say something wrong."

"That's good," Clint replied, "but then it will just be Miss Rose picking at me," he said morosely.

Everyone laughed. Clint grinned and turned away. "I'll have them right out, Robert."

Robert was almost breathless by the time Clint had paraded the twenty horses past him, their hides gleaming from the thorough brushing the boy had given them to rid them of the road dust from their trip. "They are amazing," he breathed. "My brother and I worked for years to breed horses of this quality, but I'm afraid these horses are even finer than what we produced." He turned to Abby. "How did you do it?"

Abby shook her head. "Clint did it. I just bought what he told me to buy. I brought him the papers and information on horses that were for sale, and he did the rest."

Robert turned to Clint. "How did you do it? Two years ago..."

"I knew nothing," Clint agreed. "I done been doing—I have been doing a lot of studying since then. Pretty much anything I could get my hands on," he admitted. "Daddy thinks I don't know how much he sacrificed to make sure he kept me in books and the breeding registers, but I know. I won't let anything stop me from making him proud."

Robert started to say something, but Clint held his hand up to stop him. "There's one more," he said, excitement bubbling in his voice.

"One more?"

"I saved the best for last," Clint said with a twinkle in his eye. "I'll be right back."

When Clint walked out with the bay stallion prancing at the end of the lead line, Robert could only stare. He stood and walked slowly around the horse, examining him from every angle. "He's perfect," he finally murmured. "His conformation is absolutely perfect." He continued to eye him. "He's perfectly balanced. He's a natural athlete." Robert ran his hand down his shoulder. "The head is good, he has a nice topline, and he has a big, round hip that shows how muscled he is." He moved further to the back. "His legs are strong and straight, and his hocks are well-angled and low-set."

Robert walked to the front of the horse again and gazed into his eyes. "Plenty of fire and spirit, but I don't think there is a mean bone in this horse's body." He stepped back again. "He's perfect!" he repeated. "The combination of his bloodlines with the mares you just showed me will produce astounding foals."

"That's what I thought," Clint agreed eagerly. "I couldn't see him to be sure before we bought him, but his bloodlines suggested he would be worth the price."

Robert turned a questioning look on him, before he turned back around to stare at the horse. "What is his name?"

"His name is Eclipse. He's a son of Lexington," Clint said proudly.

Robert tore his eyes away from the horse and turned to Clint. "Did you say what I think you said?" He ran his hand down Eclipse's neck. "He's a son of *Lexington*?"

"I take it that's good?" Carrie said, aware the war years had taken her far from the subject of equine bloodlines.

"Not good," Robert corrected. "Amazing would be a better term."

Clint nodded eagerly. "Lexington was bred in Lexington, Kentucky. He is a racehorse who won six of his seven race starts. He is a son of Boston, another Thoroughbred legend."

Robert added on to his information. "Lexington is known as the best race horse of his day. Unfortunately, he had to be retired in 1855 because of bad eyesight, but it's not genetic because he hasn't passed it on to his progeny. He's claimed the title of leading sire in North America many times since his retirement." He turned around to stare at Abby. "Should I ask how much he cost?"

Abby shrugged. "I wanted to make sure my investment would yield adequate results. I trusted Clint's judgment."

Robert turned and slapped Clint on the shoulder. "You did a great job," he said, his voice suddenly thick. "I hoped to one day breed horses this fine, but I never dreamed I would start over after the war with horses of this caliber."

Clint grinned. "I told you two years ago that we would make a great team."

"So you did," Robert murmured. "So you did."

Carrie caught the deep fatigue in his eyes. "You've had your parade," she said firmly. "I would prefer not to put you back in bed again just because you completely overdid it your first day."

Robert nodded reluctantly. "I think you're right," he said, weariness dripping from his voice. He reached out and gripped Clint's hand firmly. "I'll get stronger every day," he promised.

"That's what Amber tells me," Clint said easily.

Robert chuckled. "She would know. I'll be out here every day from now on, though it will take me a while to be up to full strength."

Clint nodded. "I reckon I got lots to keep me busy." He grinned. "I mean, I imagine I have plenty to keep me busy." He shrugged. "I know how to talk correctly. All my reading has taught me that. I just never saw much of a reason for bothering, and I didn't want to sound so different from all my friends."

"When you're dealing with our buyers and breeders," Robert reminded him, "you don't want to give them any reason to think you're inferior."

"That's what Rose keeps saying," Clint muttered.

"She's right," Carrie agreed. "You're already going to know more than just about anybody who comes onto the plantation. They will respect your knowledge more, if you're speaking correctly."

"I'll work on it," Clint promised. "My goal is for Cromwell Plantation to have the finest horses in Virginia." He turned and led Eclipse back into the barn.

Robert stumbled a little crossing the yard. Only Matthew's support kept him from falling.

Moses appeared from the shadows. "Looks like you need a little help," he said casually. "Are you willing for your pride to take a little hit?"

Robert managed a smile. "I don't know that I have any pride left," he said weakly. "I also don't have any strength left."

Moses chuckled and stepped forward to lift him easily in his arms. "You're not nearly as heavy as the time I had to carry you," he said.

"Handy to have a giant around," Robert said gratefully.

******

Carrie settled Robert in for the night and then went to Janie's room. She rapped lightly on the door.

"Come in," Janie called.

"Or perhaps you can come out," Carrie teased as she entered the room. She was relieved to see much of the haunted look was gone from Janie's eyes. Her face would heal quickly. "Rose and I are hoping you'll want to go for a walk. It's a beautiful night."

Janie nodded immediately. "Will I need a coat?"

Carrie smiled. "Not tonight. It's a typical warm, muggy Virginia night, but the breeze will keep the mosquitoes away." She paused. "I will go through my clothes in the morning and make sure you have all you need."

"Carrie—"

"Shh..." Carrie said firmly. "You are my sister. I may not have had many clothes left in Richmond, but my closets are full here. I never could understand why I needed so many clothes. Now I'm just glad I have them. Please let me share them with you. It will make me so happy."

Janie's lips trembled into a smile. "I had to leave everything behind."

"Of course you did. Clothes were the least of your concerns." Carrie stepped forward and put her hands on Janie's shoulders so she could gaze into her eyes. "You were incredibly brave to escape. The last months, even before you left Richmond, have been horrible for you. You will be strong again, but it's okay to take time to heal. You're in the perfect place."

"That's what Matthew told me," Janie said softly, tears of gratitude springing to her eyes. "But I can still see the sadness in him."

"Matthew went through a terrible time. He still hasn't told anyone exactly what happened that night, but it's not necessary we know. Having said that, I do think it will be helpful for you to talk about the last months."

Janie stiffened as her face flooded with shame.

Carrie lifted her chin. "And that's the very reason you need to talk. As long as you feel shame for what Clifford did to you, you will never be truly free. Talking about it will help," she insisted. "I know it will."

Janie sighed heavily. "Can I tell you while we're walking in the dark? That way I won't have to see if you and Rose roll your eyes."

"There will be no eye rolling," Carrie said firmly, "I can't even believe you would think that, after all the times you dealt with my fears and mistakes during the war. You gave me grace and unconditional love. It's my turn to give back."

"You're right," Janie said softly as she hooked her arm through Carrie's. "Let's go for a walk."

Rose was waiting on the steps when they emerged from the house. "Look," she breathed, pointing at an almost full moon resting on the dark line of trees in the distance.

"It's beautiful," Janie breathed. "So incredibly beautiful." A smile bloomed on her face. "Let's go for a walk."

Carrie and Rose fell into step on either side of her, tucking Janie's hands into the crook of their arms. They were all content to walk in silence, relishing the breeze as it swept across their skin. Fireflies danced through the trees as a gaggle of geese flew overhead, honking at the moon. They could hear the horses snuffling in the barn as they passed.

"Jeremy is going to teach me how to ride," Janie said suddenly. "I fell in love with Saffanata on the way out here."

"*Saffanata?*" Rose asked. "What kind of name is that?"

Janie smiled. "Her full name is Sassy Saffanata Glory Be."

"Do tell," Carrie murmured, giggling. "That's quite a name. She must be quite a horse."

Janie nodded. "She's beautiful. She's the same color as Granite and she has such kind eyes. Jeremy said she is an excellent saddle horse."

"Then Jeremy is right," Carrie said firmly. "He has a natural feel for horses. That, if nothing else, would convince me he is my uncle. He didn't spend a day of his life around horses until he got here. He and Granite make an incredible pair. He doesn't have Robert or Clint's knowledge yet, but he will. I'm glad he's going to teach you to ride." She didn't add that everything they could do to build Janie's confidence would help her recover from her marriage to Clifford.

Janie turned to Rose. "Matthew told me you're pregnant again."

"I am!" Rose said joyfully. "I can hardly wait for John to have a little brother or sister."

"Do you care which?"

"Not a bit. It's enough to know this baby of mine is going to be born free, not only because of the Emancipation Proclamation, but free because the Constitution says so." Rose's voice was rich with passion.

"Rose..." Janie's voice was suddenly strained.

Rose turned to her. "Tell me," she invited, continuing when Janie hesitated again. "I know there is trouble coming," she said simply. "There's already a lot of trouble happening for the freed slaves. The more I know, the better I'll be equipped to deal with it—both Moses and I."

Janie stopped and stared out over the fields, watching as the silver light from the moon danced over the softly swaying oats and wheat. All she really wanted to do was forget every word that had ever come out of Clifford's mouth, but she knew the danger of trying to stuff pain away. It always came back, usually worse than before, because refusing to acknowledge it gave it additional power. She took a deep breath and started talking.

Carrie and Rose both held a hand while Janie talked, but they said nothing to interrupt her. The moon rose high in the sky, casting an even brighter light as it changed to a gleaming white, wrapping them in a cocoon of safety and comfort.

Carrie battled the rage inside her as Janie told them of the constant abuse, humiliation and degradation. She clenched her free fist when Janie told them in stark detail of the night he hit her, leaving out nothing about what was going on around the South to the freed slaves.

"Clifford turned into someone I didn't even recognize," Janie finished, her voice a mixture of anger, pain and sorrow. "I still can't believe I actually married him."

Carrie spoke for the first time. "He was nothing like that when you married him," she protested.

"I wanted to believe that for a long time," Janie said, "but the truth is, that the end of the war simply released what had always been there. I just didn't see it because I wanted to be in love."

"But..."

Janie lifted her hand to stop Carrie's words. "I appreciate your loyalty," she said warmly, "but I was only able to start planning my escape when I was willing to face the truth. I know I'm not alone in marrying a *soldier*, not just a man."

"You mean that you weren't able to see past the soldier lying in the bed," Rose replied thoughtfully. "You weren't able to see him as a man."

"That's right," Janie said. "I'm sure there are tens of thousands of women like me right now, in both the South and North. We married men going into battle or wounded from battle. When I forced myself to look at it honestly, I realized I would never have married Clifford under different circumstances. Once I did, I gave up all my rights."

"Until you took them back," Carrie said grimly.

"Yes," Janie agreed. She took a deep breath and stared out over the fields. "I'm starting all over again, but I don't feel the panic I did every day I lived in that house. I don't know what I'm going to do, but I'm trusting I'll find my way."

"Mama used to tell me I was like a caterpillar," Rose said. "That's true for all of us."

"A caterpillar?" Janie asked in an amused voice. "Should I be concerned I'm being compared to a fuzzy worm?"

Rose grinned. "Mama and I were out walking in the woods one morning, when we found a caterpillar spinning a cocoon. It was a Sunday and we didn't have to be back, so we sat right down there in the woods and watched it. The caterpillar used what was inside it to spin a white cocoon that completely encased it. I remember her telling me it would come out a butterfly, but I knew that couldn't be true, because I had watched a worm wrap itself up. I figured it was the first time my mama was going to be wrong."

Rose gripped Janie's hand tightly as she talked, relishing the warm breeze that made her think of the countless nights she had sat outside with her mama. "It was about three weeks later when mama sent someone up to the big house to get me. I thought something was wrong, because she never sent for me in the middle of the week. I remember running all the way down there," she said with a soft laugh. "Mama had cut off the limb with the cocoon on it and brought it back to her cabin. She was sitting in front of it when I got there. I sat down with her, and we watched as that cocoon slowly cracked open. I was so amazed when a butterfly crawled out. It had to lay there for a while, until it got strong enough to fly, but pretty soon that little thing flew out the window." She shook her head. "It still makes me feel awe to know that can happen."

"And your mama had a lesson to go with it," Carrie said.

"Always," Rose agreed with a chuckle. "She told me I was just like that caterpillar. I was growing awful fast, but the time would come when life would wrap me up in a cocoon because I needed to change. When that happened, I was going to go through a complete transformation. God was going to break me down completely, so that I could become something brand new and beautiful. She told me everyone has to go through it."

Carrie nodded. "She told me the same thing one day. She also told me that since I wasn't really a caterpillar, I shouldn't be surprised if I had to go into that cocoon more than once. She said we all go through different seasons of life, and that we have to become new people for each one."

"Thank you," Janie said softly. "That's exactly how I feel. I wonder what happens in the cocoon?" she mused. "I wonder if it hurts terribly to change from a caterpillar to a butterfly."

Rose shrugged. "I just know I'm not usually having fun when I go through a transformation," she said wryly. "It usually hurts, or it's at least uncomfortable."

Janie nodded and gripped both their hands tightly as she inclined her head toward the edge of the woods.

Carrie sucked in her breath as she watched a herd of deer step out into the fields. Tiny fawns pranced on the edge of the woods, their white spots glowing in the moon, while their mothers grazed next to them. Two huge bucks with wide racks of antlers stood guard, testing the breeze with raised heads. "They're so beautiful," she whispered, shivering as the magic of the night wrapped itself around her.

The three women stood quietly for a long time.

"I'm ready," Janie said suddenly. "I don't know what really happens in a cocoon to turn a caterpillar into a butterfly, but I know being trapped in Clifford's house has turned me into a new woman. I spent a lot of my time terrified, but I also learned to respect myself, and that I was strong enough to do what was needed to change my life. I still don't know what is coming next, but being out here with both of you tonight has made me realize I'm not afraid of it anymore."

Carrie grinned and threw her arms around Janie. Rose wrapped both of them in her own warm embrace. Suddenly, all three of them began to laugh. Their laughter echoed against the woods and came shimmering back to them, encircling them with life that pulsed through their being.

When they finally quit laughing, Carrie turned her face to gaze into the moon. "We are powerful women," she said quietly. "We are going in different directions, but our spirits will always be united as one, no matter where we are, or what we're doing. The war has changed everything. Women have opportunities they have never had, but we're going to have to continue to fight hard to be treated with respect and equality."

"You've been talking to Aunt Abby," Rose observed. "She's right. I also know that freedom, whether you are black or white, means responsibility. Especially when you have opportunities most people can only dream of."

"Like the three of us," Janie said quietly. "The decisions we make aren't just about our own lives. They're about the lives of all women."

Carrie nodded somberly. "It's a heavy load to carry sometimes."

"Leading sure is more fun than following along in the pack," Rose said firmly. "Moses and I talk about that a lot. I don't know what the years are going to bring, but I'm quite sure we're not going to just wait and see how it impacts us. We're going to lead the way into change as much as we can."

"While putting your lives into grave danger," Janie said in a troubled voice. "The men with Clifford talked about terrible things that are happening."

Rose frowned, but her voice was strong and resolute. "No matter what we choose to do, our lives are going to be in grave danger because of the times we live in. Our biggest concern is that we can both hold our heads high at the end of each day and know we're living a life our children can be proud of."

"I'm right there with you," Carrie vowed.

"Me, too," Janie chimed in. "We will let nothing stop us from moving forward."

Chapter Twenty-Seven

Carrie tapped lightly on Abby's door, her heart bursting with excitement. She saw a mirror of her joy when Abby opened the door. "It's finally here! You're getting married."

Abby grinned, her gray eyes dancing. "Having you excited about it gives me as much joy as the wedding itself," she confided. "I can't tell you how long I've dreamed of having a daughter. I've thought of you as one since the first summer we were together. To have it become official is almost more than I can absorb." She took hold of Carrie's hands. "I hope you know I'll do everything I can to make your father happy. I never dreamed I would love another man, but I discover that my love for him keeps growing every day. Your father is quite extraordinary."

"I couldn't agree more," Carrie replied. She started to say something else but stopped.

Abby looked at her closely and pulled her down beside her on the bed. "What is it?" she asked.

"Your wedding day is hardly a time to ask the question that popped in my mind," Carrie protested. "I'm confident you've already thought about it. We can talk another time."

Abby gazed at her and smiled. "You read the women's rights journal that Jeremy brought back yesterday."

Carrie sighed. "Yes," she admitted.

"And you're wondering if I'm crazy to give your father control over all my assets."

"I definitely don't think you're crazy," Carrie protested. "I know my father, but..." She struggled to pull her thoughts together. They had been rampaging in her head ever since she had read the article.

"You didn't know that under law, every penny you make and any control of property actually belongs to Robert since you're married," Abby guessed.

Carrie shook her head. "I'd never thought about it."

"Does it bother you?"

Carrie fought to think clearly. "It's not that I don't trust Robert," she said slowly. "It's just that I don't believe anyone has the right to decide what I can or cannot do with what I have worked to create."

"Go on," Abby encouraged.

"Clifford saw Janie as property. He believed he could do anything he wanted with her."

"And legally he was right," Abby observed.

"Which makes the laws completely wrong," Carrie said angrily. "They must be changed."

"Agreed," Abby said calmly.

Carrie stared at her. "Which brings me back to—"

"Your father and I."

Carrie nodded. "Aren't you afraid?"

Abby smiled and squeezed her hand. "As I said before, your father is an extraordinary man. We talked at length about my assets and holdings. He was a little put off that he was marrying such a wealthy woman, especially when he is struggling to re-establish his own wealth. And I wasn't willing to relinquish control of what I have worked so hard for."

"How did y'all resolve it?" Carrie asked breathlessly.

"All my properties and income have been put into a trust in my name," Abby explained. "The laws have already changed a lot about a wife's rights to property, but they still have a ways to go. In the meantime, women have to be smart. If they choose a husband well, like I have, the husband will be smart, too."

"So the trust protects you?"

"Mostly," Abby admitted. "While the assets remain in my name, the law says your father has control over everything as long as he is alive."

"Oh."

Abby smiled. "It goes back to making a good choice. Your father and I talked about it. I've never once thought he was after control of my assets, but just to make me feel comfortable, he created a document relinquishing his right to any control. The only exception will be the factory, because we are going to build and run it together as true partners."

"Marriage can be complicated," Carrie said with a frown.

"That it can," Abby agreed, chuckling.

"Yet you're willing to do it."

Abby nodded thoughtfully. "Marriage is a risk. Any kind of relationship or partnership is a risk. You make the best decision you can, and then you live with the consequences. I believe it's a balancing act. I treasure my independence as a single woman, but I also miss the joys and fulfillment that comes from sharing my life with someone I love deeply. I have found that again with your father. I have taken steps to be wise, but I won't let my fears keep me from living a life filled with love."

Carrie smiled. "And my father is the luckiest man in the world, because he's getting a woman who is loving, beautiful *and* brilliant." She could think later about fighting for women's rights. Today, she was going to focus on making Abby's day perfect.

She stood and moved over to where Abby's dress was hanging on the door. "It's lovely," she breathed, as she ran a hand down the light yellow dress trimmed in cream satin. "Can I help you get ready?"

"I would love that," Abby said eagerly.

Carrie moved toward the door. "I brought assistants." She opened the door to reveal Rose and Janie waiting outside. "I'm hopeless with hair, but Rose is a magician."

"And I just don't want to miss any of the excitement," Janie laughed.

"Oh, Janie," Abby murmured. "This must be so hard."

"Not at all," Janie said firmly. "It gives me hope. You have found true love twice. It helps me believe that I may someday find a man worthy of me," she said smugly.

Abby laughed. "You have come a long way."

Janie nodded, suddenly somber. "I know better than to think all the pain and regret will go away so quickly, but that doesn't mean I can't celebrate love when I see it." She waved her hand toward the chair in front of the oak armoire with a massive mirror. "It's time to let Rose do her magic."

Abby smiled and seated herself. "No woman ever had a more perfect wedding party," she said softly. "I am all yours, Rose."

One hour later, after much talk and laughter, Abby was ready. She had tears in her eyes when she gazed at herself in the mirror. "Oh my..."

"You are absolutely beautiful," Janie said with awe.

Abby stared at herself. The yellow dress hugged her slim figure, illuminating the golden glow the sun had given her in the last weeks, and making her gray eyes seem even bigger. Her soft brown hair was pulled up into a loose bun on top of her head. Loose tendrils curled lightly around her face, but she knew it was the look of sheer joy that made her beautiful. "I do believe you're right," she whispered, almost stunned with the sheer delight shining from her eyes. "I never believed I would feel this way again."

"The day is only going to get better," Carrie proclaimed. "While we've been up here, everyone else has been downstairs getting everything ready."

"I do believe I remember saying that things should be simple," Abby protested.

"Yes, I remember that, too," Carrie agreed. "I also seem to remember saying I would do it my way. You are marrying *my* father, the least I can do is attempt to make it the most special day of your life."

Tears filled Abby's eyes. "I didn't really have a wedding with Charles," she admitted. "My family was appalled I was marrying a Northerner, so they ignored the whole marriage. He didn't have family, and I hadn't made many friends yet, so it was rather a solitary event."

Carrie wrapped her arm around her waist. "Not this time!" she declared joyfully. "You're going to be surrounded by people who love you. I know if we were in Philadelphia, the church would be overflowing with people, but *hundreds* of people couldn't equal the love all of us feel for you.

A light tap sounded at the door. "Everything is ready," Jeremy called.

Carrie turned to Abby. "I believe that is our cue."

Rose and Janie both kissed Abby on the cheek and promised they would see her downstairs.

Abby turned to Carrie. "Since you seem to be in control of this wonderful day, I am yours to command."

"Could you repeat that, please?" Carrie teased. "It may be the only time I hear you say it."

Abby laughed and then twirled in front of the mirror. "I feel like a girl again," she said, her eyes shining brightly. "Please take me to your father. I don't believe I can wait another minute."

Carrie grinned, took her hand, and led her to the top of the stairs. As soon as they appeared, Janie began to play the piano softly.

Matthew, who had been waiting in the alcove at the top of the stairs, stepped up to Abby's side. "It would be my great honor to give you away, Mrs. Livingston," he said gravely, his eyes twinkling with fun.

Abby smiled and reached up to kiss him on the cheek. "I can't think of anyone more perfect."

Carrie squeezed her hand. "I'll see you downstairs." She turned and ran down the stairs, smiling with delight when she saw what everyone had done to the parlor. There was hardly a spot that wasn't full of vases of fresh-cut flowers. Greenery hung over all the doorframes and windows, and fresh air blew in, turning the parlor into a fragrant fantasy.

"You've outdone yourself, daughter."

Carrie whirled around and stared at her father, resplendent in a dark gray suit. His face was tanned and relaxed, his eyes dancing with pleasure. "Father! You look magnificent."

"I'm glad you approve," Thomas replied. "Thank you for making this day so special. Everything looks wonderful."

Carrie smiled. "Nothing but the best for my father and his wonderful new bride, whom I adore as much as I do you."

"I know," Thomas said softly. A sudden shadow flitted through his eyes.

Carrie tucked her hand in his arm. "Mother would approve," she said quietly. "She loved you so much. I know she would want you to be happy. And," she added before Thomas could respond, "I believe she knows you will always love her. She knows you're moving into a new season of life, but you will always treasure the one that came before."

Thomas took a deep breath. "How could I ever deserve such a wise and loving daughter?"

Carrie laughed and kissed his cheek. "You forgot brilliant and talented," she teased. She took his hand and led him to the front of the room, smiling at the minister who was waiting in the doorway. When everyone was situated, she nodded at Janie again to switch the music—the sign for Matthew to lead Abby down the stairway. Then she took her seat beside Robert.

"Everything is perfect," Robert whispered.

Carrie's heart felt like it would explode with joy when she looked into Robert's vibrant eyes. He wasn't back to full strength yet, but he was spending hours in the barn every day and had begun to ride again. He had put on weight and the lines on his face were growing dimmer every day. The white pallor of his illness had been replaced with a healthy tan. She knew that by fall, he would look like the man she had married.

A murmur in the room made her swing her eyes to the stairway, but she looked away to watch her father, her heart singing when she saw his eyes blaze with love and wonder. His eyes were locked on Abby as she floated down the stairs. Carrie knew everyone else had ceased to exist for him.

Abby held his eyes as she walked into the parlor on Matthew's arm and took her place beside him.

******

When the day had dawned clear and with little humidity—a rare treat on a Virginia July day—Carrie moved the feast and dancing to the backyard to take advantage of the breeze and cooler temperatures. Little tables with white tablecloths were scattered around the yard. While the parlor wouldn't hold everyone on the plantation for the wedding, everyone was invited to the reception.

The yard rang with laughter and the squeals of children. All the men's families had arrived from the contraband camps in the last couple weeks. They had insisted on providing the music for the event. A joyous mix of black spirituals and modern music spilled from their fiddles, banjos and harmonicas.

The food was a sight to behold. Annie and Polly had been cooking for days, aided by many of the new women on the plantation. Long buffet tables placed under the trees groaned under the load of the piles of food that grew with every trip to the kitchen.

Lush gardens had provided huge platters of fresh vegetables. There were plates of fried chicken and Virginia ham surrounded by serving dishes full of deviled eggs, and steaming biscuits wrapped carefully in towels to keep them moist. Churns full of butter rested beside mountains of cornbread, and pies and cakes of every imaginable kind tempted anyone who came near.

The afternoon and evening passed in a haze of dancing, laughter, talking, and never-ending games of chase. Jeremy had ordered in several sets of croquet, a new craze up north since 1860.

Carrie grinned at Matthew as she hit his ball out of bounds and then promptly put hers through the wicket. "I do believe I like this game," she said innocently.

"Show off," Matthew muttered, his eyes bright with laughter.

"Perhaps you should play with one of the children," Carrie suggested. "You might have a better chance of winning."

Matthew laughed loudly. "We'll see. The day is still young. Have you never heard that pride goeth before a fall?"

Carrie grinned impishly as she struck her ball smartly through another wicket. "I don't seem to be the one falling."

Jeremy left the dancing and walked over to join them. "Is she beating you, too?"

"So I'm not the only male here to have my pride knocked around?" Matthew asked.

"Afraid not," Jeremy assured him. "No one has beaten her yet."

"That's only because she hasn't played me," Robert said as he joined them. "Carrie has a fierce competitive streak, but it's time for her to go down."

Carrie merely smiled and handed him a mallet. "Give it your best shot, Captain Borden. I will be happy to add you to my list of those I have vanquished."

"We'll see, Mrs. Borden... We'll see."

"Good luck, old man," Matthew said with a chuckle. "She obviously never learned the lesson that proper women are supposed to let men win."

"And on that note, it's time for me to assure all of you that I have not the faintest desire to be a *proper* woman," Carrie tossed over her shoulder as she hit her ball out of the double wickets to start a new game. "Win on your own merits, or prepare to be vanquished."

"Proper women are so boring," Robert said blithely, "but I warn you, I play to win."

"That's what they all said," Carrie said loftily, her eyes dancing with fun.

******

All the families had drifted back down to their cabins. The tables were empty of food, and all the musical instruments had been put away. The sun had set, kissing the sky with a haze of gold and purple that seemed a fitting end to such a magical day.

Carrie and Rose sank down into the rockers on the porch and closed their eyes.

Janie walked out onto the porch. "Are your eyes closed from contentment or exhaustion?"

Carrie cracked one open and managed a smile. "A little of both."

"Speak for yourself," Rose said. "It's a lot of both."

Carrie cocked her head and nodded. "She's right." She waved a hand at another rocking chair. "Join us. It's perfectly okay if you want to groan at some point."

Janie smiled and joined them. "It was an absolutely perfect day. Your father and Abby looked so happy and so much in love."

Carrie forgot her fatigue for a moment as she smiled. "Yes, they did. Every aching muscle was completely worth it."

"Oh please," Rose replied, opening one eye to peer at her. "Your muscles are aching because you spent the whole afternoon dancing and defending your title as the queen of croquet."

"That's true," Carrie said, satisfaction ringing in her voice. "I love to dance, and I love to win. It was definitely a perfect day."

"You didn't even let your husband win!" Janie said with mock dismay.

"I'll take her on my own when I'm stronger. She won't hold her title for long."

The women gasped and began to giggle as Robert's voice drifted down from the window over the porch. They looked up to see him staring down at them, a wide grin on his face.

"Do women always gloat over their victories?" he asked, curiosity shining in his eyes.

"These women do," Moses answered as he strolled out onto the porch. "They have joined together to spurn every proper way to protect a man's pride. I'm not sure what happened, because I'm sure Sarah taught Rose the right way to treat her husband."

"Hmm..." Robert said thoughtfully. "I'm quite sure Carrie's mother taught her. In fact, I'm rather certain it was her goal in life."

"That she failed at quite miserably," Carrie said playfully.

"And my mama never told me to be less than I am," Rose added. "If I happen to be better than a man at something, they're going to have to get used to it."

"Amen!" Janie agreed.

Moses looked up at Robert and shrugged his shoulders. "Do you see what I mean? We don't stand a chance."

Robert grinned. "Good thing we both like strong-willed, obstinate women."

Carrie suddenly felt like crying. She couldn't believe Robert and Moses were bantering like two old friends. She had seen them together many times since they had talked about their fathers' deaths, but she hadn't realized their relationship had evolved into such an easy friendship. When Rose reached over and squeezed her hand, Carrie knew she was thinking the same thing.

Moses settled down on the stairs, his back against the railing. Matthew and Jeremy wandered out to join them. Robert was close behind.

Silence fell on the group as all of them allowed the night air to wash over them.

"Has it really only been three months since the war ended?" Carrie asked, breaking the silence. "It seemed like it would last forever, but now that it's over, it seems like it was so long ago."

"That's because we're protected out here on the plantation," Matthew answered, heaviness tingeing his words. "There are plenty of places here in the country where people are surrounded by daily reminders of the war."

"And our people are fighting for their freedom every day," Rose said softly. "I love being here on the plantation, but I wonder when the trouble will reach us."

"I'll be able to keep you better informed soon," Matthew replied quietly.

Carrie turned to gaze at him. "You're leaving?"

Matthew nodded. "Yes. The last weeks have been wonderful. It's been six weeks since the *Sultana* went down. I felt like my entire soul died that night, but being out here has allowed me to see things differently."

"Are you going back to the paper?" Jeremy asked.

"No," Matthew said firmly. "My days of roaming around the country as a reporter are over."

"You talked at one time of starting your own paper," Robert said. "Is it time?"

"Not yet. That may come, but I don't believe the time is now." Matthew took a deep breath. "I've been approached by a publisher in New York to write a book about what life is like in the South right now. I've decided to accept."

"That's wonderful!" Carrie exclaimed. "You're the perfect person to do it."

"Why?" Matthew held her gaze. "Why am I the perfect person to do it?"

Carrie knew that even though Matthew had made his decision, he still needed affirmation he had made the right one. "Because you care about everyone equally," she responded instantly. "You love both the North and the South. You see the wrongs with both, but you also see what's right. You are the perfect person to tell the story about what is happening with the freed slaves because you are committed to the truth. You'll tell the stories of the veterans, and you'll make people realize the South is full of people just like them - people who are trying to rebuild their lives."

Matthew nodded slowly. "I hope so. That's what I want to do. It's the reason I said yes."

Rose gripped his hand tightly. "I will never forget the day you saved me from Ike Adams. I looked into your eyes, and I knew I could trust you, even though I didn't even know who you were. Your words on paper will make an entire country trust you to tell them the truth, even if they don't like what they're hearing."

Matthew flushed as he looked around the porch. "I wish the whole world could have friends like all of you are to me."

"When do you leave?" Janie asked.

Matthew glanced at Jeremy.

"Matthew and I are leaving in two days," Jeremy responded. "Now that the wedding is over and my big brother is hitched, I'm moving into Richmond to manage the factory. Matthew and I are going to share the east wing of the house."

"I'll use Richmond as my base," Matthew explained. "I'll travel as much as I need to, but it will be my choice each time."

"We'll miss you," Carrie murmured, "but at least you'll be close. I know we'll see each other often."

"A new season," Janie said softly. "Now that the war is over, each of us is having to rebuild our lives, just like we're having to rebuild our country."

A thick silence fell on the porch as dreams and hopes swirled through the darkness.

******

Thomas moved toward Abby and pulled the pins from her hair gently, catching her soft hair as it cascaded down her back. "You're so beautiful," he said, his eyes glowing with love. "I can hardly believe you're my wife."

"And I can hardly believe I am now Mrs. Abigail Cromwell." Abby reached up to stroke his cheek. "I am so blessed to have such a handsome, loving and intelligent man to share the rest of my life with. I predict we are going to have many amazing adventures."

"Let the adventures begin," Thomas said with a grin.

"They won't all be fun," Abby said soberly.

Thomas nodded. "I know. We're heading into a hothouse of controversy and anger by moving to Richmond, but we both know it's the right thing to do." He ran a brush through her hair, admiring how it gleamed in the lantern light flickering through the room, the breeze making shadows dance across the bed. "As long as we're together, we'll be able to handle anything," he said firmly.

Abby smiled. "I do believe you're right, Mr. Cromwell."

"You'll find I'm right about many things," Thomas replied, laughter dancing in his eyes. "Any man smart enough to win you as his wife must be quite a man."

"Right again," Abby murmured, standing and turning into his arms. "Now, if you don't mind, I would like to take action on all the things I've been thinking and dreaming about for the last two months."

Thomas grinned, swept her into his arms, and carried her to the bed. He laid her down gently, his eyes darkening with passion. "Beautiful," he said as he gazed down at her. "So very beautiful..."

Nothing more was said for a long time.

Chapter Twenty-Eight

"It is brutally hot today," Carrie exclaimed, brushing back her hair as she fanned herself on the porch. "I can't believe it's almost September."

"It doesn't seem to be bothering Robert and Clint," Rose responded, as she pulled her rocking chair into the last remaining bit of shade on the porch.

"Nothing seems to bother them," Carrie replied, her eyes shining with pleasure as she watched them working Eclipse in one of the arenas. "Sometimes I can't believe that's my husband out there."

"He looks wonderful, Carrie. And he seems so happy."

"He's completely himself again," Carrie stated.

"Are the nightmares still bothering him?"

Carrie nodded, watching Robert as he moved up next to Eclipse and stroked his gleaming neck. The man and horse had developed a powerful bond. He would perform well for Clint, but his love belonged to Robert. "Yes. They don't happen as often, but when they come, they are terrible. All I can do is hold him until he quits shaking."

"Will he talk about them?"

"More and more. At first he didn't want to say anything, because he didn't want to put the images in my head. I finally convinced him that talking would release their power."

"And you?"

Carrie sighed. "I still shudder at all Robert has endured. I wish we could all go back and make different decisions in the years leading up to the war, but we can't. If our leaders could have known what the consequences of their decisions would be, I wonder if they still would have done it." She shook her head. "It doesn't matter now. We can't relive the past. All we can do is make the most of the present, and try to make better decisions in the future."

"From Matthew's latest letters, it doesn't seem to me that Southern leaders learned much from the war," Rose said, her eyes flashing with anger. "And with President

Johnson still in charge because Congress is not in session, things just seem to be getting worse."

Carrie nodded, knowing the peace pervading the plantation was not being echoed across the rest of the country. "I know," she agreed heavily, "but I learned during the war that I couldn't control anything but my own actions."

"You don't care what's happening?" Rose asked with disbelief.

Carrie turned to gaze at her. "You know better than that," she said evenly, knowing the news Matthew was sending about worsening conditions for many of the freed slaves was increasingly hard for Rose and Moses to hear.

Rose reached forward to grab Carrie's hand. "I'm so sorry," she cried, tears springing to her eyes. "I know you care every bit as much as I do." She shook her head. "Not doing anything is about to drive me mad."

"The school is almost done," Carrie reminded her. "Robert and Clint have been going there every evening to help the rest of the men. Gabe has been a lifesaver. I don't think there is anything that man doesn't know about building."

Rose took a deep breath. "You're right. Abby and your father have been fabulous about sending supplies. The school isn't fancy, but it's going to hold at least one hundred students. I don't think it will be long before I'll have to bring in an additional teacher, but I'm going to handle it all at the beginning, with June working as my assistant."

"Which should assure you that you're not sitting back and doing *nothing*," Carrie reminded her gently.

"You're right," Rose agreed.

"But...?" Carrie asked quietly. Rose gazed at her but didn't answer. "It's not enough," Carrie answered for her.

"It has to be," Rose replied. She held a hand to her stomach, which was just showing the beginning of a bulge, and then looked down at where John played in the yard with two of the workers' children. "It has to be enough," she repeated almost desperately.

"It's a season," Carrie reminded her. "You can't possibly know what is coming in the future. Remember your mama telling you that you had to bloom where you were planted when you made the decision not to escape?"

Rose nodded thoughtfully, a small smile playing on her lips. "She reminded me I was the only one who could determine my destiny. When the time was right, Moses and I escaped and started brand new lives." She managed a small laugh. "I also know that if things changed and we weren't here anymore, my heart would break to lose you again."

Carrie stared off into the distance, her gaze drawn north. "The time is coming Rose, but we'll never lose each other again. Distance may separate us, but a war and armies won't keep us apart."

"You're getting restless," Rose observed. "Being here is not enough for you either." Her eyes widened. "I've been so concerned with myself that I didn't recognize your own angst."

Carrie smiled. "I wouldn't call it angst. My heart still longs to be a doctor, but the war also taught me to make the most of what I'm living right this minute. Yes, I want to go to medical school, but it also brings me such joy to watch Robert get strong. My heart sings when I watch Clint ride and see his confidence growing every day. And little Amber is a wonder. Robert is teaching her to ride, and she's taking to it like she was born on a horse."

"The two of them together are pure joy to watch," Rose agreed. "Amber told me you're taking walks in the woods together."

Carrie nodded. "I'm teaching her everything your mama taught me. Amber is a natural healer." She shook her head. "I wish I could have started learning at her age. She soaks it up like dry ground soaks up the rain."

Suddenly, Rose shaded her eyes and looked off into the distance. "Expecting company?"

Carrie shook her head. "Father said he and Abby would be out to visit in September. Jeremy is busy in the factory, and the last I heard, Matthew headed down to Georgia for a story." She stood and walked to the edge of the porch, watching as a wagon worked its way down the drive.

Moments later, Robert was standing next to her. "Where is Janie?" he asked quietly.

Carrie frowned. "You think it's Clifford?" There had been no word from Janie's husband. It had become easy to pretend nothing was going to happen.

"I don't know. Do you know where she is?"

"She went down to help some of the women can vegetables. She's determined to learn how to do it herself," Carrie said with a smile. "I don't expect her back until around dinner."

Robert nodded but remained beside her as the wagon drew close enough for them to realize there was a man driving, with three other men in the back. "Let's see what they want," he said, stepping down to meet them.

"Hello," Robert said cordially. "Welcome to Cromwell Plantation."

The driver nodded with relief. "I'm glad we found the right place. Are you Thomas Cromwell?"

Robert shook his head. "No," was all he said.

Carrie knew he was being cautious because of reports of violence coming in from all over the country, but a quick glance into the back of the wagon told her the story of why they were here. She stepped forward. "Thomas Cromwell is my father. My name is Carrie Borden. How can we help you?"

The driver wiped the sweat off his face. "We're here looking for you, Mrs. Borden." He looked into the back of the wagon. "We hear you know how to doctor."

Carrie stepped off the porch and approached the wagon, grimacing when she saw the flushed, feverish eyes of the three men staring back at her. "Take that wagon into the shade," she ordered briskly. She looked up at Rose. "Please ask Annie to bring out several pitchers of cool water."

Robert took her hand as the driver pulled the wagon around under the shade of the oak tree. "Can you help them?"

Carrie sighed. "I don't know," she admitted. "I'll do the best I can." Her mind raced, as she considered how she could help them with virtually no medical supplies.

"You'll help them with what you have," Robert said firmly. "I believe in you."

Carrie took a deep breath. "Thank you," she breathed.

Amber ran up and skidded to a stop. "What can I do to help, Carrie?"

Carrie stooped down to look her in the eyes. "Please run up to my room and get my medical bag. And then stay close because I'm going to need you to get some things out of the cellar."

She turned to Robert. "Please come with me. It will help them to know you've gotten well after being so sick." She took his hand as she walked over to the wagon and leaned over the edge.

"Hello," Carrie said gently, not allowing her face to show alarm at the condition of the three men who were obviously veterans. "Y'all don't look like you feel very good."

"Don't reckon we do," one whispered. He was bone thin, his face flushed with fever and his eyes bright with desperation. He was also missing a leg below the knee.

Carrie decided to start with him. "What's your name, soldier?"

The man's scrawny shoulders straightened just a little as she acknowledged his service to the Confederacy. "Joe Whistler, ma'am."

"What's wrong, Joe?"

Joe took a deep breath, and set his teeth as he pulled back his pant leg and revealed an ugly red infection spreading from his stump. "It hurts pretty bad, Mrs. Borden."

"I'm sure it does," Carrie said gently. "How long has it been this way?"

"A couple weeks. I lost it during the fighting at Petersburg. It seemed to be doing okay, but then it started hurting even worse. My wife says it's infected."

"She's right." Carrie's mind raced as she tried to remember what herbs and remedies she still had in the basement.

"Can you help?" Joe asked, his voice hoarse with pain.

Carrie reached down to take his hand. "I'll do everything I can," she promised. Then she turned to the next man. "What's your name, soldier?"

"Alfred Whiteside, ma'am. I didn't want to come here today."

"Why not?" Carrie asked, gazing at the slender blond who certainly had to still be in his teens. He had all his limbs, but she recognized the look in his eyes.

"Don't see no reason for living," he said weakly, apathy dulling his voice as much as his eyes.

The wagon driver spoke up. "His mama put him in my wagon this morning when she heard I was coming to look for you. She lost her other three boys. She begged me to bring Alfred."

Robert stepped forward. "Hello, Alfred. My name is Captain Robert Borden. Where did you last serve?"

Alfred stared up at him, his eyes showing the first spark of interest. "I served up until the end, Captain. Right before General Lee surrendered, I got real sick with pneumonia, but I was there at the end."

"Me, too," Robert replied.

"You were there at the end?"

"Yes, but I also got pneumonia. It almost killed me."

Alfred eyed him. "It don't look like you've been sick."

"Not now," Robert agreed. "I was sick for a while, but even when I started to get better, I didn't want to live. I lay in bed for two months more than I needed to, because I couldn't find a reason to get out of it."

Alfred looked at Carrie. "Ain't she your wife, Captain?"

"Yes."

"Seems like a good reason to me," he said with a faint smile.

Robert laughed. "You're right about that!" Then he sobered. "I thought the war had taken everything from me. My health was gone. My home was gone. My livelihood had been taken away from me."

Alfred nodded. "I sure understand that," he said weakly. "My family had a nice little farm before the war. We didn't have a lot, but we had enough. We all worked the farm—me and my brothers. Now my daddy and my brothers are all gone, and I'm the only one left. The farm was destroyed by them Yankees. Me and my mama live in a little shack we found that didn't have anybody living in it. No one's thrown us out yet."

"Your mama loves you," Carrie reminded him. "That's why she sent you."

"I know. It just ain't enough to make me care," he admitted.

"You let Carrie help you," Robert said gently. "Then you and I will talk."

Carrie turned to the next man when Alfred nodded. "What's your name, soldier."

"Bobby Haystack, ma'am. I remember you."

Carrie searched her memory but couldn't pull his face out of the thousands of soldiers she had treated. "Were you at Chimborazo?"

"No, ma'am. I was in the trenches around Petersburg last winter."

Carrie's lips tightened as she remembered the horrors the soldiers had been forced to endure through the brutal weather. "I'm sorry," she whispered.

"I saw you when you and your friends came through with the wagons of supplies to keep us warm. You helped a lot of the fellows." He nodded at Robert. "I recognize you, too, Captain Borden. You were one of the few officers who stayed with their men in the trenches. It meant a lot to them."

Robert nodded. "What's wrong, Bobby?"

Bobby sighed and motioned down to the bottom of the wagon where a blanket was covering his legs. "I suppose Joe and I have the same problem," he replied, pulling back the blanket. "By the time you got there with the supplies, Mrs. Borden, it was too late for me."

Carrie couldn't stop the gasp that sprang from her lips when she saw the bright red infection swarming with maggots. Bobby had lost both of his feet during that brutal winter.

"I know it looks real bad, Mrs. Borden. I thought about just letting the infection kill me, but then I heard someone saying you were back on the plantation. Lots of the fellows have talked about how you took care of them, so I decided to see if you could help me. I got a wife and two little boys that need me. The other two just came along for the ride." His voice faded away as fatigue and pain made him tighten his lips. He sagged against the side of the wagon.

Carrie nodded, trying to think clearly. "I'll do everything I can, Bobby," she said. She knew Bobby and Joe didn't have long if she wasn't able to bring their infections under control. She discarded her brief thought that she could get them to Richmond. They would never survive the trip.

Annie appeared at her side. "What you need done, Carrie?"

Bobby's eyes cleared slightly as a sneer formed on his lips. "Your niggers call you by your first name, Mrs. Borden?"

Carrie stiffened as she held his gaze. "My *friends* call me Carrie. There are no niggers on Cromwell Plantation, Mr. Haystack. If you believe you can treat my friends with respect, I will do everything I can to help you. If you think that will not be possible, I'll let you go now."

Bobby stared at her and then lowered his eyes. "I'm sorry, Mrs. Borden."

Carrie took a deep breath, wondering if she was making a grave mistake to let these men on the plantation. She met Robert's eyes across the wagon and saw his slight nod. He believed she should help them, so she would do all she could.

"Driver, please take the wagon over to the barn." She turned to Robert. "You and Clint take the men upstairs to the room. Be sure to open all the windows. We had it cleaned out last week so it should be suitable. I'll send Annie over with blankets. They'll have to lie on the floor for now, but I'll have some of the men make some beds this afternoon." She gazed down at the men. "They won't be anything fancy, but they will get you up off the floor."

All three of the men nodded.

"We're grateful for anything," Joe said weakly.

Carrie smiled. "I know you are," she said gently. The only way to fight the prejudice pulsing through these men was to show them another way of living. No one changed the way they saw things until they had the opportunity to see them differently. It had been that way for her, and now she was going to give these veterans a chance to see how the South could be, if they changed their beliefs.

She watched as the wagon pulled over to the barn, and then she nodded at Amber, who was standing over to the side with her medical bag. "Please come help me, Amber."

Amber ran to her side. "We going out into the woods, Carrie?" Her eyes were bright with intensity.

Carrie smiled. "No, not unless we have to. We're going down into the basement."

"What's down there?"

"Bottles of herbs and concoctions I made years ago," Carrie said, grateful beyond measure that some of it was still there. She turned to Annie. "Please go into the garden and pull several large onions. I'll need them sliced up."

"To pull the infection out," Annie said, her wise eyes shining.

Carrie paused. "How do you know that?"

"My mama taught me the magic just like Old Sarah taught you," Annie replied. "I don't know it as good as you, but I know a bunch."

Carrie nodded. "Can you help me and Amber up in the barn room?"

"You just tells me what to do, Miss Carrie. I'll do it."

******

Clint ran up to Carrie as she was emerging from the house, her bag full of herbs from the basement. "Me and Robert got the men up into the room," he said, his breath catching. "I don't think they was too happy to be carried upstairs by a black person, but they didn't make a fuss."

"They'd better not have," Carrie said crisply. Her voice softened. "Thank you for helping, Clint."

"Is there anythin' else I can do? Robert sent me over to find out."

"Yes. Please ride out into the fields and ask Moses to have two of the men make three simple beds. We need to keep those men off the floor. Then I'd like you to go to the cabins and ask Janie to come back. I could use her help."

"Yes, ma'am," Clint responded. "I'll get them back here as fast as I can," he said, excitement shining in his eyes.

"And have fun doing it," Carrie said in an amused voice.

Clint ducked his head but not fast enough to hide his smile. "I reckon that's true," he answered, and then turned and ran.

Carrie chuckled and turned when Annie called her name. "Are the onions ready, Annie?"

"They sho 'nuff be. I done mashed them up into a paste, and I got some rags and warm water ready to take out."

Carrie breathed a sigh of relief. "Thank you. I'm also going to need some long strips of sheeting to secure the poultices to their limbs. We don't have long to get their fever down," she said grimly.

"They don't look good, sho 'nuff," Annie muttered. She turned when Amber ran out onto the porch. "Go back into the kitchen and get them onions and water, Amber."

Rose walked out on the porch with a huge platter. "I have it all, Annie. It's too heavy for Amber to carry." She smiled down at the little girl. "Let's do it together."

"Yessum, Miss Rose," Amber replied. She reached for the other side of the platter and grinned up at Rose. "I done finished reading that new book you gave me last night."

"You did what?" Rose asked, cocking an eyebrow.

Amber grinned. "I meant to say that I finished reading the new book you gave me last night."

"Much better," Rose said fondly. She looked at Carrie. "Go on. We'll be right there."

Carrie turned, lifted her skirts, and strode rapidly across the yard to the barn. Memories swept through her when she climbed the stairs. She avoided the room over the barn as much as she could. Even though she was happy that Miles, the slave who had taken care of her father's horses, had escaped to freedom, the memories still hurt. *He had taught her how to ride...how to care for the horses...how to learn to love them as much as he did.* The memories swirled around her like the dust motes dancing in the air when she pushed open the door to the room. She shoved them out of her mind and prepared to help men who thought her friends should still be slaves.

"We made them as comfortable as we could," Robert said, staring down at the men with pity in his eyes.

"Thank you," Carrie replied. "I sent Clint to go get two men from the fields so they could make beds."

"What's first?" Robert asked.

Carrie smiled, grateful for the help. They didn't have much time. Rose and Amber appeared in the doorway with the platter.

"Annie will be right here with the cloth strips," Rose said.

Carrie nodded. "We have to treat their infections first," she said crisply. "Annie has already made the poultice for us. Both Joe and Bobby are going to need a fresh poultice every hour to draw out the infection."

Amber sniffed the large bowl. "This ain't nothing but onions, Carrie!"

"That's right," Carrie agreed. "Onions are wonderful for pulling out infections. There are medicines that will do the same thing, but I've never seen a medicine that works better than an onion right out of the garden." She worked as she talked, dipping the rags in warm water and gently bathing Bobby's stumps.

She gazed at Bobby with compassion. "Cleaning it is going to be painful, but the poultice will soon provide some relief."

Bobby gritted his teeth and stared at her, his eyes glazing over with pain. "I can take it," he gasped.

Carrie was appalled by the condition of his amputations. This man should be in a hospital somewhere receiving treatment. Anger flared in her as she thought of the tens of thousands of men suffering all over the South. She knew President Lincoln had passed an act shortly before his death that would care for the Union soldiers and provide benefits, but there was no such treatment being offered to the Confederate soldiers. They were caught in a no-man's-land as the country struggled to recover from the war. She gritted her teeth as she wondered how many would die before a solution was found.

She breathed a sigh of relief when Bobby passed out from the pain. She would give him a drink mixed with valerian root to help with the pain when he came to, but unconsciousness was the best thing for him right now.

Carrie glanced over and saw that Joe had passed out from the pain as well. Alfred had merely closed his eyes to block out the brutal reality. She had learned during the long months with Robert how to tell when someone was either unconscious or simply choosing to disengage. She saw Robert watching Alfred with deep sympathy. She knew her husband was the best person to help the struggling soldier once they got his fever down.

When Annie walked into the room, Carrie pointed to the buckets of cold water Robert had brought up. "We have to get Alfred's fever down."

Annie nodded, her eyes serious and focused. "Yes, ma'am, Miss Carrie. I done brought enough wraps for everything, but you gonna have to buy some new sheets the next time you're in town," she said ruefully.

Carrie smiled. "I'm used to replacing sheets used for treating patients." She watched for a moment as Annie pulled back Alfred's clothing and began to bathe his face, arms and legs with the water. Satisfied the boy was in good hands, she turned her attention back to Bobby. She carefully applied the onion poultice to both his inflamed stumps and then carefully wrapped them with the strips of cloth.

She beckoned to Rose. "Please come work on bringing his fever down. I'll put the poultice on Joe's leg."

Rose stood to follow her bidding, her eyes sad as she stared at the men.

Carrie understood, but now was not the time to think about the stupidity of the war that had done this to them. She had to put all her energy into saving them. She heard sounds on the stairs and smiled with relief when Janie appeared. She saw her take in the situation with a glance.

"What do you need me to do?" Janie asked.

"Help Rose with Bobby," she said. "We'll change their poultices in an hour."

Janie nodded calmly. "It's a good thing you planted a lot of onions this year."

Carrie chuckled. The situation these men were in was horrible, but it was wonderful to work with Janie again doing what they loved best. Silence fell on the room as everyone worked, wrapping and unwrapping the rags almost as fast as they put them on. Robert kept them supplied with buckets of water. Clint joined in the effort as soon as he returned with the assurance that the beds were being made and would be delivered shortly.

The battle to bring down their fevers went on for several hours. Alfred was the first to respond. "He's sleeping now," Annie said. "This poor boy done been to hell and back, ain't he?"

"That's the truth," Robert muttered.

Joe was next to respond to the cold rags. He didn't regain consciousness, but as the fever broke, the deep lines on his face relaxed and his breathing became more regular.

Carrie was overjoyed when she heard the rumble of thunder in the distance. "There is a storm coming," she exclaimed gratefully. "It will break this terrible heat, and help them sleep better tonight." Her hands continued to move methodically as she fought to bring Bobby's temperature down.

Janie replaced Amber, pushing the exhausted little girl aside gently. "You've been wonderful, honey, but I'll take over now."

"I can still do it," Amber said stubbornly, her lips trembling with fatigue.

"I know you can," Robert said as he scooped her up in his arms, "but you've done all you're going to do for one night. I can't let my assistant collapse on me. The horses need you, too, you know."

Amber giggled and reached up to pat Robert's face. "I knows what you're doing, Robert, but I don't reckon I got enough in me to stop you." She laid her head against Robert's chest and was asleep before he even walked out of the room.

Carrie gazed after them, love flooding through her for both of them, and then turned back to Bobby. She knew by the look on Janie's face that both of them were aware Bobby might not make it. The infection spreading from his amputation stumps had spread through his entire body.

The storm blew through, bringing with it violent thunder and lightning. Carrie barely registered the fury exploding over their heads, but she was totally aware when the hot, sultry air changed to a refreshing breeze that cooled the room.

Her concern deepened when Bobby's fever refused to abate. His breathing became labored, and his chest strained for air. His legs began to twitch from spasms as the infection spread further. She and Janie wrapped and unwrapped the bandages as fast as they could, but they knew they were losing the battle.

"Come on," Carrie whispered. "Come on..."

She knew the minute they had lost the fight. Bobby's stiffened body relaxed and his legs stopped moving. He released his final breath and his face went lax, the lines of pain disappearing into the relief of death.

"He's gone," Janie said softly.

Carrie settled back in her chair and stared at his now peaceful face. "Yes."

Robert walked into the room with another bucket of cold water. He stopped when he saw the look on Carrie's face. "He's dead?"

"Yes." Carrie took a deep breath. "It's for the best," she said slowly. "The infection had destroyed too much of him. Even if we could have saved him, he probably would never have spent a day out of bed." She shook her head but didn't say anything else, not wanting to infect the other men in the room with her thoughts.

She gathered up her supplies and motioned for Janie and Robert to join her as she left the room. "Alfred and Joe will sleep tonight. I'll come back up and check on them later."

******

Moses was waiting on the porch when they all trudged wearily up the steps.

"You lost one," he said softly.

Carrie nodded heavily. "Bobby. The infection had taken too much of him."

"The others?"

"Their fevers are down, and they are resting," Carrie said. She collapsed into the chair Moses pulled out for her, watching wearily as the rest followed suit. "They both will have a long recovery, but I believe they'll make it if they want to."

Silence fell on the porch, but Carrie's anger continued to grow. "It's such a waste!" she finally burst out. "Such a complete waste!" She stood and strode to the edge of the porch, listening as droplets of moisture fell from the trees that had been doused in the storm. "Do you hear that?" she demanded.

"Hear what?" Janie asked, confusion evident in her voice.

"Silence. Peace." She turned back to all of them. "We're living in a fantasy world out here. *I'm* living in a fantasy world," she cried angrily. "There are tens of thousands of men just like Bobby in this country. Who is going to help them? The government may want to, but there are too many that are going to fall through the cracks. There are men sent home from the war, who are sitting in their homes waiting to die because they can't get help. It's not right."

"So what are you going to do?" Robert asked quietly.

"What *can* I do?" Carrie asked, desperation filling her voice. "There are so many!"

"You reach the ones you can," Rose said firmly. "You bloom where you're planted."

Carrie whirled around and stared at her while her mind raced. She struggled to catch her breath. All the while, she stared into Rose's eyes, finding the strength she couldn't find in herself. Finally, she settled back down in her rocking chair and managed a small chuckle. "I believe I said those exact same words to you not long ago."

"I believe you did," Rose agreed calmly. "It's much easier to say them than it is to live them, but the words are completely true."

"But how?" Carrie murmured, staring toward the lantern light flickering in the room over the barn. The small space had worked in an emergency, but it surely wasn't a solution.

"I'm glad you asked." Moses' deep voice broke the night.

Chapter Twenty-Nine

Carrie turned to stare at Moses.

"I talked to the men tonight, after they got done in the fields. They were heading over to work on the schoolhouse. Your father sent another load of lumber. We weren't sure what to do with it, but now we have a plan," Moses explained.

Carrie gazed at him, not at all sure what this had to do with her.

Moses smiled. "As soon as the men are done with the schoolhouse in a few days, they are going to add on another large room. It won't be great as a hospital because there are times of the day it will be pretty loud," he admitted, "but I reckon it will make a good medical clinic."

Carrie gasped. "A medical clinic?" Her eyes grew wide. "Attached to the school house?"

Moses nodded. "It will be on the main road, so it will keep people off the plantation. It will be easy for them to find, and they won't have to go into Richmond to get help."

"A medical clinic..." Carrie repeated, the beginnings of a smile on her lips. She turned to Rose.

Rose nodded firmly. "Bloom where you're planted," she repeated. "There are so many people you can help. Yes, it will be open to the veterans, but you can help anyone who needs it."

"I'm not a doctor," Carrie protested. "Why would they come to me?"

"The same reason those men came," Robert said. "They'll come because they know you can help them."

"Bobby died," Carrie reminded him. Tears filled her eyes, even though she knew he was finally free of the unrelenting pain.

"Yes, but only because he didn't get help in time," Robert responded. "And Joe and Alfred are going to make it. The word will spread."

"I don't have medicines or equipment," Carrie argued, though her mind was exploding with ideas.

Rose smiled. "And you're already thinking of ways to deal with those problems," she said. "I can see your mind working right now."

Carrie grinned. "You sound just like your mama."

"So you know my mama would tell you the same thing," Rose replied, her eyes twinkling.

Carrie turned to Robert. "I'll need to go into Richmond for supplies." Her mind was working rapidly. "I need to talk with Dr. Wild, if he's still in Richmond."

Robert nodded. "We'll ride in next week," he promised. "I'm sure your father and Abby will be thrilled to have us for a visit."

Carrie nodded thoughtfully. "Joe and Alfred should be okay with me being gone by then. I believe Annie can take care of whatever they need." Then she turned to Moses. "How long will it take to build the clinic?" she asked breathlessly.

"The school will be done in three days. We'll have the clinic finished in two weeks."

Carrie turned to look at Janie, who was watching her with a huge smile on her face.

Janie held up her hand. "You don't even have to ask. Of course I'll help." Her face broke into a joyful smile. "It will be like old times," she said.

"Except that *we'll* be running it," Carrie whispered. Her earlier anger had dissolved into exciting plans and possibilities.

******

Carrie settled down at the dresser, her mind whirling as she stared into the mirror that had challenged her so many times throughout her life. Even though she knew the secret behind its gilded edges, it had no less power to draw her in and make her want to be all she could possibly be.

Robert came up behind her and put his hands on her shoulders. "What do you see in there?" he asked quietly.

Carrie smiled, joy cascading through her that she truly had her husband back. "I see a happy woman with a husband who believes she can do big things like run a medical clinic."

Robert reached down, picked up her brush, and began to stroke it through her hair, his eyes holding hers in the mirror. "Want to know what I see?"

Carrie nodded, her skin tingling.

"I see a beautiful woman who can do absolutely anything she sets her mind to. I see a woman who has incredible compassion and caring in her heart." Robert leaned down and kissed the top of her head. "I see a woman who is going to be a doctor," he finished firmly.

Carrie stiffened and opened her mouth, but Robert held his finger to his lips to keep her silent. "I see a woman," he continued, "who is going to have the chance to go to medical school because her husband wants it for her almost as badly as she wants it for herself."

"You do?" Carrie whispered. Robert nodded, still holding her gaze as the lanterns flickered, casting glowing light on the mirror, and making it shoot sparks back at her as they reflected in his eyes. "How?" She wanted so much to believe her dream could come true, but she truly couldn't see how it could happen.

"We'll figure it out, Carrie," Robert assured her. "I know you've been studying ever since Abby brought you all the books. I saw your calm proficiency when you were treating the men today. The world is changing. It needs you. It needs women doctors."

Carrie stared into his dark eyes. "You really mean that, don't you?"

"With every fiber of my being," Robert replied. "I'm well. Whether I go to Philadelphia with you for medical school, or whether I stay here on the plantation until you graduate, we'll figure it out." He held up his hand as Carrie opened her mouth again. "I know you'll argue that we've already had too much time apart, and I couldn't agree with you more, but I also know you have given up so much of who you are. First, it was because of your mother's illness. Then the war stole four years of your life." He took a deep breath. "Then you put aside all of your desires again to take care of me."

"But—"

"No buts," Robert said firmly. "I already know you did it because you love me and because you're my wife. But now it's my time to give back. Yes, I'll miss you every second if we decide it's best to be apart, but you waited for me during four years of war. I'll wait for you to get your medical degree, and then we'll live the rest of our life. We'll figure out every step of the way how to blend our lives and our passions, because our love is strong enough to support both of them."

Carrie stared at the reflection of his strong face in the mirror and had a sudden impulse. She jumped up from the chair. "Care to join me on an adventure, Mr. Borden?"

Robert raised an eyebrow. "What do you have in mind, Mrs. Borden?"

Carrie grabbed two blankets, lifted a lantern from the wall, and reached forward to open the door to the tunnel. "It's a beautiful night on the river," she murmured softly, reaching up to kiss Robert's lips.

Robert grinned. "Lead the way, Mrs. Borden."

Minutes later, they were pushing through the door that led out onto the banks of the James River. Twinkling stars reflected on the almost still surface of the water. A crescent moon hung suspended as fluffy clouds drifted across its surface. Crickets and frogs, silent when they had pushed out onto the beach, tuned up their orchestra again. A coyote howled to its mate in the distance.

Carrie and Robert carefully laid the blankets down on the shore and then Robert lowered Carrie, settling down beside her.

"Thank you," Carrie whispered. "Thank you for coming back to me. Thank you for loving me, and thank you for believing in me." She stroked his face, gazing into his warm eyes that reflected the moon, and then she claimed his lips in a long kiss. When she finally pulled away, she smiled. "I've always dreamed of loving you right here on the James River."

Robert's eyes darkened with desire as he pulled her close.

******

Rose stared at the simple, gleaming white schoolhouse tucked back into a grove of trees. An overhang protected the entrance, and a white picket fence outlined the front yard. The shining windows reflected back the early morning sun, and glistened off the bell that had been hung to announce classes and recess. A small field off to one side had been designated as a play area for the children. The other side, the home of the medical clinic, was framed and roofed. One of the walls was completed.

"Moses..." Rose whispered. "It's perfect!" He had insisted she stay away for the last two weeks because he wanted to surprise her. Tears filled her eyes. "It's what I always dreamed of."

Moses grinned. "You think I wasn't listening when you told me your dreams? I had the men build it as close to the picture you painted for me as I could."

"It's so perfect..." she repeated in a whisper. She saw a sign over the door and moved close enough to read it. "Oh... Oh..." She couldn't force any more out of her mouth. All she could do was focus on breathing as her heart pounded in her chest. She stared at the sign.

The New Beginnings School.

"Moses," she finally managed. She turned to him, finding her voice. "That's exactly what this is. It's a new beginning for us. It's a new beginning for all the children and adults who will learn what they need to know in order to live in a brand new country and a brand new reality." She reached up and stroked his face. "Thank you is so inadequate, but just know my gratitude springs from the deepest core of my being."

Moses smiled, cupped her chin, and stared into her eyes. "I know it is perfect for now, Rose, but I also want you to know this is just a season."

Rose looked at him with confusion. "What do you mean?"

"You're going to be the most amazing teacher the New Beginnings School ever had," Moses said firmly, "but I know you're bigger than a little school in the country."

Rose shook her head. "I'm soon to be the mother of two children."

"Who need to see their mama become all she was meant to be, so they have the courage to do the same thing."

Rose stared at him and shook her head. "I don't see a way, Moses. I won't deny I would love to go to college and become a true educator, because you would know I was lying, but I'm learning to be content with not having that. I told Carrie she needed to bloom where she is planted—that's what I'm doing," she said bravely. "I know I can make a huge difference in the lives of the people who come to this school."

"You're right," Moses agreed. "But—"

Rose interrupted him. "What about you and the plantation? How can you run a plantation if I'm in school? Running Cromwell is *your* dream. I can't ask you to give that up."

Moses shrugged. "I love what I'm doing here, and I love being half-owner, but I can't say it's totally my dream. My dream has always been to own my very own farm," Moses replied. He stared out over the woodland surrounding the schoolhouse. "Look, I don't have the answers. I know we're to be here for now," he said confidently. "I know our second baby is going to be born on Cromwell Plantation, and I know you're going to found the New Beginnings School. I know I'm going to bring Cromwell Plantation back, and I know we're going to create a model for how plantation owners and the freed slaves can work together." He shook his head. "What I don't know, is what is going to happen one year from now...or two...or three. I just want you to know I'm determined not to have things just one way. Your dreams are as important as mine. We'll figure out a way to make both our dreams come true," he said. "I believe our love is strong enough to support both of them."

Rose smiled softly. "That's what Robert told Carrie," she murmured, brushing her tears away.

Moses smiled. "Who would have thought the two of us would be friends," he mused. "If nothing else, it should make you know that anything is possible."

"Oh, it does," Rose answered. "It definitely does." She turned to the schoolhouse and stared at the framework of her current life. Then she turned away to the road, and stared down the dirt surface until it disappeared into a bend, somehow knowing it represented her future.

A call coming from down the road told Rose they wouldn't be alone for long. She turned to Moses and pulled his head down to meet her lips. "Thank you for everything," she whispered. "Thank you for my school, but mostly thank you for loving me so much."

"With all my heart," Moses said as he deepened their kiss.

Rose pulled back, laughing. "I have a school to run, Mr. Samuels."

Moses frowned, his eyes dancing. "Do you think you can show your appreciation later, Mrs. Samuels?"

Rose stroked his cheek. "Oh, you can count on it. You most certainly can count on it."

******

"Are we interrupting?" Carrie asked coyly as she walked up with Janie and June.

"Yes," Moses said with a sigh, "but since there are forty children showing up in an hour, I guess it has to happen."

Rose laughed and stepped up to the entrance. "Ladies?" She took a deep breath as the four of them linked hands and stepped up onto the porch of the New Beginnings School for the first time. June would be teaching with her; Carrie and Janie had come to celebrate opening day and finalize any preparations.

As soon as they stepped through the door, Carrie turned and grabbed Rose in a tight embrace. "You've come a long way since teaching in the woods around a campfire in the middle of the night," she said as she stared around in delight. "This is wonderful!"

Rose gazed around her, tears once more springing to her eyes. She looked at Carrie silently, unable to form words.

The room was simple, but it had everything that was needed. There were enough desks and benches for one hundred students. Every desk had chalk, a chalk slab to write on, and a book. There was a shelf along one wall that held hundreds of books, and the front wall was a giant chalkboard for the teacher to use. A small desk stood to one side. Fresh air streamed in through the large windows, along with ample sunshine.

Carrie understood what Rose was feeling. She wrapped an arm around her and scanned the room. "Your mama knows," she said finally. "I just know she's up there laughing and dancing around, because her baby girl has done got her own school now."

Rose laughed and wiped away her tears. "You're right," she said happily. "Mama knows." She took a deep breath as she looked around. "There's not really anything to do," she said. "Moses and the rest of the men thought of everything."

"Well, let's say Abby sent detailed instructions," June said with amusement. "I was here every night with Simon to make sure they followed them just as she wrote them. She wanted it to be perfect for you, Rose."

Rose sighed. "Is this whole day nothing but a conspiracy to make me cry?" she demanded. "Abby said she was going to make sure we had everything we needed. I'd say we have all that and so much more."

"I'd say there are a lot of teachers who would be very jealous if they could see inside your school," Janie observed, "but the only important thing is how many kids you're going to help."

"Kids *and* adults," June added. "Now that they're free, I think there are going to be as many adults as children here—maybe more. I've talked to a lot of them passing by as the schoolhouse was built. They're so excited to learn how to read."

Rose smiled. "The classes start for adults next week. At first, I thought I should wait until after the harvest, but Simon convinced me the adults want to start now."

June nodded. "They're willing to work all day, come to school at night, and go with little sleep," she confirmed. "After being denied education their whole lives, they're not about to pass up their opportunity now. You know, I love watching children learn how to read, but watching adults make sense out of letters for the first time in their lives is even better." She stared around the room. "I remember when you taught me how to read after I got to the contraband camp. That first moment when all the letters came together to form words I could read was one of the best moments of my life. It opened up a whole new world to me."

Rose walked over to stare out one of the windows. "Education means everything to our people," she said quietly. "Nothing will truly change until the freed slaves are able to control their own lives. They can't do that without knowing how to read, and write, and do math."

Janie turned from where she was standing by the door. "We've got some eager children," she called over her shoulder.

The other three women walked over to join her. They all started laughing as they saw the line of children pressed against the wooden fence, their eyes wide with excitement as they stared at their new school.

"No reason to make them wait," Rose said, walking out to meet them. "Hello, children," she called.

"Hello, Miz Samuels!" they called back.

Rose shivered. After spending most of her life with no last name at all, it was still such a thrill for her to hear it. She stooped down to look into the face of the smallest child, who couldn't be more than five. "What's your name?" she asked gently.

"I be Sarah," the little girl said solemnly.

Rose smiled. "I believe that's the best name I know, Sarah. My mama had the very same name." Sarah stared back at her new teacher, her black eyes as solemn as her voice. "Are you glad to be at school, Sarah?"

"Oh, yessum, Miz Samuels!" Sarah's eyes glowed. "My mama told me she got beat real bad when she was my age 'cause she wanted to read. She done tole me I should be gladder about comin' to school den I eber been 'bout anythin' in my life. I reckon I am, sho 'nuff!"

Rose smiled, her heart dancing with pure joy. She stood, and held out her arms toward the children. "Welcome to the New Beginnings School. The first thing we'll do is separate you by age, and then I'll assign desks." She clapped her hands together sharply. "I'd like everyone in a straight line please."

*****

Once Rose had everyone at their desks and had introduced all the children to June, Carrie and Janie, she moved over to her desk and settled on the edge of it, wanting to be as close to the children's eye level as possible. "I'm going to start school today by telling you a story," she began. "In fact, I'm going to tell you a story every single day."

Sarah raised her hand.

"Yes, Sarah."

"I sho do like stories, Miz Samuels!"

"I'm glad, Sarah. So do I. Some people think stories are just things you make up, but there are also true stories about people I want you to get to know. Those are the stories I'm going to tell you."

Rose had thought for so many years about her own school. She had envisioned the first day. She had dreamed about what she would start with, knowing that teaching the children to read and write wasn't enough. She wanted to teach them to be proud of themselves and their heritage. She wanted to plant dreams in them and make sure they knew they could do anything they wanted to with their lives. She opened her mouth and began...

"Forty-three years ago, there was a little girl born into slavery in Maryland."

Rose was interrupted by a wildly waving hand. "Yes, Amber?"

"That's where I was born, Ro... I mean, Miz Samuels!"

"That's right, Amber," she agreed.

Rose knew she had to take firm control of the class from the beginning. "I will want to hear all your experiences and answer your questions at the end of the story, but until I'm done, I would like everyone to just listen." She smiled. "Can you do that?" Forty heads nodded solemnly. "Good. Thank you." She returned to her story, starting over again...

"Forty-three years ago there was a little girl born into slavery in Maryland. When she was little, they called her Minty. Her master was not kind to her, and she received lots of beatings. Even as a little girl, she dreamed about how things would be different if she wasn't a slave."

Rose could tell by looking into the faces of the children, that many of them had dreamed the same thing. She paused and asked a question. "Is there anyone in here that is twelve years old?"

Several of the children raised their hands.

"When Minty was about your age, she was in town to get some supplies. She saw another slave owned by another family, who had left the fields without permission. His overseer found him and demanded that Minty help him capture the boy. She refused."

Wide eyes stared back at her. She knew all of them were thinking about the overseer on whatever plantation they had come from. Only Sarah was too young not to have some memory of that. The little girl had been only a year old when her parents had escaped to the contraband camp.

"The boy she was trying to help started to run away. The overseer, not able to stop him, threw a heavy weight at him. He missed. Instead, the weight hit little Minty in the head."

Every child in the room gasped and leaned forward a little more, their bodies pressed up against their desks as they listened intently.

"Minty was carried back to her house, bleeding and unconscious. She didn't receive medical care for two whole days. She lived, but from that time forward, she had seizures and would fall asleep without warning. She also began to have visions and really powerful dreams."

Several of the children nodded their heads knowingly. Rose knew there were other women, like her own mama, who had the visions. She was sure the children knew some of them.

"Little Minty grew up and got married to a man named John Tubman. At some point, though I don't know why, she changed her name to Harriet. She also started dreaming about escaping slavery. She got her chance when she was in her late twenties." She glanced around the room and her eyes lighted on one of the older students. "How old are you?"

"Far as anyone knows, I be sixteen, Miz Samuels," the girl said shyly.

Rose nodded. "Thank you. About the time you were born, Harriet Tubman escaped." She allowed a silence to build. "And then she went back." She waited for the gasp to die down. "It's true. She escaped the first time with two of her brothers. Her brothers had second thoughts, probably because they were afraid of being caught, and they went back, forcing Harriet to go with them."

She smiled at the looks of righteous indignation on the faces staring up at her. "Harriet escaped again," she told them. "This time she didn't take her brothers," she said with a grin, laughing when everyone's faces lit up.

"Have any of you heard of the Underground Railroad?" Rose asked. Every child in the room nodded. Rose knew some of them had escaped through the Underground Railroad, just like she had, or they had heard about it through friends. "Well, Harriet escaped through the Underground Railroad. Once she got free, she loved being free so much that she decided to help other family members escape to freedom, too. By the time the war started, she had made the trip with the Underground Railroad *thirteen* times," Rose said dramatically. "She rescued *seventy* of her friends and family from slavery. No one she helped rescue ever got caught."

She paused for a long moment, letting the importance of what Harriet had done sink in. Then she continued. "When the war started, and it became much easier for slaves to go free, Harriet started helping the Union Army. She started out as a cook and nurse, but then she served as an armed scout and spy."

"A *woman*?" Amber gasped. She slapped her hand over her mouth when she realized she had interrupted.

"A *woman*," Rose said firmly. "I'm going to be telling you stories about all kinds of people in the days ahead, but I want all of you in this room to know you can do *anything*. It doesn't matter whether you are male or female. Harriet Tubman was just five feet tall. She had a disability because of her head injury that would have made most people give up. She risked her life time and again, because she cared so much about her friends and family living in freedom like she was." She paused again and swept the room with her eyes. "She *believed* she could help them, so she just went out and did it."

Rose walked around the room slowly, touching many of the children on the shoulder as she passed them. "Every single one of you sitting in this room has a dream. I happen to believe God gives us dreams because he knows we can make them come true. We usually have to work real hard at it, but I believe no matter what your dream is, you can make it come true."

She let her words linger in the air as she walked back to the front of the class. "Now it's time to start learning all the things that will enable you to *make* those dreams come true," she said firmly. "We're going to start with the letters of the alphabet."

******

Two days later, Carrie and Robert rode into Richmond on Granite and a sorrel mare named Shandy. They had laughed and talked all the way, grateful for a relatively cool day in September. They had not had time to notify anyone of their arrival, but knew they would be welcomed.

Both of them grew silent as they rode into the city's business district. The streets were crowded with people on foot. Just a few horse-drawn omnibuses carried loads of passengers. It had been almost four months since Carrie had been in the city, but this was Robert's first time viewing the destruction.

"You tried to prepare me," Robert finally said, "but I don't think anything could. My God, it seems as if the whole city was on fire."

"It felt that way," Carrie admitted, able to remember every detail of that horrific night—the flames, the explosions and the sheer terror of everyone in the city. "If the Union Army had not arrived when it did, I suspect the fire would have indeed consumed all of Richmond."

"So in taking the city, they saved it," Robert said.

"Yes," Carrie said quietly, "though I have a feeling that in the future, it will be portrayed differently."

"If they hadn't come down to take Richmond, none of this would have happened," Robert replied, anger sparkling in his eyes as he stared at the grim outline of destroyed buildings.

Carrie could only imagine his feelings if he had seen the city four months earlier. There was still so much to be done, but great progress had been made. She understood his anger, but... "And if the South hadn't seceded, they would have had no reason to come here," she said. "If we could have done the same thing to Washington, DC, we would have done it gladly."

Robert gazed around him and heaved a heavy sigh. "You're right," he admitted. "There was not a way for the war to end with anything but destruction. When people make decisions from passion, it seldom ends well." He shook his head. "At least it's over."

"It isn't over," a voice said firmly.

Startled, Carrie and Robert looked down at a man standing close enough to overhear their discussion.

"Excuse me?" Robert replied. The gray haired, middle-aged man addressing him had on a business suit that had seen better days, but his posture was still erect, and his eyes glittered with defiance.

"See that wall over there?" the man asked.

Robert and Carrie looked over at the burned-out building.

Carrie tried to remember what had once been there. "It used to be a clothing store," she recalled suddenly. "I've bought many things there."

"Yes," the man agreed. "It was my store. I lost everything the night the fires burned Richmond. I don't have a penny to my name, and no one is offering to help me rebuild. Northerners have come down and stocked the remaining storefronts with products we couldn't even get into the city during the war, but what good does it do?" he asked bitterly. "No one has any money to buy anything. Before the war ended, anything you could find was ridiculously expensive, so Richmonders couldn't afford to buy them. Now, our prices are lower than anywhere in the North because no one has any money, so they still can't afford to pay for them. Nothing is leaving the stores the Yankees decided were worth their investment. They keep lowering the prices, but what difference does it make? Broke is broke."

Robert frowned. "What are people doing? How are they eating?"

The man shrugged. "Just like I am," he said. "The government is providing food supplies. They distribute tickets, and then we all stand in line waiting to get enough cornmeal to keep us from starving. There are gardens all over the city, but most people are still hungry."

Robert nodded, remembering his conversations with Matthew before he left. "What do you think of the new military governor, Pierpont?"

"I think he's honest, and I think he's trying to help," the man answered. "He got the Richmond government back in operation, and he seems to understand that he can't possibly govern a state under a republican form of government, when the vast majority of its people are disenfranchised and can't hold office," he said with a scowl. "The men who could make a real difference are still waiting to be pardoned by *President* Johnson," he said sarcastically.

Carrie thought about Abby. "I understand there are a lot of Northerners who are coming down to invest in businesses."

Again the man nodded. "That's true. It's hard to tell if it's good or bad yet. They at least got one of the banks open again. Some of us have been able to get loans, and I know they're trying to increase funding to help rebuild the city." His voice was bleak. "I haven't been able to borrow a penny."

"I also understand Tredegar Iron Works is almost back to full operation," Carrie said, trying to find the positive in the destruction that surrounded them.

The man peered at her. "You seem to know a lot about the city," he said, looking closely at Granite and Shandy. "Those are fine horses," he added, his eyes narrowing suspiciously. "Are you Yankees?"

Robert answered for them. "I assure you we are not. I am Captain Robert Borden from Virginia."

"And I am Carrie Borden. My father worked in the Virginia government during the war."

The man's eyes narrowed. "Your father is...?"

"Thomas Cromwell," Carrie answered proudly, surprised when anger flashed in the man's eyes.

"Cromwell..." the man muttered angrily. "He and his wife are building that new factory down by the river."

"That's right," Carrie said evenly. "Do you have a problem with that?"

"I have a problem with a new factory going in that wants to hire niggers," he said.

"You believe only white people should have jobs?" Carrie asked.

"I believe the nigger needs to know they will never be equal to whites," the man said bitterly. "Your father seems to think he can get away with paying blacks the same wages whites will get."

"If they do the same work, they should receive the same pay," Carrie responded, biting back the angry words that wanted to spew from her mouth.

The man stiffened and glared at her. "Do you agree with your wife, *Captain*?" he asked, casting a glance at Robert.

"And if I do?"

"Then you need to go live up north where they love niggers," he said with a sneer.

Robert managed to smile calmly. "I believe I'll stay here in the South, and work to change people's ignorance," he said.

The man's face flushed red as his eyes flared with rage. "We may have lost the war, but we do not intend to have our country run by niggers," he spat.

"And I don't think any of them have designs on running the country right now," Robert replied. "They simply want to live their lives and also make a living."

"Then they should go back out to the plantations and do what they were born to do!"

"Be slaves?" Carrie asked. "I believe that was abolished."

The man snorted. "Slavery may be dead, but niggers can't do anything more than work as laborers. They were meant to be controlled by the white people. If they're not slaves, then they need to be on the plantations under the control of people who can help them survive."

Carrie sighed. The war may be over and slavery abolished, but it was clear the way people believed had not changed. "The freed slaves believe they can take control of their lives now," she replied, trying to remember that anger only fueled anger. It wouldn't do any good to respond to this man's anger with anger.

"That's ridiculous!" the man snorted. "Left to their own devices, the niggers will cease to exist in a hundred years. They've never been able to take care of themselves, and they certainly can't now."

Carrie smiled softly. "My experience tells me very differently."

"Yes," the man snarled, his face twisting into an ugly mask. "I've heard about your experiences, Mrs. Borden."

Chapter Thirty

Carrie stared at him.

"Your father was the laughing stock of Richmond when it was discovered you had let all your slaves go free. We felt terribly sorry for him," the man said.

Carrie tensed. "And yet my *father* still has a viable plantation, and he is here in town to build a new factory," she shot back, instantly sorry when the man's rage deepened to something that scared her. She was also sorry she had let the man's anger inflame her own.

"You little..."

Robert moved Shandy forward. "That will be all," he said, his voice deep with anger. "You will not disrespect my wife."

"Your *wife* should learn her place," the man growled.

Carrie was suddenly aware there were many people listening. Their faces were a mixture of angry sympathy and disdain. The few blacks close enough to hear the interchange had started to edge away, sensing the growing danger.

"My *wife* is one of the most intelligent women I know," Robert shot back. "You could learn a lot from her." He looked at Carrie, his eyes saying it was time to go. "I believe we have engaged this charming gentleman long enough, Carrie." He nodded his head. "Have a nice afternoon," he said, nudging Shandy forward.

Carrie was more than happy to nudge Granite into a trot to follow him. Several blocks passed before either said anything. "I'm sorry," Carrie finally said, her breathing back to normal. "I know I shouldn't have let him make me angry."

"I would have thought you were deaf if you hadn't gotten angry," Robert replied. "The man was an idiot."

"That idiot is going to be part of the Richmond business district my father and Abby will have to deal with on a regular basis."

"Yes," Robert replied, "but that is no reason not to confront ignorance with the truth. I'm quite sure your father and Abby have dealt with these feelings already, and I'm also quite sure they knew what they were getting into before they started this venture."

Carrie was quiet for several blocks. "They're going to be in danger, aren't they?" When Robert just looked at her, she knew he was trying to temper his response. "Don't bother to figure out an easy way to say yes." She sighed, glad when the blackened shells of the business district faded behind them, giving way to the neighborhoods leading to her father's house.

******

Abby had just stepped out onto the porch when Carrie and Robert rode up. "What a lovely surprise," she called. She stepped back into the house. "Thomas, come out here!"

Carrie and Robert were dismounting when Thomas strode onto the porch. "Carrie! Robert! What are you doing here?"

"Can't I just have missed my father and his wonderful wife?" Carrie asked lightly.

Abby narrowed her eyes. "You could, and I believe you have, but your face tells me it is more than that."

Carrie laughed. "It's a good thing I like the fact that you can read me like a book."

She smiled as Micah stepped out on the porch. "Would you mind taking Granite and Shandy in the back?"

"I'd be happy to," Micah replied, his eyes shining as he looked at the horses. "Granite looks like himself again," he said with satisfaction, "and that mare is sure a beauty!"

"That she is," Robert agreed. "They both have earned some feed and hay."

"I'll take care of it," Micah promised, as he took their reins and led them around to the stable.

"I'm afraid I gained you an enemy today," Carrie said regretfully as the four of them walked into the house. When her father raised an eyebrow, she told them the whole story. "I don't know who he was," she said when she finished.

Thomas sighed. "Marcus Summers. He is a man eaten up with bitterness."

"So you know him?" Robert asked, taking the glass of tea May offered him with an appreciative smile.

"I'm afraid so," Thomas answered. "He and his family were quite wealthy before the war. He did well, even throughout the war, by raising his prices exorbitantly, but he lost everything in the fire."

"I made things worse by pointing out how well you are doing," Carrie said regretfully. "I'm so sorry I lost my temper."

"The man could make a saint lose his temper," Abby replied archly. "I almost have a hole in my tongue from biting it."

"But at least you bit it," Carrie said remorsefully. "I'm afraid I said what I thought."

"Don't worry, Carrie," her father said immediately. "It was just a matter of time. He has been looking for an opportunity to start a fight ever since we got here. Maybe it's time it came to a head."

"But what will happen?" Carrie asked, her face creased with worry. "It seems he could be a dangerous man."

Thomas paused, causing Carrie's worry to deepen. "Father?"

"What will happen, will happen," Thomas finally said with a casual shrug.

"What does that mean?" Carrie cried, suddenly frightened.

Thomas hesitated, exchanged a long look with Abby, and then sat down in the chair by the fireplace. "Richmond is a powder keg right now," he said. "They are struggling to come back from financial ruin. At least half of the city is surviving because of federal support programs. The Freedmen's Bureau is here to provide assistance and programs for the freed slaves, but that seems to be enraging the white population even more."

"I think *terrifying* them is a better description," Abby added. "Their fear is making them angry. They can't figure out a way to keep the blacks under control, so their anger is growing. They feel they've lost total control of their lives, so they are lashing out at anyone they can lash out at."

"But the army is here to keep control of things," Carrie argued, hoping that meant protecting Abby and her father.

"Yes," her father agreed calmly, "but they can't be everywhere at once."

Carrie saw the flash of anger on Abby's face and turned questioning eyes toward her.

Abby hesitated and then began to speak. "The government seems to be overwhelmed as well," she said. "The soldiers are here to keep control, but too many of them don't see the freed slaves as people who should have equal rights. They may not think they should be slaves, but they believe they have to stay in their place."

Carrie sighed. "I thought the Freedmen's Bureau was in place to make sure they were taken care of."

"They are," Abby agreed, "but there are over two million freed slaves, and not nearly enough people in the Freedmen's Bureau to take care of things. Things in Richmond are bad, but they are much better than other parts of the country."

Carrie sighed. "We simply don't know what's going on when we're out on the plantation."

"It's probably a good thing," her father replied ruefully.

"It might be more comfortable," Robert agreed, "but it leaves us feeling rather out of the loop."

Jeremy walked in just then. "What loop would you like to be in?" he asked as his face broke into a grin. "Welcome to Richmond!"

Warm hugs were exchanged. Jeremy glanced over his shoulder. "Matthew should be here any moment. I ran into him on his way from the train station, but he had a stop to make. He'll be thrilled you're here."

May walked in with a plate of cookies. "I put some more chicken on to fry," she said happily. "It sure is nice to have a full house again!"

******

"So you still haven't told us why you're here," Abby said an hour later, when dinner was finished.

"I need to find Dr. Wild," Carrie said, her heart fluttering with excitement as she took another step toward turning her idea into reality. "I'm going to start a medical clinic."

"That's wonderful!" Abby cried. "I'm sure there is a story that goes with this decision."

Carrie nodded and told them about Joe, Alfred and Bobby. "I realize I'm not a doctor yet, but someone has to help them," she said. "Moses and the men are finishing the building this week. I'm hoping Dr. Wild is still here, and that he can help me with supplies."

"He's still here," Matthew said. "I interviewed him a week ago about the plight of veterans in the Confederacy."

"Then you know how terrible it is," Carrie said.

Matthew's face darkened. "I do. The number of war casualties is far from being final. Men are dying every single day, and there will be many more that die in the years ahead. But that's not all. There are many struggling with depression and alcohol addiction. They have lost everything, so their families are suffering as well." He frowned. "It's as big a problem for the North as it is for the South. There are benefits in place for Union soldiers, but the government is struggling to figure out how to handle so many men's needs, as well as the families who have been left behind."

"People in rural areas are suffering more," Abby said. "They don't have access to even the limited programs the cities have." She smiled at Carrie. "Your clinic will help."

Carrie sighed. "I hope so. I know it's such a small drop in the bucket, but..."

"At least it's a drop in the bucket," Abby said firmly. "And it will mean everything to the men and the families you help."

Carrie nodded. "I believe so. Janie is going to work with me, and Annie is going to help as well. We'll do everything we can." She turned to Matthew. "I told Rose and Moses we would bring back all the information we could about what is happening with the freed slave situation."

Matthew stared at her and shook his head. "I'm afraid there is not much good news," he said heavily. "There are certainly bright spots of hope, but they seem to be overshadowed by the problems and the hatred."

"But the Freedmen's Bureau..." Carrie protested.

"Is so hampered in what they can actually do," Matthew said. "Most of the people involved care deeply about the freed slaves, but their number is so limited." He hesitated. "And there are some who seem to just be drawing a paycheck. They're eager not to create waves and are letting the Southern states have their way."

"*Their* way is to put freed men back into slavery!" Carrie said angrily.

"Something like it," Matthew agreed. He looked at Thomas. "I took your advice and contacted Perry Appleton. I just got back from their home in Georgia."

"Louisa's husband?" Carrie asked. "How are they? I haven't heard from her in so long."

Matthew frowned. "I'm afraid this has been a difficult year for them. They got through Sherman's march through Georgia with their house intact, but everything else, including all their cotton ginning equipment was destroyed. They kept their spirits up, believing a good crop of cotton from their neighbors would help them begin again, but the weather in the Deep South has been terrible, and the neighboring plantations are finding it difficult to hire labor to work the fields. The crop yields are not what anyone hoped for."

Thomas frowned. "I didn't realize. I haven't kept track of much outside of Virginia. The weather here has been perfect this summer."

"I've spent a lot of time the last few weeks with plantation owners," Matthew revealed. "The ones who are left anyway."

Thomas nodded. "I know many of them have walked away from their land because everything has been destroyed. Their houses and barns are gone, along with all their animals and their tools. They don't have the heart to try again."

"Tens of thousands of them," Matthew agreed. "Some are leaving the country, while others are going north or heading out west to start over."

"What is happening with their land?" Robert asked.

Matthew shrugged. "It depends on what day you are asking." His eyes flashed angrily. "There have been a lot of promises made that I fear will never be kept." He paused. "I'll see if I can make sense of what is becoming an increasingly complicated situation. When we were at war, hundreds of thousands of acres of land was confiscated from its owners by the Union Army."

"The plantations?" Jeremy asked.

Matthew nodded. "Yes. Most of them were very large plantations confiscated from owners who were financing the rebellion. During the last couple years of the war, and in the months since the war has ended, the lands have been given to freed slaves who have fought for their right to that land because it was their labor that built it."

"Like down in the Sea Islands," Carrie said. "I remember reading about it in a journal that came last month."

"Yes," Matthew replied. "When General Sherman took Savannah, he promised four hundred thousand acres of land to the ten thousand freed slaves who had followed the Union Army across Georgia. Each of them got forty acres, and many of them got tools and a mule as well. They have worked hard and have created an independent community." He stopped to gather his thoughts.

"I've heard great things about that community," Abby said.

"They've done a remarkable job," Matthew agreed. "I met with some of them while I was in Georgia. Unfortunately," he said with a sigh, "everything is different now."

"How?" Jeremy asked.

"Congress passed a law in March of this year that gave the Freedmen's Bureau the mandate to redistribute these lands. Now this is where it becomes totally frustrating," Matthew explained. "When President Johnson issued his amnesty proclamation in May, it included political immunity as well as return of confiscated property, but it did not include landowners with property worth more than twenty thousand dollars."

"Which would be all the plantation owners," Thomas observed. "I happen to be one of those, which makes me even more grateful Cromwell was not taken."

"Yes," Matthew replied. "After Johnson's proclamation, the head of the Freedmen's Bureau, General Howard, asked Attorney General James Speed how this affected the bureau's mandate to distribute land to the freed slaves." Matthew reached for his notebook and flipped through it until he found what he was looking for. "Howard got a response back in June. *'The Bureau Commissioner has authority, under the direction of the President, to set apart for the use of loyal refugees and freedmen the lands in question; and he is required to assign to every male of that class of persons, not more than forty acres of such lands.'*"

"That's a bad thing?" Abby asked, confusion shadowing her eyes.

"Definitely not. General Howard acted quickly to make it happen. He ordered an inventory of lands available for redistribution and resisted the plantation owners' attempts to reclaim property. Until very recently, the Freedmen's Bureau controlled eight to nine hundred thousand acres of plantation lands previously belonging to slave owners. Then he created a directive within the bureau."

"I believe that's the Circular Thirteen I heard about," Thomas said. "It raised quite an uproar here in Virginia."

"I imagine it would have," Matthew answered. "Based on the attorney general's authorization, Circular Thirteen explicitly instructed bureau agents to prioritize the congressional mandate for land distribution over Johnson's amnesty declaration. In the final section it was very clear. It said the pardon of the president will not be understood to extend to the surrender of abandoned or confiscated property, which by law has been set apart for refugees and freedmen. General Howard made land distribution the official policy for the entire South."

"I know that must be so difficult for the plantation owners," Abby said sympathetically, "but it does seem a fair consequence to the war." She reached over and squeezed Thomas' hand. "I'm sorry, dear. I'm sure we disagree on that."

Thomas sighed and shook his head. "I hate it," he agreed, "but I also realize we *lost* this war, and it's also true that something has to be done, to help more than two million slaves that are now free. There are simply no easy answers."

"It gets more confusing," Matthew said. "Right after General Howard issued Circular Thirteen, he went on vacation in Maine. While he was gone, our President Johnson began to counteract the order almost immediately by restoring land to an estate owner in Tennessee."

"His home state," Jeremy observed.

Matthew nodded. "It seems the president and the attorney general don't see eye-to-eye. Two days ago, Circular Fifteen came out. It has Howard's name on it, but my sources assure me it was written by Johnson himself." He sighed. "The bottom line is that it was rewritten to support Johnson's policy of land restoration. In many places, it has ended the policy of land redistribution entirely."

"What does that mean exactly?" Abby asked slowly.

"Like I said, it depends on what day you are asking," Matthew answered, "but right now, it means that our president is going to go back on all the promises made to the freedmen. Most of the lands are held by freed slaves down in Georgia. My understanding is that they will be able to harvest their crops, but then they must relinquish their right to the land, because the government will give it back to the original owners. They must either agree to work for the former owners, or be evicted."

"They can do that?" Carrie asked in a shocked tone. "Give it to them and then just take it back?"

"It seems our President Johnson does whatever he wants," Matthew answered.

"What about the Congress?" Jeremy asked.

"Until they come back into session in January, their hands are tied," Matthew said wearily. "Many of them are out of their minds with rage and worry, but Johnson is using this time to press his agenda as strongly as he can."

Abby frowned. "Doesn't he realize his agenda will be overthrown once Congress is back in session? I cannot imagine them letting this continue. There are too many congressmen who fought for the slaves. They're not just going to sit back."

Matthew shrugged again. "I wish I could sit inside our president's head for a day. Perhaps then I could understand him. Unfortunately, I can't. And whether his agenda is overturned in four months or not, it will have already done a tremendous amount of damage. President Johnson is no friend of the black person, and based on what I'm seeing, I don't believe he is a friend of the United States either. I'm afraid his actions are going to reverberate through history for generations to come."

A heavy silence fell on the room.

"At least things are a little better here in Richmond for the freed slaves," Jeremy said, finally breaking the silence.

Carrie looked up, almost desperate for words of hope. "How?"

"You heard about blacks being deported out of the city and of all the vagrancy laws?" Jeremy asked.

Carrie nodded, feeling her anger rise again.

"Over three thousand blacks filled The First African Baptist church here in the city, back in June to approve a formal complaint to the president. Then several of them wrote a letter to the *New York Tribune*." Jeremy reached down beside him. "I have a copy of the paper here." He flipped pages until he found what he was looking for. "Here it is. In part of the letter they complain of the '*mounted patrol, with their sabers drawn, whose business is the hunting of colored people.*'" He put the paper aside. "You can read it all later. The most important part, is that the letter and the formal complaint drawn up at the church were delivered to President Johnson by a delegation headed by Fields Cook."

Carrie looked thoughtful. "I know that name. Isn't he a black barber in town?"

"Yes," Jeremy replied. "He's also a local church leader. He has gotten very involved in politics here in Richmond."

"You said it helped?" Robert asked.

Jeremy nodded. "The complaint was part of the reason General Ord was replaced as the head of the Army of Occupation here in Richmond. General Alfred Terry, who took his place, struck down the city's discriminatory vagrancy laws and announced the army would treat all inhabitants as equal before the law. Then Secretary of War Stanton stepped up in July and instructed Southern commanders to discontinue pass requirements and forbade the army to hinder blacks' freedom of movement."

"That's wonderful!" Carrie exclaimed. "At least *something* positive is happening." She paused when she looked closely at Jeremy's face. "Tell me the rest," she said quietly.

Jeremy sighed. "Those are indeed positive steps, but I'm afraid it doesn't change the basic assumption underpinning military policy."

"And that would be?" Robert asked.

"The Freedmen's Bureau believes that the interests of the South, the nation and the freedmen themselves, would best be served by all the freed slaves going back to plantation labor. They can be free, but they belong on the plantations."

"Even if they don't want to be?" Carrie asked. "And even if the plantation owners don't pay them correctly or if they abuse them?" She was remembering everything Janie had told her. "How is that any different from slavery?"

"It's not," Jeremy said. "It's also not easy to come up with answers."

"And you see it from both perspectives?" Matthew asked.

"I do," Jeremy responded. "I have tremendous empathy for the slaves because of my heritage, and because of how wrongly they have been treated. I also understand the financial ramifications of what will happen if labor can't be found for two million freed slaves, or what will happen if Southern agriculture completely falls apart."

"The freed slaves don't want to work on the plantations anymore?" Robert asked. "Not even if they are receiving wages?"

"If only it were that cut and dry," Jeremy responded. "I've talked to so many of the freed slaves since I've been back in the city. From everything I have learned, I don't believe they are against working. The plantation owners are saying the blacks are lazy, and must be made to work like they were in slavery."

"With overseers and whips," Carrie said with a scowl.

Jeremy nodded. "That's their basic belief," he agreed. "The owners want things to pretty much remain the same, and the freed slaves are not willing for that to happen. They are demanding to receive fair pay, and they want the freedom to come and go. If they think they are being treated unfairly, they just walk away."

"Seems reasonable," Aunt Abby said, her eyes flashing.

"It is," Jeremy agreed again. "The problem is, that most of the plantation owners don't have anything to pay them, and they are terrified of losing control, so they are reverting back to their old ways."

"Like in Louisiana and Texas, where they are murdering blacks in order to scare them into compliance," Carrie said bitterly.

Jeremy nodded heavily. "I wish every plantation owner was like Thomas. If they would treat the workers with respect, and share the profits of the harvest with them, everyone could be satisfied. I also believe that in the end, everyone would make more money—even the plantation owners—because their productivity would be so much higher."

"But that isn't happening? I don't know a lot about it, but isn't that what sharecropping is all about?" Carrie asked.

"In an ideal world, it is the perfect answer," Jeremy replied. "But we don't live in an ideal world. No one will know for certain until harvest time, whether the sharecropping arrangements are working."

Carrie watched him closely. "You don't believe they will."

Jeremy managed a slight chuckle. "Abby is not the only one who knows how to read others like a book." He frowned. "No, I don't believe it will work. Oh, if everyone was like Thomas it would be fabulous, but I suspect most of the owners are going to short the freed slaves and give them barely enough to subsist on, so they can keep them under their control. Sharecropping will, I'm afraid, become just another word for slavery."

"So what do we do?" Carrie asked.

"We fight," Jeremy responded immediately. "We continue to fight for the freedmen's rights. We continue to fight to rebuild the South into something we can be proud of again."

"With men like Clifford and his friends, it's going to be a long uphill battle," Carrie said.

"It always has been," Abby responded. "We fought for so long for abolition, but those of us who understood the South knew the battle that would come after would be just as long."

"It's not only Southerners who are creating the problem," Thomas said. "I have a feeling there are just as many prejudiced people in the North. They just didn't have the opportunity to own slaves. Matthew is right—they may not believe the blacks should be enslaved, but neither do they believe they should be offered equality."

"You're right," Abby said immediately. "I don't believe prejudice is a Northern or Southern problem. I believe it's a human nature problem. People always want someone else to look down upon. I see it not only between racial groups, but also between ethnic groups." She paused. "We just have to hold on. The Congress will begin to turn things around when they come back into session. I've heard from several of my friends in Washington, DC. They are incensed with President Johnson and believe he is doing the exact opposite of what Lincoln would have done."

"Does that matter?" Robert asked. "He is president now."

"Yes, it matters," Abby replied. "Thank goodness in a democratic government, it is not possible for one man to call all the shots. Johnson is taking bold steps now, but he is fighting a losing political battle. He doesn't have the votes or the support to keep pressing his agenda in January. Lincoln knew how to work with people and pull them to his way of seeing things. He garnered true support—the reason he was able to pass the amendment to abolish slavery. Johnson, on the other hand, just plows through and runs over anyone in his way. I'd heard he was rather a loner."

"Which is not the formula for an effective president," Matthew observed.

"It most certainly is not," Abby said forcefully. "I believe Congress will stop him, but he will certainly do damage in the meantime." She took a deep breath. "I'm going to have to believe Congress will do their job. I'm going to focus on mine."

"Which is building the factory," Thomas said. "The building starts going up in two weeks. Then the equipment will arrive. We'll start training people on it even before the building is ready so that we can get the advantage on any competition."

Abby nodded. "We'll all do our part. Matthew will tell the stories and make sure people know the truth. Jeremy will run the factory and make sure the blacks are treated equally and with respect. Robert, you are starting a whole new string of fine Virginia Thoroughbreds, and Carrie, you are going to start a new medical clinic. We are all doing our part to rebuild a South we can be proud of."

A breeze blew through the parlor, blowing the curtains and causing the lanterns to flicker. Silence fell as each of them absorbing all they had talked about. The breeze carried a hint of fall, but it also carried a hint of bigger troubles coming their way.

Chapter Thirty-One

Spencer was waiting outside the next morning when Carrie stepped onto the porch, grateful for the bite of fall in the air. It had been a long, hot summer. A coat was not yet needed, but she relished the cooler temperatures. "Good morning, Spencer!" she called brightly.

"How do, Miss Carrie," Spencer replied warmly. "How's Miss Janie?"

"She's wonderful," Carrie replied. "Being on the plantation has been good for her." She told him of their plans to start a medical clinic.

"Then we're heading down to Jackson Hospital to find Dr. Wild, ain't we?" Spencer asked.

"Yes, we are,"

Carrie leaned back in the carriage to enjoy the ride. The leaves were still bright green, but it wouldn't be long before the cooler temperatures teased the golds and reds from them. She thought of the lush fields at Cromwell. The wheat and oat crop was doing well, but if this early cool spell was any indication, they would have a frost before they could harvest the tobacco. She knew, though, that it was just as likely they would settle into a long Indian summer that would produce a bumper crop and boost everyone's profits. Only time would tell.

Carrie frowned as she thought about all they had talked about the night before, but decided to force it all from her mind. She couldn't change politics, but she could help people get better. Eager to get home and prepare the clinic, she ran through her plans in her mind.

She was in a much better mood by the time they pulled up in front of the hospital. Minutes later, directed by helpful personnel, she was knocking on Dr. Wild's door.

"Carrie!" Dr. Wild stepped forward and embraced her warmly. "It's so wonderful to see you." He paused. "How is Robert?"

Carrie knew he was afraid to ask. He had seen Robert's refusal to live and get well. "You wouldn't recognize him," she said happily. "Actually, you probably would! He looks just like the man I married, except he has a little more gray in his hair. We rode in from the plantation so I could talk to you."

Dr. Wild beamed. "You could not have given me better news today," he said enthusiastically.

Carrie looked at him closely. "You've been receiving mostly bad news, haven't you?"

Dr. Wild nodded. "Yes, I'm afraid that's true."

"I thought you were going to leave Richmond after the war," Carrie said. "I was surprised to find you still here."

"I wanted to, but I find the need is still too great."

"The veterans," Carrie said softly. "It's why I'm here. I came to ask for your help."

"I'll help you if I possibly can," Dr. Wild responded. "What is it you need?"

Carrie told him the story about Bobby, Joe and Alfred. "There are so many veterans who need help, but that's not all. There are virtually no medical services for the freed slaves, unless they are closer to the cities where the Freedmen's Bureau has offices. And the families of the veterans have no resources either."

"It is a bleak situation," Dr. Wild agreed heavily.

"I'm not a doctor yet..."

Dr. Wild shrugged. "You weren't a doctor when we worked side by side at Chimborazo either. What do you want to do, Carrie?"

"I'm planning on opening a medical clinic next to the school we just built," she said, watching him to get his initial reaction.

"You just built a *school*?" Dr. Wild asked.

Carrie explained about Rose opening a school for the area children. "They're building a large room for the clinic onto the schoolhouse," she explained. "I'm going to make sure people know I'm not actually a doctor, but I believe many will want me to help them."

"You're right," Dr. Wild agreed. "What you did for Joe and Alfred will make the word spread quickly. Once they actually visit you, they will realize you know as much, or more, than any certified medical doctor."

Carrie flushed. "Thank you."

"I'm speaking the truth," Dr. Wild replied. "I think it's a wonderful idea. There are so many who need help. Even if they could make it into the city, we don't have enough services to take care of everyone." He gazed at her warmly. "You're here for supplies."

"Yes. I am prepared to pay for them, but I didn't know who else to turn to."

"You came to the right place," Dr. Wild assured her. "How long are you in the city?"

"We'd planned to return tomorrow, but we can stay longer if needed."

"That won't be necessary. Come by the hospital in the morning, and I'll have everything you need." He paused. "I hope you are still using your herbal remedies."

Carrie looked at him. "I am, but why is that important? Surely it is easier to get drugs now."

"Too easy," Dr. Wild said, anger sparking in his eyes. "We have over a hundred soldiers in the hospital right now who are addicted to morphine. I don't deny they needed it for their pain after amputations, but the addiction will kill them as certainly as the infection would have. It will just take longer." He turned to stare out his window. "If it's not morphine, it's alcohol. I don't blame the men for wanting to forget the hell they went through, but the alcohol is destroying them and what is left of their families." He took a deep breath. "I fear we will have hundreds of thousands of addicts, both North and South, within the next ten years."

Carrie frowned. Morphine had been the drug of choice all through the war because it was the only thing that could relieve the soldiers' pain. There had been so many times it had been the only choice to silence the screams of agony from bullet wounds and amputations. "What are you using now?"

"I don't have an answer yet," Dr. Wild admitted. "Right now, everything I read substitutes another drug. I read in a journal yesterday about something called *Vin Mariani*. It's a mixture of cocaine and wine."

"Is it working?" Carrie asked

"I don't know. I agree that morphine addiction is bad, but I'm not sure substituting one drug for another is the answer." He shook his head. "I'm trying to detox as many men as possible."

"How?" Carrie asked eagerly. She was quite sure she was going to run into the issue. She had been using valerian root with Joe and Alfred, but they hadn't come to her addicted to morphine.

"It's not pretty," Dr. Wild said bluntly. "If a soldier is addicted to morphine, they will start going into withdrawal after about twelve hours without the drug. They will have mood changes, becoming very restless or anxious. Twelve hours more and they will probably develop the full syndrome of shaking legs, nausea and cramps. This stage can last two to three days. Many times I have found the men in a fetal position, sweating and vomiting. The whole process, before they feel themselves again, usually takes seven to ten days."

Carrie watched him closely. "There's something else you're not telling me."

Dr. Wild sighed. "Even if you get the morphine out of their system, the odds are they will find a way to use it again if they can. It evidently is highly addictive."

"But if they're not under medical care, how can they get it?"

"An addict can often find a way," he said ruefully. "They will steal from hospitals or medical supply companies. Oftentimes, they'll buy it from other soldiers." He sighed. "The morphine can kill them as easily as their wounds can—perhaps even more easily. It's going to be a problem for a long time."

Carrie nodded thoughtfully.

Dr. Wild changed the subject. "Are you still hoping for medical school?"

"Yes." Carrie told him about the medical books Dr. Strikener had sent her. "I've been studying them every day." She thought about everything Robert had said. "I don't know when it will happen, but I believe I'll become a doctor."

Just saying the words filled her with a stronger sense of purpose than she had ever felt.

******

Robert was standing on the porch reading a letter, when Spencer drove Carrie up to the house. She could hardly wait to tell him her news. "Robert!" she called as she stepped out of the carriage and gathered her skirts.

He smiled. "I take it by the look on your face that he said yes."

Carrie was beaming as she ran up the steps. "He did! We can pick up the supplies in the morning, before we head back to the plantation." She threw her arms around him and lifted her face for his kiss.

"Congratulations," he said warmly. "Of course, I already knew he would say yes."

"So you said," Carrie murmured. After so many years of being without her husband, she didn't think she would ever get used to the feel of his warm lips on hers. "I love you," she whispered.

Robert's arms tightened. "And I love you."

When Carrie finally stepped back, she looked at the letter he still gripped in one hand. "News?"

Robert nodded and led her over to the porch swing. "Would you mind terribly if we didn't go right back to the plantation?"

Carrie eyed him, noticing a light in his eyes she wasn't quite sure she could identify. "Where are we going?"

Robert smiled. "How about a trip to lovely Oak Meadows?"

Carrie gasped. "Oak Meadows!" She pushed all thoughts of the clinic out of her mind. She had dreamed of seeing Oak Meadows for years, and Robert hadn't been home since Matthew convinced the Union officer not to destroy it. "When do we leave?"

Robert chuckled. "Aren't you anxious about getting back to work on the clinic?"

"Anxious isn't the right word," Carrie replied. "I think eager would be more appropriate."

"Okay. Then aren't you *eager* to get back to work on the clinic?"

"Yes," Carrie replied, "but not nearly as eager as I am to see my husband's boyhood home, and discover where he grew up."

Robert took her hand. "It will be so strange to be there without Mother," he said gruffly.

Carrie held his hand tightly, letting memories of his mother and the brother he lost during the war sweep through him. "She'd be so glad you lived to come home," she said gently.

Robert nodded but corrected her. "Not *home*," he said. "Home is Cromwell Plantation now. That is where my future is."

Carrie let out the breath she hadn't even been aware she was holding, relief sweeping through her body. She would not have hesitated to go to Oak Meadows with Robert, but it would have been difficult to leave everything behind. "What will you do with Oak Meadows now?" she asked quietly.

Robert lifted the letter. "Until last night, I thought the letter I sent a few weeks ago was pointless, because I was quite sure Oak Meadows would be redistributed to the freed slaves. I had come to a place where I was okay with that. When Matthew told me President Johnson had changed everything, I felt bad for the slaves, but I also felt relief that I wouldn't lose it," he admitted.

Carrie nodded. "You would be something less than human if you hadn't felt that way," she told him. "You poured your whole life into Oak Meadows."

"Yes," he agreed. "I did." He held the letter up again. "Now someone else is."

Carrie stared at him. "What do you mean?"

Robert took a deep breath. "I've decided to sell Oak Meadows," he said.

Carrie sat back and stared at him, unable to find words.

Robert smiled. "I received an offer about a month ago."

"I didn't know," Carrie murmured.

"The letter came when you were out of the house. I decided not to say anything, because I didn't want either of us to get our hopes up."

Carrie was puzzled. "Why would I get my hopes up about you selling Oak Meadows?"

Robert brandished the letter again and grinned. "Because the money that will come from the sale will be used to expand the horse program at Cromwell and..."

Carrie poked him as the silence lengthened. "And *what*?" she demanded. "You know I am not a patient person."

Robert's grin widened. "I have heard the only way to gain patience is to simply practice when you need it. I'm helping," he said innocently, his eyes bright with laughter.

Carrie raised a fist and turned to him. "Robert!"

His grin dissolved into laughter, and his eyes shone with excitement. "The money from the sale will also be used to put you through medical school when you're ready," he said triumphantly.

Carrie gaped at him, searching for words as tears filled her eyes. "Medical school?" she whispered.

Robert nodded. "I already know your father and Abby would have made it possible for you to go, but it's important to me to know I can make my wife's dream come true." He tilted Carrie's face up so he could gaze into her eyes. "When you're ready, there is nothing to stop you from becoming Dr. Borden."

Carrie threw herself into his arms. "Thank you," she cried. "Knowing you believe in me...knowing you really want me to become a doctor means everything to me."

Robert cocked a brow. "I thought I convinced you of that on the banks of the James River."

Carrie flushed and grinned as she met his eyes. "Maybe I just need to convince myself," she replied. She stood up and walked to the edge of the porch to stare out over the yard. "Dr. Borden," she said softly. Her voice strengthened as she imagined going to class and learning all she could learn. "*Doctor* Borden." She stared at Robert. "I believe I like the sound of that."

Robert stood and swept her into his arms, silencing her with a deep kiss. When he finally pulled back, he held out a hand to her. "How about if we leave for Oak Meadows tomorrow?"

******

Three days later, Robert and Carrie turned down the final road toward Oak Meadows just as the sun was sinking low toward the horizon. They would have made better time on Granite and Shandy, but they had decided to leave them in Richmond and bring a wagon, so Robert could take any heirlooms from the house before he turned it over to the new owners.

"Do you know when the buyers are going to be here?" Carrie asked.

Robert smiled, something flashing in his eyes that she couldn't interpret. "I believe they're already here," he said casually.

"*Before* they buy it?" Carrie asked. "Isn't that rather odd?"

"*Yankees* are odd," Robert replied, chuckling lightly.

"Is it true that many of the deserted plantations are being bought up by Northerners?"

Robert nodded. "It's true. They're the only ones in the country with money," he said. "It's also true that the vast majority of them served in the Union Army. It seems that while they were down here destroying our land, they also fell in love with it."

Carrie raised her eyebrows at the note of bitterness Robert couldn't keep out of his voice. She laid a hand on his arm. "Are you sure you want to sell Oak Meadows?" she asked quietly. "No papers have been signed. It's not too late to change your mind."

"I won't change my mind," he said. "I know you heard the bitterness in my voice. Most of the time I'm okay with what is happening, but that's because you and I are so much more fortunate than most other Southerners. We had a home to return to, and we had Abby to invest in our dreams. We are the very rare exception. I think about all the men I served with who are returning to nothing." He stared at the horizon and scowled, falling silent.

"Robert?"

"There's something I haven't told you," Robert finally said. "I planned on telling you during this trip, but I just can't seem to find the words."

"Straight out is usually best," Carrie replied, laying her hand on his leg as she braced herself for what she was sure was bad news.

Robert nodded and gripped the reins so tightly the veins stood out on his hands. "Georgia is dead," he said bluntly, shaking his head. "She died during the march from Richmond to Appomattox."

Carrie stiffened as her eyes filled with tears, but she remained silent. After so many months with no word, she was sure something had happened to Georgia, but she had learned to accept the fact she may never know. Memories filled her mind of the slight woman who passed herself off as a man to go into battle with her brother. Carrie had moved her into her father's house to protect her from discovery when she was wounded in battle. She had nursed her back to health and taught her how to read so she would have a better chance at a future. Tears slid from her eyes as she realized Georgia would *never* have a future.

Robert glanced at her. "She got sick during the long winter," he said. "I made sure she got one of the coats and a pair of gloves when you brought them down in the wagon."

"But she had warm clothing when I sent her back to the field," Carrie cried.

"Yes, but she had already given them away to a soldier she believed needed them more," he answered roughly.

Carrie nodded, knowing that's what Georgia would have done.

"I did my best to help her," Robert said, his voice breaking. "She wouldn't let me do much..."

"She was proud," Carrie said softly. "And she didn't want anyone to suspect what she really was."

Robert nodded. "I was hoping that when spring came she would get better, but she was already so weak. The long march when we left Richmond was too much for her," he said hoarsely. "She lay down on the side of the road and died one night in her sleep. She didn't have any more to give. One of my men informed me in the morning." His voice broke again. "I couldn't even bury her," he said regretfully. "Grant was after us, and Lee kept us moving as fast as we could."

Carrie squeezed his hand, knowing this was just one more of the scars he would carry with him for the rest of his life. "Thank you for telling me," she said gently. Her voice grew firmer. "Robert, you did all you could. Alex told me how often you chose not to eat so that the men—and woman—you commanded could eat." She bowed her head as images of Georgia's laughing face filled her mind.

Robert stared out at the horizon. "Georgia kept the book you gave her. She read it every chance she got. She told me you convinced her reading was important, and that she didn't want to get rusty."

Carrie managed a smile. "She was an extraordinary person. It would have been so easy for her to simply put on women's clothing and never go back into battle. She cared too much about the men she served with not to help, even though she was certain the South would lose."

The wagon rattled on, both of them silent as they let their thoughts be calmed by the late afternoon coolness.

******

The sun had slipped below the tree line when they turned into the gates of the plantation. Carrie sucked in her breath when she saw the horse pastures spreading out, surrounded by wooden fences. The fields were overgrown, wildflowers swaying in the breeze, and many of the posts and boards lay on the ground, but Carrie knew just how beautiful the pastures would be when the fences were repaired, and horses were once more romping through the fields. "It's beautiful," she said softly as her eyes settled on the mountains rising above the valley.

Both of them remained silent as they wound their way down the rutted road lined with towering oak trees. The leaves had begun to take on a hint of color, but the Indian summer Thomas and Moses had hoped for kept Virginia firmly in its grip. Carrie gazed up as they rolled through the tunnel formed by their mighty branches. "Oh, Robert..." She gripped his hand as they rounded the final curve and saw the sprawling house nestled at the foot of a bluff. "How can you bear to give it up?"

Robert squeezed her hand. "Oak Meadows is my past," he said, gazing around to take it all in. "You and Cromwell Plantation are my future." He smiled. "My mother would like knowing Oak Meadows will give me the chance to start over again on my own terms."

Carrie looked at him. "Without Abby's help, you mean?"

Robert shrugged. "A man likes to know he can take care of his family. Abby did a tremendous thing. I will always be grateful, and she will always do well with her investment, but I have big plans."

Carrie smiled up at him. "And I believe in you completely."

"And that, my dearest Carrie, means everything to me," Robert said simply.

Carrie caught movement out of the corner of her eye, and turned her head in time to see a woman emerge from the barn.

"Hello!" the woman called.

Carrie watched as a woman, clad in breeches and a blouse, hurried up to them. She was immediately drawn to the open brown eyes and wide smile.

The woman reached the wagon and smiled up at them. "Hello, Robert," she said warmly.

Carrie had only a moment to wonder at the easy familiarity the woman used with Robert. Surely someone about to purchase land would call the owner Mr. Borden.

"You must be Carrie!" the woman said enthusiastically. "I've wanted to meet you for so long."

Carrie stared at her and then turned to look at Robert questioningly. She gazed back at the woman. "And you are?" she asked politely.

The woman looked at Robert and laughed. "You still haven't told her?"

Chapter Thirty-Two

Now Carrie was even more confused. Before she could say anything, her attention was diverted by the sound of a galloping horse. Moments later, the horse slid to a stop next to the wagon.

"Hello, Mrs. Borden," the man said warmly.

Carrie stared at the slim figure on the towering Thoroughbred, his strong shoulders backlit by the setting sun. "Captain Jones?" She held her hand to her mouth to control her gasp.

The woman chuckled. "Robert hasn't told her."

Robert turned to Carrie. "I wanted to keep it a surprise," he explained.

Carrie was still trying to make sense out of the turn of events. She stared at Robert, looked back at Captain Jones, and then swung her gaze back to the woman. Her mouth moved, but no sound came out.

The woman laughed gaily and stepped forward. "I will never understand why men think it's a good idea to stun their wives," she said, glaring at Robert briefly before she laughed.

"You're Captain Jones' wife?" Carrie managed.

"Heaven forbid!" the woman exclaimed, her eyes dancing. "I am this old man's sister. My name is Susan."

Carrie finally found her voice. "Susan!" She now understood the instant attraction. "I've heard about you as well. I understand you keep the state of Pennsylvania in a frenzy with your rather unladylike habits."

Susan chuckled. "Now that may be the best compliment I have ever received," she said cheerfully.

"It was most certainly meant as one," Carrie assured her.

"I've heard about your exploits foiling my brother's attempt to steal your Thoroughbred. I would love to have seen you jump him across that fence bareback—and in the moonlight!" she added, her eyes wide with admiration.

"Nobody steals my horse," Carrie said calmly, stepping down from the wagon. "Now, would someone like to tell me what is going on here?" She looked up. "Captain Jones?"

"It's not my story to tell, but the war is over. How about if we leave off the Captain Jones part? My name is Mark."

Carrie smiled. "I'm thrilled to do away with the formalities," she said brightly. "Please call me Carrie." Then she looked up at Robert. "Out with your secret!" she demanded.

Robert chuckled, and jumped down from the wagon to wrap an arm around her waist. "It seems Matthew told our Yankee Captain all about Oak Meadows when he heard Mark was interested in investing down here after the war."

Susan jumped in. "At first Mark was interested in a cotton plantation, but it didn't take me long to convince him we could make much more money, and have much more fun, managing a horse plantation. We own a small place in Pennsylvania, but I've always dreamed of running a place like this." She took a deep breath of the fragrant air and gazed up at the mountains. "I don't believe I've ever seen a more beautiful place."

"If you can close your eyes to all the destruction surrounding us," Robert snapped, and then apologized immediately. "I'm sorry. I grew up in the Shenandoah Valley. It's still a shock to see it like this."

Susan nodded. "I understand, Robert," she said gently. "This whole stupid war has been such a waste, and I realize it will take the South a very long time to recover. I can only imagine what I would feel if this was my home."

Carrie's liking for this non-traditional, caring woman intensified. She stepped forward and hooked an arm through Susan's. "How about if we go for a short ride before it gets completely dark? I'm dying to see this place." She glanced at Robert. "You can give me the complete tour tomorrow, but after three days on that wagon seat, I'm dying for a ride, and I would love to get to know Susan better."

Robert nodded in amusement.

"I would love to," Susan replied immediately. She turned to her brother. "Do not talk one word of business until we return," she ordered.

Mark chuckled. "Far be it from me to forget for even a second that we're business partners!"

Susan appeared satisfied and walked to the barn, emerging minutes later leading a tall black mare with one gleaming star.

"Oh, Susan!" Carrie cried, reaching forward to stroke the horse's face. "She is magnificent."

Susan smiled. "I raised Silver Wings from a foal," she said proudly.

"This is the horse you're using to beat all the men," Carrie guessed.

Susan smiled smugly. "They believe their horses can out-jump my mare. We teach them differently."

Mark chuckled. "She didn't name her Silver Wings by mistake. This lady really does seem to fly over jumps."

Susan grinned. "I must admit, however, I've never tried to jump her over a solid six-foot fence bareback," she said. "Nor have I ever jumped her with a bullet in my shoulder."

Carrie grinned. "I'd say we have a lot of stories to exchange," she said happily.

Mark vaulted off his chestnut gelding and handed her the reins. "Thunder has plenty of energy left. Riding him will save time."

Carrie allowed Robert to boost her into the saddle. She looked at Susan. "Lead the way!"

******

Four days later, Robert and Carrie drove the wagon, full to the brim with family heirlooms Carrie insisted he keep, back down the drive. He had been prepared to leave everything, but she convinced him he would want memories of his boyhood home.

"What a wonderful time," Carrie breathed as she turned to wave goodbye to Mark and Susan again. She had spent most of her time in the saddle either riding with Robert or Susan. Robert had taken her to all his secret, special places. They had picnicked by the stream, laid under the stars in the meadows, and stood on the same bluff Robert had looked down from when Matthew saved Oak Meadows. They had wonderful meals with Mark and Susan, staying up late to talk and laugh around the fireplace that warded off the early autumn chill. "It was the honeymoon we never had," she said softly, knowing she would carry the memories with her for the rest of her life.

Robert smiled and leaned over to kiss her. "I'm thankful every day that the war is over, but this last week with you has released something in me that has taken my gratitude to a new level."

"Because you know you're not going to be called into battle tomorrow," Carrie replied, remembering all the wrenching goodbyes when she couldn't possibly know if she would ever see her husband alive again.

"Yes," Robert murmured. "I can't even begin to tell you what it was like to be in the midst of so much death and destruction. The memory of your face was the only thing that kept me going so many times, but I always felt guilty bringing your perfect beauty onto a battlefield."

Carrie ached as she saw the haunted look flicker in his eyes. His nightmares were getting better, but she wondered if he would ever be completely free from the memories that assailed him when he closed his eyes. "It's over now," she said gently.

Robert took a deep breath and shook his head. "You're right," he said firmly. "Sometimes it reaches out to grab me and suck me back into the darkness, but it happens less and less," he said with relief.

"Are you regretting selling Oak Meadows?" she asked, wondering if the loss was triggering the new wave of memories.

"No," Robert responded immediately. "If anything, I am more convinced than ever that I've done the right thing. I'm ready to walk away from my past and create a brand new future with you. I love Oak Meadows, but there is a part of me that wonders if the horrible things that happened here would ever completely release me. I've changed so much, but I don't want reminders of those times." He stared off into the distance. "I will always want Clint to work with me. I couldn't imagine bringing him or Amber to a place where I had a little boy killed." His face clouded.

Carrie leaned against him. "We all have done things we regret," she said tenderly. "But not enough of us change our lives so that we'll never repeat those things. You have." She reached up and turned his head so their eyes would meet. "I'm very proud of you."

Robert leaned his forehead against hers. "Thank you," he whispered.

When they reached the gates of Oak Meadows, he stopped the wagon and turned for one final long look. Then he turned his face toward Richmond and headed home.

******

Rose sang softly as she walked to school. June had left earlier, to prepare the classroom so Rose could spend more time that morning with John. She frowned as she thought about the fever making him cranky—he had cried when she left that morning. Janie had promised to take care of him, but she couldn't get his imploring eyes out of her mind. How had her own mother stood it when her little girl was moved into the big house, and she'd only been able to see her on Sundays? She would go mad if she couldn't be with John every day.

Gazing up the road, she wondered when Carrie would return. She had received the letter about her and Robert's trip to Oak Meadows, but it had been more than two weeks since they had left. The medical clinic was complete, and people stopped by every day to find out when they would start seeing people. She knew, though, that the biggest issue was how much she missed her best friend. After nearly four years of separation, she treasured every moment they had together. Rose knew the day would probably come when they would be apart again, but she certainly wasn't ready for it to happen any time soon.

Rose sighed and forced her mind to focus on other things. She scolded herself for being melancholy when she had so much to be thankful for. There were now sixty children in her school, with eighty adults coming seven nights a week. The adults came in tired and dirty from their work, but very few of them missed a night. They were determined to get the education that had been withheld from them for their whole lives. She and June were switching off nights so she could spend time with John, but she knew her schedule couldn't continue for long now that her pregnancy was advancing. She still had more than three months to go, but she had learned her lesson the hard way at the contraband camp when she had almost lost John because of exhaustion. She wouldn't allow that to happen again.

Rose scowled when she realized her mind had once more drifted into dark thoughts. What was wrong with her?

"Miz Samuels! Miz Samuels!"

Rose was jolted out of her thoughts by a high-pitched little voice. She recognized Sarah racing down the dusty road toward her. She knelt down and caught the young girl's hand as she drew near. "Hello, Sarah," she said calmly, able to breathe more easily when she didn't see trouble in Sarah's eyes.

"Miz Samuels! It done happened, Miz Samuels!"

Rose smiled at the unrestrained excitement and joy in Sarah's eyes. "What happened, honey?" she asked quietly.

"They came together," Sarah cried. "Just like you said they would! All them letters just came together!"

Rose sucked in her breath. "You're reading?"

"Yessum! I done read to my mama out of dat book you sent me home with—the one about the horses." Sarah's eyes shone with pride. "My mama done cried and cried when I read to her. She said she'd been dreamin' about readin' most all her life, from the time she was about my age. I reckon I sho made her happy!"

Rose laughed and hugged Sarah warmly. "You made your mama *and* me happy," she assured her. There was simply nothing that gave her more joy than helping someone learn.

"Mama learned how to read last week," she confided. "She and Daddy both came home and sat right down by the fire readin' to each other. I heard her tell my daddy that she feels like she's been walkin' in the dark her whole life, and now it's like a big ole sun is shinin' on her all the time!"

Rose made no attempt to stop the tears flowing down her cheeks. She might be tired, and she might miss Carrie, and she might wish she didn't have to leave John when he was sick, but suddenly it was all worth it again. Helping her people walk from darkness into the sunshine was all she wanted to do.

Sarah frowned and patted her cheek. "You be okay, Miz Samuels? I didn't make you feel sad did I?" Her tiny face puckered with worry.

"Not a bit," Rose assured her with a watery laugh. "You've made me happy!"

Sarah peered at her and nodded. "Then them be happy tears!" she announced brightly.

Rose smiled and hugged her closer. The little girl would never know how much she had needed her news that morning.

******

Rose settled into a rocker on the porch, grateful for the cool breeze blowing over her body. It was October, but Indian summer still had Virginia in its grip. John, his fever gone, was snuggled on her lap with his head resting on her shoulder and his big eyes drowsy. Rose hummed softly as she rocked her son, smiling tenderly when she felt the baby in her womb give a kick. Moments later, John's body went lax as he fell asleep.

"It's a perfect evening," Janie said softly, speaking quietly so she wouldn't disturb John.

"That it is," Rose said contentedly, drawing in deep breaths of fragrant air that carried the smells of the freshly cut oats and wheat. A call from down the road made her turn her head. She smiled when she spotted Moses and Simon striding rapidly down the road. "They must have good news, or they wouldn't be moving so fast," she observed.

Moses was grinning when he strode up onto the porch, Simon right behind him. Both of them reached for the pitcher of water, poured tall glasses, and downed them before they settled into two of the rocking chairs.

"The harvest is finished," Moses announced, his white teeth flashing in a wide smile.

"Congratulations!" Rose cried. The men and their families had all been working hard the last week to harvest the crop of oats and wheat. She had ridden out several nights ago, to watch them cut the stalks and bind them together into shocks. Not wanting to take a chance on rain ruining the crop, they had worked late every night to haul the shocks in wagons into one of the barns. Soon they would take the wagons to the local thresher.

"Is it a good crop?" Janie asked.

Simon nodded. "It's a good crop." His eyes were shining.

A good crop meant good wages for all the men. "All of you deserve it," Rose said warmly. "Everyone has worked so hard."

Moses nodded. "Just a couple more days and we'll harvest the tobacco. It could be cut now, but it wouldn't be as high a quality. I'm determined to make this first crop as profitable as I can. Next year, most of the fields will be planted in tobacco."

Rose knew he had been spending hours poring over reports from the years before the war. Thomas' office, now her husband's office, had become his sanctuary as he studied all the records and profit sheets. Her heart swelled with pride, but she felt a catch in her heart when she looked over and saw Simon staring out over the pasture, a hard look on his face. There was something in his posture that worried her.

"Simon?" she asked gently. "What is it?"

Simon glanced at Moses and then turned to look at her, a shadow of sadness in his eyes. "A friend came through a couple days ago. He served with me and Moses. He lives down in South Carolina." His sadness dissolved into a scowl. "I should say *lived*."

"Bad news?" Rose asked.

"I'm afraid so. We must have gotten all the rain that the Deep South didn't get. The drought has about destroyed the cotton and rice crops," he said heavily. "It's making a bad situation even worse."

Moses stood and poured another glass of water. "The freed slaves were already struggling. They agreed to work in exchange for a portion of the harvest profits. Now there won't be anything. Families who were already starving will have a difficult time making it through the winter," he said heavily. His eyes flashed anger. "Families who are trying to leave and find a better opportunity are being beaten and whipped."

"What?!" Rose cried. "Isn't anything being done to stop it?" When Moses shrugged and averted his eyes, she became more frightened. "What aren't you telling me?" she asked sternly. "I will not be protected from knowing what is happening."

Moses sighed. "Samson told us the plantation owners down there are determined to treat the freed slaves just like they did before we were free." He stopped talking, his face tight with tension as the silence thickened.

"What he doesn't want to tell you," Simon said bitterly, "is that Samson snuck away one night because he saw some of his friends murdered for saying they were going to leave. Others were killed because they weren't working the way the owner wanted them to, or they had the audacity to dispute their labor contracts." He scowled and got up to pace around the porch. "One of the men in our unit refused to be bound and whipped when the owner found him coming back onto the plantation after going to church."

What's wrong with that?" Janie asked indignantly.

"He didn't have a pass," Simon said flatly. "The owners don't want any of the laborers leaving the plantation. When he refused to be bound and whipped, the man pulled out a pistol and killed him." His eyes were heavy with grief. "They killed Otis."

Rose gasped and began to cry. "Will it ever end?" she whispered. "What will ever make it end?"

Moses crossed to her, and took her hand but remained silent. Rose knew he was battling his own grief and fury, and she also knew he didn't have any answers to give.

*****

Annie walked out onto the porch with a platter of warm cookies. She usually brought food onto the porch and returned to the kitchen, but tonight she settled down into the remaining rocker and handed the platter to Rose.

Rose stared down at the cookies but shook her head. "Thank you, but I'm not hungry," she murmured, wiping the tears from her eyes as she pulled her son closer, relishing the comfort his warm body gave her. She stared at him, wondering if freedom was going to give him a better life, or if it was merely going to change the way white people made his life miserable.

"Ain't no good to be thinkin' like that, Miss Rose," Annie said quietly.

Rose had learned to appreciate the wisdom Moses' mama had. "How do you know what I'm thinking?"

"I was listenin' to Moses and Simon talkin'," she admitted, her eyes sad.

"Then you know how we feel," Moses growled, his eyes burning with tears as he thought of Otis' full, laughing face. Otis had served under his command for two years. He'd been so proud to run away from his plantation in South Carolina to join the army, and he'd been full of such grand plans for how he was going to live his life as a free man. He bit back a groan as he envisioned Otis standing up against the plantation owner. He felt his heart skip a beat as he imagined him being shot in cold blood simply for going to church.

"I know what you be feelin'," Annie agreed. "I also know it ain't gonna help you none."

Moses frowned. "How could we possibly feel anything else?" Then he stopped short, realizing his mama had felt what he was feeling for far more years than him. The image of his daddy's broken body hanging from a noose in the clearing roared into his mind. "I'm sorry, Mama..." he whispered. "I know you know how we feel."

Annie nodded. "I done did a heap of talkin' with Miss Abby when she be here. She told me all about how them people up north fought for us to be free." She paused. "They had to fight for a long time. Did you know folks started trying to stop slavery way back even before I was born? They been fighting it since before the

Revolutionary War. It done took a real long time for them to get slavery done way with." She took a deep breath. "Lots of our people died while folks was trying to get things to change."

Rose listened carefully. "What are you saying, Annie?"

"What you think I be saying, Rose?"

Moses snorted. "I told you she was just like your mama, Rose."

Rose smiled, remembering all the times Sarah had answered her questions with questions of her own. She recognized the value of thinking through things, so she let Annie's words flow through her mind. She thought of all the people who had fought slavery, while it seemed to do nothing but grow more pervasive and violent. She thought of laws passed, while even more slaves were smuggled into the South to begin lives in bondage. She thought of all the slaves killed and beaten, while owners carried the belief it was their right and privilege to do whatever they wanted with their property.

"Nothing is over yet," Rose said slowly. "The amendment abolishing slavery is a big step toward freedom, but it's going to take a very long time before our people are truly free." She stared out into the distance. "Many more of our people are going to die because the battle is far from over."

Annie nodded. "That be the truth of it," she said calmly.

"So we sit back and watch people die, saying it's just the way things are?" Simon cried angrily, clenching his fist.

"I sho 'nuff hope you *don't* do that," Annie said, "but feeling hatred ain't gonna hurt nobody but you." She reached over and put a hand on Simon's fist. "I learned a long time ago, that the only way to keep from going completely mad was to forgive people."

"Forgive—"

Annie held a finger to her lip to stop Simon's outburst. "I remember a time when I thought forgivin' them people that killed my Sam was pure craziness. I couldn't imagine forgivin' the beatin' that crippled my bright little girl, or killed my other baby daughter."

"How did you do it?" Rose whispered.

Annie smiled. "I learned forgiveness ain't 'bout makin' an excuse for the wrong somebody do. It be about stoppin' what they done from destroyin' my heart."

A deep silence fell on the porch while everyone pondered her words.

Janie was the first to break the silence. "How long did it take you?"

Annie sighed. "It took me a good long time, Miss Janie. There be some days I thought I done let it go, and then somethin' or somebody would bring it right back up. It would burn right into my heart just like at the beginnin'. But every day done got a little better," she said. "I had to make a decision ever' single day not to let them destroy my heart." She stroked Simon's hand tenderly. "Once you let them destroy your heart, you ain't got nothin' left to live for," she said firmly.

Annie stood and walked to the edge of the porch, and then turned back around to face them. "We all be free on paper, but it gonna be a good long time before we be free in people's eyes, especially down here in the South. Lots of our people gonna suffer. Lots of them are gonna die," she said heavily. "It just be the way of things. We keep fightin' it," she added firmly, "but if we do it with hate in our hearts, we ain't any diff'rent from the ones who be doin' the killin'."

Moses stared at her and slowly nodded. "You're right. When I heard about Otis, and when we talked about it tonight, I felt hatred for white people." He looked at Janie apologetically. "I know that's wrong, because I know so many white people who are wonderful, loving, caring people."

"Hatred ain't a color issue," Annie said. "It be felt on both sides. I figure hatin' be the easy choice to make."

"How do we fight it?" Rose asked. She smiled at Annie. "I'm asking all of us. I think you're right that it's going to take a long time, and there are going to be a lot of deaths. So the question becomes, how do we fight it and not hate?" She gazed down at John nestled against her breast. "How do we make America better for John and little Simon?" She thought about all the children in her school. She envisioned the faces of all the adults who were so determined to learn. She thought about their perseverance in the face of fatigue and hardship.

Rose remembered something Sarah used to tell her. "Mama used to say that she was already free, because somebody might own her body, but no one could own her soul and her mind."

Annie nodded. "Your mama was right."

Moses stood and stared out over the fields, drinking in the sight of the plantation he had come to love. "How long?" he asked. "How long will we have to fight?"

"I figure we's gonna have to fight all our lives," Annie said bluntly. "I think it be a mite easier for John, but he gonna have to fight, too. I reckon his chilun and all his chilun's chilun gonna be fightin', too."

Moses whirled around and stared at her. "You don't think it will *ever* end?" he asked with disbelief.

Annie looked at him sadly. "Once you start somethin' evil, it be 'bout impossible to stop it, Moses. The very first slave that done be brung here set somethin' evil in motion. People had to stop seeing us as human in order to keep us as slaves. Theys had to believe we's were less than them, so they's could feel good 'bout takin' care of us," she said. "There be generations of people who done believe that. They's gonna teach their chilun, and then they gonna teach their chilun."

"So there's no end?" Moses demanded, slamming his fist against the porch column. "I refuse to believe that!"

"Oh, it gonna get better," Annie said calmly. "Now that the slaves be free, they's gonna show what theys can do, and who theys can be. They's gonna make white people have to question what theys really believe. Some of them gonna change their minds in time."

Moses took a deep breath. "So we have to show white people what we're really capable of," he said slowly.

Rose stood up and moved beside Moses, slipping her hand in his. "We've been proving ourselves all our lives. We'll keep right on doing it. And we're going to help others prove themselves," she said. "You are showing plantation owners what can happen if they treat their workers fairly."

"And you and Miss June teaching all them folks how to learn," Annie said proudly. "They's gonna hold their heads up high, and then they ain't gonna be afraid no more."

Rose turned and looked at Annie closely. "That's really the key isn't it?" she murmured. "As long as black people are afraid, we're easy to control. When we stop being afraid, because we know we're more than what white people believe we are, then they will lose their power over us."

Annie nodded. "I reckon that be true, sho 'nuff."

Janie stood and moved over beside Moses and Rose. "I believe that is true for everyone," she said quietly. "I know it was easy for Clifford to control me, because I had started to believe I was who he told me I was. When I realized that wasn't true, I was able to take action to control my own life. He lost his power over me."

"Ain't nothin' more powerful than fear," Annie agreed. "I reckon every person alive gots to fight it every day of their life. I learned a long time ago that I's couldn't control what was goin' on in my world, but it for sure weren't going to control *me*."

Moses stepped over and pulled his mama up from the chair, wrapping her closely in his massive arms. "I love you, Mama," he said gruffly. "The best thing about the war ending was getting you back."

Annie smiled and patted his shoulder. "I reckon that be true, sho 'nuff," she said. "I knows you be growin' up 'cause now you be smart enough to listen to your mama!" She chuckled and stepped back. "Now, are you young'uns gonna eat these cookies or not?"

A holler from down the road made everyone lean forward.

Moses looked at Janie and nodded toward the door, but she shook her head firmly. "I'm done with being afraid of Clifford," she said. "There's not a thing he can do to me with all of you here."

Annie stepped up and laid a hand on her arm. "Bein' careful ain't the same as bein' afraid, Miss Janie. From what I hear, your husband be an angry man." She glanced around the porch. "There be a bunch of people here he would like to hurt. He be more likely to do it if you not doin' what he wants."

Janie gasped. "Of course, Annie. I never thought about it like that. I wouldn't put all of you at risk for anything in the world." She quickly moved into the house and peered out from the window, watching as the horses got closer. Her heart pounded against her ribs as she wondered if Clifford had finally come looking for her. She suddenly realized she was almost looking forward to it. She was tired of being afraid. As she waited, she was aware it was time to file for a divorce and deal with whatever ramifications came. It was time to quit hiding.

******

Everyone on the porch waited for the wagon to get close enough to identify the occupants.

A wide smile broke out on Rose's face. She shifted John into Moses' arms and ran down the stairs. "Carrie!" she cried. "You're home!"

Carrie was laughing when she leapt from the wagon to embrace Rose. "I missed you so much!"

"Oh, I missed you, too." Rose smiled up at Robert. "Welcome back," she said. "Thank you for bringing my best friend home."

There was a wild flurry of welcome, and then everyone sprang into action to carry things in from the wagon.

Carrie smiled with contentment when she finally settled down in one of the rocking chairs with a cool drink in her hand. She gazed around at all her friends. "I love going away, but I think coming home is always the best."

Chapter Thirty-Three

Carrie smiled when she walked out on the porch to find frost glistening on the pastures, each blade of grass sparkling like a diamond under the early morning sun. The almost-bare limbs of the trees created gray sculptures that seemed to be posing, showing off their splendor, now that the leaves had drifted to the ground to lay at the base of their trunks. Granite lifted his head and snorted at her before he lowered it again to continue grazing. Carrie sighed with contentment.

Moses stepped out beside her, a hot cup of coffee nestled in his huge hands. "Indian summer has officially ended," he commented as he took a sip.

"But not before you got the tobacco harvested," Carrie said gladly. "I do believe I'm ready for some cold weather. I can hardly believe it's November. Life always seems to slow down when summer is over. I'm ready for a change of pace."

Moses chuckled. "Don't tell the men that. I've given them a list of work to be done that will keep them busy the entire winter. There is so much to do to be ready for next year. Now that we're not spending every minute in the fields, we can finally get to all the needed repairs."

Carrie nodded. "I know the women are busy canning and putting food away. The long fall produced a huge bounty within the gardens, as well. I was down at the cabins yesterday. Everyone seems to be happy."

"They're happy," Moses replied with deep satisfaction. "I can remember all the nights I spent with my men around the fires last winter during the siege at Petersburg. We spent hours talking about what our lives would be like in a year." He chuckled. ""Even in their wildest dreams, the men couldn't have imagined this."

Carrie smiled. "Father said the oat and wheat sold for a good price. He already has a buyer for the tobacco."

"The profit margin was good," Moses agreed, his eyes lighting with pleasure. "I wish you could have seen the men's faces when I gave each of them their share. Just getting paid every month was something they had never experienced. Actually receiving a percentage of what they worked so hard to produce was almost more than they could believe."

"How do you think they'll spend it?" Carrie asked.

Moses looked at her. "They won't," he said simply. "I've been teaching them everything your father has taught me. He sends me books every week."

"I see you up late in the office every night studying," Carrie commented.

"I want to learn everything I can. When Thomas said he would mentor me, I didn't fully realize what that meant. I do now. I realize your father is giving me a tremendous gift. I don't want to waste it. Sometimes my brain feels like it will explode, but I can't ever seem to get enough." He took another sip of coffee. "The men are all saving their money so that someday they can have places of their own," he said gravely. "All of them have that dream."

"Of course they do," Carrie responded. "I think every human being dreams of owning something for themselves." She gazed up at Moses. "I imagine that includes you," she said quietly.

"I'm half-owner of Cromwell," Moses replied, not quite meeting her eyes.

"Yes, but it's not something you can pass on to John, and you're not free to sell it. I believe it's more accurate to say you own half the profits."

Moses looked at her sharply but saw nothing except understanding. "Have you and Rose been talking?"

"Don't we always?" Carrie asked calmly. "But, no, Rose and I have not talked about this. I just see the restlessness in your eyes sometimes. Or at least I think I do." She paused. "Am I right?"

Moses met her eyes. "I reckon you are, but it's not something I intend to do anything about for a while. I don't even know that I'm *supposed* to do anything. I'm happy here. Rose is going to have another child in two months. The plantation is doing well, and I'm learning so much."

"I know," Carrie replied, holding his gaze. "I mostly just want you to know that I realize things may not always remain the same. There are going to be changes for all of us. Sometimes I wish all of us could be satisfied to remain on the plantation, but I don't think any of us are like that."

Moses narrowed his eyes. "You're restless, too."

Carrie smiled slightly. "I know I should say I'm not. The clinic is doing well. We're seeing more people every day. I treated seven veterans yesterday, but I also saw ten members of the black families. I'm doing what I love to do, but..."

"It's not enough, because you still want to be a doctor."

Carrie saw no reason to hide the truth from Moses. He could see into her heart almost as well as Rose. "That's true." She frowned. "I also feel guilty because I want to go to medical school. Who will take care of these families if I leave? What will happen to them?"

Moses didn't pretend he had an answer. He reached down to squeeze her hand. "You'll know," was all he said.

Carrie sighed, realizing his simple statement was the truth.

******

Robert was heading out to the barn after finishing up some paperwork in the house, when he heard the sound of hoof beats coming down the drive. His eyes narrowed when he identified the rider. He turned to the barn just in time to see Clint emerge with Eclipse for his morning workout. Without saying a word, he waved Clint back into the barn. He saw Clint peer down the road before quickly turning and disappearing again.

Robert took a deep breath and waited until the rider pulled up to the bottom of the porch.

"Hello, Robert."

"Clifford," Robert said evenly.

"You're looking well," Clifford said, his eyes shifting nervously as he gazed around the plantation. "I'm glad you're better."

Robert just looked at him. "What are you doing here, Clifford?"

A red flush crawled up Clifford's neck as his eyes sparkled with anger. "I came to get my wife," he said, no longer making a pretense at civility.

"What makes you think she's here? I can imagine a lot of places a wife could go when she no longer wanted to be abused and beaten by her husband."

"I don't know what that little idiot has been telling you..." Clifford began.

Robert stiffened and held up his hand. "Janie is one of the finest women I know," he said firmly. "You will not talk about her that way."

"She's my wife," Clifford retorted. "I'll talk about her anyway I choose."

Robert looked at him carefully. "I take it you got the divorce papers."

Clifford snorted. "Total nonsense. I've come to take Janie back to North Carolina."

Robert remained silent again, staring at Clifford as he struggled to maintain control.

"Divorce is not an option," Clifford said angrily. "Our laws protect marriage as a sacred institution."

This time it was Robert who snorted. "Which seems to be considerably more than how you view it," he said caustically.

"Janie has been filling your head with nonsense," Clifford shot back. "I have never beaten her."

"I suppose the bruises and welts on her face appeared magically," Robert said, his anger growing as he envisioned Janie's face the day she had arrived.

Clifford shrugged. "Sometimes it is necessary to remind a woman of her place."

"And sometimes it is necessary for a marriage to end in divorce. I believe this is one of those times."

"There are laws to protect marriage," Clifford said haughtily, his eyes narrowing with hatred.

"Let's see," Robert mused, well versed in the laws since he had gone to Richmond to handle Janie's divorce two weeks earlier. "Divorce is a much easier process since the end of the war. It seems there are many unhappy couples, so the courts have eased up on their restrictions. If you live in South Carolina you're out of luck because they refuse to allow divorce under any circumstances. If you marry in North Carolina, and you happen to be the guilty party, you're forbidden to remarry during the lifetime of the innocent party." He smiled slightly. "That could make things rather uncomfortable for you."

"Why, you—"

"Of course," Robert continued calmly, "I suppose it's good for you that you married in Virginia, and it's also good that divorces are much easier to obtain now." He paused. "You being a lawyer, I'm sure you know that."

"The courts acknowledge the right of a husband to treat their wife any way they want to," Clifford said, fury shining in his eyes as he struggled to maintain his dignity.

"They certainly used to," Robert agreed, "and I'm aware there are judges who hold that view in every state. It's rather pitiful how women are allowed to be treated in some courts." He gazed at Clifford. "It's a good thing for Janie that the judge in Richmond actually has a brain. It seems he agreed she didn't have to continue to be abused." He relaxed, discovering he was actually enjoying himself as Clifford grew more panicked.

Robert moved onto a lower step to put himself at eye-level with Clifford. "I suggest you sign the papers you have in your pocket and be done with it. No one wants you here, Clifford. Janie doesn't. I don't. Carrie doesn't. In fact, I can't think of anyone who does."

Clifford sniffed. "Carrie has told me I'll always be welcome."

Robert clenched his fists as he battled the urge to knock the sneer off Clifford's face. "That was before you abused and beat the woman she loves like a sister. Any welcome you had on any Cromwell property has long disappeared." He took a deep breath. "It's time for you to leave, Clifford. You can sign the papers now, or I'll have my attorney come to Raleigh to take care of it."

Clifford looked at him carefully and swung from his horse. "I'm not leaving without Janie."

"You're leaving," Robert repeated quietly.

Clifford snarled and tensed. "I don't know who you think you are, Borden!"

"I think I'm someone who knows Janie is far too good for the likes of you," Robert responded, holding himself in check, while waiting for the moment he knew was coming. He smiled when Clifford drew his fist back. He was hoping for a chance to dish out some of what Clifford had dished out on Janie. Before Clifford could even throw a punch, Robert's fist slammed into his face. He quickly followed it with two more blows, the stomach punch doubling Clifford over as he gasped for breath.

Robert stared down at him. "Beating a woman does not make you a fighter," he said coldly. "Now, I've asked you to leave, and I've told you to leave. If you don't want more of the same, you will get on that horse and ride out of here now."

"You won't get away with this," Clifford growled, struggling to catch his breath.

"If you ever step foot on Cromwell Plantation again," Robert said sternly, "you'll get much more than what I've given you today." For just a moment, pity mixed with the anger, causing him to shake his head. Janie had *loved* this man at one time. "Why, Clifford? Janie is an amazing woman who would have been a wonderful wife. Were you always like this, or did the war do this to you?"

Clifford glared at him before he stood straight, gathered his reins, and slowly remounted his horse, desperately trying to hold on to any dignity he had left. "What do you know, Borden? You and your nigger-loving wife!"

Robert stiffened, his eyes blazing with anger. "Get off this plantation, Clifford. Don't ever return or you will be sorry." His heart pounded as he fought to retain control. All he really wanted to do was haul Clifford from the saddle and beat him to a pulp. He took a step forward and reached for the reins.

Clifford's face whitened as he realized he had gone too far. He snarled before he turned and galloped off.

Robert took several deep breaths and then turned toward the barn. If Clifford went by the school, Janie would be in danger. He started to run, hoping that by cutting through the woods he could reach the school and clinic before Clifford.

Clint rode up just then, skidding to a stop.

Robert gasped with relief. "Give me your horse," he said sharply.

"It's okay, Robert," Clint said. "I rode to the clinic. Carrie and Janie are on their way home now. Through the woods," he added. "I told them to stay off the road."

Robert sagged with relief. "How did you know?"

Clint shrugged. "I figured that man had to be the one who beat Janie. Did you give it to him good? I wanted to wait around for the show, but I decided you would want me to go get Carrie and Janie so he couldn't find them."

Robert grinned and thumped him on the shoulder. "Thank you," he said fervently. "And yes, I gave it to him good."

Carrie and Janie emerged from the woods behind the barn, their faces set and anxious. They both looked relieved when they saw Robert talking to Clint.

"Robert!" Carrie cried. "What happened?"

Now that he was sure Carrie and Janie were safe, Robert began to relax. "Clifford was here," he said sternly.

Janie gasped, looking around fearfully.

"He's gone," Robert said. He answered the question in Janie's eyes. "He got the divorce papers and didn't take kindly to them. He seemed to think he could convince you to go home with him."

"Robert gave it to him good!" Clint exclaimed.

Annie was hurrying across the yard to where they were standing. "He certainly did," she called proudly, her black eyes shining. "I don't believe that coward of a man will be back here again." She smiled at Robert. "Where'd you learn how to fight like that, Mr. Robert?"

Robert flushed. "I had boxing classes in college," he admitted. He smiled as he remembered the look on Clifford's face. "Let's just say people will know he was in a fight that he lost."

Carrie giggled. "I'm so sorry I wasn't here to see it," she said.

"Carrie Borden!" Janie gasped, but she couldn't stop the giggle that escaped. "You gave it to him good?" she asked hopefully.

Robert nodded. "I'll send my attorney to Raleigh next week. I'm certain he'll return with signed papers. If nothing else, Clifford knows you have friends who are going to make sure he never touches you again." He shook his head. "He fights like a girl," he said contemptuously.

Laughter erupted from everyone as the tension disappeared.

When the laughter died away, Janie looked at all of them, a bright sheen of tears in her eyes. "Thank you," she whispered. "I felt alone every single moment I was in Raleigh. It's so wonderful to be with friends who care so much."

******

Carrie watched Robert as she got ready for bed later that evening. "You're worried about something," she finally said, putting her brush down and turning to him.

Robert walked over and lifted the gleaming hair from her shoulders, burying his face in it for a long moment. "So very beautiful," he said softly before he lifted his eyes and met hers. "I'm worried about Clifford," he admitted.

"I thought you told us he wouldn't be back," Carrie said, her heart quickening.

"I didn't want to scare Janie," he admitted. "Clifford is a dangerous man. Alone, he is nothing but a coward, but he's also a man who thrives off power. Janie leaving him is a threat to his power. I'm concerned about what he will do to retain his reputation. If he has his eye on a political office, it won't look good that his wife left him."

"So he would force her to come back for appearance's sake?" Carrie demanded angrily. "We won't let it happen!"

"No, we won't," Robert agreed instantly. "It would be helpful if Clifford couldn't find her at all. I believe he'll sign the divorce papers, but I want Janie out of his reach."

"How?" Carrie asked quietly.

Robert put his hands on her shoulders. "I think it's time for you to go to Philadelphia to check out the medical college," he said quietly. "Take Janie with you."

Carrie stared at him. "Go to Philadelphia? *Now?*" She tried to analyze the feelings tumbling through her heart.

Part of her pulsed with excitement, but there was just as big a part that was totally resistant. "Robert, I..." She shook her head slowly. "It's not time."

"I hope not," Robert replied, "because I will admit I don't want you to go yet, but I think it best if Janie leaves for a while, and I can't think of another way to make it happen."

"Without her knowing she is in danger." Carrie finished the words he didn't say, her throat tightening as she remembered the bruises and welts on Janie's face, and the terror in her eyes when she first arrived.

"Yes," Robert said heavily. "I'm afraid I wasn't quite truthful with Clifford. I convinced him the Richmond judge was in favor of Janie's divorce request, but I don't know that for certain. Because so many women are requesting divorces now that the war has ended, he agreed to the petition, but I'm not sure what he will do if Clifford presses it." He sighed. "The truth is that divorce law is left up to every state to interpret. From what I have learned, each judge basically has the freedom to decide how they want. I've read cases of judges sending women back who have been more horribly abused than Janie." He scowled. "I won't let that happen to her."

"Of course we won't!" Carrie cried, fury raging in her heart at Clifford. "Why won't he just leave her alone?"

"I think he will in time," Robert replied. "The cost and time of trying to fight it here in Virginia will become more than he can bear, especially if he can't find her. He'll have no way of knowing she has gone to Philadelphia."

"You've talked to Father and Abby about this," Carrie guessed.

"Yes," Robert admitted. "We talked about it when I went to file the papers for her. Abby offered her home in Philadelphia if it is needed."

Carrie filtered this new information through her mind. "When should we leave?" she asked.

Robert took a deep breath. "In the morning," he said sadly. "I wouldn't put it past Clifford to come back soon. It makes sense to fight it here before he has to go back to North Carolina. Since he is an attorney, he may have friends he can convince to make Janie go back."

Carrie gasped. "*Tomorrow*? What about the clinic? What about our patients?"

Robert took both her hands. "I realize this isn't a good time." His brow creased with worry. "I just don't know what else to do," he said with a helpless shrug of his shoulders.

Carrie realized what an impossible situation he was in. She also realized what a sacrifice he was making to let her go away. Hard on the heels of that realization was the very real possibility that Janie could be dragged home or hurt again if Clifford returned. Pushing aside any other feelings, Carrie squeezed Robert's hands and nodded. "Thank you for caring so much about Janie," she whispered. "How long do you think we should stay away? I will miss you every moment we're gone, but I believe you're right."

Robert closed his eyes with relief. "One month," he said. "Thomas and I agree that will be long enough to take the wind out of his sails, and also make him realize it will be best for him to move on."

Carrie trembled but nodded. "There's only one thing," she said, suddenly realizing it was the only way they could do this.

Robert cocked his brow.

"Janie has to know the truth about what is happening. She is not a child. She is a grown woman, who has already had to fight for her freedom. She may be frightened, but she is strong enough to deal with this. There will be no secrets."

Robert nodded slowly. "You're right."

Carrie put down her brush and rose from her seat. "I'll go talk to her now. We'll be ready to leave in the morning." She stood and wrapped her arms around Robert. "I said there was only *one* thing, but actually there is one more," she said lightly, forcing herself to focus on the night she had left and not all the ones without her husband that loomed ahead.

"And that is?" Robert asked, kissing her softly.

"I want you waiting for me when I get back," she said, running her hand down his chest and deepening their kiss before she stepped away with a sultry laugh.

"Oh, you can count on it, Mrs. Borden. You can definitely count on it."

******

Rose and Moses were there to tell them goodbye the next morning, when they stepped out onto the porch long before sunrise.

Rose wrapped Carrie tightly in her arms. "Be safe," she whispered. She stepped back and laughed lightly, putting her hand on her stomach. "My baby is telling you to be safe, too. He or she seems quite insistent."

Carrie laid her hand softly on the growing mound. "I'll be home long before this little one is born," she promised.

"And I promise to let all your patients know you were called away on an emergency, but that you'll be back as soon as possible," Rose replied, glad the darkness was covering the tears she had vowed not to shed. She turned and wrapped her arms around Janie. "You're going to be okay. Clifford won't be able to hurt you."

Janie nodded bravely. "I know," she said, surprising everyone with the strength in her voice. "I'm done being afraid of him, but I'm also wise enough not to make decisions that will put me, and all of you, in danger as well." She managed a light chuckle. "Besides, I've always wanted to visit Philadelphia!"

******

One week later, Carrie and Janie stood outside a restaurant taking deep, appreciative breaths. "It sure smells like Opal's cooking," Carrie said, leaning back to look up at the sign perched over the door of the simple storefront. "*Southern Goodness,*" she read. "This is the place."

Carrie could hardly believe so much time had already flown by. Once she got over the shock of so suddenly leaving Cromwell, it was easy to enter into the spirit of the adventure. She hadn't been in Philadelphia since the summer before the war—that amazing summer that brought Abby into her life, and changed everything she felt and believed.

Janie shivered and pulled her coat tighter. "Is it always so cold here?" she asked.

Carrie laughed. "The Farmer's Almanac said this winter is going to be brutal," she informed her cheerfully. "Look at the bright side. When you get back to Virginia, you may think it's actually warm."

"I'm more interested in being warm *now*," Janie retorted good-naturedly. "Are we just going to stand outside this restaurant, or are we actually going in?"

Carrie responded by pushing open the door, smiling when the warmth from the large pot belly stove in the middle of the restaurant pushed out to blast her face. She was immediately charmed by Southern Goodness. The décor was very basic, but it was warm and friendly. Small tables were covered with red and white checked cloths, and lanterns cast a warm glow through the entire place. She wasn't surprised when an instant silence fell over every table, as people turned to stare at them. She smiled brightly, knowing they were probably the only white people to ever enter the restaurant.

It didn't take long for the silence to be broken.

"Carrie! Carrie, is that you!" Opal bustled out of the kitchen, her ample body clothed in a crisp apron, her eyes shining with delight. "And Janie!" she cried. "Well, if you two ain't a sight for sore eyes. Sit yourselves down and tell me what you're doing here in Philadelphia." She leaned over the counter and yelled. "Eddie! Get out here. You won't believe who just walked in our door."

Conversation resumed as everyone realized the two white women were Opal's friends. Eyes were still trained on them, but now there were merely curious instead of suspicious.

Beaming, Opal seated them at a table and then rushed back into the kitchen, appearing moments later with a huge platter of fried chicken, mashed potatoes and steaming biscuits slathered with butter.

Carrie closed her eyes with delight as she took the first bite of a biscuit. "Annie is a wonderful cook, but no one makes biscuits like you do," she confessed.

Opal ducked her head, her eyes shining with pleasure. "Now you two tell me what you're doing up here."

Her face grew stern as Janie told her about Clifford. "Ain't no man got a right to hurt a woman," she said firmly. "If my Eddie were to lay a hand to me..."

"Opal would probably hurt me worse than I could hurt her," Eddie said, as he stole up behind her and kissed the top of her head. Then he moved around her and gave both Carrie and Janie a hug. "It's so good to see you two. I never imagined we would have you in our restaurant."

Carrie looked around her and noticed every table was full. "You seem to be doing well."

Eddie nodded. "We gots Aunt Abby to thank for that, for sure. She gave us the money to get started, but more importantly, she talked a friend into renting us this building. It's in a perfect location. We been making money since the very beginning. The kids help when we need them, but we're keeping them in school as much as we can. The kids are all real bright, but those two Sadie's are something else. Both of them want to go to college."

Opal shook her head. "Can you imagine that?" she asked proudly. "It ain't been long at all since all of us be slaves. Now these two girls are in school and talking about going to college."

"How is Susie?" Janie asked. "Zeke?'

Opal shook her head sadly. "Susie ain't heard nothing at all about Zeke. We knows there a bunch of soldiers got killed that were never identified. Me and Eddie think Zeke has to be one of them, but Susie refuses to give up hope." Her eyes shone with tears. "It breaks my heart to see her disappointed every single day when she doesn't hear from him. She was in here working till just a little while before you came in. She opens up the restaurant every morning about five o'clock. She leaves when lunch starts so she can go to school."

"Her heart is broken," Eddie said heavily, "but she's determined to go to school and become a teacher like Rose. She's gonna do it, too!"

"So you're glad you left the South?" Carrie asked, saddened by the news about Susie, but knowing the girl was strong enough to handle yet another loss, especially since she had her daddy back.

"We sure are," Eddie said firmly. "It ain't perfect up here, and there still be lots of people who think we're just dumb niggers, but there are opportunities here that we wouldn't never have found in the South. Especially not in Richmond. We made the right decision."

Opal nodded her head. "I wouldn't want to be anywhere else," she agreed. "I just wish it weren't so *cold*," she said dramatically. She laughed heartily. "Now you two tell me everything that is going on down in Virginia." She glanced toward the kitchen. "I have sweet potato pie for dessert."

Carrie grinned at Janie and leaned forward. "There is so much to tell you..."

Chapter Thirty-Four

"This is it," Janie murmured, as she gazed up at the looming, three-story building at 229 Arch Street. "The Female Medical College."

Carrie's heart pounded as she stared at the building, and watched the female students hurrying in and out of its doors. "We're looking at the first college in the world specifically established to train women for the degree of doctor of medicine. There were just eight women who received degrees during their first graduation in 1851. Dr. Hannah Longshore was one of them. Abby told me about her. She was Philadelphia's first active woman doctor." Awe filled her face. "So much history has been made here. So many women have changed the course of medicine and the future for women. It's an honor just to be standing here."

"And four years ago," Janie added, "they established the Woman's Hospital of Philadelphia, to offer medical and surgical care for women by women. It was the first-ever woman's hospital."

Carrie nodded. "They knew they had to expand clinical experience for the college's students." She thought about all she had learned during her long years at Chimborazo. "They train nurses, too." She and Janie watched as two women strode by, their heads together in serious discussion, their arms loaded with books.

"Are you ready for your interview?" Janie asked. "It's almost time for you to go in."

Carrie took a deep breath. "I don't know if I'm ready or not," she murmured. "Standing outside and thinking about being a doctor is very different from actually walking through those doors and applying for medical college."

"You're meant to be a doctor, Carrie," Janie said firmly. She gave her a little push. "Being late is hardly a good first impression."

Carrie looked at her for a long moment, nervousness clutching her throat.

"You walk in there with your head held high," Janie scolded. "You probably already know more than most of the doctors who have graduated!"

Carrie seriously doubted that was true, but she straightened her shoulders, lifted her head, and sailed in through the doors, her heart pounding with excitement. She could hardly believe she was actually walking into the Female Medical College, clutching a recommendation from Dr. Strikener and a letter from Dr. Wild.

٭ ٭ ٭ ٭ ٭ ٭

Two hours later, Carried emerged from the building, her eyes a little glazed as she absorbed all she had learned. Janie was just walking up from the opposite direction, her cheeks glowing from the cold, but her eyes strangely bright. "You haven't been waiting outside all this time, have you?" Carrie asked.

"No," Janie replied. "I've kept warm." She grabbed Carrie's arm. "Well?"

"The interview went well," Carrie replied. "It was almost surreal," she admitted. "After working alongside only men during the war, it was rather strange to be surrounded by women who are actual doctors. I felt both intimidated and validated," she confessed.

"They were impressed with you, weren't they?" Janie demanded. "Come on, Carrie, tell me the truth."

"They seemed to be," Carrie acknowledged. "That may have just made it harder. I'm afraid of letting them down."

"Nonsense," Janie snorted, grabbing Carrie's hand. "Carrie, this is what you want. You've wanted it for years." Her eyes were confused. "Why are you holding back?"

Carrie looked at Janie, tears glistening in her eyes. "Yes. This is what I want." She thought back to five years ago. "When I was in Philadelphia before the war, I didn't get to come here. I toured the University of Pennsylvania, but I didn't know about the Female Medical College. When I left to go home, I thought I would be coming right back. Abby and I had made so many plans..."

"And then your mother became ill and died. And then you had to run the plantation because of your father's grief." Janie's voice sounded a little impatient. "What does that have to do with now?"

Carrie ignored her question, still lost in the past. "Then there was the war," Carrie said heavily. "And now I'm back on the plantation with Robert."

"He supports your desire to come to medical school," Janie reminded her.

"I know," Carrie said.

"So what is wrong?"

Carrie shook her head. "I'm not sure..." She stared up at the building as the truth filtered into her heart. "In spite of the fact I've spent my whole life rebelling against Southern tradition, there is a part of me that feels guilty for leaving Robert to come to school," she admitted, scowling as the truth of her acknowledgement hit home.

"And you'll miss your husband..."

"Of course," Carrie said. As she stared at the building, her heart pounding with excitement, she knew it wasn't missing Robert that was holding her back. "I love Robert with all my heart."

Janie reached for her hand. "Robert wants this for you."

"I know he does," Carrie whispered.

"Then you just need to get over it," Janie said firmly.

Carrie stared at her, smiling at the determination shining in her friend's eyes. Janie had seemed to grow stronger every day they were out of Virginia. Carrie had watched during the last ten days, as Janie bloomed into a woman she liked very much but wasn't sure she recognized. "Just like that?" she asked quietly.

"No, not just like that," Janie responded. "You never change *just like that*. It's never easy." She gripped Carrie's hand more tightly. "Carrie, it was your words that gave me the courage to escape Clifford, even though it took me months before I could accept the truth of them. Southern tradition told me I was a failure as a person if I was a failure as a wife. Southern tradition told me my life was over as a woman if I got a divorce."

"None of that is true," Carrie said.

"You're right," Janie agreed easily. "It is just as true that you leaving Robert long enough to become a doctor doesn't make you a bad wife. Especially," she said with a laugh, "when your husband *wants* you to do it so badly." She peered into Carrie's eyes. "You're afraid," she said softly.

Carrie wanted to deny what Janie said, but all she could do was drop her eyes and stare down at her hands. Her friend had helped her through so many times during the war when fear threatened to swallow her. She struggled to make sense of the feelings swarming in her mind and heart. "I had to be strong for so long during the war. There were times I thought it would never end. Now that it's over..."

"There is a part of you that wants things to stay the same. You want to stay on the plantation, run your clinic and be with your husband."

Carrie's defiance flared. "What's wrong with that?"

"Not a thing," Janie said calmly. "If it was *enough.*" She tilted Carrie's head up to meet her eyes. "But it's not. You also want to be a doctor. You want to come to school in Philadelphia, where you can meet other strong women who share your dream. You want to study with them. You want to learn new things from women doctors who have led the way for you. You want to be an *actual* doctor."

Carrie looked back at the building, her heart yearning to experience what Janie was describing, but a stubborn part of her also wanting long nights around the fireplace with Robert. She wanted to watch Rose's children grow up. She wanted to walk to her clinic and treat her patients, listening to the voices of small children learning on the other side of the wall. She wanted to ride into Richmond any time she wanted, to visit her father and Abby. After five years of almost constant turmoil, she yearned for a period of normalcy and consistency.

The vision drew her in, but...

"It's only two years," Janie reminded her. "And you'll be able to go home during parts of it."

"I know," Carrie whispered.

"Remember *why*, Carrie."

Carrie turned questioning eyes toward her friend. "Why?"

"Why do you want to be a doctor? What has kept the dream alive?" Janie squeezed her hand and fell silent.

Carrie sat quietly, knowing this was the real question that had to be answered. Visions of her father's slaves, and all the times she had helped them filled her mind. She saw her mother lying on her bed, slowly wasting away until she died. Memories of each soldier she had treated during the war rose up to beckon her. She thought of the thousands of veterans who would need help in the years to come, and the communities of freedmen struggling to get medical care. She envisioned Robert's proud face as he talked about her being a doctor.

She took a deep breath, knowing that once again she was letting her fears stop her. Suddenly, Sarah's wise face rose into her mind, and she could feel her calm voice reverberating in her heart. *"Ain't nothin' wrong with fear unless you let it stop you, Carrie girl. God done got big things for you to do, girl. You can sit in one place and ignore that, or you can stare down them fears and go do what you gots to do."*

"You're right," Carrie said finally. "I'm coming back to be a doctor," she said firmly.

"When?" Janie asked, a broad smile breaking out on her face.

Carrie closed her eyes for a moment. "I'll start in April," she said, a feeling of freedom and excitement washing over her as she said the words out loud. She tipped her head back and laughed loudly, watching as the wind whipped dead leaves in a dance over her head. "I'm going to start medical school in April," she said again, more loudly this time.

"I'll be here waiting," Janie replied.

It took a moment for Janie's words to filter through her excitement now that she had made her decision. She turned and stared at her friend's dancing blue eyes. "What did you say?"

"I said I'll be here waiting."

Carrie kept staring at her, trying to decide what she meant.

Janie grinned. "I was content being a nurse for a long time. I watched you all those years at Chimborazo, and I didn't think I could ever be a doctor because I didn't have your confidence." She held up a hand when Carrie tried to interrupt her. "I almost let Clifford destroy me, but I found the strength to escape. Doing that...coming here...seeing the college... It's made me realize I want the same thing. I want to be a doctor," she said boldly. "I'm going to stay here in Philadelphia and study every book I can get my hands on. I'm also going to get a job in the hospital as a nurse, if they'll have me. When you're ready to come, we'll start medical college together." She dipped her head. "While you were in your interview, I talked with someone in admissions," she confessed. "They assure me my experience will qualify me for medical school."

When Janie opened her mouth next, she answered the question in Carrie's mind. "Aunt Abby is an angel. I'm borrowing the money from her for school. She wanted to give it to me, but I couldn't accept it. It may take me a while, but I will pay it all back," she finished firmly.

Carrie sat silently while Janie's words seeped into her brain. Suddenly, she jumped up, grabbed Janie's hands, and began to whirl her in a circle, laughing loudly. "A doctor! We're going to be doctors *together*!" Her mind began to swirl with plans. "We'll live at Abby's house. We'll help each other study. We'll keep each other company when we're lonely. We'll have other students come over for dinners..."

She collapsed onto the bench shivering in spite of her excitement, pulling her coat close as the wind picked up. Metal-gray clouds scuttled across the sky, sinking lower as she watched. The images of medical school swirled as wildly as the clouds, threatening to overwhelm her. It wasn't until just that moment that she realized how much she had dreaded being in Philadelphia alone. She would still be leaving so much behind, but she would have Janie!

Janie tilted her head up to stare at the clouds. "I think Abby's house sounds quite wonderful right now."

Her eyes were bright with excitement, but her cheeks were red from the cold.

"It's going to start snowing soon," Carrie said, pushing aside the images when she realized Janie was shaking. "Let's go someplace warm."

They chattered excitedly all the way back to Abby's house, planning what life would be like as they both studied to become doctors.

******

Matthew trudged up the stairs to Thomas' house, heavy-hearted in spite of how glad he was to be home. Darkness had fallen, making the glowing light from the lanterns even more appealing. The air was rich with the smell of burning fires. Even in the dark, he could see the white plumes of smoke curling from the houses surrounding him. He had been gone for almost a month. Each day had brought him to a new level of despair and anger.

Abby was sitting in a chair pulled up close to the fireplace in the parlor when he walked in. "Matthew!" she cried. "I didn't know you were coming tonight. Why didn't you telegram us?"

Matthew shrugged. "I just decided to come home yesterday. I didn't want to waste time on a telegram," he said wearily.

Abby sprang up to give him a warm hug. "My dear boy," she murmured. She pulled him over to the other chair and pushed him down into it.

Matthew, in spite of the feelings rampaging in his soul, smiled. "I don't know if I'll ever get too old not to want you to call me your *dear boy*. I always know I'm home when I hear that."

Abby reached for one of his hands. "You'll never be too old, because I will always be this much older, and you will always be my dear boy," she said tenderly. "You've had a difficult trip," she observed as she took in his exhausted eyes.

Matthew sighed. "We're living in difficult times. I don't think it's possible for me to have any other kind of trip. I don't regret contracting to write this book, but there are times I wish I could hide away, and not be aware of all that is happening in our country."

Abby smiled. "That would last for a short time, and then you would go mad sitting in ignorance."

"Either way I lose," Matthew said.

"Tell me," Abby invited gently, warm concern filling her eyes.

Matthew glanced at the clock. "Will Thomas and Jeremy be home soon?"

"Yes. I left the factory early. The last pieces of equipment were installed today," she said proudly. "We're opening for business in mid-January."

Matthew forgot his own problems for a moment. "Congratulations!"

"Thank you. Thomas and Jeremy stayed behind to do some work on one of the machines. They should be along shortly."

"If you don't mind, I'll wait for them to come. I only want to have to say all this once."

Abby frowned. "That bad?"

Matthew nodded heavily. "That bad."

Heavy footsteps told him he would have to talk about it soon. He wasn't sure if he wanted to hold it in, pretending it wasn't really happening, or if he wanted to tell it all with the hope it would lose some of its weight when it was out of his mouth. Not that it mattered. Abby, Thomas and Jeremy needed to know.

Abby continued to watch him with concern and then pressed a kiss to his forehead, hurrying into the kitchen to let May know there would be one extra for dinner.

Thomas and Jeremy greeted Matthew and headed into the dining room.

"We're starving!" Jeremy announced, his face flushed with excitement. He turned to Matthew. "Did Abby tell you about the equipment?"

"She did. Congratulations."

"It's been so amazing to see the building emerge from all that burned-out rubble," Jeremy exclaimed. "I can hardly believe we're just weeks away from opening. I always thought finance was satisfying, and I still feel that way, but being part of bringing a business together—especially with my brother and sister-in-law—

is an amazing feeling." He glanced fondly at Thomas and Abby, his eyes shining.

Matthew could feel Thomas preparing to ask him about his trip. "Have you heard from Carrie and Janie?" he blurted. He sincerely wanted to know, but he also wasn't ready to talk about everything.

"Carrie is coming in on the train in three days," Thomas answered. "Janie has decided to stay in Philadelphia," he explained. "She is going to start at the Female Medical College in April." He decided to let Carrie share her own news.

Matthew whistled. "Janie is going to become a doctor?"

Thomas nodded. "I know Carrie is eager to tell us the whole story when she gets here. We're heading out to the plantation for Christmas the next day."

Matthew stared at him. He had completely forgotten Christmas was so close. He grimaced. Could Christmas really happen in a country where so much evil was running rampant?

Thomas frowned. "Matthew? Is something wrong?"

"No talk until after dinner," Abby said firmly. "Matthew has had a rough trip. He's going to tell us about it, but not until he has a full stomach."

Silence fell on the table as they ate. The wind kicked up outside the window, brushing the limbs of the magnolia trees against the screens in a weird type of orchestra. Sparks flew from the fire as gusts blew down the chimney.

Matthew felt some of the horror of the last weeks leave his body as the warmth and camaraderie soothed his soul. After so many years of living alone between assignments, it was wonderful to have a home to return to. By the time May placed coffee in front of him, he was ready to talk.

"I suspected things were going to be bad under President Johnson, but I didn't foresee them being this bad." He hesitated. "I think Micah and May should hear what I have to say."

Abby got up and walked to the kitchen. Moments later, Micah and May had pulled up chairs at the table, their eyes wide with questions.

"The last month has been a steady supply of one revelation after the other," Matthew began. "None of them have been good."

"Where have you been?" Thomas asked.

"I spent time in Georgia, North Carolina, Mississippi and Florida. I talked to correspondents who have been in the other states to make sure I had a complete picture." He scowled, trying to force aside his feelings for the moment as he reported what he had discovered. "There are times I truly hate politics, and this is one of them, but understanding the political scene is the only way to understand what is happening. I'll try to make it as simple as possible."

Micah shook his head. "Don't you worry none, Mr. Matthew. Me and May might not speak so good yet, but we been keeping track of what be happening around the country. We read the paper every day," he informed them.

Matthew stared at him. "You do?" He winced. "I'm sorry if I sound condescending. I know how intelligent you and May are."

"Don't you be worrying none. There's still way too many of my people that gots no idea of what's going on. I'm hopin' that will change in time, but I don't reckon it's going to change fast enough for them to be ready for what's gonna happen."

May nodded. "You's gonna tell us about the Black Codes, ain't you?"

Matthew sat back in his chair and stared at her. "Yes."

"You's go right ahead. I'll admit all that political talk done be real confusing. If you can make sense of it for us, I would be mighty appreciative," May said, "but I know that don't change what is happening."

Thomas looked around the table. "I'm embarrassed to admit I may be the most ignorant one here. I've been so involved in getting the factory up and running, that it has been easy to ignore what is going on in the country. I've enjoyed washing my hands of politics, but I have a feeling I've made a grave error. I have no idea what you're talking about."

"I'm afraid I'm guilty of the same thing," Jeremy admitted. "The last six weeks have been a total blur."

"As they have been for me," Abby added. She took a deep breath. "Tell us everything, Matthew.

"President Johnson's Reconstruction Plan has been a complete failure," he began. "Back in May, when he excluded Confederate leaders and disloyal wealthy planters from political affairs, there was hope there could be a true change in Southern politics."

"Because of the pardons he required for anyone who had property worth more than twenty thousand dollars," Thomas said.

"Yes. At first, Johnson was very cautious about granting them. By September, they were being issued wholesale, sometimes hundreds a day. Right now there are thousands of men in leadership whose only agenda is to do everything they can to rebuild the New South with the same agenda as the Old South."

"Not all of us," Thomas said. "I received my pardon in October."

"You are a very rare exception," Matthew said. "No one can completely understand why Johnson has abandoned the idea of depriving the prewar elite of its political and economic control. From everything I have learned, I suspect he has decided cooperation with the planters is indispensable in order to secure white supremacy in the South, as well as his own reelection."

"Some of the fellows here in Richmond figure President Johnson be a little put off by how much we be willing to fight for our freedom," Micah commented laconically. "He told some fellow over in England that we need to be kept in order while we *'receive the care and civilizing influence of dependence on the white man.'*"

He smiled at the surprised look on the faces surrounding him. "It's best to memorize some of what I be readin'." He shook his head. "There's lots of folks here in Richmond who want things to be different."

"They're about to get worse," Matthew said with a scowl. "Micah is right. Our president believes only planters can supervise and control the black population. Since he believes that, he also decided the planters could not be barred from a political role in their states." He took a deep breath. "This whole last three months has been a series of one state convention after another, followed by Democratic elections, because each state supposedly passed Johnson's requirement for restoration into the Union."

"Did they?" Abby asked. She shook her head. "I can't believe I even have to ask that question. I should know what is going on!"

Matthew reached over and patted her hand. "It's a full-time job to know what's going on in our country right now. Yes, they passed the requirements, but I'd say it was more by adhering to the letter of the law. They surely have turned their noses up at the spirit of the law." He scowled. "But then so has our president," he said angrily. "President Johnson has made it very clear he favors a white man's government. He has confirmed time and again that he is against giving blacks the right to vote. His stance has inspired Southern whites of all political persuasions to rally to his support."

Abby stared at him. "What does he intend to do about winning the Northern vote?" she asked with disbelief dripping from her voice, her eyes wide and angry. "Surely he realizes he is taking a stance against everything the North fought for. Congress went back into session a week ago. They will not let it stand." She fervently hoped she was right.

Matthew shrugged. "It seems the new Southern leaders are predicting just such a breach. They are calling for the formation of a new party to rally around *their* president and sweep away everything that opposes him."

"They're mad," Abby said bluntly.

"I hope so," Matthew replied. "In the meantime, a whole series of Black Codes have already gone into effect around the South."

"That's what we been hearing," Micah said. "They ain't in Virginia yet, but I knows they's talking about them."

Thomas shook his head. "Perhaps I was unwise to step so completely out of politics. I don't even know what you're talking about. Keep going," he said heavily.

"The Southern leaders have decided that since black labor can no longer be controlled by plantation owners, it must become the job of each state. They are firmly convinced that the only way to bring any kind of order back to the South is to make sure the freed slaves are still under control."

Micah nodded. "They's real upset that we want to control our own money. They's also mad because we ain't willin' for them to have the right to beat us into doing things their way," he said bitterly. "When Moses was here a while back, he told me about Otis being shot 'cause he weren't going to let himself be whipped." His hands trembled. "There be lots of that going on."

Matthew clenched his fists. "He's right. President Johnson has guaranteed the white South a virtual free hand in regulating their own internal affairs, especially in regard to the freed slaves. The South interprets states' rights as the right and power to govern the black population as they please." He stared into the flames of one of the lanterns for a long moment. "Enter the Black Codes. At their core is the decision to replace the old slave master with the state. The *state* will now enforce the labor contracts and plantation discipline. The *state* will punish blacks that don't comply."

"All they've done is return things as close to slavery as they can!" Abby said angrily.

"I'm afraid that's true," Matthew replied. He pulled out a sheet of paper. "The best way to tell you about the Black Codes is to read how they are impacting the blacks where they have been put into force. They started in Mississippi, but they are now in force throughout the entire Deep South. There are slight differences in each state, but they are all very similar." He began to read.

"*All Blacks are required to possess each January, written evidence of employment for the coming year. If they leave their jobs before their contract expires, they will forfeit wages already earned, and also be subject to arrest by any white person. If any person offers work to a laborer already under contract, they risk imprisonment or a fine of five hundred dollars.*'"

"Preposterous!" Jeremy snorted.

"There is much more," Matthew replied.

"*Blacks are forbidden to rent land in urban areas. Vagrancy—a crime whose definition includes the idle, disorderly, and those who misspend what they earn—can be punished by fines or involuntary plantation labor.'"*

Shocked silence fell on the room.

"'In South Carolina, blacks are barred from following any occupation other than farmer or servant unless they pay a high annual tax that very few can afford. The plantation laborers must work from sunup to sundown; and there is a ban on leaving the plantation, or entertaining guests, without the permission of the owner.'"

Matthew paused. "Florida's code was drawn up by a commission whose report praised slavery *as a kindly institution* deficient only in its inadequate regulation of black sexual behavior." He rolled his eyes. "They have made *'disobedience, impudence and disrespect to their employer a crime. Blacks who break labor contracts can be whipped, placed in stocks, or sold for up to one year's labor.'"*

"Matthew," Abby whispered, tears filling her eyes.

Matthew folded the sheet of paper and placed it on the table. "There's more, but I think that gives you the scope of it," he said angrily.

"These are laws?" Jeremy asked with disbelief. "That President Johnson has approved?" He shook his head.

"Our president has lost any semblance of control over Southern politics. The sad thing is I think he realizes it, but he has no idea how to reclaim it. He's become little more than a puppet of the new Southern leadership."

"*Congress* will reclaim it," Abby retorted.

"I believe so," Matthew agreed, "but so much damage has already been done. Congress reconvened a week ago. It remains to be seen what action they take, but it is for certain that untold numbers of black people are suffering terribly right now."

"*Eight months,*" Abby said quietly, her voice trembling. "It was eight months ago today that President Lincoln was killed. I knew the results of his assassination would be terrible, but I didn't envision this." She looked at Micah and May. "I'm so sorry," she whispered. "I'm so terribly sorry that your people are suffering this way."

May reached over and squeezed her hands. "Don't you be sorry, Miss Abby. It's 'cause of folks like you that we be free at all. It ain't gonna be easy, but we're going to keep fighting."

"And we'll fight with you," Abby said firmly. "I believe President Johnson has seriously underestimated the determination of Northerners to ensure the war was not fought for nothing. The North believes it is important that the South acknowledge its defeat, that slavery be ended, and that the lives of the former slaves be much improved."

"What about voting, Miss Abby?" Micah asked. "If things gonna really change, the blacks got to have the vote."

Abby sighed. "I believe that, Micah, just like I believe women should have the right to vote, but I don't know what it will take to make either of those two things happen. Very few states in the North, even though they abolished slavery years ago, have also given blacks the right to vote. I believe that right, like the abolition of slavery, will happen in time, but I also believe it will be another long-fought battle."

Abby decided to change the subject. "You'll be going to the plantation with us, won't you Matthew? I know our country is in chaos, but I understand Christmas on Cromwell is something very special."

Matthew smiled, realizing she was trying to lighten the mood. In truth, there was nothing that could be done, and there was going to be no real movement on anything until after the beginning of the new year. "It is indeed special," he agreed. "I have wonderful memories of the Christmas I spent there. I would be honored to join you."

"Wonderful!" Abby said enthusiastically. "Carrie arrives in Richmond on Monday afternoon. We leave the next day for the plantation.

Chapter Thirty-Five

Sam and Annie stood in the doorway of the house and took deep breaths, their eyes shining with pleasure.

"It smells just like the woods in this house!" Annie exclaimed. She walked over slowly to gaze up at the towering cedar tree Moses had hauled into the house earlier. Then she looked around at the garlands of greenery draped over every doorway and window, and the vases of holly decorating every mantle and table. "I think this be the prettiest thing I ever seen!" she exclaimed.

"You ain't never seen a Christmas tree before?" Sam asked.

Annie shook her head. "Ain't never been inside a big house at Christmastime," she admitted, "but I don't remember seeing a tree ever go inside one."

Sam grinned. "Wait until you see it decorated. Then it really be something." He took another deep breath. "Christmas always be Miss Carrie's favorite time of the year. I didn't guess I would live to see me another one with all the family home, but I sho 'nuff be glad I'm here."

"They should be here any minute," Annie said excitedly. She lifted her face to take another breath. "My nose tells me them pies about ready to come out of the oven. We got a whole table of bread and corncakes already baked up." She shook her head. "Me and Polly been cooking for days, but I reckon it will disappear right fast."

"There will be a lot of people here," Sam agreed happily. He glanced in the direction of the cabins. "The men and their families already have the barn ready for the dance on Christmas Eve."

Annie shook her head. "That be another tradition?"

"You ain't never been to a Christmas dance?" Sam asked with disbelief.

"I heard about 'em, but I ain't never been on a plantation that let 'em happen," Annie replied. "How long you been on Cromwell Plantation, Sam?"

Sam creased his brow as he thought. "Goin' on 'bout seventy years now," he said slowly. "I be born here, like my mama and daddy before."

"You been here a long time. You don't know what it's like at other places," Annie said with a scowl.

Sam smiled. "Oh, I know all about it," he said. "I know exactly how bad some folks been treated during slavery." His eyes twinkled. "Rose told you how so many of the folks from here escaped on the Underground Railroad?"

"'Course she did," Annie replied. "She never did figure out how that conductor knew to come here." She looked more closely into Sam's eyes, her own eyes widening. "You?"

Sam nodded. "I done helped with the Underground Railroad for a long time. I made a lot of trips into Richmond for Mr. Cromwell." He paused, laughter dancing in his eyes. "Let's just say I made more stops than I was told to." He shook his head. "I never told my Rose girl about any of that. I figured she couldn't get into trouble for somethin' she didn't know nothin' 'bout." His eyes misted over with memories. "Our people got a long way to go, but we sure have come a long way."

Annie grinned. "Well ain't you a source of surprises, Sam!" She frowned. "How you feelin' lately? You was moving pretty slow when I got here, but you seems to be movin' even slower now."

Sam shrugged. "I'm gettin' older every day," he said calmly. "Don't reckon I know how many more days I got to get older." He looked around the room again. "I sure be glad I get me another Christmas, though." His eyes brightened. "I reckon it's gonna be the best one ever. Hard to believe we'll all be in the big house together with the Cromwells, Rose, Moses, little John, all the folks down in the cabins..." He shook his head with disbelief. "The slaves always be brung up to receive their gifts every year, but they never were treated like nothin' but slaves. We livin' in a new world, Annie."

"Only some of us are, Sam," Annie said heavily. "I know most of our people ain't havin' a Christmas like this."

"I reckon you be right," Sam agreed. He grabbed her hand. "But there ain't no reason for us not to enjoy every minute of it," he said. He started toward the kitchen. "You figure one of them pies be ready for me to test it? I sure don't want the family to eat somethin' that ain't passed the *Sam Test*. Opal made that my official job when she be here," he said gravely.

Annie chuckled and pushed through the kitchen door, smiling broadly when the fragrant heat blasted her face. Sam was right. This was going to be the best Christmas of her life. She'd dreamed for so long about being with her babies again. Now she had Moses, Rose, June, and two handsome grandsons, with another baby on the way. It only made sense to enjoy it.

******

The porch was full of people when Jeremy pulled the carriage to a standstill. "Merry Christmas!" he called.

Carrie, Thomas, Abby and Matthew emerged from the mound of blankets they had burrowed under for the ride. Their noses were red from the cold, but all of them were grinning with excitement. "Merry Christmas!" they yelled, as everyone on the porch echoed back their greetings.

Carrie ran laughing into Robert's arms, reaching up to touch his face as she gazed into his eyes. "Robert!"

"Welcome home, my love," Robert murmured huskily. "I missed you."

Minutes later, they were all huddled in front of the fire with cups of hot cider and coffee warming their hands as they all talked over each other to share the news.

Annie and Polly bustled back and forth from the kitchen, putting out platters of cookies.

"Dinner will be served in one hour," Annie called. "Don't nobody be spoiling their appetite," she said sternly, her eyes dancing as she stared at everyone.

Thomas was laughing as he stepped away from the fire and went to stand next to the tree.

Abby joined him there. "We've only been here a few minutes, and I already know this is going to be the best Christmas of my life," she said softly.

Thomas nodded. "I'd almost forgotten how wonderful Christmas was here," he agreed. "My first wife always knew how to make it special, but when she died…"

"The magic died with her," Abby replied, putting her hand in his.

"Yes. Carrie tried to make it up to me the year before the war started, but I couldn't feel anything. All I wanted to do was escape back to Richmond and forget I ever lived here."

"And now?"

"And now I am quite happy to create wonderful new memories with you, dearest Abby." Thomas squeezed her hand warmly and looked around. "I also find it quite amazing that this colorful group of people is actually all my family. I think back to who I was just a few years ago… I can hardly believe the changes."

Abby smiled. "It gives me hope for the rest of the country," she replied. "I'm going to hold to our decision not to talk about all the horrible things happening, but it doesn't stop me from thinking about it and determining to feel hope for the future."

Thomas smiled. "Carrie told me what you said when you all learned President Lincoln had been assassinated. It helped her so much." He looked thoughtful. "You told her all of you would survive that darkness, just as you survived the darkness of the war. You would be *carried forward by hope*. I believe that statement is just as appropriate now."

Abby leaned into his solid warmth, still amazed this man was her husband. "You're right," she agreed, her own words sinking into her heart and giving her comfort. "We will be *carried forward by hope*."

******

Once Carrie had been warmed by the cider and blazing fire, she looked up at Robert. "Care to go visit Granite with me?"

Robert held out his hand. "Only if I get to kiss my wife in the barn."

Carrie chuckled. "I'm quite sure that can be arranged," she murmured, batting her eyes at him playfully. She was grateful for her thick coat as they walked across the yard toward the barn. "We left snow in Philadelphia. I think it has followed me here."

Robert grinned. "Amber is praying for a white Christmas. She'll be a happy little girl if it happens."

Carrie cast a practiced eye at the sky. "Oh, it is most definitely going to happen. I predict it will be falling by the time we're done eating." She tucked her hand in Robert's, so grateful for connection after more than a month apart. "Where are the kids now?"

"Down in the cabins with the rest of the children, though Clint would be appalled if he heard you call him a kid. Amber appointed herself the *Mistress of Tree Decorating*. She and the other children have been collecting things for the last week. They are going to decorate the tree in the house, but they also have one in the barn for the dance. She is more demanding than any officer I ever served under," he said ruefully.

"You're so proud of her you can hardly stand it."

"That's the truth," Robert said cheerfully. "When we have children, I hope our little girl will be just like Amber."

When they walked into the relative warmth of the barn, Robert pulled her into his arms and claimed her lips. The only sound for many minutes was the snuffling of horses and an occasional stamp of an impatient hoof. Finally, a shrill whinny broke the quiet.

Carrie pulled away laughing. "I do believe that's Granite."

Robert nodded. "He's telling me I've kissed you quite long enough, and that I'll have another chance tonight. He's demanding his turn now."

Carrie ran to the stall, slipped inside, and threw her arms around Granite's neck. "Hello, boy," she said softly, sudden tears filling her eyes as she felt his solid warmth. He nickered gently and rubbed his massive head against her shoulder. She took a deep breath and tried to calm her heart. When she finally looked up, Robert was staring at her.

"You're going back."

Carrie blinked back her tears, walked over, and took his hands. "I have been accepted," she said quietly. "I start in April."

Robert blinked his eyes and grinned. "Congratulations!"

Carrie continued to look at him. "Do you really feel that way? Are you truly happy?"

"Did you think I would change my mind?"

"No, but I..." Carrie stopped, unable to find words. She glanced around the barn, knowing how much she would miss it. The idea of leaving Robert—of leaving Granite—tore at her heart.

"I will miss you every second," Robert said, "but I meant what I said before. Our love for each other is big enough for both our dreams." He tilted her chin up until their eyes met. "You have three months before you have to leave. We will make memories every day. You will see Rose's baby born. We will cram enough love into these months to carry us both through the separations. And then, when it is all over, you will be *Dr. Carrie Borden*," he said proudly.

Carrie relaxed. He was right. She wasn't saying goodbye. They would still have months together. She intended to make the most of them.

"What about Janie?"

Carrie grinned. "She was so happy when you wired the news that Clifford signed the divorce papers. It confirmed her decision."

"What decision?"

"Janie and I are going to be in medical school together!" Carrie beamed as she told him the story, telling him how she had almost let her fears stop her from accepting a place in the next class.

Robert stroked her face. "You and Janie have always been able to be strong for the other when you need it. I'm glad you'll be there together."

"I'll be able to come home on visits," Carrie reminded him. "The course is only two years." It sounded like forever when she said it, but she also knew how fast it would go by, because she would be busy doing what she loved every single minute.

"And I know how to get on a train to come visit my wife in Philadelphia," Robert said. "Don't forget I went to college there. I have many places to show you when I come. And lots of stories to tell you, that I should keep to myself..." he said with a laugh. "I'm quite sure Matthew was hoping you would never hear some of them!"

Carrie suddenly felt as light as a snowflake in a brisk breeze. She was acutely aware she wasn't walking *away* from anything. Rather, she was walking right *into* a wonderful adventure. She pulled away and twirled in a circle, her arms spread wide. "I'm going to be a *doctor!*" she called, laughing as Granite hung his head over the stall door and snorted loudly.

* * * * * *

Everyone was finishing dinner when they heard a shrill voice outside. "Robert! Robert!"

Robert pushed away from the table. "I'm no prophet, but since Amber sounds extraordinarily excited, I have a feeling the snow Carrie predicted is falling."

Carrie laughed. "Amber has been praying for snow," she explained to everyone.

"Me, too!" Rose exclaimed, leaping up to rush for the window. "It's snowing!" she called.

Moments later, all of them, wrapped tightly in their coats, were standing on the porch, admiring the flakes swirling through the air. Amber twirled in circles on the lawn, her head back and mouth open wide to catch as many flakes as she could. "It's snowing! It's snowing!" she sang. She looked up at Robert, a radiant smile on her face. "I told you God would send snow," she yelled. Then she resumed her twirling as they all laughed.

She stopped her spinning and called up to them. "I'm going down to the cabins, so I'll have someone to play with. I already know all the rest of you are just going to *look* at the snow." She whirled and began to run, disappearing around the curve moments later.

Thomas smiled over at Carrie. "So, daughter, how much snow do you predict we'll have?"

Carrie grinned back at him. "According to everything I learned from my esteemed planter father, I predict we'll have at least a foot."

"A foot? So early in the season?" Abby asked, startled. "I would expect this in Philadelphia, but I thought the heavier snows came later in the winter here."

"Normally they do," Carrie agreed, "but this is going to be a hard winter."

"And you know that how?" Abby asked with amusement.

Carrie winked at her father. "It's not hard. You just need to watch the signs nature gives you. I knew back in August, because the cornhusks were thicker than normal. I was certain in September when the acorn crop was more abundant than usual." She smiled. "Then there was the early departure of geese and ducks this year."

"Not to mention that caterpillars are even more fuzzy than usual this year," Thomas added, "and I've been watching the squirrels in Richmond. They started gathering nuts early this year, just like they did last year."

A moment's silence fell on the group as memories of the past winter filled their mind.

Robert shuddered as he remembered the long nights spent freezing in the trenches around Petersburg. He forced himself to smile. "The best thing about *this* Christmas is that we're all together in a warm place."

Rose stepped up beside Carrie and wrapped her arm around her waist. "Abby promised me last year that we would all be together for Christmas. I could hardly believe it, but she was right."

Abby stepped up on the other side of Carrie. "One day you girls will realize I'm always right," she said lightly. "Except for those rare times when I'm terribly wrong," she added impishly.

Thomas frowned. "What? I believed you when you told me you're always right. Do I need to reconsider my marriage vows?"

"Not if you expect to receive Christmas gifts," Abby retorted. "They could be exchanged for a bag of coal at any time."

Everyone laughed as they continued to watch the snow. Plans were made for the fun they would have in the morning, when the sun came out on what they knew would be a winter wonderland.

******

Carrie was up early the next morning, already sitting by the fire when Rose walked down the stairs. She smiled and pulled the other chair close to hers. "This feels like the last Christmas we had together here," she said when Rose settled next to her.

"Except we won't have to worry about hiding all the missing slaves from your father, and Ike Adams won't be showing up," Rose reminded her. She thought back to how worried she had been when Moses and some of the other men rode off to stop Adams from meeting Carrie's father and revealing their secret.

"We've been through so much," Carrie said softly, reaching over to take Rose's hand. She smiled when she looked down at her friend's bulging stomach. "You shouldn't have to wait much longer."

Rose nodded. "I'm so glad you're home. Polly assures me she is an excellent midwife, but I couldn't imagine having this baby without you."

"And there was no way I was going to let you," Carrie said. "I missed little John being born. I wasn't going to miss this one. My calculations say this one will arrive in the middle of January."

Rose smiled, but there was a shadow in her eyes. "I see you looking around here like you're compiling memories. You're starting medical school soon, aren't you?"

"In April," Carrie told her, understanding when tears filled her best friend's eyes. "I struggled with the decision for so long, Rose. I wanted to wait longer. I didn't want to leave so soon. I will miss you so much." She looked around the room glowing with warmth and holiday cheer. "I will miss everything so much," she whispered. "But when I got there..."

"You knew it was where you belonged."

"Yes," Carrie admitted. She struggled to explain. "I met other women who are doctors. I met women who are changing history. I met strong women who have had the courage to do whatever it takes to make their dreams come true." She paused. "I was afraid to say yes," she confessed. "I almost didn't, but then I saw your mama..." Her voice trailed off.

"And she told you there ain't nothing wrong with your fear unless you let it stop you," Rose said with a sigh. "She told you God has big things for you to do, and that you gots to stare down them fears and go do what you gots to do."

Carrie chuckled, tears filling her eyes as she nodded. "Yes."

"I know you have to become a doctor, Carrie. I know it takes going to school to do that. But I'm not going to lie and say I won't miss you every second," she said fiercely. "I hate the war that kept us apart for so long, but I can't hate your becoming a doctor." She shook her head. "Maybe it's just that you're leaving first."

Carrie looked deeply into her eyes, not needing Rose to tell her she wanted to go to college and become an educator. "It's coming, Rose."

"I believe you're right," Rose agreed as she stared into the flames. "I wish I could see into the future and know when it will be." She shook her head and laughed. "And if I had a crystal ball that lets me see into the future, I would probably be so terrified I would never get out of this chair."

Abby walked in just as Rose was finishing her statement. "I think that is quite true. I'm grateful life takes me one day at a time. Most of the time I think I can handle that much. Then there are the times I'm quite sure I can't!" She looked between the two of them. "Carrie told you she's starting medical school," she guessed.

Rose nodded.

Abby settled into a chair. "You girls have something time and distance will never change," she said gently. "Life pulling you apart now doesn't change the fact that for most of your lives you grew side by side. Your roots will always be tangled. Your hearts will always be meshed. You will always know when the other is sad or happy. That bond carried you through four years of war when communication was impossible. Two years of medical school when you can visit and send letters will seem like nothing after what you've endured."

Carrie smiled. "You're so right, Abby." She looked at Rose. "The last four years have made us afraid that every time we are apart it will be for a long, long time. But that's not true, I'll be back every chance I get. Robert is here. You are here. Moses is here. My *family* is here."

"You're right," Rose finally said, tearing her eyes away from the flames. "But that doesn't mean I have to be happy about it," she said defiantly.

"No," Abby chuckled, "You certainly don't have to be happy about it, but I'm looking forward to taking you and your two children to Philadelphia as soon as the little one is ready to travel. I'm thinking summer would be about right."

******

Everyone had been banned from the parlor while Amber marshaled her troops to decorate the Christmas tree.

Suddenly, she appeared. "I need you, Robert," she said imperiously. "It's very important."

Robert hid his smile and nodded seriously. "Is there a problem?"

"Nothing that your long arms can't take care of," Amber said confidently. "Please come with me."

Robert winked as he followed her obediently out of the room. Carrie smiled as memories of other Christmases floated through her mind. "I had Moses carry down all the boxes of ornaments," she said, "but I do believe Amber gathered just as many from the woods. I haven't seen what she and the children have created, but I know they carried in bags of acorns, pinecones and dried flowers. I'm glad Moses cut such a huge tree."

"I'm quite content to just sit here," Rose said lazily, staring out the window at the bank of snow nestled up against the tree line. The flash of red cardinals and vibrant blue jays was the only color in the black and white scene spread out before her. "It made me tired just watching all of you play out there today. John and Simon are sound asleep already, though they made me promise to wake them up when the tree is finished." She laid her hand on her stomach. "I loved watching the snow, but my little one and I are content to wait until next year to play in it."

Abby smiled. "It's been a very long time since I built a snowman. The streets of Philadelphia aren't exactly conducive to playing in the snow." She sighed with contentment. "I even made a snow angel!"

Amber raced into the room, her black eyes snapping with excitement. "It's time!" she cried. "It's time!" She danced in place, her pigtails bouncing on her shoulders.

Rose smiled and walked into the next room to wake John and Simon. They were still yawning when they walked out holding her hands, but their eyes were wide with excitement.

Robert appeared behind Amber and scooped her up onto his shoulders. "Lead the way, oh Mistress of Tree Decorating," he said solemnly.

Amber giggled, holding her head high as they all created a processional into the parlor.

"Oh!" Carrie gasped, staring in wonder.

"Pretty!" John cried.

Simon stared up at it, his eyes wide with awe. "Christmas tree!"

The ten-foot-tall Christmas cedar was beautiful. The children had started by using everything in the attic to decorate the tree. It was dressed with cotton balls, gilded nuts and berries, paper garlands, colored pieces of glass and white lace. But then Amber had taken it from beautiful to spectacular by adding tiny sculptures the children had created from pine cones and nuts. Swatches of pink, white and blue dried flowers nestled in the branches. To finish it off, she had directed the placement of hundreds of tiny white candles that were gleaming and twinkling in the otherwise dark room.

Everyone stood silently, stunned by the simple beauty, and then they broke into loud clapping for the twenty children who had decorated the tree. They were lined up against the far wall, their faces split with smiles as everyone applauded their work.

Thomas reached up, plucked Amber off Robert's shoulders, and whirled her in a slow waltz around the room before he brought her to a stop in front of the fireplace. "You, Miss Amber, have created the most beautiful Christmas tree I have ever seen." He bowed to her deeply. "Thank you."

Amber giggled, her eyes wide. "You're welcome, Mr. Cromwell. I reckon you've given me the best home I ever had. I be real grateful. I ain't had to be afraid for even one second since I been here. And I got all the people I love best right here around me."

Thomas stooped down to look her in the eye. "I feel exactly the same way, Amber. I have all the people I love best right here around me."

Carrie's eyes filled with tears as she exchanged a long look with Rose. She knew both of them were feeling the warm love pulsating through the room, wrapping around them like a warm cocoon and transforming them from the inside out—preparing them for whatever was ahead.

Thomas stood and cleared his voice. "I believe it's almost time for the dance down in the barn."

Carrie looked at Rose and then back at her father. "Are you going?" Her father had never gone near one of the Christmas dances.

"Yes," he said simply. "I won't stay long because I don't want to hamper anyone's fun, but I do have an announcement I want to make."

Carrie shook her head when Rose looked to her. She had no idea what her father was going to do, but one glance at the excited gleam in Abby's eyes told her his wife certainly did. She was certain of it when Abby refused to look at either one of them.

"You folks go on down," Sam said, as he slipped into the room quietly. "I'll put out all the candles on this very beautiful tree," he said. "You did real good," he told Amber proudly.

Amber beamed and skipped over to take Sam's hand. "I'll stay here and then go down to the dance with you, Sam."

Sam shook his head. "Not this time, Amber," he said lightly. "I believe I'll be staying up here. I'm just going to look at this purty tree and rest a little while."

Rose looked at him sharply. "You've never missed a Christmas dance, Sam!" she protested.

Sam smiled. "Why, that ain't true, Miss Rose. This be the first Christmas dance in four years. These old bones don't want to go out in the cold tonight." He kissed Rose on the cheek. "You go down and dance with that fine husband of yours. I'll keep an eye on the boys in case they wake up." He looked down at them. "If I don't miss my guess, they'll be asleep in the shake of a lamb's tail."

Rose tried to push down the uneasy feeling in her heart. He had spent more Christmas Eves dancing than she had living. She just didn't want to admit how old he was getting. Sam had been her rock for her whole life.

Carrie pressed up against her side. "We'll come back and check on him after my father makes his announcement."

Rose nodded reluctantly. "And you really don't know what your father is going to say?"

"No idea." She looked up at Robert as he brought her coat. "Do you know what father is going to announce?"

"I haven't a clue."

Moses overheard the last of the conversation as he walked up. "I don't know either," he confessed, "but I sure am curious. Let's get down there!"

Chapter Thirty-Six

Music was already swirling through the barn when they arrived. Banjos, fiddles and harmonicas were beating out the spirituals that had sustained black people during their long years of bondage, and would continue to sustain them in the years ahead. The barn was bulging with families from the plantation, and with friends they had invited to share the festivities. Matthew and Jeremy had already arrived and were deep in conversation.

Thomas stared around the barn when they walked in. "I had forgotten others would be here," he said.

"Is that a problem?" Moses asked.

"Of course not! This is their home. They are free to invite others to join us. It's just..."

"That you wanted to tell them in private," Moses guessed. He could tell by the light in Thomas' eyes that whatever he had to say was important.

"Yes."

"Will it take long?"

"No more than a few minutes," Thomas assured him. "Abby and I would like to tell them together." He glanced at Carrie and Rose. "I would like both of you to join us."

"I'll gather them in Simon and June's cabin," Moses said promptly. "Just the men?"

"Yes. They can tell their families afterwards."

Carrie and Rose were as curious as the men who had all gathered by the time Thomas and Abby opened the door and walked in. No one said a word while they walked to the front of the cabin next to the fireplace and gazed at everyone in the room.

Thomas cleared his throat. "I want to begin by saying thank you. If all of you in this room had not been willing to work for so little in the spring, I doubt Cromwell Plantation would have had a crop at all. Because you *were* willing, we have had a surprisingly good year— certainly better than other plantations in the area."

Carrie watched as proud smiles lit the men's faces. She knew how much their share of the profits had meant to them. They all hoped to own their own land someday, and were glad for a chance to earn the money for it.

"I'm aware our government made promises to the black population they are not going to keep," Thomas continued. "Families that thought they would have land and a home of their own, have discovered that is not true and will not *be* true."

The men nodded somberly.

Thomas smiled. "I spent years in politics. I could make this long-winded, but I won't." His silver hair shone in the firelight as everyone chuckled. "There are ten families here on the plantation. Mrs. Cromwell and I have set aside four hundred acres on the north edge of the plantation. It will be divided into ten equal portions. Each of you will receive forty acres, and enough lumber to build a house and a barn." His gaze swept the room. "Though I sincerely hope all of you will continue to work for me for years to come, I want to make it clear this land is yours. You've worked hard, and you've earned it."

Shocked silence met his announcement. The only sound in the room was the crackle of the fire.

Thomas' gaze swung to Moses. "I suggest you allot a number to each forty-acre plot, and write them down on a strip of paper. Each man can pull a slip out of the bag in order to keep it completely fair."

Moses' eyes were as wide as everyone else's in the room, as he nodded. Suddenly, he found his voice and walked forward to grip Thomas' hand firmly. "Thank you." He paused. "I know I'll think of more to say when the shock wears off, but thank you is enough for now."

One by one, the men—some with tears in their eyes, and all with joy exploding on their faces—came up to shake his hand.

"Thank you, Mr. Cromwell."

"Merry Christmas, sir.

"This means the world to me, Mr. Cromwell."

Shock still hung in the air when Thomas smiled broadly, took Abby by the hand, and walked from the cabin. Everyone stared around the room until the reality of what had happened truly sank in.

Carrie laughed when the joy finally erupted. She didn't know what was happening in the barn, but there was surely a lot of dancing happening in the cabin. She was so glad she was here to see it. The pride and love she felt for her father expanded her heart until she was afraid it might explode.

Moses grabbed Rose and swirled her around the room gently, his face almost splitting from his grin. "He couldn't have given them a better Christmas present," he said hoarsely, leaning down to speak into her ear.

"Indeed he couldn't have," Rose agreed happily, thrilled beyond measure that these men who had led such hard lives, and paid such a difficult price for freedom, finally had something they could call their own.

Simon bowed to Carrie and spun her into a wild dance of celebration. Suddenly he broke away. "I have to go tell June!"

Within seconds, all the men were heading toward the door. "We have to tell our wives," they called back.

Moses, Rose and Carrie followed them more slowly. They were almost at the barn when Abby appeared out of the shadows.

"Carrie!"

Carrie tensed, somehow knowing what she was going to say before she said it. "Sam?"

Abby nodded. "He was collapsed in the parlor when we got back."

Carrie and Rose were running toward the house even before she finished her sentence. They knew Moses would make sure Abby got back safely.

Thomas had carried Sam into the downstairs bedroom when they arrived.

One look told Carrie he didn't have long. She took his hand tenderly. "Hello, Sam."

"Hello, Carrie girl," Sam gasped, his breath labored. "I ain't feelin' so good." He peered into her eyes. "You done always told me the truth, Carrie girl. I ain't got long do I?"

"No," Carrie said gently, grief making it difficult to talk. This gentle man had been part of her family for her whole life. He had protected her and kept her out of trouble. He had covered for her when she was doing something he knew her mother wouldn't want her to do. His great heart had finally given out. "I'm so sorry," she whispered.

Sam shook his head with difficulty. "Don't you be sorry, Carrie girl. I done led me a good life. I done know I couldn't live forever, but I sure am glad I gots to have one more Christmas in the big house."

Rose groaned and dropped down on her knees beside him, tears streaming down her face. "Sam..."

Sam laid his hand on her head and smiled. "It be okay, Rose girl. I'm gonna go see your mama," he gasped, his face twisted with pain, but his eyes peaceful. "I'm gonna tell her all about how you be living free with Moses, and all about that fine baby boy named after her man. John gonna dance in heaven when he finds out," he said. "And you's about to have another fine baby."

"But, Sam..." Rose cried brokenly.

"Shh... Rose girl, you don't need me no more. You was just like a daughter to me, but my days of takin' care of you be over. You's all grown with a fine family." He looked up with a trembling smile as Moses and Abby entered the room.

"I'm going to miss you so much," Rose murmured, taking his hand as she leaned forward to kiss his leathery, wrinkled skin.

"You cry all the tears you need to, Rose girl, but don't cry them for me," Sam said slowly. "I reckon I been here as long as I needed to be, but now I'm ready to go on home." A burning light appeared in his eyes as he gazed slowly around the room, imprinting all the people he loved in his mind and heart, sending them a blessing with his loving gaze.

Then he closed his eyes and gave his last breath. Peace settled over his face like a veil.

Carrie sagged against her father, but found there was too much peace in the room to shed tears.

Rose leaned forward and gathered Sam into her arms, holding him tenderly.

Silently, everyone filed from the room, leaving them alone.

Only Moses remained, standing quietly with his hand resting on Rose's shoulder. He knew what Sam had meant to her. He knew losing Sam was almost as hard as losing her mama.

"He lived a full life," Rose said quietly, finally breaking the silence. "He told me a long time ago, that he was ready to go whenever God was ready to call him home." A smile trembled on her lips. "I remember him telling me that death might end a life, but the memories of that life will never end."

She reached up a hand. "Will you help me up?" she asked.

Moses grabbed her hand and pulled her up easily, surprised when she gasped. "Rose?"

Rose stared at him, stunned surprise in her eyes. "You should go get Carrie," she said slowly, looking down as a puddle appeared on the floor. "I believe we're going to have another baby."

Moses froze. "Isn't it too soon?"

"Evidently not." Rose smiled. She pushed at him. "Go get Carrie and then come back and help me upstairs."

"Can you make it upstairs?" Moses asked, fear filling his eyes.

Rose laughed this time. "I'm an old hand at this now," she said calmly. "We have plenty of time. That is, if you can quit staring at me and go get my midwife."

"A baby!" Moses kissed her and then turned and ran from the room.

Moments later, Carrie rushed into the room, Abby on her heels. "It's time?"

"It's time," Rose agreed, a strange look on her face as she looked down at Sam. "It's so odd to have a new life right on the heels of death," she murmured. "It's almost as if God is giving me a new baby to fill the emptiness." Suddenly, her face twisted with pain.

"The first contraction?" Carrie asked.

Rose nodded, smiling reassurance as Moses rushed in with Thomas. "If you two fine gentlemen would help me upstairs, I would greatly appreciate it."

When Rose was comfortable in her bed, Carrie turned to Moses and began to bark orders. "I want several basins of hot water, and the pile of sheeting Annie has already cut up." She turned to her father next. "Please bring me the extra blankets out of my and Robert's room."

"Oh..." Rose moaned, as she clenched her fists and lay back against the bed rails.

Carrie turned to look compassionately at Moses. "Your wife will be fine," she said firmly. "Now go get that water and the rags. You are no good to me standing in this room," she said sternly.

"Yes, ma'am," Moses said weakly, turning and almost running from the room. They heard his heavy footsteps receding down the hall.

Rose smiled weakly. "*Men.* It's a good thing God didn't make them the ones who had to bear children. I'm sure the Earth would have been unpopulated a very long time ago!"

Abby laughed. "That's the truth of it." She stepped forward and took Rose's hand. "Is there anyone else you want here?"

"June," Rose said immediately. "She was there with John...when I almost didn't make it." The look on her face was peaceful and confident. "This time is going to be a breeze. Oh, and I want Jeremy waiting with Moses. My twin has to be one of the first to see his niece!"

"And you know this time is going to be a breeze because..." Carrie asked, praying Rose was right. She had heard the terrifying story of John's birth.

"And you know it's going to be a girl?" Abby asked. "How could you...?"

"I just know," Rose answered casually. Then her face grew serious. "God took Sam, but he's sending this baby as his Christmas gift."

Carrie smiled tenderly. "A Christmas baby. I can't think of anything more wonderful." She stepped back as Thomas appeared with the blankets. "Leave them on the chair," she directed. "Please wait outside. Knock on the door when Moses arrives with the water, and then I would appreciate it, if both of you would wait downstairs. And please go get June and Jeremy."

"Banished to the living room once I'm done being an errand boy?" Thomas said with mock disgust.

"Unless you would prefer the porch," Carrie replied sweetly.

Thomas rolled his eyes and gave Rose an encouraging wink. "I'll keep Moses sane until you have this baby," he promised.

Rose nodded, but immediately leaned forward as another rush of pain caused her to cry out. Fear pushed through her peace, as she remembered the agonizing pain from before and just how close she had come to death. Was it going to happen again?

Carrie waved her father from the room and sprang into action. Moments later, she looked up at Rose. "This little one is in a hurry. How long were you in labor with John?"

"Hours," Rose whispered.

"Not this time," Carrie promised her. "Relax. Everything is going perfectly."

Rose relaxed, knowing Carrie would never tell her anything but the truth.

A gentle tap sounded on the door.

Abby reached out to get the water basins, smiling encouragement when she saw Moses' panicked eyes. "Go downstairs, Moses. Everything is fine here. It won't be like the last time," she promised.

Moses relaxed just a little. "Are you sure?"

Abby nodded. "I'm sure." Then she closed the door and carried the water to the bedside table to wait for Carrie's orders.

A peaceful silence fell over the room. The wind picked up outside. The crackling of the fire as Abby fed it wood to keep the room warm was the only other sound. Carrie hummed as she made the preparations.

"This is so different," Rose said suddenly. "When I had John, I was in a tiny little cabin on a hard bed. I was terrified and so very exhausted." She gazed around the room and then looked at Carrie and Abby. "I feel so peaceful and safe."

"You should," Carrie said calmly. "From what I can tell, you will have another child in about an hour."

"An *hour*?" Rose asked with disbelief. She doubled over as another contraction gripped her. "Okay," she gasped, when it finally ended. "Maybe an hour. That one was strong."

Another light tap on the door announced June's arrival. She chuckled when she entered the room and saw Rose sitting up in bed with a confident look on her face. "I guess Thomas was right. I really didn't have to run all the way. You look good." She sobered and took Rose's hand. "I'm so sorry about Sam."

Tears glistened in Rose's eyes, but she brushed them away. "My baby will know all about Sam," she said quietly. "He treated me like his daughter from the minute I moved into the big house when I was only five. He never let on that he knew I was taking books from the library, and he managed to hide the fact that I was taking candles so I could read at night." A smile trembled on her lips. "I remember all the times he covered for me when I was out teaching school in the woods. I found out from Annie, that Sam was the one who arranged to have Mr. Jamison from the Underground Railroad come through here. He never told me. And he didn't leave because he had promised my daddy he would look after me."

"He loved it here," Carrie said. "He's been so happy living here in the house with Opal and the kids for the last several years. He told me it was better than being free, because he didn't have to worry about anything. He figured he was too old to run away and start over. He wanted to die right here."

"I know," Rose whispered. "Mama used to talk to me a lot about the circle of life. She'd tell me that every time something died, something else was being born." She patted her stomach. "My baby is the circle of life for Sam. He would be so happy to know that."

Abby smiled tenderly. "Oh, I think he knows," she replied, taking Rose's hand. "He knows."

Rose gasped as another contraction gripped her. "Ohhh!" she cried, sweat breaking out on her beautiful face. Her eyes were wide when she looked at Carrie.

Carrie bent down for another examination. "I was wrong," she said lightly. "It will be less than an hour." She looked up with a grin. "I can see this little one's head already. It's obviously in quite a hurry."

"You can?" Rose gasped, bearing down as another contraction ripped through her. She clenched her teeth as she fought to control the scream.

Abby smiled. "You scream if you want to. It will terrify the men, but they should have to suffer *some*. You're the one doing all the hard work. They can deal with a little terror."

Rose relaxed enough to laugh, and then she screamed loudly as another contraction hit.

"Push!" Carrie urged her. "Your baby is almost here." She locked eyes with Rose and smiled. "Push!"

Rose, taking strength from Carrie's eyes, *pushed*, and then collapsed back against the bed, knowing her work was over.

******

Carrie worked swiftly. She cut the umbilical cord, cleaned the baby gently, and wrapped it warmly in the soft blanket Annie had sent up. A brilliant smile on her face, she carried the baby to where Rose lay staring at her.

"You have a daughter," she said gently, tears of joy streaming down her face.

Rose reached out her arms. "A daughter?" she asked with awe. "I have a daughter?"

Carrie nodded. "You have a beautiful, perfect daughter."

Rose pulled the blanket back and stared down at the miracle gazing up at her. "Hello, daughter," she crooned. "My beautiful, beautiful little girl." She paused for a moment. "Will you get Moses and Jeremy?"

Carrie nodded at Abby.

Moments later, Moses was standing over the bed. Jeremy and Matthew hovered at the door. He reached down and took his daughter from Rose's arms. He held her gently, gazing down tenderly. "Hello, little girl," he whispered. "Welcome to life."

He turned and beckoned to Jeremy. "Come hold your niece."

Jeremy moved forward, his face lit with wonder, and reached out his arms to gather his niece close. He smiled at Rose. "Well done, sister."

Moses settled down on the edge of the bed and kissed Rose warmly. "Well done indeed," he murmured.

Carrie watched all of them for a moment, her heart pounding with joy. "Do you have a name for her?" she asked.

Rose looked up, her smile as bright as the snow outside, now that the clouds had cleared and the moon was gleaming down. "Samantha Hope Samuels," she said softly. "Samantha because she is the circle of life for Sam. Hope because she is the symbol for the hope that keeps my people moving forward to a better life. And Samuels because freedom has allowed me to have a last name."

Rose cuddled her baby. "Samantha Hope Samuels is proof God still has faith in humans," she murmured as she looked at Abby. "It's just like you told us." She sighed as her daughter gurgled, and pressed into her breast. "I believe it now more than ever. *We will be carried forward by hope..."*

To Be Continued...

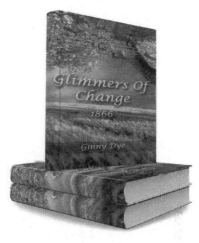

Available Now!
www.DiscoverTheBregdanChronicles.com

*Would you be so kind as to leave a Review on Amazon?
I love hearing from my readers! Just go to
Amazon.com, put Carried Forward By Hope into the
Search box, click to read the Reviews, and you'll be able
to leave one of your own!*

Thank you!

The Bregdan Principle

Every life that has been lived until today is a part of the woven braid of life.

It takes every person's story to create history.

Your life will help determine the course of history.

You may think you don't have much of an impact.

You do.

Every action you take will reflect in someone else's life.

Someone else's decisions.

Someone else's future.

Both good and bad.

The Bregdan Chronicles

Storm Clouds Rolling In
1860 – 1861

On To Richmond
1861 – 1862

Spring Will Come
1862 – 1863

Dark Chaos
1863 – 1864

The Long Last Night
1864 – 1865

Carried Forward By Hope
April – December 1865

Glimmers of Change
December – August 1866

Shifted By The Winds
August – December 1866

***Many more coming... Go to
DiscoverTheBregdanChronicles.com to see how
many are available now!***

Other Books by Ginny Dye

Pepper Crest High Series - Teen Fiction

Time For A Second Change
It's Really A Matter of Trust
A Lost & Found Friend
Time For A Change of Heart

When I Dream Series – Children's Bedtime Stories

When I Dream, I Dream of Horses
When I Dream, I Dream of Puppies
When I Dream, I Dream of Snow
When I Dream, I Dream of Kittens
When I Dream, I Dream of Elephants
When I Dream, I Dream of the Ocean

Fly To Your Dreams Series – Allegorical Fantasy

Dream Dragon
Born To Fly
Little Heart

101+ Ways to Promote Your Business Opportunity

All titles by Ginny Dye
www.AVoiceInTheWorld.com

Author Biography

Who am I? Just a normal person who happens to love to write. If I could do it all anonymously, I would. In fact, I did the first go round. I wrote under a pen name. On the off chance I would ever become famous - I didn't want to be! I don't like the limelight. I don't like living in a fishbowl. I especially don't like thinking I have to look good everywhere I go, just in case someone recognizes me! I finally decided none of that matters. If you don't like me in overalls and a baseball cap, too bad. If you don't like my haircut or think I should do something different than what I'm doing, too bad. I'll write books that you will hopefully like, and we'll both let that be enough! :) Fair?

But let's see what you might want to know. I spent many years as a Wanderer. My dream when I graduated from college was to experience the United States. I grew up in the South. There are many things I love about it but I wanted to live in other places. So I did. I moved 42 times, traveled extensively in 49 of the 50 states, and had more experiences than I will ever be able to recount. The only state I haven't been in is Alaska, simply because I refuse to visit such a vast, fabulous place until I have at least a month. Along the way I had glorious adventures. I've canoed through the Everglade Swamps, snorkeled in the Florida Keys and windsurfed in the Gulf of Mexico. I've white-water rafted down the New River and Bungee jumped in the Wisconsin Dells. I've visited every National Park (in the off-season when there is more freedom!) and many of the State Parks. I've hiked thousands of miles of mountain trails and biked through Arizona deserts. I've canoed and biked through Upstate New York and Vermont, and polished off as much lobster as possible on the Maine Coast.

I had a glorious time and never thought I would find a place that would hold me until I came to the Pacific Northwest. I'd been here less than 2 weeks, and I knew I would never leave. My heart is so at home here with the towering firs, sparkling waters, soaring mountains and rocky beaches. I love the eagles & whales. In 5 minutes I can be hiking on 150 miles of trails in the mountains around my home, or gliding across the lake in my rowing shell. I love it!

Have you figured out I'm kind of an outdoors gal? If it can be done outdoors, I love it! Hiking, biking, windsurfing, rock-climbing, roller-blading, snow-shoeing, skiing, rowing, canoeing, softball, tennis... the list could go on and on. I love to have fun and I love to stretch my body. This should give you a pretty good idea of what I do in my free time.

When I'm not writing or playing, I'm building I Am A Voice In The World - a fabulous organization I founded in 2001 - along with 60 amazing people who poured their lives into creating resources to empower people to make a difference with their lives.

What else? I love to read, cook, sit for hours in solitude on my mountain, and also hang out with friends. I love barbeques and block parties. Basically - I just love LIFE!

I'm so glad you're part of my world!

Ginny

Join my Email List so you can:

- Receive notice of all new books
- Be a part of my Launch Celebrations. I give away lots of Free gifts!
- Read my weekly BLOG while you're waiting for a new book.
- Be part of The Bregdan Chronicles Family!
- Learn about all the other books I write.

Just go to www.BregdanChronicles.net and fill out the form.

Made in the USA
Lexington, KY
18 March 2016